A VERY PLAIN YOUNG MAN

BOOK TWO

THE HAPGOODS OF BRAMLEIGH

CHRISTINA DUDLEY

In memory of Evelyn,
on Karen D.'s behalf

RICHARD HAPGOOD = AUGUSTA ARBUTHNOT

- ELFRIDA
- ALICE = JOSEPH TIERNEY
- MARGARET
- EDITH

HUGH HAPGOOD = HARRIET MORROW

- LIONEL
- HARRIET
- ROSALIE

THE
Hapgoods of Bramleigh

PROLOGUE

For I have lost my honour, lost my fame,
And stained the glory of my Royal house,
And all to bear the branded name of Mistress.
—John Dryden, *All for Love* (1677)

Lady Wimpole had worked herself into a state.

Her thin, ruffled muslin wrapper pulled tight about her, auburn hair loose and streaming, she flew to the balcony to greet her lover. "At last! Oh, Frederick! How could you keep me waiting when I summoned you so urgently?"

The gentleman scaling her ivy trellis tilted his golden head back to regard her, the look on his classically handsome face more exasperated than concerned. "And see how I have come. For your sake have I abandoned a very promising hand at the club and braved the ire of my fellow gamblers, who felt I should stay and let them win back their money." Pausing to pluck a leaf from his cravat, he asked, "Honoria, was it truly necessary that I enter by these means? Your footman has been admitting me through the front door these several months."

"But, Frederick—it is Rodney. I believe—I believe he suspects!" Her voice dropped to a whisper as she clutched her throat.

"Of course he suspects, darling," her lover replied, swinging himself over the balcony railing and dropping lightly to his feet beside her. She instantly threw herself against his chest, burrowing into the highly-starched folds of his neckcloth as she sobbed. Grimacing, he detached her. "There, there. I must already answer to my valet for the damage done by the cursed ivy—let there be no saltwater bath added to it."

"Frederick—how can you be so calm and heartless?" Lady Wimpole demanded. "Do you care nothing for my reputation?"

Running his hand over her bottom, he gave it a playful slap. "I care for your reputation every bit as much as you do, Honoria. Which is to say, almost not at all." Protests bubbled to her lips, but he stopped them with a kiss. "Come. Let us retire, and then you will tell me your sad tale."

Torn between her desire to prolong the scene and her desire for Frederick Tierney's handsome person, the latter carried the day, and it was not until she was tumbled beneath him that she remembered her crisis.

"Frederick."

"Mm?" He was half asleep, one arm thrown across her hip.

She ran her eyes admiringly down him. He was beautiful. From tip to toe. Her own husband Rodney Braithwaite, Lord Wimpole, had red bumpy skin like a plucked fowl and was narrow where he should be broad and expansive where he should be lean. Not so Frederick Tierney, whose enviable form could have been the model for Townley's *Discus Thrower* in the British Museum.

"Frederick! Do wake up."

With a sigh, he rolled onto his back, pulling up the bedclothes before tucking his arms behind his head. He said nothing, only raising his eyebrows to indicate his attention.

"It is as I said—Rodney suspects!" Lady Wimpole propped herself on one elbow so that she could clap her hands together and wring them appealingly. "I fear he will, in his jealous rage, slay either me or you."

"Pardon me," said her lover. "Are you speaking of Rodney *Braithwaite*?"

"Of course I am! How can you jest at such a moment, Frederick?"

"I could not be more serious. I own myself astonished that he could summon such ardor—even for the sake of your spotless honor, my dear."

"Rodney is an exceedingly fond husband," she bristled. She had pictured her pronouncements of doom being received quite differently. In one imagining, Frederick Tierney clutched her to him and shouted defiance to the stars, before begging her to run away with him, while she wept and protested that she could not so yield to sin. The Frederick Tierney lounging beside her, however, showed no sign of perturbation, and—to her annoyance—his sleepiness was returning.

"Naturally Lord Wimpole is fond of you," he yawned. "Or, as fond as a man of his phlegmatic disposition can be. But one does not look to the Rodney Braithwaites of the world for towering passions and deaths by duel."

Gathering her injured pride about her, Lady Wimpole reached for her wrapper and flounced from the bed. "You are a monster. I regret—yes—I regret losing my heart to you." Her speech ended in a choking sob as she turned away, shoulders shaking.

Unheard by his weeping lady, Frederick Tierney stifled a groan and reached for her pillow, covering his face with it until he could either master his expression or die of suffocation—he wasn't particular. It was the chief flaw of women that they were everlastingly prone to tears. Whether they felt grief, anger, fear, or simply desired to evoke a reaction, tears were the result. Why this must be, only the gods could explain, but Frederick had had enough for one day. First there was the letter that morning from his mother, blurred and puckered by evidence of her distress, and now this. And to think his mother and his mistress were both weeping for the same reason: that he had chosen to involve himself with a married woman! At least Lady Wimpole might have the grace to be cheerful, she being the married woman in question. But perhaps, no matter how cheerful the woman, or however often she declared that she sought only amusement and nothing more—perhaps all love affairs ended thus, in tears and recriminations.

Having failed to suffocate, Frederick set the pillow aside and blinked up at Lady Wimpole's apricot-tinted ceiling. *Was* the love affair ending, then?

Why, he supposed it was.

Honoria, for all her beauty and charm, showed a growing penchant for theatrics, which he found distasteful. Frederick thought that, if it should ever fall to his lot to have a lover weary of his company, he should win her back with a glittering display of what attracted her in the first place. There would be no pleadings or arguments or acts of desperation, such as women in his experience resorted to.

Another frown distorted the perfect lines of his face. Well, so be it. Honoria Braithwaite had been a pleasant lover for a time, but all good things must come to an end.

With one hazard, he would send two balls into the pocket: his mother would be glad he ceased to keep an adulterous mistress, and his adulterous mistress would be glad her husband could no longer threaten her with exposure.

Taking leave of Lady Wimpole would be a tricky matter, however. She was not the Haymarket opera dancer, to be bought off with a necklace, or even Mrs. Gurdy, the self-styled widow actress whom Frederick dallied with until her troupe took itself off to the provinces the previous summer. Lady Wimpole was a wealthy gentlewoman whose complacent husband sat in the House of Lords, and neither Wimpole would make a welcome enemy.

Assuming an air of appropriate gravity, Frederick rose to a sitting position and patted the bed to beckon her. She came, but indicated her continuing displeasure by showing him her back, letting her draperies droop becomingly.

"Honoria."

The wings of her shoulder blades rounded, as if she hunched to protect herself. "You care nothing for me, Frederick."

"What utter nonsense. Of course I do. Have I not said time and again that I love you? You are a beautiful, warm, charming woman." And if Wimpole ever left her, Frederick added inwardly, she had dramatic talent enough for a career on the stage. He gave her wrapper a twitch. "Look at me, Honoria. I have greatly enjoyed your company."

In a flash, her rounded back stiffened and she whirled to glare at him. "'Enjoyed'? Why do you speak of it as something past? Do you no longer enjoy my company?"

A mistake there. His eyes gleamed as he gave her a placating smile. "A mere slip of the tongue. Come—tell me what Braithwaite has said or done, to worry you."

Relenting, his mistress crumpled against him and regarded him with dewy eyes. "Oh, Frederick! You know how cold he can be. How the very sight of him chills my bones. His eyes—the eyes of a dead fish!"

"Aptly put," he mused. "Lord Wimpole's eyes do share that flat, blank quality. My brother and I used to dig out the eyes of the fish at dinner and hide them on each other's plates. Under the greens, or tucked in the pudding. I once made the brilliant success of burying one in Joseph's blancmange."

Lady Wimpole's only reply was a reproachful furrowing of the brow, and Frederick politely added, "But I digress. Do continue, my dear."

"You know what I suffer, Frederick. I have told you many a time of his indifference to me." (She had.) "Even after I bore him little Anna—and I was equally disappointed with a daughter—he acted as if I were to blame. As if I had done it on set purpose! How can a wife bear such a husband?"

The tears flowed forth again, and Frederick patted her shoulder, but it was too familiar a subject to rouse any stronger display of sympathy. His mind wandered back to his mother's letter. *I know Lady Harding to be a busybody, Frederick, but I fear the details she shared about your conduct were too specific and shocking for my peace of mind. Please write at once to reassure me...*

"Honoria—" Frederick interrupted that lady's muffled blubbering "—you know I regret that Lord Wimpole has not proved the husband you wished, for all his 'fondness,' but you have me on tenterhooks. Why did you summon me tonight?"

Dashing her tears away, Lady Wimpole straightened. She pulled her wrapper tight and tied the sash. Crying had reddened her eyes and nose, and Frederick thought he would never have imagined her thus, when he had first seen her at the Morreltons' rout in January. There she had been dashing and flirtatious, snapping her fan at him and tossing witticisms. She had quite put in the shade the less worldly young ladies who competed for his attentions. Dance followed dance; conversation followed conversation; flirtation followed flirtation. Not a fortnight after their meeting she became his mistress.

Frederick felt some twinges of guilt at first. He had been raised in a conservative household, and his mother was the granddaughter and niece and grand-niece and cousin of clergymen, but—he argued with himself—whom did he truly harm? Lady Wimpole was willing enough. Her husband Lord Wimpole cared only for his speeches and committees when Parliament sat, and for his books and debate clubs when it did not. The child—the thought of the child gave him particular discomfort—the child was too young to be aware of what passed. Frederick had only seen the Honorable Miss Anna Braithwaite once, in the care of a nursemaid, as he rode in the Park.

No, he had ignored his scruples, putting them from his mind until repetition of the offense dulled his sensitivity, only to have them resurrected once more when he received his mother's letter. It had not been the first reference Mrs. Tierney made to her son's escapades, but the timing of this particular epistle worked in her favor. By this point, the charms of Lady Wimpole had faded with familiarity. Frederick knew her now for an unhappy beautiful woman, shut out from her husband's affections and uncertain of herself beneath her veneer of enchantment.

Lady Wimpole took a deep breath, her eyes fixed beyond him on the brocaded bed hangings. "Rodney asked me whether we should dismiss the nursemaid and search for one more—more nurturing."

As always, the mention of the child pricked at him and made his voice rougher. "I fail to see what bearing this has on the matter, Honor—"

"Do you not see? He criticizes me! He might as well have said, 'I find you deficient as a mother.'"

"I rather think he found the nursemaid deficient."

"But if the nursemaid is deficient and he must point it out to me, he implies that *I* am deficient. I told him so. I told him I took great umbrage and that he had better keep to his own concerns."

Frederick shut his eyes and thanked the gods he had no domestic controversies to embroil him.

"And Rodney replied that, as I seemed too busy with *my* concerns, he felt he must speak up. Oh, Frederick! How my knees quaked and my breath left me when he said this!"

Again, Frederick was surprised by a ripple of sympathy for the battered Lord Wimpole. Honestly, if Lady Wimpole had fallen to his, Frederick's, lot, instead of Rodney Braithwaite's, he would not be surprised if his own eyes went dead and fishy after a year or two.

"Calm yourself," he urged her. "Lord Wimpole's remark seems innocent enough."

"Innocent! You cannot know, Frederick—you were not there. You have no idea his power to fix one with his gaze. To speak fair words and all the while, to bubble and *seethe* underneath."

"I admit such a picture of your lord beggars my powers of imagination, but do not let this prevent you from continuing. You were saying—he fixed you with his cold, fish-like eye and accused you of the sin of busyness—"

"And I cried, 'What can you mean by this? What concerns have ever prevented me from the fulfillment of my duties?' And Rodney said, 'I am sure your concerns are best known to yourself.' And I declared, before fleeing his presence, 'That they are, and you would do best to stay out of them.'" Her revelatory scene now disclosed,

Lady Wimpole heaved out another sob and pitched herself against her lover yet again. "So you see? We are suspected, Frederick! We are discovered!"

If he were truthful, Frederick Tierney would have to say he did not see at all. He did not see why on earth she was so overwrought, and he did not see how she could wrangle such sinister implications from her husband's humdrum speech, Lord Wimpole's purported bubbling and seething notwithstanding. But if he were to bring this chapter of his life to a close, Frederick realized, he would do best to take her words at their value.

He sat up even straighter and pushed a pillow behind his back before saying, "Ah, my love. We knew this moment would come."

"Did we?" She popped up again, dabbing her eyes with the coverlet.

"How could we not?" he pursued. "When one considers how much time we have spent together, even in open flirtation before the eyes of society?"

"I—I suppose. Lady Keith did say to that pernicious Kate Montrose that things were come to a pass, if handsome scoundrels such as you were allowed to roam London freely, preying upon the married and unmarried women alike."

"Did she?" Frederick grinned. "What a grand old dame! I will be sure to prey upon her next."

"Frederick! Lady Keith is sixty, if she is a day, and she was never accounted a beauty, even in her youth."

He bit the inside of his cheek. This would be the other wearing characteristic of his dear mistress: for a woman so gifted with wit, she was singularly devoid of humor.

"How right you are," Frederick rejoined agreeably. "I had better not make the attempt. But you see what I mean, do you not, Honoria? We have become the talk of the town. Naturally hints of our doings have come to the astute Lord Wimpole's notice."

"What then will we do? You will not fight him, will you, Frederick?"

"Fight him? Why should you suggest such a course? Lord Wimpole has not wronged me in the least."

"But—but—" she ducked her head and peeked at him from under her lashes— "Rodney possesses what you most desire."

That he did not, but Frederick knew better than to say so. He reached for her hands and took them both in his, stroking the backs of them and endeavoring to arrange his face in lines of regret. Lady Wimpole admired the picture her elegant white hands made in his strong ones and took heart. He must love her to distraction!

"It will ever be my misfortune," began Frederick after a decent interval, "that Lord Wimpole made your acquaintance before I did—that he made you *his* before I might have offered you an alternative—"

"Oh, Frederick! Do you mean that, if I were free, you would have married me?"

Weighing the possible consequences of such a declaration, he decided it would be a safe enough venture. "Can you doubt it, Honoria?"

Gracious Lord, that unstopped the fountain again. The woman was become a veritable watering-pot. While she sobbed and hiccupped and gazed adoringly at him through bleary eyes, he pushed himself up from the bed and rifled through his discarded frock coat for his handkerchief, holding it out to her.

"Th-thank you, love," she gasped. "Oh! Must you get dressed? I could fetch you one of Rodney's dressing gowns."

Frederick shuddered at this suggestion, not only for its symbolism, but also because he dressed fastidiously and had no taste for Lord Wimpole's sober blacks and unflattering cuts. He shook his head and continued to button his drawers before reaching for his pantaloons. There were some speeches a man must make in his life which required the dignity of clothing.

"But I *was* too late to make you mine," he went on. "And I cannot bear to be the cause of pain to you—"

"...Pain to me?" echoed his lady wonderingly. "No—Frederick! You are my only source of joy in life—in my hollow union with Rodney."

"Listen to me, Honoria. How can your union with Rodney—with Lord Wimpole, rather—be otherwise than hollow, if we persist in our doomed love?"

"Rodney is a cold, passionless man! He is incapable of love of any kind. I would rather have our doomed love than none at all." Here she grasped at his shirtfront. "I beg you, Frederick—do not be noble—"

"And think of little Anna," he broke in, his voice changing. "You would not have her raised under this cloud. How can she love and respect her parents and choose wisely for herself, if we continue in this?"

Lady Wimpole drew herself erect, her hands falling to her sides. The sudden seriousness in his voice raised doubts in her heart. Had he not been sincere when he claimed to love her? If he had, why did he sound different now? Why did his speech have the ring it was missing before—the ring...of conviction? But if he did not love her—

She shook this off. It did not bear thinking of. Of course he loved her. He must speak so now from other impulses. She watched him as he fastened his braces and tied his neckcloth in an easy knot. For a man who prized his valet's ministrations, Frederick Tierney dressed himself with remarkable skill. How many women's bedsides had he left in just such a manner, to be so practiced?

"You, too, accuse me of being a bad mother," she whispered.

"I do not. It is because I know your desire to be a good mother that I appeal to that instinct now."

"But—my love—how can you bear to give me up? No matter how many husbands or daughters are sacrificed?"

"'The world well lost,' eh?" he smiled.

"Wh-what?"

"You know," he said. "The Dryden play. Though I fear you are the Antony in this situation, and I the Cleopatra. Never mind."

"How can you talk of the theater at such a time? I forbid you your nonsense. Pray, Frederick—speak from the heart—you would urge me return to my enforced solitude? You care nothing for my sufferings?"

"I care a great deal for your sufferings and wish them of the shortest possible duration," he rejoined, dropping a kiss on the top of her head and stroking her hair. "And a woman such as you will never want for friends or companionship. With time and effort, you may even win over your husband."

But Lady Wimpole threw off his tokens of tenderness, her own softness giving way to anger, as her doubt of his love blossomed into fear. "You do not pull the wool over my eyes, Frederick, for all your fine words!"

"My dear lady—!"

"This is how you dispose of me, after months of sharing my bed? I know you now for a heartless reprobate and regret ever taking up with you."

"Do compose yourself, Ho—"

"Permitting you to—I should have Rodney take a whip to you—you Fiend!" She flew at him, her fingernails clawing the air, and a startled Frederick Tierney held her wrists out of striking distance with one hand as he reached for his frock coat with the other.

"Honoria—"

"Get out!" she shrieked. "All your talk of plays and not causing me pain and 'doomed love'! I hate you! I wish I never set eyes on you! I will have Rodney pass a law in Parliament to run you from the kingdom, you—you—"

What name Lady Wimpole finally bestowed on her erstwhile lover was drowned in Frederick's ears by the balcony doors slamming after she shoved him out, her sherry-colored eyes flashing in such a fetching way that he momentarily considered appeasing her for one last meeting of minds, as it were.

But alas.

He might be foolish, but he was no fool.

Smoothing himself into his navy blue coat and tut-tutting over the sad crease it had received, Frederick Tierney made his departure.

Chapter One

So much as I have gathered by report

and common heare-saie.

—W. Harrison, *The Description of England* (1577)

Upon returning home from her younger sister's wedding, the unmarried Miss Elfrida Hapgood sat before the looking glass and took stock.

She was accounted by most who met her as the loveliest young lady in the county, lovelier even than the Honorable Miss Birdlow, daughter of Viscount Lord Marlton, though Miss Birdlow had the advantage in fortune. Miss Elfrida Hapgood was exactly the right height for fashion; she had exactly the right shade of golden hair and blue eyes, and the pleasing regularity of her features was matched by the pleasing symmetry and curves of her form. She knew these things about herself and did not underestimate their value, but she took little interest in them, except sometimes to wonder why beauty was accounted so important in her world. Being possessed of weak eyesight herself—a condition she tended to deny and which she had not yet taken steps to remedy—Elfrida could rarely get a good look at a person until after she had already formed an opinion on him. An opinion based on other—and to her mind more telling—evidence. A man's words. His actions. His reputation.

No—beauty was worth little. If she could have chosen at birth, Elfrida would have preferred Miss Birdlow's fortune—not from any covetousness on her own part, but because then she might live comfortably at home with her parents and sisters, free from the burden of marrying.

Marrying. There was the rub.

Elfrida leaned closer to the mirror, rubbing at a smear on the glass. When one shared a bedroom with a sister like Alice, mysterious smudges might be anything from crushed insect to fish slime, and Elfrida felt a catch in her throat to realize she would never again have to wonder. The chamber was now solely her own.

Her sister Alice had seemed eager enough to marry, but that was Alice. Alice never did anything by halves. When their father forbade her the study of the natural world—Alice's ruling passion—the girl had dressed as a boy and continued her activities. And when Alice met the very first gentleman who shared her particular interests, she fell head over ears in love. Fortunately for her, the compromising situation which led Mr. Joseph Tierney to offer for Alice was shortly followed by the offer of his heart.

And now the Reverend and Mrs. Joseph Tierney were married and bound for their parsonage in Buckinghamshire, having dispensed with a wedding breakfast that they might reach Bath by evening.

And here she sat.

Turning her eyes away to the window, she gazed out on the grounds of the Bramleigh estate, blind to the weeds that sprouted between the paved stones of the walkway and the bedraggled shrubs and flowerbeds. Her sisters teased her for her poor vision, but the condition had its benefits. Elfrida's world held only gentle, gauzy shapes and soft, blurred faces. There were no harsh lines, no offensive details. She moved in a dream landscape.

And yet, for a shortsighted young lady, Miss Elfrida Hapgood saw the world with astonishing clarity.

She saw that she was born of an ancient and respectable Saxon family, whose wealth in heritage was not equaled by wealth in actual monies. She saw that her father had married her mother for that woman's beauty in youth, and that his early admiration had long given way to resigned sufferance. She saw that her mother's tendencies to extravagance, and her father's inability to refuse her, led to the destruction of the Hapgood finances and the family's present straits. She saw that her mother's younger brothers, Elfrida's uncles Alec and Alwyn Arbuthnot, shared their sister's tendency to profligacy and added to it a taste for scandal. She saw that her mother's retreat into imagined invalidism some years past had inadvertently rescued the family from the financial abyss, but that her father took small comfort because he still had four—three, now—daughters to provide for and marry off, if anyone would have them. And finally she saw that even the relief of disposing so well of Alice was coupled with the strain to come up with her marriage portion. The Hapgoods must be especially, especially thrifty now.

With all the righteousness of youth, Elfrida could not imagine what led people to such passes. She vowed to herself that she would never fall prey to the fleeting wiles of beauty, as her father had. She would never let money pour through her fingers, as her mother had. She would never tolerate or support, as her parents did, the wild habits of men like her uncles, who gambled and wenched and lacked a fixed purpose in life. If she could not live out her days quietly in her father's house, she would marry someone with whom she might. A steady, sensible, kind man. He need not be handsome. With her eyesight, handsomeness or plainness need only be regarded when the man was within two feet of her, in strong light.

Her sisters called her practical, and Elfrida considered it a compliment of the highest order. She would rather be practical than beautiful, and if she was both, she would make her beauty serve her practicality. With little else to recommend her, she must shift as she might. Elfrida cherished no romantic illusions.

All of which explained why Elfrida alone, of every woman in attendance at the Marltons' Midsummer Ball three days prior, resisted the spell cast by one Mr. Frederick Tierney, brother to her new brother-in-law. Three days earlier, sister Alice and brother-in-law Joseph had *not* been married. In fact, three days earlier, marriage between the two of them appeared impossible, as Alice had sent a letter jilting her betrothed. It had only been the momentous events at that very Midsummer Ball that set all to rights.

Three days earlier, with a Midsummer moon high in the night sky, Elfrida had been dancing with the silent Mr. Norman DeWitt when a ripple of excitement swept the ballroom. Heads turned; necks craned; lorgnettes and quizzing glasses rose; fans flashed to hide whispering lips.

"Whoever can that man be?"

"How handsome he is!"

"Hmmph! Fine feathers, I say."

"Lucky Miss Birdlow—see how he bows over her hand and asks her to dance!"

"He must ask her to dance, naturally. I'm sure the viscount gave him no choice in the matter."

"Let us stop halfway down on the next promenade, that we might be closer to them."

Elfrida's gaze sought her partner's, when the figures of the dance brought them together again, and she found him raising question-ing eyebrows. *Did she, too, wish to force her way closer to the newcomer? If so, he would be happy to oblige.* For someone who rarely spoke, Mr. DeWitt managed to express much. She shook her head in reply, giving him a rueful smile. What would the new arrival think, the way the dancers were criss-crossing and bunching up to have a better look at him?

When she glanced the man's way again, she perceived only a streak of golden hair, the dark blue of an evening coat, but it was not long before more information worked its way down the chain of dancers.

"He is Mr. Frederick Tierney—brother to that Mr. Tierney the naturalist. The Mr. Joseph Tierney who disgraced himself with that hoyden Miss Al—" The voice broke off when its owner was hissed at and reminded of Miss Hapgood's proximity. Elfrida, knowing her sister had severed the connection between the Tierneys and Hapgoods, affected not to hear.

"He's the *older* brother," went on another. "The heir. To his father *and* a baronet uncle."

"How beautiful he is! I've never seen such fine tailoring."

"A little overdone, to my mind. Embroidered waistcoat, my eye!"

"Has he any fortune? The younger brother hadn't."

"Modest, modest. But expectations of more from the uncle. Possibly three thousand a year, there."

"Oh! How old, precisely, is the baronet uncle?"

Here the music ended, and Elfrida did not catch whether Fortune favored Mr. Frederick Tierney with an elderly, ailing uncle who would soon drop off entirely, or a strapping man in his prime. Mr. DeWitt took her hand and accompanied her to the refreshment table.

"Lemonade or tea, Miss Hapgood?"

"Lemonade, please."

"A sandwich?"

"No thank you, Mr. DeWitt."

Their exchange having exhausted Mr. DeWitt's conversational powers, they stood in companionable silence, watching the antics of their neighbors. Elfrida loved to see the sheen of sarsenet by candlelight, the indistinct forms of the men and women fuzzing and blurring as if in the turnabout at the Taunton fair. From this whirl, one figure withdrew and emerged, growing more distinct as he approached. It was Mr. DeWitt's older brother Roscoe.

"Miss Hapgood." He sketched a bow before rounding on his brother. "What ill luck! Why the devil must we suffer the brother, as well?"

"Are we suffering?" came the mild reply.

"I thought I should have to restrain Miss Porterworth physically from throwing herself at him."

"She always did like yellow hair," said Norman.

The black-haired Roscoe looked thunderous at this. "She is an innocent! What could she know of men like this Frederick Tierney?"

"I venture she knows as little of him as we do. Another lemonade, Miss Hapgood?"

"I beg your pardon, Norman," snapped Roscoe, as Elfrida signaled her refusal. "Your habitual silence in company isolates you. I've learned more than enough of the man in the last few minutes. Lady Grafton says he leads the devil's own life in London. Something about opera dancers and actresses and even a liaison with one 'Lady W'—"

With a sharp throat-clearing, Norman interrupted his brother.

"Come now," Roscoe chided him, frowning apologetically at Elfrida nonetheless. "With her sister Miss Alice's recent adventures, Miss Hapgood is woman of the world enough to hear such tales, are you not, Miss Hapgood? But I suppose it would not please you to hear what is said of your future brother-in-law's brother?"

"There's many a slip, 'twixt cup and lip," Elfrida said evasively, thinking Alice's broken engagement would soon be fodder for gossip. "But I would prefer you not discuss my sister, at any rate, Mr. DeWitt."

"Very well. Forgive me." Roscoe dismissed Alice with a flick of his fingers. "But, as I was saying, Miss Alice's misdoings cannot compare to those of our latest upstart visitor. Mr. *Frederick* T—"

"A-*hem!*" coughed Norman, with alarming violence. Elfrida eyed him in concern. But before she could ask him if, perhaps, he were the one in need of more lemonade, she caught a new voice, low and warm and musical, tinged by amusement.

"I thank you, Mr. Birdlow. I would greatly appreciate any introductions to your charming guests and neighbors."

Startled, she glimpsed around Roscoe's shoulder the newcomer almost upon them, accompanied by Lord Marlton's son, the Honorable Mr. Frank Birdlow. Elfrida's surprise was nothing, however, to Roscoe DeWitt's. That gentleman fairly jumped out of his morocco pumps, and Elfrida was hard put to stifle a giggle. Her laughing eyes swept Mr. Tierney's in the briefest of moments, and while he was not close enough for her to discern his expression, she saw his eyes were blue, a shade perhaps two degrees paler than her own. How much had he overheard? It hardly mattered. He would guess they were talking about him from their elaborate discomfort.

Before she could frame her face into proper blankness for an introduction, she found Roscoe DeWitt grabbing her gloved hand and crying, "Miss Hapgood! Our dance!" He gave a ruthless jerk to her arm to set her in motion, and fairly thrust her into the line.

"Mr. DeWitt!" hissed Elfrida, rubbing her elbow after she was released. "I do not recall you asking for this dance or my consent to it."

"I meant to, when I came over," he declared, as they took hands and went around.

"I rather think you came over to complain about Mr. Frederick Tierney."

His shoulder, when he passed her on the straight hey, shrugged in annoyance. "You wanted to be introduced to such a man, did you, as he's to be your brother?"

Elfrida had to wait until they were slipping in a circle to reply. "I would rather not have the choice taken from me, sir."

Roscoe's mouth thinned, and they did not speak again. In the whirl of the dance Elfrida spared a glance in the direction of the refreshment table. Mr. Tierney was tall enough that she could discern the golden blur of his hair. He appeared to be having a lively conversation with Mr. Norman DeWitt, of all people, and Miss Porterworth. That young lady threw back her head and laughed at something Mr. Tierney said, giving him a rap with her closed fan.

"Handsome, isn't he?" whispered the young lady next to Elfrida in the line, whose name she did not know.

"Everyone believes so," murmured Elfrida.

The young lady sniffed, thinking that the beautiful girl need not put on airs, simply because Mr. Frederick Tierney had more than once looked her way. The girl had likely never had a season in town, as she herself had, after all.

"When I was in town this last spring," the young lady said emphatically, "I recall how all the other girls were wild for him. An acquaintance of mine made quite a cake of herself, in pursuit of him, but he was taken with some peeress, the more shame to her."

To Elfrida's relief, the young lady and her partner took hands for the promenade. The Hapgood family having been gossip's victims the past few weeks, Elfrida had no interest in hearing another person's supposed crimes.

But there was more to come. As she wove through the line, passing hands with Mr. DeWitt between each couple, she caught more bits, usually hushed when she drew near: "...gambled on a horse..." "...belongs to two clubs..." "...tailors battle for his custom, though he don't pay..."

She wondered that so much could be known of a stranger who had never before come among them, and decided he must have been living the very life in London, if so much had filtered out to these distant reaches. Why, if half the things said of Mr. Frederick Tierney were true, he must out-Arbuthnot both her uncles, Alec and Alwyn, in wild living and prodigality!

If such were truly the case, she would prefer *not* to know the man, and it was fortunate Alice had jilted his brother. But suppose this Frederick Tierney were to be introduced to her? In the course of the evening, it would be impossible to avoid, the Hapgoods being one of the first families of the county, whatever the recent problems caused by the squire's second daughter. And, if Elfrida were introduced to Mr. Frederick Tierney, he would be obligated to ask her to dance.

Her brow furrowing slightly as she proceeded automatically through the steps and figures, she considered this. There would be no polite manner of declining, if Mr. Tierney were to ask, and Elfrida admitted to herself that she would like to satisfy her curiosity with a closer inspection and evidence of her own gathering. Any deeper acquaintance, however, was entirely out of the question, and it was a mercy the two families would not be connected, after all.

To her mingled relief and disappointment, the introduction never came to pass. The Hapgood family's attendance at the Midsummer Ball was abbreviated by a new scrape of her sister's, and the squire rapidly gathered his two girls for a hasty departure.

"Such behavior out of you, Miss," their father railed at Alice, once in the barouche. Their uncle had been left behind to make his own way back to Bramleigh (a punishment for the share he had in Alice's latest escapade), and the squire left Hal up alone to drive, that he might wag a finger in Alice's face and give her the full benefit of his shaggy, frowning brows. "How came you to be in this draggle-tailed condition? If that betrothed of yours didn't already have his head in the noose, I should challenge him over this!"

"Joseph did nothing wrong," Alice replied dreamily. "And he says we will be married as soon as he can arrange it with Father Thomas." Her fingers went to her lips, as if remembering a recent touch there. "He will call tomorrow, to make his explanations and ensure I have suffered no lasting injury."

"I thought you had meant to jilt him," said Elfrida mildly. "Have you changed your mind?"

"Jilt him, Miss?" roared the squire. "After the pains we took to protect your reputation?"

"I had jilted him," Alice murmured. She contemplated the shocking state of her torn hem and gave a small smile. "But he loves me, and I have reconsidered."

Elfrida sat back, shaking her head over her younger sister's follies, and they drove home to the blusterings of their father and the creaks and rattles of the ancient carriage.

As promised, Mr. Joseph Tierney called on his beloved the next day and the day following. And on the third day, he and Alice were wed. The Hapgoods kept to themselves during this time, the sisters busily preparing Alice's limited trousseau, and Elfrida heard no more of Mr. Frederick Tierney than one comment Joseph let fall: "My brother would have come to pay his respects and be introduced, but he received some troubling correspondence to which he must attend straight away." What this correspondence treated on, Elfrida was too polite to enquire and Alice too preoccupied. If their younger sister Margaret had been present, she would surely have pried more information from him, but she was not, and that was as far as the matter got.

Some rumpus belowstairs roused Elfrida from her thoughts, driving out the memories of the past few days. Whatever had passed at the Midsummer Ball, it was over, and this was now. Alice and Joseph were married and embarked on their new life, and Elfrida was left to pick up the threads of the old.

She heard doors slamming, raised voices, hurrying footsteps, the steps being taken two at a time. Before her chamber door was flung open, she knew it was Margaret. The coltish fourteen-year-old flew in, eleven-year-old Edith at her heels.

"Elfie! Elfie!" Margaret cried. "You will never guess—he is come at last!"

"Will you try to speak to him long enough that I might take his likeness?" added Edith breathlessly.

"Who is come?" asked Elfrida, not stirring, except to pluck a shred of lint from her skirt.

"Don't be maddening, Elfie," Margaret frowned. "You know very well we mean Mr. Frederick Tierney—"

"Mr. Frederick Tierney? Why should he bother now?"

"—And you must entertain him because one of the hounds has an ear infection and Papa is down at the kennels."

"Won't it be strange to call him 'Mr. Tierney,' when 'Mr. Tierney' has always been Mr. *Joseph* Tierney to us?" added Edith.

"Strange indeed," said Elfrida. "But Margaret, cannot you send Hal to fetch Papa?"

"There isn't time!" Margaret fairly shrieked. "Edie and I saw him—Mr. Frederick Tierney is trotting up the drive on the handsomest horse, and you know how Hal can dawdle. If you do not come down *immediately*, Dorcas will say Papa is at the kennels, and Mr. Tierney will go there directly, and we will not meet him." She thrust Elfrida's embroidery hoop at her and gave her a shove.

"I do not see why he has come," Elfrida wondered. "Joseph and Alice are gone, and there is no wedding breakfast."

"Because he is now *family*!" insisted Margaret with exasperation. "It's only right. Elfie—don't make me drag you..!"

"Should not we tell Mama?" Elfrida persisted, digging in her heels and grabbing the door jamb.

"There isn't time!" her sister repeated. "Mama said she was half-dead from Alice's wedding this morning and was not to be disturbed on any account, not even for the Second Coming."

With a droop of resignation, Elfrida released the door jamb. She knew when arguments were lost. Besides, Margaret spoke truth: Mr. Frederick Tierney was now family, of sorts. The introduction would take place eventually, and better here in the Bramleigh drawing room, where she was effective mistress, than in a ballroom, where she must clasp hands with him and speak or not speak. Margaret's presence, at the very least, would preclude lengthy silences.

As ever, what was unpleasant had best be got over quickly.

Smoothing her hair, Elfrida took Edith by the hand and led the way downstairs.

Chapter Two

Heav'n has no Rage, like Love to Hatred turn'd,
Nor Hell a Fury like a woman scorn'd.
—William Congreve, *The Mourning Bride* (1703)

Mr. Frederick Tierney had indeed intended to make Miss Hapgood's acquaintance at the Midsummer Ball. But he had been ambushed by the wide-mouthed and flirtatious Miss Constance Porterworth and, that he might be spared further coquettish raps from that lady's ivory-handled fan, he asked her to partner him for a quadrille.

"La!" cried Miss Porterworth, with one final, smart, smack to his breast and a lavish fluttering of lashes. "What would people say? I must share you with the rest of the company. You have been standing here conversing with Norman and me an age, I'm sure."

Frederick rather thought Miss Porterworth responsible for the lion's share of the conversation, but he was willing to avail himself of the excuse she offered. "Well, if you think it would be looked askance on…" His gaze wandered again Miss Hapgood's direction. Her graceful figure was dropping in a curtsey to that rude young man who had hustled her away just as Frederick approached.

"I daresay we shall brave it," said Miss Porterworth quickly, laying a plump hand on his arm. "I myself fear nothing. Lead on, Mr. Tierney."

Too well-mannered to protest, he obeyed. Their presence caused a stir as they took their place in the square, and Frederick was compelled to feign ignorance of the swell of whispers and heads craned their direction. He lost sight of Miss Hapgood in the rush of motion, nor did he see her as the couples went through their sets of figures. By the time he could deposit Miss Porterworth at her mother's side and look about him, the Hapgoods had made their departure.

It was not Miss Hapgood's beauty alone which caught his attention, though Frederick admitted to himself that she rivaled any of the wealthier and better-dressed women of his acquaintance. It was that, in the fleeting instant when her gaze crossed his, he was startled by what he did and did not find there. Absent were the usual flirtatiousness, curiosity, challenge, desire. He had been pursued by women since he was fourteen and encountered the full range of their battery. There were the ones like Miss Birdlow, who held themselves aloof but watched him expectantly under lowered lids. There were the ones like Miss Porterworth, who thought to attract his notice with extravagant displays of person and personality. There were the

Lady Wimpoles, who employed subtler methods of wit and held out hints of worldliness and experience to lure him. And there were the awkward girls in their first Season, who scarcely opened their mouths but who stared at him helplessly like bedazzled calves.

Miss Hapgood fit none of these categories. Her violet-blue eyes held only mirth when they turned on him, as if the two of them shared a joke. It *was* amusing—how the rude young man leapt like a deer at a musket shot. The elder Mr. DeWitt must have been saying something most reprehensible about him, and the way the man fairly kidnapped Miss Hapgood afterward confirmed it. No—she was not flirting, not trying to catch his eye. She was merely having a laugh. And before he could recover and throw any sympathy or admiration into his own look, she had passed by him.

No matter. Surely he would find her eyes often upon him, and he would be ready at the next opportunity. Having driven Joseph down on a whim, Frederick had not decided how long he would stay in Somerset. Certainly he had no desire to return to town and the histrionics of Lady Wimpole; nor did he wish to be soon in Buckinghamshire again to face his mother. News of Joseph's engagement had distracted her from her anxieties on Frederick's behalf, but he could not be so fortunate a second time. No, he would accept the viscount's offer of hospitality and stay a while. A flirtation with a pretty girl would pass the time most pleasantly.

His resolution was confirmed the morning after the ball. After the Hapgoods decamped so hastily, Frederick found the affair rather flat. He danced with the prettiest young women in the room, accompanied Miss Birdlow to supper, and was altogether the toast of the evening, but when Lord Marlton informed him that his brother Joseph had left the ball not long after the Hapgoods, Frederick pleaded travel-weariness to depart early, assuring the viscount that both Tierneys would return the next day.

When he awoke, late morning sunlight filtered through the bleary windows of the inn chamber, and he found Joseph dressed and pacing the floor.

"What on earth happened to you, brother?" asked Frederick, noting the black eye and squares of sticking plaster below Joseph's thatch of curling brown hair. "Was the inn beset by brigands while we slept?"

"At last! I worried you might sleep the day away and was just thinking I would leave you a note. Never mind about these," Joseph added, touching the injuries. "I had something of a set-to with my dear Alice's uncle last night, but all was made clear and set to rights. We are to be married in two days' time."

"You and Miss Hapgood, I presume," said Frederick dryly. "Not you and the pugilistic uncle."

"Just so."

Frederick sat up and stretched, and Joseph politely went to the window as his brother made water. "I am the happiest of men, Frederick," Joseph went on. "You will all love her. The dearest girl—clever and winning and affectionate. We are exactly suited for each other. Only think! She has loved me all along."

"Joe, I beg you. Remember I am hearing this twaddle on an empty stomach."

Joseph laughed outright, before wincing and rubbing his face. "Was it not you who accused me some days ago of being too cold when I spoke of her? But very well. I will not assault you with my happiness. I mean to forward our luggage to Pattergees and send our men ahead when they arrive, but I myself will steal over to Bramleigh to visit my betrothed."

"Bramleigh?" Frederick paused in the buttoning of his shirt. "I—should like to meet this paragon of yours. She will be my sister now, you know."

"I do know. But I suspect you will have other matters to attend to this day." Putting a hand into his frock coat, Joseph retrieved a packet of letters and tossed them on the rumpled bed. "Forgive me—the address was so ill-written on the first that both the innkeeper and I thought it was intended for me."

His brows drawing together, Frederick took up the opened missive and inspected the hand. The writing was bold but blotted and hurried, as if the writer struggled to command himself. That was to say, *her*self. He sank back onto the bed, running troubled fingers through his locks. "You read this, you say?"

"Enough to know it was not, in fact, addressed to me."

"Sadly, no." Holding the tear-stained paper gingerly, Frederick read:

> *My heartless love –*
> *I cannot believe you have let us part on such terms! A*
> *mere lover's quarrel, I thought it, but then when I sent*
> *for you this morning, I find you have left town! Cold,*

cruel, marble-breasted villain! To woo me with words of love—to take from me my precious honor and my [illegible]. How could you treat me thus? If I hear not from you, if I discover my fears to be true, I vow I will rend your [illegible] [illegible] from your [illegible], and what is left after my revenge, Rodney will [illegible] with his bare hands!

Coward! I am no nameless wench of the stews to be cast aside as the whim takes you!

Believe me when I say you will regret your treatment of

H. B.

Frederick gave a sigh and folded the letter carefully before reaching for the next. "I suppose our father had this post forwarded from Stone Halt."

"Mm," said Joseph. "See the hand again which wrote the Patterton address. Mother's."

Frederick made no response, although his shoulders slumped. He ran a finger under the wax seal of the second letter, dated the same day as the first.

Darling Frederick –

Do forgive me the excess of emotion which characterized my earlier letter. I was overwrought and no sooner did the footman post it, than I wished it back and burned in the fire. Of course you must have been called away by pressing business, and I am so womanish as to let my fears run away with me. We have had our first quarrel, but you need not worry. I have forgiven you entirely and only wish to be once more in your arms to assure you of my love.

I hope you will pardon me writing you at your family estate. I did not want you to go another hour in doubt of me.

May you show the same courtesy to your own

H. B.

An improvement on her first epistle, he thought, but Frederick would have felt more cheerful if there were not a third to be got through. Observing that the hand on the last was even wilder than on the first, he braced himself and broke the seal.

F—

How can you not have responded to me? The man who claimed to love me to distraction would not have suffered my distress one instant, when it was within his power to alleviate it! Am I to understand that you fed me on untruth? That you promised me all, that you might rob me of my virtue? You spoke to me of being a good wife, as if pretending to such with R would not give the lie to all that has gone between you and me. And as to my child, would not you, a man who claimed such love for me, out of that love be a better father than such as she now has? I cannot, cannot believe that you would betray me thus. If it were so, you would be the greatest monster womankind has known. You would deserve it, if all my sex were to turn on you and rend you to pieces, to trample you to [illegible], you base, [illegible] miscreant!

R has noticed my peevishness and despondency. He speaks of making a "summer progress" through the country, as if he were the king. I loathe him. I long to throw our love in his face.

Write to me quickly, or come to me. If you do not, I cannot answer for the consequences. I swing like a pendulum between rage and fear, despair and longing. I will cover you with kisses or I will murder you. Or murder you and then take my own life.

Forgive the foolish passions of your very own

H. B.

Frederick passed a hand over his brow, feeling the beginnings of a headache. Had he spoken so carelessly of love to Honoria Braithwaite? Admittedly he had made no effort to deny words of love, when she put them in his mouth. He had been fond of her, yes. And was fondness really so far short of love?

"Frederick?" prompted Joseph, taking a seat beside him.

"Help," his brother answered, "I seem to be caught in a John Webster play."

"Are you in earnest? Do you really seek my help?"

Two blue eyes fixed him, followed by a rueful smile. "Dear brother, unless, in your study of natural history, you have come upon a vixen who threatens her straying fox with tears, with beatings, with murder, with cajolery, with guilt, and with self-slaughter, I fear you cannot help this particular fox with this particular vixen."

"I am sorry to hear it," returned Joseph. "Foxes and vixens of the animal variety are far more predictable creatures, however. The males rarely stray. When they choose a mate, it usually lasts their lives long."

"How pleasant for them," said Frederick acidly. "Mating for life with this particular vixen is out of the question, unfortunately. Or perhaps I should say *fortunately.*"

"Because you do not care for her?"

"That, and because she is already married."

Joseph said nothing, too conscious of how any remark on the subject he could offer would likely be received, especially since he had only recently taken orders.

Frederick rose and moved restlessly about the room. "I cannot expect you to understand, Joe. You have ever been the good son—your temporary rebellion against becoming a clergyman notwithstanding. No—do not protest—you know it to be so! Only see how you marry this Alice Hapgood of yours, out of duty, and to protect her reputation."

"There you are wrong," declared Joseph, springing to his feet. "I may once have spouted such nonsense as 'duty' and 'reputation,' but I am heartily ashamed of it now. I marry my Alice for no other reason than that I love her with all my being. Why do you suppose I threw myself at the uncle last night?" Shaking his head, he gave a humorless laugh. "I thought him a rival for her affections. Smile if you like, but I suspect if Alice really had been eloping with another man, I should do more than hound her with tear-stained letters."

"And I should think the more of you that you did," insisted Frederick. "Such vigor becomes a man. But this language from the pen of a woman...Only read these!" He waved the letters at his brother.

After a hesitation, Joseph complied, withdrawing to the dim light from the casement. Frederick saw him shake his head once. Bite his lip. When he had finished, he folded the letters neatly and laid them on the bureau.

"Frederick—" his brother's voice was serious. "I have no notion of what has passed between you and this person, but I hope you will take care in your response. If I understand correctly, she was no serving maid to be trifled with."

"She is Honoria Braithwaite, Lady Wimpole."

Joseph drew a sharp breath. "Not the wife of Lord Wimpole, the 'Silent Saint'?"

"The same," said Frederick grimly.

"Why, I admired his committee work for the Slave Trade Act! Wilberforce praised him as the best worker behind the scenes in the House of Lords. Said something about Wimpole quite turning the tide there—"

"Yes, exactly so," Frederick cut short this glow of enthusiasm. "Wimpole, the 'Silent Saint,' whose efforts played a part in rescuing countless thousands of unfortunates from being sold in slavery to serve the British Empire. *That* Wimpole. And I have cuckolded him."

"I say," frowned Joseph. "What a shabby return to make such a great man." Seeing his brother's eyes narrow, he added, "Of course, I know only as much of him as one reads in the papers—but how did such a man marry such a woman as—that?" He indicated the letters.

"He married as I suppose all men do," Frederick said, shrugging into his frock coat with impatience. "He chose as beautiful, wealthy, and clever a wife as fortune afforded him."

"And see how she has repaid him," muttered Joseph.

"If you are *quite* done moralizing, Reverend Joseph..."

"Nonsense, Frederick. I have not yet begun to moralize. Tell me—does Lord Wimpole know about your affair with his wife?"

"Possibly. But he is not the sort of man to do more than cut me publicly, if even that. He is a politician, after all."

"Lady Wimpole, however, threatens to be far more impolitic," said Joseph. He watched Frederick wrestle with his neckcloth before the glass. "Do you truly consider your relationship with her at an end, Frederick?"

"Completely and utterly. I grant you, she can be charming, and I lost my head for a time, but she has since proven too melodramatic for my taste." He paused in tying his mail coach knot, all too aware of his brother's averted gaze. "You, like she, think me heartless, do you not?"

"I do not think so highly of you as I have at other times," Joseph said simply. "Whatever the woman's tendency toward melodrama, I suspect some true feeling underlies it, and if you have played a part in her unhappiness—"

"I ought to play a part in remedying it?" Frederick broke in curtly. He threw the neckcloth aside in frustration and yanked a fresh one from his open valise. "That is impossible. She has taken some damn-fool notion that we should run away together, and I will not."

"Nor would I suggest that," rejoined Joseph.

"Then what do you suggest?" Frederick crumpled the second cravat in a ball and hurled it against the window. "You see that, if I tell her the truth—that I do not love her nor never have—that I bedded her because I thought her an amiable, willing partner and no more—there is no telling what she might do! More poisonous letters, to be sure. But then—she may decry me to Braithwaite until he has no alternative but to take action. She may make London too hot for me ever to return—"

"You must not be so painfully honest with her then," Joseph interjected, taking the third neckcloth from his brother's hands and managing it himself. They were equals in stature, Joseph being slighter in build, but they shared the same quickness and easy grace. Hazel eyes met blue ones. "You must write and say otherwise. That though you cared for her at one time, guilt has overwhelmed you." He grinned. "No—wait—she may not find that credible."

"I did feel guilty," Frederick protested. "From time to time. One could not grow up with our family and not think, whether one wanted to or not, that adultery was a sneaking, shameful thing."

Joseph only raised an eyebrow and then winced again, touching his bruised face. "Pray, do not make me skeptical, in my condition."

"I have it!" cried Frederick, snapping his fingers. "I will write that, though I cared for her at one time—cared deeply, say—and will always remember her with fondness and respect, I was compelled to give her up because I have yielded to family pressures. My brother now a clergyman, et cetera, et cetera."

"Leave me out of it, Frederick, I beg you. I would just as soon not have this woman turn her anger on me."

"Then I will say I must give her up because, as the sole heir of both my father and my uncle, I felt it incumbent on me to take a wife."

Joseph here gave a bark of a laugh. "Better, in that case, to say you felt guilty, Frederick. In comparison, it might strain her credulity less."

"All right, all right." Frederick paced the length of the small chamber. "Not that I feel it *incumbent* on me to take a wife, then. Too vague. I will say, rather, that I am shortly to be married.

Yes—that by the time fate ever brings us together again, I will have a wife. Therefore, she and I must sunder our ties and cleave to our spouses for the good of all, and so on and so forth. That's it! I will say I am to be married."

"To whom, if I might ask?" Joseph said. "I need hardly point out that, if you say you are shortly to be married, and then you show up in town next season still *unmarried*, will you not make matters worse?"

"Perhaps she will have chosen a new lover by then," Frederick suggested, not looking convinced himself. He sighed. "I suppose you are right. I should at least have a betrothed in tow, if I dare to show my face again."

"Lord Marlton did introduce you to Somerset's finest last night, did he not?" Joseph teased. "What do you say to the Honorable Miss Birdlow?"

"I could not possibly think as highly of Miss Birdlow as she thinks of herself."

"Her bosom friend, then, Miss Porterworth?"

"There certainly was a great deal of bosom there," said Frederick, "though rather less of 'friend.' No, perhaps I will follow your lead, brother, and choose one of the delightful Hapgood daughters. Perhaps...the eldest?"

The grin vanished from Joseph's face. "I would not have you jest about my wife's family."

"Who jests? If Miss Alice Hapgood has succeeded in captivating you, why should I not find her elder sister equally so?"

"Did you flirt with her, Frederick?" Joseph demanded. "With Miss Elfrida Hapgood?"

"Is her Christian name Elfrida? How peculiar. But—to answer your question—I did not. We were not even introduced."

His brother relaxed, taking Frederick's shoulder in a firm grip and giving it a shake. "Very well, then. I know how irresistible the fair sex finds you, Frederick, and I would prefer that you not dally with the heart of my soon-to-be sister." The corner of Joseph's mouth twisted wryly. Not that he could imagine Miss Hapgood heartbroken and screeching about like this Lady Wimpole, but if anyone could reduce a sensible young woman to a puddle, it would be his brother Frederick.

Releasing him, Joseph took up his beaver hat. "If we are agreed on that matter, I will leave you then to your imagination and your correspondence. What woman you choose to torture next is your own affair, so long as it is not Miss Hapgood. Your misadventures have kept me too long this day from the first object of my heart. Fare you well."

"Good-bye," murmured Frederick, after the door closed behind him. Dragging the little deal table across the floor to the window, he rapped his knuckles on it. He would ask the innkeeper for paper and ink after he looked about for some breakfast. What exactly he would write remained to be seen, but one thing was clear.

If he wished to make Miss Elfrida Hapgood's acquaintance, it had better wait until his brother was married off and out of Somerset.

Chapter Three

He seemed to want no introduction, but was going to salute my daughters as one certain of a kind reception.
—Oliver Goldsmith, *The Vicar of Wakefield* (1766)

Some women were best seen by candlelight, but Elfrida Hapgood was not one of them. Her fair and flawless complexion bore well the light of day, and the beams penetrating the admittedly clouded windows of the Bramleigh drawing room only served to enhance the rich hues of her hair. Moreover, Elfrida always took care to choose the chair most in the sunlight, not from vanity, but that she might see her embroidery more clearly.

She was seated there when the raw-boned and inquisitive young maid threw open the drawing room door with a flourish, bellowing, "Mr. *Frederick* Tierney!"

"Ah. I beg your pardon," he began, glancing at the three young ladies who rose to greet him. "I thought the squire was at home." Nor was there any sign of the mother, but Joseph had mentioned the woman was seldom in company, having pretensions to invalidism. The morning's wedding, and all that led to it, must have finished her.

"There was an ear infection," breathed little black-haired Edith. She was a delicate creature, probably still in the schoolroom, and her cheek was smudged with something dark, as if she had been sweeping chimneys.

"I regret to hear that," said Frederick. "I hope he will recover quickly, though he looked well enough this morning."

"Not *Papa*," cried the older Margaret, shaking her head at her younger sister. "There is nothing wrong with *Papa's* ears. Edie means the hounds. Caractacus—the dog—has the ear infection, and Papa is in the kennels with Mr. Frick, attending to him."

"Attending to Mr. Frick," Frederick said, a gleam in his eye. "How kind."

"Not attending to Mr. Frick!" corrected Margaret once more, marveling at his slow wits. "Attending to Caractacus."

"Margaret," said Elfrida simply, and her sister hushed.

Frederick availed himself of the opportunity her speech afforded and turned toward Miss Hapgood, whose calm, unreadable violet gaze was fixed on him. He thought, however, he dictated a twitch about her lips. That amusement again.

He bowed. "I find propriety's dictates in this instance almost absurd. We are not introduced. But in the squire's absence, who will perform the necessary offices? We are nearly related, you know. I am Frederick, the brother of Joseph, who married your sister Miss Alice not three hours ago. Miss Hapgood, I had the pleasure of seeing you at the ball, although we did not meet."

Elfrida curtsied and gestured toward her sisters. "My sisters Margaret and Edith."

When all had found seats again, and Elfrida and Margaret took up their embroidery frames, a silence fell. Frederick felt Edith's eyes on him, but when he looked her way, she dropped her gaze and returned to whatever she was sketching. She reached up to brush hair from her face, and he then understood the smudge on her cheek.

"Miss Edith, are you an artist?" he asked.

"I—I?" Guiltily, she dropped her charcoal stick, which left a black daub on the window seat cushion. A hasty rub at the blot only made it worse.

Margaret sucked in her breath and stared up at the ceiling, but Elfrida came to Edith's rescue. "She is, Mr. Tierney. We are very proud of Edith's talents, but she can rarely be prevailed upon to exhibit her work to any but the immediate family. Are you a great connoisseur of art?" It was Elfrida's experience that most people delighted in talking of themselves, and she hoped, by throwing Mr. Tierney this question, to be spared further effort for the remainder of the fifteen-minute call. Why he had come to call in the first place was another question. His brother was gone; Mr. Frederick Tierney had no business in Somerset—should he not be on his way? Back to his London life of gambling and prinking and courting scandal with married women?

She thrust her needle through the muslin, drawing the bright green floss after it. Even in the strong light, if she could not hold her hoop closer, she trusted herself with no more than stitching the grass beneath the shepherdess's feet.

"Sadly, I am...not...a great connoisseur of art," replied Frederick. He flicked a speck off the knee of his breeches. "And with the war off and on, there has been no opportunity for a Grand Tour, to develop any incipient connoisseurship. However this lack of mine, Miss Edith, makes me the very best friend an artist might have. I find something to love in everything."

"If you mean to flatter her," said Margaret, before her younger sister could respond, "that is not the way to do it. To find something to love in everything only means you lack discernment."

This would not do, after all, Elfrida decided—letting Margaret's tongue run loose.

She rose with no appearance of hurry (compelling Mr. Tierney to spring to his feet as well) and gave the bell cord a tug. When Elfrida seated herself again, it was beside her sharp-tongued younger sister, and she took care to arrange her skirts that she might press Margaret's foot if the need arose. As Margaret occupied the chaise directly across from Mr. Tierney, his blurred features took on more substance. There was a fine, straight nose to accompany that golden hair, and a firm jaw above the points of his shirt. Elfrida had, moreover, the suspicion that he had just been looking at her, his gaze withdrawn the instant she turned toward him.

Another silence swallowed the company. With her back to the light now, Elfrida accidentally ran the needle through the shepherdess's foot, and she bit the inside of her cheek in annoyance. She tried again. "How long do you intend to stay in Somerset, Mr. Tierney, now that your—our—brother Joseph and sister Alice have gone?"

"I cannot say. The viscount has invited me to stay as long as I like. And, as I have never before been in Somerset, I am curious to look about me."

"Do you find Miss Birdlow beautiful?" Margaret blurted. Elfrida slid her foot over and pressed *down*. Margaret gave something like a chirp.

"I do," said Frederick. "Very."

This was not the answer to win approval from the younger Hapgoods, who believed no one in the county could hold a candle to their Elfrida. Margaret's lips pressed together and Edith frowned at her drawing. Elfrida only worked at pulling out the offending stitch, her brow serene.

"You rang, Miss?" The maid-of-all-work Dorcas burst in, hair coming loose and her face red.

"Yes," said Elfrida. "We should like—"

"To fetch the squire?" Dorcas interrupted. "I set Hal on it. Going to the kennels, that is."

"Thank you." Only the faintest color in her cheeks betrayed Elfrida's impatience. "And we should like some tea, as well."

"'Tisn't time for tea," pointed out Dorcas. "Nor dinner. Button'll have a fit."

"We have a *guest*, you know," hissed Margaret, nodding Frederick's direction as if the maid might have forgotten admitting him a few minutes earlier.

Dorcas looked blank, and Elfrida mouthed an unladylike oath. With only three servants at Bramleigh, they often complained of overwork, and Alice had been wont to keep them happy with little gifts of fish and birds and game, garnered during her wanderings out of doors. Today must begin a new regime.

Assuming her firmest tone, Elfrida said, "Tea, please, Dorcas. Tell Button it is my express wish. Mr. Tierney has just come from Pattergees, and while we may not provision him as luxuriously as the Marltons, I hope we may still prove hospitable."

That did the trick. Dorcas' elder sister Tabby was in service at Pattergees, and the comparison to that great estate roused the younger's competitive spirit. The girl sketched a clumsy curtsey and withdrew.

Another pause followed. Elfrida's bosom rose and fell. Good gracious! How would they fill the requisite fifteen minutes? This man spoke less than Mr. Norman DeWitt! Perhaps she should just let Margaret rattle on. The worst that could happen would be that Margaret so offended Mr. Tierney that he never called again. Would that be so terrible? Alice and Mr. Joseph Tierney were safely married; it could not harm them now, if the in-laws were not on intimate footing.

Though his expression gave no hint of it (he appeared, rather, to be contemplating the faded fabric of the window draperies), Frederick was also struggling. He could not say why or how, but this Miss Hapgood put him at a disadvantage, with her calm demeanor and concentration on her blasted embroidery. The two younger stared at him frankly enough, Miss Margaret critically and Miss Edith awestruck, but he was not here to charm schoolroom girls. Even the haughty Miss Birdlow over at Pattergees studied him while feigning indifference. That was it—Miss Birdlow feigned indifference, while Miss Hapgood...who knew what she was thinking? The few times her glance fell on him, her eyes were vague, unfocused. As if her mind were elsewhere. But where could her mind be? Did handsome, eligible gentlemen call so frequently on her that she could hardly differentiate one from the next, nor did she trouble to? He should like to see her laugh again, as she had at the ball, but his feeble attempts at jests this afternoon left her untouched. Miss Porterworth would have burst her stays, laughing at that bit about the squire and Mr. Frick.

He cleared his throat. "What lovely grounds you have here." A lie. They were rather unkempt, but one could detect traces of their former glory beneath the runaway greenery. And some might interpret the botanical dishevelment as a display of the picturesque. "Do you favor landscapes, Miss Edith?"

Edith shook her head dumbly, and it was Margaret who answered, "Never. Edie paints portraits."

"Are you working on a portrait there?" he persisted.

Edie slapped a hand to cover her picture, as if he had threatened to snatch it from her.

"It's of you, I imagine," Margaret went on. While Elfrida did not instantly smash down on her sister's toes, Margaret scooted her foot away nonetheless. "You're very handsome." She delivered this pronouncement without a trace of coquetry, as if she merely observed he wore polished boots.

"Oh!" said Frederick. In his surprise he added, "Do you think so?"

"Everyone does," piped up Edith.

"Or *nearly* everyone," Margaret amended, throwing Elfrida an arch look. That very morning, after the wedding, when Margaret had asked Elfrida what she thought of Frederick Tierney, Elfrida had declared him "a very plain young man." But that was Elfrida: making a parade of how little beauty swayed her opinions.

Before Frederick could digest this interesting piece of information, little Miss Edith had made up her mind about him. She jumped from her window seat and held her paper out. "It is you, you see. I hope you don't mind. We don't often have male models, besides Papa, and I'm sure I already have captured Papa in every attitude and mood and pose imaginable."

"Which isn't many," put in Margaret. "He's either gruff, gruff, or gruff." Bounding up herself, she slapped the back of the chaise, frowning like Hades and shaking her fist. "Where has my riding crop got to? If Hal's misplaced it, I'll have that boy cut up and put in a pie!"

"Margaret!" cried Elfrida. But Frederick caught it again then—that flicker of amusement which made her blue eyes dance. In an instant it was repressed, and her chastened sister resumed her seat, Elfrida sliding over so as to be nearly against her.

To cover the awkwardness, he took the charcoal likeness from Miss Edith and examined it. And for the second time in as many minutes, he was nonplussed. This was no childish attempt he held.

The outlines were rough, yes, and smudged in places, the crown of his hair only hinted at, as well as the line of his neck disappearing into his shirt points, but she had captured something. A cast to his eyes. In them was no expression he imagined himself showing the world—no coolness or self-possession or disdain. Rather, his eyes were almost...wistful. Frederick felt unclothed to look upon them.

Edith registered his dismay and went scarlet. "You don't like it. It's—it's—not finished. It's rough."

"Not like it!" exclaimed Margaret, now up in arms over this slight to her baby sister. Pushing Elfrida away, she sprung up to see the sketch over Mr. Tierney's shoulder. "I can't imagine why not. That would be like saying you didn't like yourself, Mr. Tierney, because it is *exactly you*."

"I did not say I did not like it," he rejoined quietly, as Elfrida tried to glare Margaret into sitting back down. "The skill of it took me by surprise—that is all."

At once, all was forgiven. Edith looked like she might cry with pleasure, and Margaret plopped onto the chaise and clasped her hands smugly. "It is no surprise to any of us. Our old drawing master said Edie could be the Angelica Kauffman of our age."

"If she were not moored in this backwater, he also said," Elfrida spoke up. "Miss Kauffman had the benefit of living in Rome and London. She had the friendship of Sir Joshua Reynolds and the royal family."

"I don't want to be friends with them," said Edith stoutly. "That would be scary. Or to live anywhere but Bramleigh. But I should like to attempt a classical scene one day, like Miss—Mrs.—Miss Kauffman did."

"And why should you not?" said Frederick. "No matter who your friends are, or where you find yourself."

"Because we never see anybody," Margaret said, with a baldness that made Elfrida grip her embroidery frame till her knuckles whitened. "Edie has girls enough to be her models—she has been drawing Elfie and Alice and me since she could hold a pencil—and Papa would do for Zeus, if Edie made him taller"—she shook off Elfrida's hand, which had flown to her wrist warningly— "though really he reminds me more of Hephaestus because he is so stocky. But, you see, there are no Apollos or Adonises or Areses to be had."

Before Elfrida could do more than wish a great earthquake would split the ground beneath them and swallow up Bramleigh, furnishings and all, the drawing room door banged open to admit Squire Hapgood, followed by Dorcas with the tea tray.

"Mr. Frederick Tierney? Richard Hapgood. You are welcome to Bramleigh," muttered the squire, executing a bow, though Elfrida could see from her father's red face and knit brows that he was irked to be summoned from his ailing hound to greet someone who could have paid his visit far more conveniently any day before the wedding.

"I thank you, sir. I am sorry to hear about your Caractacus."

The squire's lip almost trembled, but he managed a curt nod. "Frick says a little goldenseal, a little almond oil, and he'll come 'round."

Elfrida half expected Mr. Tierney to say, "Frick will come 'round?" (and Frederick nearly did say it), but he managed to resist, and everyone was able to resume their seats while Dorcas deposited the tea tray with a clatter before her. Elfrida poured Mr. Tierney a cup, and was on the point of asking if he took milk or sugar, when the squire absently took the cup from her hands, tipping some of the hot tea into the saucer to cool it.

"You've met my girls then—except the one your brother made off with," said the squire, making an effort.

"I have." Frederick accepted the next cup Elfrida poured, refusing any additions to it. Giving her a slow wink, he too poured some of the tea into the saucer. "Charming young ladies. We were discussing Miss Edith's artistic talents."

"Hmmph. Yes. A pat hand with the pen, my little Edie."

The squire slurped his beverage from his saucer. A mortified Margaret was about to remonstrate when Frederick followed suit, slurping even more noisily, if that were possible. Elfrida ducked her head to hide her smile, her indignation at being winked at nearly forgotten. She did, however, turn her body away from Mr. Tierney and resume her needlework, to calm the flutter his insolence aroused. Her father might not have the manners of a viscount, but he was a good man and did not deserve to have his daughters *winked at*, even in jest.

The tea seemed to revive their father because he looked suddenly at his guest, as if only then realizing what he represented. "All talented, my girls," he resumed. "Edie with the pencils and paints, Margaret with—uh—with—ahem! That is, and Alice, in her way, in natural history. (Not a ladylike pursuit, Alice's, but your brother seemed to like it.) But my Elfrida here—quite the incomparable—"

"I was just saying, before you entered," interrupted Mr. Tierney smoothly, "that I would be glad to sit for Miss Edith. She was deploring her lack of male models, and, while I cannot boast such talents as your daughters possess, I have been told I stand still remarkably well."

Here Elfrida choked on her tea and Margaret was obliged to pound her on the back.

"Stand still?" repeated the squire, puzzled. He could not see what the handsome young man was about, making up to him about Edith. He, Richard Hapgood, was as eager as any gentleman in financial straits to marry off his daughters advantageously, but Edie was a mere ten or eleven, and Frederick Tierney was five-and-twenty if he was a day. For Elfrida, now, any man between twenty and fifty might do, but that was because she was nearly of age. A father had his standards.

"Wouldn't be proper," declared the squire. "Young chit still in the schoolroom, drawing strange gentlemen."

"Not to contradict you, sir, but I take exception at being called 'strange.' I am, after all, the brother of your son-in-law. And if, perhaps, Miss Hapgood and Miss Margaret would submit to being present at the sittings, there could be no objections on the grounds of propriety."

"Hmmph." The squire frowned. This Mr. Frederick Tierney was a slick one—there was no telling if the innocence was an imposture. But if the squire were to judge by the gossip abroad at the Midsummer Ball, he would do best to keep his chicks gathered close. On the other hand, the man could hardly work mischief in a drawing room with *three* daughters present, and being thrown together for hours at a time might wake him to Elfrida's charms.

"I suppose," he conceded at last. "If my daughters were all present. Might be able to rouse my wife from her deathbed to come down, as well."

"Is Mrs. Hapgood so ill?" said Frederick, startled.

"Ill? What? Nah. Though her imagination threatens to carry her off any day now." The squire rubbed his hands together and glanced none too subtly at the clock. "I'd best see how Frick's applications are going. Crack is a lively one, and he may need help holding him down."

Frederick took the hint and rose to his feet. "Miss Edith, what time shall I come?"

"Oh—" Edith looked to her sisters in alarm, but Margaret only raised her eyebrows and Elfrida continued to stitch away. "If you please—the morning light would be best. Perhaps ten o'clock? To-morrow or Monday?"

"Ten o'clock tomorrow to begin with," agreed Frederick. He made his bow and the squire marched him to the door, nodding in salute after the gentleman untied his horse and took himself off. Then he clapped his hands together and hurried back to the drawing room.

"Papa!" wailed Margaret, winding her arm through his. "Must you take your tea like that, pouring it in your saucer and making such a noise when you slurp it? I'm sure that's not how they do it at Pattergees."

"Confound Pattergees," said her father. "And this fancy Frederick Tierney took it that way, too."

"I'm sure Joseph never did," Edith said.

"I think Mr. Frederick Tierney took his tea that way to keep you company, Papa," said Elfrida, remembering the wink. "And made such a noise drinking it, that Margaret might not be embarrassed."

"Hmmph. Courteous of him," answered her father doubtfully. "Do you like him, Elfrida? I think I prefer Alice's Joseph—this Frederick is too tailored and silly for my taste—but I daresay most women would prefer him."

"Thank you, Papa," said Elfrida, as if she were being offered a second cup of tea. "I do not think I will try to attach him."

"Now, now. I spoke too hastily, Elfie. I did not mean he would not do for a husband. All women must bear with a few faults. He's well enough to look at, and I suppose he has more money than Joseph. You could do far worse."

Laying aside her work, she glided over to take his other arm and to lean her cheek on his shoulder. "Thank you all the same. You speak as if I had only to snap my fingers, and Mr. Tierney would offer for me. But, even if that were true, I should prefer a different sort of husband. You would not have me marry anyone like my uncles Alec or Alwyn, would you? I fear Mr. Tierney is most Alec-and-Alwyn-like. And you admit my uncles would not make good husbands, however much we might love them."

As the squire loved his profligate brothers-in-law very little indeed, he found her argument highly persuasive. Imagine if his eldest's marriage, instead of bringing financial relief, only served to place another burden on the quarterly rents!

Giving a shudder, he patted her hand and dropped kisses on her head and Margaret's. "Very well, then. Let there be no more Tierneys marrying Hapgoods. Didn't care for that one much at first sight anyway—popinjay air and something cunning about the eyes. But I suppose he is related to us, somewhat. For Joseph's sake we must suffer him. Let us hope he will come some few times and then carry away Miss Birdlow, instead."

With this benediction, their father shook them off and made for the kennels again, to watch over his beloved hound.

Chapter Four

Their tears..pierce the hearts
of their pittying neighbors.
—Thomas Hubbart, *A Pill to Purge Formality* (1650)

"No wedding breakfast!" Miss Constance Porterworth echoed to the Honorable Miss Agnes Birdlow. "How irregular."

"Irregular is precisely the word I would use to describe the Hapgoods," Miss Birdlow replied. The two friends were walking the formal gardens of Pattergees, Miss Birdlow's arm linked through Miss Porterworth's. They were an odd pairing: Miss Birdlow with her queenly height and lofty beauty, and the much shorter and fuller Miss Porterworth, of the snub nose and wide mouth. But Miss Birdlow had learned long ago that a young woman could have no dearer friend than one whom she cast utterly in the shade. If only

Constance were not inclined to coquette so outrageously with every man she encountered, she would be perfection indeed.

"But Mr. Joseph Tierney explained it," Miss Birdlow went on, as they trailed along the curving broderie spirals of the parterre. (She longed for her father to replace the old-fashioned *jardin à la française* with a wilderness and some Gothic ruins.) "He said they chose a small wedding supper the day before, that he and Miss Alice—that is, that he and Mrs. Joseph Tierney—might be able to get as far as Bath by nightfall."

Miss Porterworth gave a long sigh. "A wedding journey! Only think."

Her friend shrugged. "I should prefer not to take mine in a borrowed gig, but I suppose if you are a mere respectable clergyman setting up house, you do well to practice economy."

Too wise to answer immediately, Miss Porterworth gave an amiable titter. She privately thought Agnes' scorn of the borrowed gig hinted at sour grapes—after all, had they not, some weeks ago, hoped Mr. Joseph Tierney might sweep one of *them* off in a gig, borrowed or not? He had been even poorer then, having no living to speak of, but they had all been willing to entertain the thought of winning him.

When they reached the stone-paved Goose foot, from which several *allées* radiated like points of the compass, Miss Porterworth plopped down on the circular bench. "One good thing about Mr. Joseph Tierney borrowing his brother's gig," she declared, "is that he did not also borrow the brother. It is my opinion that Mr. Frederick

Tierney is twice as handsome as the younger, and twice as eligible. What is Mr. Joseph to him?"

Miss Birdlow hesitated, digging the point of her parasol between the pavers. She wanted to hug her disdain of Mr. Joseph Tierney and his pathetic wedding journey a little longer, but the temptation to talk of the other Mr. Tierney was too great. She dropped beside Miss Porterworth. "Mr. Frederick Tierney is indeed far handsomer."

"And now he is without his gig! And come to Pattergees! How I envy you, Agnes! Cannot you ask your father if I might visit for a fortnight?"

"Of course you may. I needn't ask Papa; I will simply tell him."

Miss Porterworth clasped her gloved hands and beat an excited tattoo with her little feet. "What fun we will have! You must tell me all about him."

"Well, he only came from the inn yesterday—Mr. Joseph Tierney said his brother left Buckinghamshire in a hurry and therefore had much correspondence to attend to, before he had leisure to look about. But last night he joined us at supper—Mr. Joseph being at the wedding supper, of course—and quite charmed us all."

"Do tell, Agnes! What did he wear? His waistcoat at the ball was divine."

"The one he wore last night had the tiniest stripes, green and tan-color, and my brother Frank was struck dumb by the beauty of Mr. Tierney's cravat. Frank said his man would never be capable of such a creation. It was sculpture."

"Sculpture," breathed Miss Porterworth, shutting her eyes.

"And he talks more than Mr. Joseph Tierney ever did," Miss Birdlow said. "And on more interesting topics than trees and insects. Mr. Frederick Tierney is a man of the world. He has lived in town and seen every play and opera. He knows so many people, and all the right sort of people to know." She sniffed and gave her parasol a twirl. "For all her tricks and stratagems, that Miss Alice—Mrs. Joseph Tierney—has only managed to have herself buried alive in rural Buckinghamshire for the rest of her life."

Miss Porterworth, who never had a London season like Miss Birdlow, still clung to romantic notions about society. "So true, Agnes. I did not think of that. Of course—Papa says we are great fools to go on about Mr. Frederick Tierney so. He said the man is nothing but a rakehell, and not a very wealthy one at that."

Stiffening, Miss Birdlow said in a quelling tone, "I am sure my papa would never tolerate a rakehell under our roof. Mr. Tierney cannot help being popular and arousing jealousy and gossip."

"I daresay you are right," answered her friend, chastened. Her lower lip protruded, however, to have her father's opinion so summarily dismissed, and it was with a hint of mischief that she added, "And Papa would be right to be jealous, I suppose. There is not a chance Mr. Frederick Tierney would look my way, if you were nearby."

"Stuff and nonsense!" objected Miss Birdlow, blushing nevertheless.

"He did dance with you at the ball."

"He could not do otherwise, when Papa introduced us." Stabbing the pavers with her parasol, she got to her feet and paced the circumference of the Goose foot. "And I had to pay for it—when Geoffrey danced the two next with me, he took every opportunity to denigrate Mr. Tierney."

"Does Mr. Wynstanley persist in thinking you will be married one day?" asked Miss Porterworth. As long as she had known Miss Birdlow, she had envied her friend her cradleside betrothal to her cousin Geoffrey Wynstanley. Imagine always having one beau in reserve!

"We never speak of it. I had thought Geoffrey might, when Mr. Joseph Tierney came among us—" Miss Birdlow broke off, frowning. Geoffrey had shown signs of resentment toward that potential rival, but it all came to nothing. Mr. Joseph Tierney married Miss Alice Hapgood, and Geoffrey left for home, the day after the ball. It would serve her cousin right if, when he next descended on their corner of Somerset, he found her courted by another Tierney! Geoffrey could not expect her to wait around and wait around. Miss Birdlow was hardly certain she wanted to marry her cousin, but she was equally uncertain she did *not* want to.

Sensing her companion's conflict, Miss Porterworth obligingly turned the subject. "Where has Mr. Frederick Tierney got to today? Did he never return after the wedding at Bramleigh Chapel?"

"He did," said Miss Birdlow. "Frank took him to show him the lodge renovations. But then he—he went to call on the Hapgoods. I suppose he must."

"Yes, being related now by marriage." Miss Porterworth stood to join her friend, and the eyes of both turned in the direction of Bramleigh to the northeast. The two estates shared an entire flank, separated by a stream that gurgled and tumbled along for nearly a mile before it met the Holliton. Wooded stands alternated with grassy rising ground that became, to the southwest, the famed Blackdown Hills. Beautiful country, if anyone had an eye for it—which Miss Birdlow and Miss Porterworth this day did not.

As if summoned by the strength of their interest, a speck materialized in the distance. The two young ladies said nothing, in case it proved to be nothing or no one of interest, although Miss Birdlow could not think who but Mr. Frederick Tierney would be skirting the fields between Bramleigh and Pattergees at this hour.

The speck grew into a figure: a man in a royal blue tailcoat on horseback. Certainly Mr. Frederick Tierney. But whyever would he set his horse at a gallop on such a warm day?

In truth, Frederick had given it no thought. The bay responded to the urgency communicated by his body, and as the man's thoughts were flying, so too did the horse.

Under the squire's watchful eye Frederick had trotted sedately enough down the graveled drive of Bramleigh, but once out of sight he left the road and cut across the fields, clearing the first hedgerow with a brace and a bound.

He would marry her, he decided.

She didn't talk much, but that came as a relief after the chattering likes of a Miss Porterworth or a Lady Wimpole. Chattering was well enough in a ballroom but it made for a tedious *tête-à- tête*, and a lifetime of it would be dreadful. What Miss Hapgood did venture to say was to-the-point and utterly rational—a rare thing in a woman.

While Frederick usually preferred greater liveliness in his love affairs, marriage was no love affair. Besides—after having spent the last few days debating how best to manage Lady Wimpole's choler, he welcomed Miss Hapgood's phlegmatic temperament. With Miss Hapgood there would be no wild threats, no tears or frenzies. Of course, were she to extend that unnatural calm to the marriage bed, marital relations might prove more of a duty than a pleasure, but Frederick thought the draw of her beauty would suffice long enough to beget an heir or two.

And she was beautiful! Even more so than the very lovely Miss Birdlow, whom he really ought to try for, if he was going to be cold-blooded about the whole business. Indeed, when he holed in the Patterton inn for the previous two days, he made an effort to transfer his preference from Miss Hapgood to Miss Birdlow. The latter was wealthier, had been more in society, and was the daughter of a viscount—would she not be a more logical fit for one of his experience and interests? They could gad about town and Frederick could dispense with staying at his uncle's place in Green Street—Lord Marlton owning a perfectly good townhouse in Mayfair. Furthermore, Miss Birdlow's pride would prevent her from weeping or throwing crockery when confronted with his peccadillos. They would make a fine, typical couple.

And yet a second evening spent with Miss Birdlow, in the intimate bosom of her family, left him unmoved. She had continued aloof, and he had conversed and flattered and flirted some, fully aware of the admiration she hid behind those lowered lids. If he chose to care for her, those eyes said, she would not repulse him.

But he did not care to. He found himself still thinking of Miss Hapgood's laughing, open gaze and wishing for his brother's speedy departure. Nor had the glimpses he had of Miss Hapgood at the wedding dimmed his interest. She would not meet his eyes there, no matter how many times he glanced her way, and, before he could shake off less reticent members of the parish and force an introduction upon the family, she had gone.

The afternoon's call frustrated him. It was all well and good for Miss Hapgood to be a serene sort of person, he muttered to himself, but was a flicker of spirit too much to ask for? No, no—that wasn't the problem. She had spirit enough shelved away in that admirable figure of hers. Only see how he caught those tantalizing glimpses of amusement, and the slight flare of her nostrils when he winked at her. She had not liked that. Yes—spirit enough, but it was repressed ruthlessly beneath her calm demeanor.

But why repress it at all? Ought she not, rather, to put it on display, when he was about? To demonstrate a *little* awareness that he was an eligible young man to be won?

Frederick grimaced, his hands tightening on the reins until the bay slowed. Had he really just thought that? How insufferably vain! And yet, if he thought so highly of himself, the world had never gainsaid him. He did not need Miss Hapgood to fall over herself to please him. He did not need fluttering lashes or giggles behind fans or elaborate ploys to win his compliments. But neither would he object to some small signs of recognition. She might look at him more purposefully, for starters, and not as if her thoughts were elsewhere. She might let him know in some fashion, that she would be glad to meet him again.

The bay mare gave an impatient *whuffle* and shook her head as if she would look back at him and say, *First you drive me, and then you force me to a walk?*

"Just so," said Frederick. "I have not been considerate. You are no doubt anxious for cool water and a bag of oats." Pulling the brim of his beaver lower on his head, he looked out across the downs toward Pattergees. They were not far from the park now, and the rise he was descending gave him a good view into the gardens.

"Ah ha. Look there, Mignonne. Those two distant figures would be the Honorable Miss Agnes Birdlow and her bosom companion Miss Constance Porterworth. You see? They turn our direction. We are discovered. I suppose I might ride you right over the top of Miss Hapgood before she would look up from her embroideries, but those two—"

He broke off. Not because it was odd for a gentleman to address his horse (Frederick was often in that habit when alone), but because an idea came to him. Perhaps the taciturn Miss Hapgood could be roused to a show of spirit. Perhaps she needed only a touch of inducement. Surrounded as she was by only rather unconventional younger sisters, and isolated as she was in the county by the relative shabbiness of Bramleigh, Miss Hapgood might not be aware of the feminine arts required to ensnare suitors. She might need instruction.

And who better to provide instruction than her peers?

He could hardly expect the Marltons to host another ball, so close on the heels of the Midsummer Ball, but there might be a card party drawn up. Or an evening of music, followed by a little impromptu dance.

Let Miss Hapgood join them and learn from her more worldly neighbors.

He nudged Mignonne to a trot, raising his riding crop to salute the young ladies.

"He's coming!" squealed Miss Porterworth. "Oh...how well he sits his horse—better even than Roscoe, who is a perfect *centaur*, I assure you."

"Stop waving at him," urged Miss Birdlow. "Really, Constance, one would think you were on a sinking ship, and he the rescue vessel."

"Pooh. He will think I am friendly. At the ball Mr. Tierney remarked on my 'amiable disposition' and 'high spirits.'"

"He is quite the gentlemen," Miss Birdlow said wryly. "Now shhhh..."

"Good afternoon!" cried Frederick, swinging down from his mount and sweeping his hat off to make his bow. "Miss Birdlow. Miss Porterworth. How pleasant to come upon you here."

"We were just taking a turn in the garden before dinner," replied Miss Birdlow.

Gallantly he offered an arm to each of them, to walk back to the great house, letting Mignonne trail behind them like an overgrown mastiff.

"Have you found them all well at Bramleigh?" pursued Miss Birdlow.

"Very well indeed, save one hound afflicted with earache."

Miss Porterworth loosed a cascade of titters. "Indeed, Mr. Tierney. With the Hapgoods, the hounds are very much part of the family. If you stayed until the hunting season, you should see how the squire prizes them."

He nodded pleasantly at this, and Miss Birdlow went on, "But were they sorry to have Miss Alice Hapgood—that is, Mrs. Joseph Tierney—gone from among them?"

"I do not know. We did not speak of it."

"Didn't speak of it?" echoed Miss Porterworth. "Not talk of the wedding? How very odd. What did you speak of?"

"Oh...beauty and art, I suppose," he said, with a sidelong look at Miss Birdlow. "Miss Margaret Hapgood asked if I thought you beautiful."

"How—how—impertinent—of her!" marveled Miss Birdlow, turning her head away. "She is but fourteen or fifteen—not yet out and little in the world. I hope you did not answer."

"But that would have been impertinent of *me*," said Frederick. "Of course I answered."

After an agonizing pause, Miss Porterworth gave a hop. "And what did you say, Mr. Tierney? You must have said, of course, that dear Agnes here is as beautiful as they come."

He hid a smile to hear her regretful admission. "Miss Margaret Hapgood asked if I thought Miss Birdlow beautiful, and I said, yes, very."

"Oh," said Miss Birdlow and Miss Porterworth in chorus, though in rather different tones.

"And so the subject turned to art," Frederick barreled on. "It so happens I have offered to sit for Miss Edith Hapgood. She shows a talent for drawing."

His two companions were still recovering from his bald admiration of Miss Birdlow's beauty and could hardly comprehend this later pronouncement.

"Sit for Miss Edith Hapgood?" murmured Miss Birdlow.

"Which one is that?" asked Miss Porterworth.

"The youngest. Yes, a very decided talent that I should like to encourage while I am here."

"Oh—won't that be inconvenient for you, Mr. Tierney," said Miss Porterworth, "to spend such time at Bramleigh?"

"One must make a few sacrifices for connections," he explained. "And the Hapgoods and I are certainly connected now."

Miss Birdlow lightly removed her fingers from his arm and opened her parasol, so that she had to walk a little apart. "You must let us turn the tables, then, Mr. Tierney, and ask you what you thought of the eldest Miss Hapgood's beauty."

"She is lovely, indeed. I see why my brother spoke of the natural beauty of Somerset, although I suspect he referred to other fauna than the population. But I must say, there is a something wanting in Miss Hapgood's demeanor. A certain fire and quickness."

Miss Birdlow and Miss Porterworth exchanged glances.

"One doesn't like to discredit one's own sex," ventured Miss Porterworth, "but I have myself made the same observation with

Miss Hapgood. She would be the embodiment of feminine perfection, if only she was not so sadly wanting in liveliness."

"She has much to make her serious," rejoined Miss Birdlow, shaking her head. "The Hapgoods, while a pedigreed and ancient family hereabouts, have little fortune. The property is, I believe, entailed to a cousin of the squire's, a married man of large family who could not therefore be induced to marry one of the daughters."

"How unlucky," said Frederick. "But perhaps the cousin's wife might be so obliging as to die in the near future."

"Oh, Mr. Tierney!" cried Miss Porterworth, with an ecstasy of giggles and eye-rolling. "How naughty you are."

The trio gained the foot of the staircase leading from the entrance of the hedge maze up to the terrace, where one of Pattergees' several grooms appeared from a gap in the shrubbery to take charge of Mignonne.

When the servant was out of earshot, Miss Birdlow took up their subject again. "Not only has Miss Hapgood no chance at the cousin, but with an invalid mother she is at a disadvantage to secure another suitable match."

"Oh, yes, Miss Birdlow," agreed Frederick. "You need not explain to me the vital role of a mother in securing suitable matches. She can research them, effect introductions, encourage conversation, and smooth over so many little potential obstacles." He laid a hand on the sculpted shrubbery that formed the wall of the maze. "Like your master gardener here, she can take what is wild and unpromising, and shape it into order and a goal. Miss Hapgood is indeed at a disadvantage. You and Miss Porterworth have enlightened me. Miss

Hapgood's want of spirit must come from her relative poverty and dim future prospects."

There was something in his tone that Miss Birdlow could not like. A humming note, as if he forced down a laugh. Frederick's powers of observation being hardly less than hers, he realized he had gone too far and easily added, "But for all our newfound connection, Miss Hapgood's spirits and prospects can be nothing to me. I will do my duty and sit for Miss Edith Hapgood, but, for the rest of my stay, I imagine I will find plenty to interest me at Pattergees."

He lifted his hat at his fair companions. "I say—have we time before dinner? Do we dare to enter the maze, or should we never find our way out?"

"Ridiculous!" said Miss Porterworth, giving him a poke in the chest. "Do you not know Miss Birdlow has walked this maze since her infancy? Getting lost would be impossible, if she be with us."

"Then I beg you, Miss Birdlow—may we never be without you. Would you do us the courtesy?"

Mollified, she lowered her parasol and snapped it shut. "Very well. I had thought getting lost was half the fun. But, if you insist, I will lead the way."

He extended his arm to her, and she laid her light gloved fingers upon it, noting with irritation how Constance fairly clung to his other side. It would be a tight squeeze in places, but if Constance was not going to let go, neither would she.

And they entered the maze.

CHAPTER FIVE

He knew to rank his elms in even rows,
For fruit the grafted pear-tree to dispose,
And tame to plums the sourness of the sloes.
—John Dryden, *Works of Virgil* (1697)

Miss Elfrida Hapgood had many reasons to regret Edith wanting to paint Mr. Frederick Tierney, not least of which was that Elfie saw no good purpose in furthering the acquaintance. How could there be, when Mr. Tierney occupied such a different sphere of life? Forming an intimacy with him could only give rise to dissatisfaction on both sides. Mr. Tierney would find them a dead bore, and Elfie's younger sisters might grow attached and form wrong-headed ideas of what made a fine gentleman. It was bad enough that Margaret and Edith must be exposed to their uncles

Alec and Alwyn's conduct, but at least *there* there was no danger of them losing their heads or hearts.

But today Elfrida's objections took a practical turn: the cook Button had informed her that the cherries were "fair falling off the trees" with ripeness, along with the first of the plums. Hal had a fear of heights and could not be made to pick them all, and hadn't she more than enough on her hands, with the drying and pickling and preserving? It used to be Alice who would skip up the ladder into the branches, stuffing her apron full and emptying her store into buckets, but Alice was gone. Button said she was too fat to be climbing ladders, and Dorcas reminded Elfrida that she had only ever been a house servant.

"It must be us, then, to pick the fruit," announced Elfrida at breakfast. She placed delicate fingers over her mouth to smother a yawn. Apart from Alice, the Hapgood ladies were not generally early risers, but Elfrida had roused them all so that they could finish before Mr. Tierney came.

Bramleigh's grounds might be halfway to ruin, but the kitchen garden was reasonably well-kept, lest there be nothing to eat. Its modest confines sheltered fruit trees from apples to quince, and rows of vegetables and greens tended by the boy Hal, who, whatever his faults, had quite a hand with growing things.

Hal always reduced Margaret and Edith to whispers and helpless giggles for the way he mooned over Elfie, and this morning was no different.

"I would do this for 'ee, Miss, I would," he assured Elfrida as he placed the ladder for her. "Climb up for 'ee, but last summer I felt fair dizzy and fell out and Miss Alice had to plaster me."

"Thank you, Hal. I am sure we will manage."

"But ye must take care, Miss Hapgood. Mind your footing."

"Yes," said Elfrida. She squinted in the scattered light to be sure of herself before stepping off the ladder into the branches. Her heart was beating quickly, but she swallowed her trepidation. She did not like being off the ground herself, but she must set the example.

Soon enough Hal moved and set the ladder for Margaret and Edith, while he darted about below, picking the lowest fruit, holding the baskets for them to fill, and calling up warnings and encouragement. Margaret ate nearly as much as she picked, until Elfrida moved her to the sour cherry tree, and Edith kept stopping with dreamy looks to regard particularly beautiful fruit or blossoms.

"Come, you two," Elfrida chided, when she caught them idle again. "Think on the cherry tarts and preserves and plum wine Button will make. We are nearly finished, but we must hurry if we are to be presentable for Mr. Tierney."

"I was thinking I will have Mr. Tierney presenting you with a plum," said Edith, rousing herself and dropping one frosted, deep purple one to Hal. "Because it is not apple season yet."

"Whatever can you mean, dear?"

"For the painting—the sketch, rather," Edith explained. "I will sketch it first, and then paint it later."

"Sketch Mr. Tierney handing me a plum?"

"No, silly!" interjected Margaret. She had accustomed herself to the tartness of the sour cherries and spat out a pit before she continued. "Edie and I were talking in bed last night and have hit upon the very subject for her classical painting: the Judgment of Paris."

A few sweet cherries tumbled from Elfrida's hand, bouncing off Hal's head below. "Oh! I beg your pardon, Hal. Do bring the basket. Edith! Do you really think such a scene fitting?"

"What could be better? There are three of us and one of him. Though perhaps I might have you be both Aphrodite and Hera, Elfie, because Margaret is so tall."

"I still don't see why I have to be Athena," grumbled Margaret. "No one ever thinks she stood a chance in the contest."

"Darling," said Elfrida. She wiped her hands on her apron and carefully placed her feet on the ladder to descend. When she was safely down, she marched over to the plum tree and looked up into it. "You asked Mr. Tierney to sit for you. You did not say Margaret or I would be sitting as well, nor doing so alongside him. And such a subject! It would not be modest to make this gentleman whom we hardly know pretend to judge which among us is the most beautiful."

"But it is you, of course!" Edith insisted. "That is why you must be Aphrodite."

"That is not what I mean," said Elfrida, with a firmness that made her sister's heart sink. "It would not do to have us sit for you together. You must choose another scene. Why not have him be Apollo as you once said, playing the harp or sporting his laurels?"

The groans of her younger sisters rose in chorus. What would be the harm? Edie didn't mean to show anyone the painting. He was nearly their brother-in-law, remember! They were certain he would not think there was any impropriety in it. Apollo playing his harp would be *stupid*. How could Elfrida be so overscrupulous?

They were still arguing about it when they carried the brimming baskets to the kitchen, only pausing to hear out Button's tirade that she didn't know for the life of her how they expected her to take on such a great lot of work if more help couldn't be hired, she being too old now to be doing this alone, mark her words, with only that shiftless Dorcas to hand. After Elfrida promised to speak to Dorcas, the girls hurried upstairs to change their frocks and comb their hair. Elfrida exchanged her brown calico for a white muslin morning dress and twisted her tresses up in a high chignon. She was just pinning up stray strands when Edith entered, her battered leather portfolio under one arm and a box of pencils and charcoal sticks clutched to her stomach.

"Elfie," she coaxed, "suppose I kept my subject, but I did not have you sit at the same time? If I sketched each figure separately...? Please—this might be my only opportunity to capture a young man, unless Alice and Joseph invite me to visit. But you know the two of them will be too occupied with their work to sit still and let me sketch them."

While Elfrida was well able to resist Margaret's manipulations, Edith was another matter altogether. She was so small and asked so sincerely, the hint of tears glimmering in her gray eyes, that Elfrida found herself giving in. "Very well. I still do not recommend it, but I suppose if he may sit for you and I may be free to mend Papa's shirts and play no part, there will be little harm. Oof! Do not squeeze me so hard, sweeting. Come—if he is punctual, he will be here shortly. Let us see if Mama can be prevailed upon to come down."

Mrs. Hapgood could, in the event, though it required the combined efforts of her daughters to assist her in dressing and descending the stairs, and to arrange her comfortably in the drawing room. Dorcas must be summoned, moreover, from pitting cherries in the kitchen, to build a hasty fire that no one aside from Mrs. Hapgood would find pleasant to be near.

When Mr. Frederick Tierney arrived and was admitted by the flustered and cherry-stained maid, he found the family placed in a tableau: the squire with his hands folded behind his back, staring out a window, the girls seated at various points, two holding embroidery frames and one a book, and the mistress by the fire, already almost dozing.

The tableau stirred to life. The womenfolk rose to make their curtsies, and the squire came forward and shook hands with him, already beginning his excuses. He could never bear to spend a bright morning within doors, and, with Elfrida having already convinced him of Frederick's unsuitability as a potential husband, he saw no point in doing so. "...Caractacus still poorly, you know, and Frick not able to check on him until tonight at the soonest..."

Far from being affronted, Frederick read the squire's speedy departure entirely otherwise: to be left nearly alone with the Hapgood daughters must mean Frederick was welcome to whichever of them he chose. Nor did the mistress of the house undermine this assumption. Mrs. Hapgood was smiling, benignant, and unwilling to leave the fireside, while Edith had set up her easel some distance away, just beside the windows, that her subjects might bathe in the full light.

"Shall I assist you, madam, to a seat nearer your daughter?" asked Frederick. "Surely you will wish to see our progress here, in the service of art?"

"Oh, no, I thank you," Mrs. Hapgood replied in her fluttery voice. She pulled her wraps more tightly about her. "I have caught a sad summer cold and could not bear the draft there. But I can enjoy it all very well from this position, I assure you. So kind of you to sit for Edith, Mr. Tierney. Very kind, very kind. So like your brother Mr. Joseph Tierney."

Frederick, whose character was not often compared favorably with his paragon of a brother, found himself inexplicably pleased. And pleased as well that Miss Hapgood was privy to her mother's comment. He ventured a sidelong look at that young lady, but she was digging in her workbasket and did not appear to have heard. Most ladies would only embroider or do other decorative work if company were present, but Miss Hapgood appeared to have a heap of shirts on her lap. She had smiled, made her curtsey, given him one of her unfocused looks, and murmured something in welcome when he came in, but thereafter paid him little heed.

So that was her game, was it? Frederick drummed his fingers on his knee. She intended to stand out from every other young woman of his acquaintance by her very withdrawal. He had turned over her behavior in his mind, examining it from many angles, whenever he had time and solitude for thought, and such was his conclusion. It was a new strategy to him, to be certain, but therefore all the more intriguing. Indeed, the originality of Miss Hapgood's scheme made Miss Birdlow's cool admiration and Miss Porterworth's blatant flirtatiousness appear quite antiquated. Very well, then. He would rise to the challenge. He would lure Miss Hapgood from her remote realms; he would rouse her to reveal her interest.

He turned to Miss Edith Hapgood, who was arranging and rearranging her pencils and charcoal sticks in the tray of the easel, not knowing how to begin. Miss Margaret appeared on the point of urging her to get on with it, so Frederick said, "Shall we begin, Miss Edith? Have you decided on a subject?"

"Oh! Oh—er—yes. That is..." Edith's eyes slid over to where Elfrida sat, but her older sister did not look up from her sewing. "...That is—I thought I might make a preliminary sketch..." She cleared her throat. "Mr. Tierney, would you be so kind as to sit in that window seat, like this?" Scurrying over, she arranged herself on the cushioned seat, half turned so that she could have been about to sink on one knee. Then she pulled a plum from her apron pocket and held it up, arm bent and somewhat extended. "You see?" Springing back up, she offered him the fruit.

"Not entirely," said Frederick, taking the plum. He spread the tails of his coat and settled himself on the cushion. "Am I Tantalus, and I've finally got a hold of something? Very unconventional."

"No—not Tantalus. If you could bend your left leg a little more...a little more...and extend your right foot forward...thank you."

"I am Atalanta, then," he guessed.

Edith was already pink from having referred to his leg, and her color deepened. "Mr. Tierney, Atalanta is a *woman*. I might have got my sisters to sit for that."

"Perhaps they are not athletic enough to be convincing as the winners of a foot race," said Frederick blithely. "Sewing and embroidering and drawing being no great fosterers of strength or speed."

The Miss Hapgoods said nothing to this, not being in the habit of discussing their physical abilities with young gentlemen, and after a pause he went on. "Moreover, I have been told by some of my detractors, Miss Edith, that I have an effeminate air about me."

"Surely you mean 'effete,'" spoke up Margaret, unable to hold her tongue longer. "That you have an effete air—not an effeminate air."

"Margaret," Elfrida said in a low tone. "Mr. Tierney teases us. And it is hardly polite to accuse one's guests of being overly refined, even if you mean to defend them."

"You wrong your sister, Miss Hapgood," protested Frederick, tossing and catching the plum with his same hand. "Because I am afraid—now that Miss Margaret reminds me—that I have been accused in my life of both effeminacy *and* effeteness. It must be my taste for embroidered waistcoats or my devotion to cleanliness and grooming."

Elfrida could think of no possible reply to this, but when she saw Margaret lean forward to speak, she heard herself say, "Edith plans to paint the Judgment of Paris. You are Paris, sir."

"Ah! I see." He saw what? His tone was light, but Elfrida's brow furrowed. She could not, of course, discern his expression from where she sat. What was he thinking? That it was not a fitting subject?

"You may think it not a fitting subject," she began, in spite of herself.

"I?" he asked. "I said nothing." He gave the plum another toss and carried it to his mouth, stopping just short of taking a bite. "Certainly, Miss Hapgood, if the subject meets with *your* approval I can have no objections."

Here both Margaret and Edith gave little gasps, and Elfrida pulled the thread through her father's cuff so suddenly that it snapped. "Yes. Well," she said, aware that her face grew hot. Turning away, she rummaged in her workbasket again. From her place by the fire, Mrs. Hapgood gave a soft snore, as her head dropped to her chest.

"Perhaps I should remove my coat," Frederick went on, laying the plum on the windowsill and beginning to do just that. "For is not Paris usually in his shirtsleeves, and the goddesses altogether nude?"

Now Elfrida was on her feet, the heap of shirts rolling from her lap to the carpet, her needle still clutched in her grasp. Taking a few halting steps, she came between him and her sisters, both to read his face more clearly and from an obscure instinct to protect Margaret and Edith. Despite her high color, her eyes were steady. "Please—do not trouble yourself, Mr. Tierney. I assure you my sister has no pretensions to imitate the works that have gone before. She merely hit upon a classical subject with the proper number of figures, male and female. Edith does not even intend to sketch us all at the same time. You will be Paris now—fully clothed—and she will add—the other—also fully clothed—figures when you are gone."

By heavens, she was beautiful when she was distressed! Those for-get-me-not eyes, and the bloom of her cheeks. Frederick could hard-ly repress the grin that tugged at the corners of his mouth. The placid Miss Hapgood—discomfited and affecting the schoolmistress. She would be a pleasure to provoke.

"What a relief to my mind, Miss Hapgood," he answered, shrug-ging into his coat once more. "Your sister follows in Mrs. Angelica Kauffmann's footsteps once more—you have seen the engraving of her Judgment? No nudes to speak of, and Paris well-draped. I am glad of it. A traditional treatment would have put me to the blush."

"I am not sure it would have," was her short reply. She turned on her heel and resumed her seat, angry with herself. The man meant only to tease and upset her, and he had succeeded! *He would like to flirt with me*, Elfrida thought, *as if I were a Miss Birdlow or Miss Porterworth*. At closer range, she had caught the mischievous glint in his eye. It seemed Mr. Frederick Tierney lived up to his reputation: he had small respect for women.

Let him have his little games. If she could help it, she decided, she would not say another word.

With an agreeable smile at Edith, Frederick plucked the plum from the window sill. "I am at your command, Miss Edith."

The young artist glanced from her model to her eldest sister, but Elfrida was snipping a new thread for her needle, the pile of shirts restored to her lap. Edith then looked to Margaret, who only opened her eyes wide and raised her eyebrows, as if to say, *Get on with it, before Elfie changes her mind and orders him from the house!*

"If you please, Mr. Tierney,"—Edith cleared her throat— "Turn a shade more toward the window and lean forward slightly. No—not just your head. With your back, too. And your arm—" It occurred to her, as she sketched the line of his head and back, that she had no idea how high Mr. Tierney should hold the fruit. And she did wish Elfrida hadn't been so hasty in having Mr. Tierney replace his coat; Edith preferred her Paris in shirtsleeves. The goddesses wouldn't be nudes, of course, but Paris in a frock coat was just silly.

Of further concern to the budding artist as the sitting went on was Mr. Tierney's obtuseness, coupled with Margaret's tendency to interfere.

"Mr. Tierney," said Edith, after she had roughed out his head, torso, left arm, and legs, "could you please bring your arm down?" He was holding it nearly straight up.

"But I am seated," he protested, "while Aphrodite will be standing. Would she not tower over me?"

"She's Aphrodite, not the main mast," put in Margaret, scooting her chair closer. "And you are Paris, not Nelson's signalman."

Frederick obligingly lowered his arm to half-mast.

"And bend your arm, please," coaxed Edith. She demonstrated with her own as she held the charcoal. "You are offering Aphrodite a tribute—"

"—Not shooting her with a dueling pistol," Margaret interjected.

"Just so," said Frederick. "Shall I hold it here? Here? Or, here?" He demonstrated at different angles and elevations, the last with his elbow as high as his shirt points. "Help me, Miss Edith! Cannot you be my Aphrodite for one moment, so I do not feel so lost?"

"That would not help at all, Mr. Tierney," said Edith, "for then I could not draw it."

"Have you a giant mirror, then?" he suggested. "Such as artists have used for self-portraits?"

"None nearly large enough. And it would do no good. I am too short and the angle would be all wrong."

"*I* will supply the stead of Aphrodite," declared Margaret, throwing aside her embroidery and determinedly not looking at Elfrida. Shaking out her skirts, she tripped over to stand beside their guest.

"Ah. How appropriate," beamed Frederick. "Miss Edith, you were going to have Miss Margaret be Aphrodite, weren't you? I see now exactly the angle at which I must present the goddess with the prize."

Here Edith stamped her slippered foot, her patience giving way. "I am afraid, Mr. Tierney, that I did not intend Margaret to be Aphrodite because Margaret is too tall and—angular. I meant her to be my Athena."

"I hardly see what my 'angles' have to do with this," retorted her sister. "And we are merely assisting Mr. Tierney for the sketch. If I am too tall, I will stoop. Thus." She hunched over like a crone.

"It won't do!" insisted Edith, as Mr. Tierney proffered the plum to the crone. "Now you are too short. –No, too tall again! Lower...lower...higher...You must be Elfrida's height, or we are back where we started."

"Was Miss Hapgood to be Aphrodite, then?" asked Frederick, all innocence. "I took her for Hera. More motherly in nature. And how does Homer refer to that goddess? Oh, yes—'cow-eyed.' Cow-eyed Hera."

Elfrida stitched on. Inwardly she was beside herself at her younger sisters' conduct—at Edith for being so naïve when Mr. Tierney bated her, at Margaret for thrusting herself forward, and at both of them for arguing before this man.

"What do you mean, 'cow-eyed'?" demanded Margaret, straightening to her full height. "Elfie isn't the least bit cow-eyed. She has the finest eyes in Somerset."

"Very fine eyes, I am sure," agreed Frederick meekly.

"Margaret," Elfrida could not help hissing.

"Finer than Miss Birdlow's, for instance," Margaret went on, irked by Mr. Tierney's evident disbelief. "Has the beautiful Miss Birdlow eyes the color of violets?"

"*Margaret!*"

"She has not," Frederick admitted. "Hers are more like shards of ice. But I believe Homer meant it as a compliment of sorts. '*Boöpis*' is often translated as 'cow-faced,' when not applied to Hera. A much harder go, in my opinion. Cow faces not being equated often with loveliness. Cow eyes, on the other hand—cows have rather nice eyes. Mild and soft and liquid."

"My sister is not cow-*anything*," grated Margaret. With a sniff, she swished aside her skirts and flounced back to her seat, taking up her work again as if it offended her.

Elfrida could sit still no longer. Not with Margaret furious, Mr. Tierney bemused, and Edith trembling. The trembling worried her most; she knew in another instant it might turn to tears. Swiftly she rolled up her father's shirt and set the heap aside on the sofa. Rising, she gave Edith one touch on the shoulder before going to stand before the would-be Paris.

"Let us have the proper heights and angles, then," she said in a low voice.

Edith gave one wordless nod and tried to swallow her distress. "E—Elfie—if you could move a little closer to Mr. Tierney. And, Mr. Tierney, tilt your head back until you are looking at her face. Thank you."

Elfrida's eyes were anything but mild and soft and liquid as she regarded Mr. Tierney. This close to him, she saw him clearly enough now: handsome, ingenuous, and...pleased with himself. He had wanted her there and he had got her there. She saw the amusement in his eyes and the curl to his lips that he fought to repress. Her own lips disappeared into a line.

"It seems I was wrong altogether," he murmured, his mouth barely moving. "Not cow-eyed at all. Far too earthbound a comparison. Yours are like stars on a night with no moon."

Some of Edith's trembling seemed to make its way into the pit of Elfrida's stomach. She looked away. "How adept you are at manipulating people. Do you always get your way, Mr. Tierney?"

"That remains to be seen."

Not—another—word! Elfrida took a measured breath. She would not say another word.

A silence fell over the room, broken only by Mrs. Hapgood's even breathing and the rasp of Edith's charcoal pencil on paper.

Elfrida could not decide what to do with her body. She knew she was but a placeholder in the scene and that Edith focused on Mr. Tierney, but that did not make it easier. Especially as she knew Mr. Tierney continued to look at her. At first Elfrida crossed her arms over her middle, but then she thought that made her look afraid. Then she clasped her hands behind her, until she thought it might bring her bosom into too much prominence—and her bosom was at his eye level. To clasp her hands before her felt as if she were trying to hide that bosom, and might make him think she was thinking *he* was thinking about her bosom. At last, unable to stifle her sigh completely, she let her hands hang loosely at her sides. The man was impossible—tying her up in knots. She wished he would leave.

But Edith feared she might not have another opportunity with Mr. Tierney when this one was passed—not after her bickering with Margaret. Elfrida would certainly have something to say, afterward. Therefore she took her time capturing her subject, from the attitude of his figure, to the sweep of his hair and the long lines of his limbs. She wished she might pose him in a classical robe and sandals, that she could practice with folds and shadows, but a Paris in frock coat, breeches, and polished boots would have to suffice. His expression was peculiar, as he stared fixedly at Elfrida. She saw his eyelids droop and his lip curl. Lady Wimpole would have recognized such a look straightaway, but not inexperienced Edith. As for Elfrida, she chose not to acknowledge it, but that did not mean she was unaware of it, as every hair on the back of her neck seemed to prickle.

"I do have something to tender you, Miss Hapgood," he said at last, "if you will not accept this plum."

"Have you?" She threw a glance toward his shoulder.

"An invitation. Lord and Lady Marlton have asked me to bid you come for dinner and a card party two nights hence."

"Oh! I cannot think why that would be."

"Dinner at Pattergees!" cried Margaret, forgetting her earlier indignation. "How exciting, Elfie! You should wear your pearl jaconet. And you may borrow my lavender ribbon."

Her elder sister ignored this, but she did turn to face Mr. Tierney more fully. "I mean I do not understand why they would invite me. They never have before."

"There is always a first time," he answered easily. "Since your sister's union with my brother, and since Joseph's and my visits with them, it seems perfectly natural that those at Pattergees would be curious now to know the Hapgoods better, despite being neighbors for generations."

"Genera*tion*," corrected Margaret. "It was Lord Marlton who came into the property. We Hapgoods have been here since the Conquest, but not so them."

Elfrida shut her eyes over this latest instance of Margaret's heedless tongue. An evening—one evening—at Pattergees would be a welcome novelty, if only because she would have no one's *faux pas* to fear but her own. She had never been at that great estate alone, in the intimacy of the viscount's exalted family, and she could not say if the idea filled her with more pleasure or dread. The Hapgoods rarely dined from home.

And yet, part of her feared how flat and quiet life would be with Alice gone. She confessed to herself, moreover, that she would be curious to see how Miss Birdlow responded to Mr. Tierney's flattery.

"I have my sketch," Edith announced, laying down her charcoal and stepping back to consider. "It will do for you, Mr. Tierney. This afternoon I will reproduce it on my canvas, and later I will put in the goddesses." Pushing her stray hair from her forehead, she smudged her temple. Margaret was next to her in an instant, oohing and aahing, but Frederick and Elfrida were slower to join them.

"I would be pleased to accept their invitation," said Elfrida, her breath quickening.

He clapped his hands together. "Splendid. The DeWitts will fetch you in their carriage at five o'clock."

"Oh! What a bother for them. Hal could bring me. Or I could ride."

"No bother at all. And if you will not let the DeWitts fetch you, I will do it myself."

"Let it be the DeWitts, then."

Grinning, he rose and gestured for her to precede him. "The devil you know, eh? But let us see about this picture of Miss Edith's. I am sure we have not spent the hour in vain."

Chapter Six

A man of gallantry...who was known
to play his cards well, and to have good luck,
whenever hearts were trumps...
—Maria Edgeworth, *Belinda* (1801)

The Hapgoods were great card players. Dependant mostly on themselves for society and entertainment, all four daughters played respectable, if not downright clever, hands of whist and casino, or, if their father or mother or uncles joined them, they were equally versed in the round games of loo and speculation. Therefore, the prospect of cards at Pattergees gave Elfrida no qualms. No—the flutterings in her stomach, as she rode with the DeWitts in their sturdy, old-fashioned coach, stemmed entirely from anxiety about the company.

She liked the DeWitts well enough: kindly Sir Cosmo, his amiable wife Lady DeWitt, the sensible Miss DeWitt, and her two younger brothers Roscoe and Norman. Elfrida had known that family forever, enough time to be comfortable even with the two sons. Roscoe had imagined himself in and out of love with her once or twice, but his latest attachment was to the coquette Miss Porterworth, and Norman DeWitt had yet to show an inclination for anyone.

It was not they who made her anxious. It was her hosts. The Hapgoods may have been resident at Bramleigh centuries longer than their neighbors, but there was no denying the family at Pattergees had elegance and wealth and rank. And Elfrida was well aware that the county viewed Miss Birdlow and herself as rivals, however little the two young ladies were acquainted or in company together.

"Miss Hapgood, you are very welcome at Pattergees," said the viscount, bending over her hand.

"Thank you, my lord."

Lady Marlton only added, "What a lovely gown. I hope your family is well." Not waiting for Elfrida's response, she turned to greet Miss DeWitt.

Although some hours remained until sunset, candles were already lit in the grand drawing room. For once Elfrida was grateful for her shortsightedness—she could make her curtsies to the gathered company without being troubled by, or having to analyze, the expressions of each person to whom she was presented. Mr. and Mrs. Frank Birdlow, Miss Birdlow, Miss Porterworth—

"And you are acquainted, of course, with Mr. Frederick Tierney," ended the viscount.

"Yes," she said, as that man made her a slow and unnecessarily deep bow, raising his eyes to seek hers before he straightened up.

Fortunately, the DeWitts had been tardy in fetching her, and, as a result, their hosts were anxious to get dinner under way, that they might proceed to cards. Therefore Elfrida was spared a response to Mr. Tierney's exaggerated courtesy by the footman's entrance, and couples immediately began to pair up to walk to the dining room. She made quick calculations in her head—as a daughter of a mere country squire, she would not be paired with Mr. Tierney, the nephew of a baronet, and she was not surprised when Lady Marlton summoned him to Miss DeWitt's side. But then whom...?

"Forgive me, Miss Porterworth, Miss Hapgood," called the viscountess. "I am afraid young Mr. Sadler had to excuse himself of a sudden. The lumbago, sadly. It leaves us thirteen at table. Mr. Norman DeWitt, if you would be so kind as to assist *both* Miss Porterworth and Miss Hapgood, we should be very grateful."

As the last to enter the dining room, the three of them were left to take what seats remained. Miss Porterworth hastened to sit across from Mr. Tierney, Miss Birdlow having taken his right hand, and Miss DeWitt occupying his left. There remained two seats between Mrs. Mary Birdlow and Sir Cosmo DeWitt. Elfrida surmised that if she sat between Norman and Sir Cosmo, she might be allowed to be silent throughout the meal and free to observe the others, and she gladly let the footman assist her to that chair.

At Bramleigh, summer dinners consisted of roasted meat and a boiled vegetable, followed by fruit, but such simplicity was not for Pattergees. Here a white soup was removed for a fish course, covered in some rich sauce and accompanied by a salad of peas, lettuce and cucumbers. Roast pheasant and collops of veal came next, dumplings and damson cheese, all rounded out by cherry tarts and a plum pie. Elfrida could give little attention to the culinary parade, however, because her plan to say little and observe much was thwarted by none other than the kindly Lady Anne DeWitt.

"How does your family, Miss Hapgood," she called down the table, "with Mrs. Joseph Tierney now gone into Buckinghamshire?"

"We are well. But she will be sadly missed," said Elfrida. "I have begun a letter to her."

"And you will visit, of course, when she is settled?"

"I do not know. I am not sure my mother and sisters could spare me."

"Miss Hapgood keeps a firm hand on the reins at Bramleigh," said Mr. Tierney, chasing a pea around his plate with a leaf of lettuce. "Who knows what disaster might follow, if she were to loose her hold."

The young ladies greeted this remark with giggles.

Elfrida speared the fish on her plate with her fork. "My mother is not in the best of health," she explained to Lady DeWitt.

"What would you know of how Miss Hapgood manages Bramleigh?" Miss Porterworth teased Mr. Tierney, her mouth pursing in a charming bow. "You have spent all of one morning there." Leaning forward to see Lady DeWitt (and giving Mr. Tierney an eyeful down the neckline of her gown), she added, "Mr. Tierney was at Bramleigh yesterday to sit for Miss Edith Hapgood, who fancies herself an artist."

"Little Miss Edith?" echoed Lady DeWitt.

"It is not without warrant," said Mr. Tierney, noting the narrowing of Elfrida's eyes. "Miss Edith Hapgood is a talented creature, and I am happy to encourage her. If I can convince her to let me have the painting when it is finished, it might prove a fortunate investment."

This brought on another indulgent laugh from the ladies, and Elfrida took up her fork again, that she might not curl her hands into fists. She had rather her little sister not be a topic for discussion by strangers.

"If Miss Edith attempts a portrait of *you*, Mr. Tierney," Miss Birdlow interposed, her long lashes fluttering down to cast shadows on her cheeks "you had better buy it. Indeed, you might be the only bidder."

"I don't know about that," objected Miss Porterworth, not catching her friend's tone. "Some of us do not find Mr. Tierney too painful to behold." She followed this confession with a squeak and titter and looked about her for concurring glances.

"My sister does not paint for the eyes of the public," put in Elfrida hastily. "Merely for her own pleasure. Nor does she attempt a portrait of Mr. Tierney—as himself, I mean."

"What is the subject then, of her work?" asked Lady Marlton.

Oh, dear. Elfrida blinked and reached for her glass of currant wine, but before she could compose herself to answer, Mr. Tierney stepped in. "Like many great artists of our day, she undertakes a classical scene. You cough, Miss Hapgood—I hope you have not swallowed wrong. Yes—Miss Edith Hapgood asks me to sit for—err—Perseus. Perseus slaying the Gorgon."

Now Elfrida choked in earnest, burying her face in her napkin until she could recover. The company politely ignored her fit, going on to quiz Mr. Tierney about being a mythological hero. Roscoe DeWitt asked acidly if a Perseus in embroidered waistcoat had ever before been attempted, while the young ladies were more interested in what Mr. Tierney held to serve as Medusa's head.

"That would be a lady palm," pronounced Mr. Tierney, and Elfrida could only marvel at the ease with which he invented lies. "I hold a plant. Thus—" He demonstrated with the salt cellar. "—Because none of the Miss Hapgoods would consent to having their heads chopped off for art's sake."

"I hardly blame them," Miss Birdlow said coolly. "And certainly the Miss Hapgoods are all of them far too lovely to turn any man to stone."

However complimentary her words, the look Miss Birdlow then shot Elfrida had a Gorgonish effect of its own, and the modest demurral rising to Elfrida's lips died unspoken.

To her very great relief, Mr. Tierney's comment reminded Lord Marlton of his poor cousin Eliza, who had married a French count and narrowly escaped the Terror with her life. This exciting story naturally distracted everyone, and from the many questions put to their host, the conversation naturally proceeded to the state of the war and the recent coronation of Napoleon's brother Joseph as King of Spain. Thus passed away the meal and, Elfrida hoped, all interest in Edith's painting.

Because of Mr. Sadler's lumbago, Lady Marlton's vision of two tables for quadrille and two for ombre had given way to two quadrille tables and one larger round one for loo. With eagerness and dread the guests awaited their assignments as the servants brought candles and fresh packs of cards.

"Has anyone a preference?" asked Lady Marlton.

The older, married couples naturally formed one quadrille table, but how were the young people to be divided? For Miss Birdlow and Miss Porterworth, all depended on what Mr. Tierney chose, though he appeared in no hurry to decide. Mr. Roscoe DeWitt wanted to keep an eye on his ever-wandering Miss Porterworth, so he waited as well.

Assessing the situation with her usual rapidity, Lady Marlton said, "Agnes, you have been longing for a good game of quadrille—why do you not take this spot? Perhaps I can prevail upon...let me see...Miss Porterworth and Mr. Tierney and Mr. Roscoe DeWitt to join you. That will leave Frank and Mary for loo, along with Mr. Norman DeWitt, Miss DeWitt, and Miss Hapgood. Will that not work out well?"

Feeling the lightness of pin money in her reticule, Elfrida would far rather have played quadrille. If she were to risk her meager savings, she would sooner trust to skill and strategy than simple luck. But to object was impossible. She took her seat at the round table. Perhaps luck might be with her. If she did manage to increase her store, she might perhaps send to Bristol for the box of sample spectacles she read about—her sisters continued to insist she needed them, and perhaps they *would* be a help with her sewing.

"If you don't mind, my lady," drawled Mr. Tierney, "I feel the concentration required by quadrille would overtax my brain tonight. Could not Miss Birdlow, Miss Porterworth and Mr. Roscoe DeWitt be persuaded to join me at loo, instead?"

"Oh—well, I—certainly," agreed the viscountess, "though Mary hasn't the head for quadrille either."

"I will be happy to switch with Mrs. Birdlow," said Elfrida, rising.

"But Miss Hapgood, if you exchange for quadrille, I will be forced to do so as well," Mr. Tierney interposed smoothly. "For I promised my brother Joseph I would avenge the name of Tierney." To the company at large he added, "My brother tells me the Miss Hapgoods have won from him more in one evening than he loses in a month in town."

Annoyance flickered over the features of her ladyship and Miss Birdlow, but Elfrida did not notice and Frederick chose not to, instead taking the chair next to her as the restructured group bustled about.

"Did Joseph really say such a thing?" she ventured in a quiet voice.

"You doubt my honesty?" he whispered back, in mock alarm.

"Certainly not," said Elfrida dryly. "After all, *Perseus* was such a man of his word that he slew Medusa to fulfill a rash vow."

"Now, now. You would not have me tell them about Paris, would you? That would then lead to questions, I am certain, about who would be my Aphrodite, and what we should wear, if anything."

"What are you two whispering about?" demanded Miss Porterworth, claiming the chair on the other side of Mr. Tierney. Her gown of diaphanous blue gauze brushed against his leg as she sat.

"Strategy," he replied, without hesitating.

"No cheating!" she cried and rapped the back of his hand playfully. Mr. Tierney gave her a pained look and pretended to suck on his knuckles.

"I do not know what such an accusation wounds more," he rejoined. "My joints or my honor."

Having no quip to toss back at him, Miss Porterworth settled for an elaborate giggle that trailed off into a sort of croon.

"Do be serious now," frowned Mr. Roscoe DeWitt, taking the seat beside her, "or you will lose more than you did last time."

"And if I do?" she retorted. "I'm certain it's no one's business but my own and Papa's."

"Children, children," chided Miss Birdlow. She took up the deck and began to shuffle it expertly. "Come now—who will cut first?"

They went round the circle until Frederick drew the ace.

"I am glad for that," declared Miss Porterworth, "I do not like to deal first. People forever blame me for what they receive. Miss Hapgood, you are fond of cards?"

"I am."

"I don't mind loo. I only have to be certain I've counted my pips right, and the rest takes care of itself, leaving me free to think on other things. You must tell us about your sister's wedding! Agnes and I are agog to hear about it."

If Miss Birdlow were as eager for details, she hid it well, favoring Elfrida with a cool smile.

"There isn't much to tell," said Elfrida, examining her cards. She was grateful for the Birdlows' lavish use of beeswax candles and the bright, steady light they provided. "Father—that is—Reverend Thomas married them at the end of the service, and they took their leave in Mr. Frederick Tierney's gig."

"You misunderstand Miss Porterworth," put in Roscoe DeWitt. He waved his hand to pass and threw down his cards. "She means to ask, what did Mrs. Joseph Tierney wear?"

"I will stand," said Elfrida when it came her turn. "I believe she wore her rose dotted muslin." That is, Alice had worn one of Elfie's gowns made over, since none of Alice's own frocks were found fine, clean, or whole enough for a wedding.

"Dotted muslin," repeated Miss Birdlow. "How charming." She laid a jack of diamonds over Miss Porterworth's ten.

"Oh, Agnes!" her friend protested before turning to Elfrida again. "And were you and your sisters her attendants?"

"Yes." Elfrida trumped the hand with a queen of hearts.

"And did your mother weep?" Miss Porterworth pressed.

"She did," replied Elfrida. "But her eyes always do water, this time of year."

Mr. Tierney overtrumped her with the king of hearts and took the trick, to a chorus of groans.

It turned out Elfrida was not in luck that day, and the evening's play did not improve her opinion of loo. The luck was all with Mr.

Tierney, who took more tricks than he needed and seemed to delight in beating her trump.

Frederick, however, would not have agreed with this surmisal. He might win at cards, but his plan to expose Miss Hapgood to how young ladies should suitably express admiration of eligible young men was but half a success. Miss Birdlow and Miss Porterworth did their part, paying him unceasing attentions, in their varying styles, but Elfrida was too concerned with her cards to take proper note.

Miss Birdlow was in spirits, winning whenever Mr. Tierney did not, and his compliments on her play brought color to her cheeks. Margaret would have been in raptures over Miss Birdlow's white silk gown with its overskirt of sheer, thin stripes, now glossy, now dull. Her silvery fair hair was curled and piled atop her head and encircled by a bandeau of lace. It was not often Miss Birdlow's features expressed excitement, and she grew pink thinking how it might become her.

"How I love a game!" she declared. "It's all very well living in the country, but things grow dull at times. There are not nearly enough assemblies and parties, to my mind. Not when compared to the whirl of gaiety whenever we go up to London."

Mr. Tierney left off arranging his counters to grin at her. "You would find town dull enough in the summer, if you were there now."

"Of course I do not mean *now*," she said archly. "No one is in town *now*."

"Take pity on us who must live in the country all the year round, Agnes," grumbled Miss Porterworth, a pettish edge to her voice.

"We do have the Taunton Fair approaching," put in Mr. DeWitt. "Norman and I took Rosemary to see the players last year, and they were well worth it."

"I suppose," said Miss Birdlow doubtfully, with another look at Mr. Tierney. "Traveling players must suffice, if you have not Drury Lane or Covent Garden."

"If I'm not mistaken, the fair troupe is from London and probably composed of cast-offs from those very theaters," Mr. DeWitt growled. Throwing a card down, he tilted back in his chair and called to the next table. "Ros—! Say, Ros—weren't those players at the Taunton Fair last year a good show?"

Miss DeWitt gave her fellow quadrille players an apologetic glance before answering. "They were indeed. They performed *As You Like It.*"

"Then I should like to see them this year," said Miss Porterworth, with a toss of her chin. "Mr. DeWitt, would you and Mr. Norman take me, if you take Miss DeWitt again?"

"Of course."

"I too love a play," Mr. Tierney said, yielding the trick for once to a triumphant Miss Porterworth. "We should make a day of the fair."

Miss Porterworth looked like she might kiss him for this. "Oh, when? Mr. Tierney, name the day!"

"It was my suggestion," pointed out Mr. DeWitt, throwing in three fish and snatching the deck from her to shuffle it. "And you asked me to take you. Should not I name the day?"

Not to be left out, Miss Birdlow murmured, "With your endorsement, Mr. Tierney, I find myself tempted to go as well. The entertainment may be rustic, but it is entertainment nonetheless."

Amidst this beaming approval (and Mr. DeWitt's flattering resentment), Frederick could not help turning to gauge Miss Hapgood's response. She had none. She waited with her hands folded in her lap and her eyes fixed on the cards being dealt. His mouth tightened as he looked away. Troublesome girl. She might pretend indifference, but it was precisely that—a pretense.

"I hope they will enact a tragedy," he said. "I much prefer general slaughter to widespread matchmaking."

Miss Birdlow and Miss Porterworth attacked such an opinion, each in her own way—Miss Birdlow with a *tsk-tsk* and lowered lashes and Miss Porterworth with a laughing shriek of "How bloody-minded of you!"

Elfrida, on the other hand, felt like echoing Mr. DeWitt's sigh as she regarded the five of hearts, four of diamonds, and seven of clubs in her hand. Hopeless. After being looed seven times in succession, she had bidden farewell to her plan to order spectacles from Bristol. If she continued losing at this rate, she would land the Hapgoods in the poorhouse faster than a visit from one of her uncles! And naturally, when Mr. DeWitt flipped a card for trumps, it was a spade. Worse and worse. Imagine if she had had to write Mr. Tierney a note for the amount, at the end of the evening! Her little heap of counters was dwindling.

"I pass," she murmured, throwing her hand in.

Mr. Tierney then changed his own cards for the extra hand and, after examining it, gave a slow smile which Elfrida found aggravating. "As longtime inhabitants of these parts, Miss Hapgood," he said, "the Taunton Fair and its players must be familiar fixtures to you."

Hiding her surprise at this sudden address, Elfrida recalled her thoughts from their dire places and replied, "My sisters and I have been on several occasions."

"And do you prefer tragedy or comedy?"

She thought a moment, turning her mind to the flirtations going on around her. "I had much rather see everyone slain at the end, than joined in matches that bode ill for their future happiness."

"Why, Miss Hapgood!" cried Miss Porterworth. "Whatever can you mean?"

Miss Birdlow's face twitched. Miss Hapgood meant to put herself forward, by agreeing with Mr. Tierney—wasn't it obvious?

Elfrida wished she had expressed her opinion less provocatively, as her fellow players now hung on her response, but there was nothing to do but press on. "I mean only that, on the stage, people are forever falling in love on the slightest pretenses. They know each other little and their own hearts less."

"Do you not believe in love at first sight, then, Miss Hapgood?" asked Mr. DeWitt.

"*I* do," breathed Miss Porterworth, clasping her hands to her gauzy bosom.

Elfrida thought of her sister Alice, who claimed to love Mr. Joseph Tierney when first they met. And yet, Alice learned he was a naturalist mere minutes after coming upon him, and Elfrida knew her sister well enough to suppose Mr. Joseph Tierney's profession held even greater allure for Alice than his handsomeness.

"I think love based on so little as appearances will be of short duration," she said at last, "unless it is further fed by stouter fare, such as—respect for the other person's character."

"Well, of course," rejoined Miss Birdlow impatiently. "It would be imprudent to indulge a love, if there were not the likeness of rank or situation to support it."

"I suppose," Elfrida tried to agree, "although that is not exactly what I meant. One might be of unexceptionable social rank and still have no character to boast of. Or, I imagine, hold no consequence at all and yet be rich in character."

"I don't follow this at all," complained Miss Porterworth, "and it is your turn, Agnes."

For her part, Miss Birdlow thought Miss Hapgood had held everyone's attention long enough with her silly moralistic pro-nouncements, and she let the subject drop, only to have Mr. DeWitt take it up again.

"Well, Miss Hapgood, comedy or tragedy, you are welcome to come with us. Or do you and your sisters attend the fair with your father?"

"In the past we have usually been taken there by one of our Arbuthnot uncles—my mother's brothers. My father is not one for plays, and my mother's head cannot bear the noise of the crowds, which can be somewhat clamorous."

"These Arbuthnot uncles of yours," Mr. Tierney interposed, collecting his third of the pool, "the more I hear of them, the more I like them—especially the one who blackened my brother Joseph's eye—Alwyn Arbuthnot, I believe."

As the story of Mr. Joseph Tierney's scandalous brawl with his betrothed's uncle had been much talked of, an appreciative laugh went around the table. A line sprung up through Elfrida's soft cheek. Alec and Alwyn Arbuthnot were indeed not uncles to glory in, but it was ungracious of Mr. Tierney to remind everyone of it.

For his part, Frederick bit back a curse. His mocking comment, meant to deprecate Joseph, somehow emerged as a deprecation of Miss Hapgood's connections. *Yet how could I deprecate your connections?* he demanded silently, willing her to look at him. *When* your *connections are now, by Joe's marriage, also* my *connections?* Moreover, she had not said whether she would join their party to the fair, and he had only suggested the damned outing to include her. He had no need for traveling players.

Feeling the force of his thoughts, perhaps, Elfrida's gaze met his. The vagueness in her violet eyes sharpened into puzzlement as she tried to read him. What was he about?

Then Miss Birdlow called for the bids and Elfrida gave up, reaching for her cards.

It was not until the DeWitts' carriage was at the door and the guests donning their wraps that Frederick tried again. "Please tell Miss Edith I will come once more to Bramleigh at ten tomorrow."

"Will you?" asked Elfrida, just managing not to add, "Whatever for?"

As the good-nights rang out, he answered her unspoken question nevertheless. "I cannot imagine one sketch sufficient for her purposes. And I hope she and Miss Margaret could be persuaded to join us at the fair."

"Come, Miss Hapgood," said Mr. Norman DeWitt, taking her elbow. "We are ready for you. Last in, first out."

Nodding to Mr. Tierney and the Pattergees family, she climbed in. She was thirty shillings poorer, could not claim truly to have enjoyed herself, and now must look forward to another visit from the strange and provoking Mr. Tierney. Elfrida appreciated Lord and Lady Marlton's kindness in inviting her, but she hoped it would be a very, very long time before they saw fit to do so again.

Chapter Seven

To Sorrow sighing, and the rolling Tear,
and piteous mourning suits with dreary Chear.
—John Dart, *Complaint of the Black Knight* (1718)

Elfrida dreamed of searching and searching for her reticule in the field separating Bramleigh from Pattergees, with the woeful refrain ringing in her ears, "All gone, all gone. The money all gone." She woke and felt relief wash over her, until she remembered the shillings she had lost at loo, and her relief gave way to chagrin. But before she could think overmuch of either emotion, some weight pressed against her feet and she opened her eyes to find Margaret fully dressed and perched at the foot of the bed.

"Good morning," Elfie yawned. "Is something the matter? Was I talking in my sleep?"

"You're awake!" Instantly Margaret threw herself alongside her sister, propping herself up on her elbows to thrust her eager face close. "No—would you have said something you did not want me to hear? How was the card party?"

"For the last card party I will ever attend, it was adequate."

"Why the last?"

"They play for rather higher stakes than pins at Pattergees, and I was assigned the loo table."

"Dear me—luck all against you?"

"Almost without exception."

"You will have to trim your mourning bonnet with scraps from your workbasket then, if you have lost all your money."

At this, Elfrida left off rubbing her sleepy eyes and rose to her elbows herself. "Mourning bonnet? Whatever are you talking about, Margaret?"

No one deeply beloved by the family could have died because Margaret rolled up and hugged her knees excitedly. "News came last night. You will never believe, Elfie! Harriet Hapgood is gone!"

"Our cousin's wife?" gasped Elfrida. "But—how? Oh—the children. The poor children. Was it her consumption?"

"Not at all, although Cousin Hugh wrote that she had been in declining health in any case. Mrs. Harriet Hapgood went with her sister to Tunbridge Wells to take the water, and—oh, Elfrida!—she was run down by a carriage in the Parade, as she crossed from the milliner's to the circulating library!"

Elfrida absorbed this in horrified silence. Mrs. Harriet Hapgood's husband, their cousin Hugh, had been a fixture of her childhood.

Some ten years younger than her father, he had paid regular visits before Edith's birth, as it became clear that Bramleigh might in all likelihood pass to him on Richard Hapgood's death. He being closer to her father's generation than her own, Elfrida had no clear memories of him, other than that he was a serious, sober-looking man—not unkind. Once Cousin Hugh married, however, his visits became rarer, and Mrs. Harriet Hapgood had not been at Bramleigh above three times. When she did come, Mrs. Richard Hapgood bristled at her presence, imagining the woman must be inspecting everything from the wallpaper to the furniture to the pig pen for its value, but this was paranoia on her part. Harriet had brought a tidy settlement to her marriage and was guilty of no more than thinking the house she and her husband presently occupied might be smaller than Bramleigh, but it was a good deal newer and better kept. After the Hugh Hapgoods began producing children, their visits to Bramleigh ceased altogether, and the Richard Hapgoods had never met this new generation of cousins who would one day supplant them.

"Poor motherless children," murmured Elfrida again. "They cannot be very old yet."

"Cousin Hugh wrote they are a boy, aged twelve, and two girls, aged ten and six."

"Well, I am sorry for them. And for Cousin Hugh."

"Yes," said Margaret. She tried to assume an appropriately stricken expression but gave it up after a minute and tucked her legs under her. "At any rate, we must all don black ribbons for a month or two, Mama says, and Papa must trim his hat with crape. How glad I am that all those Birdlows and Mr. Tierney saw you with my lavender ribbon in your hair before this happened. The color suits you better."

"Mr. Tierney—" Elfrida repeated, her hand flying to her mouth. "What time is it?"

"I haven't the least idea," frowned Margaret. "But we've all breakfasted, apart from you. Why?"

As if in answer, they heard light steps taking the stairs two at a time, and, a moment later, Edith peeped into the room, her grey eyes enormous. "Elfie! Are you still abed? It's *him*. That Mr. Frederick Tierney, come again. Dorcas has shown him into the drawing room, but there's no one at all in there. Mama has not come down, of course, and who knows where Papa is—probably at the kennels. What shall we do?"

Elfrida gave Margaret a push. "You two must go down and greet him. He comes to sit again for your Judgment of Paris, Edie. I will be along as soon as I can."

"But Elfie—by ourselves? Supposing he says something improper again," protested her little sister, "or makes one of his jokes?"

"He won't," answered Elfrida firmly. "If I am not present. I am sure he will be all that is proper." She could hardly explain to her sisters that it was only herself Mr. Tierney delighted in nettling.

"Are we allowed to do something so frivolous as paint pictures, when we are in mourning?" questioned Margaret.

"I suppose it is odd," sighed Elfrida, "although painting a picture is hardly attending a ball. But it would be hypocritical of us to pretend we are sunk in grief when we were barely acquainted with our cousin's wife."

With a little further verbal and physical encouragement, Edith and Margaret were driven off, and Elfrida sank back against her pillows. She looked longingly at Alice's vacated spot and wished her sister there. She would finish her letter to Alice this afternoon—she must, if she were to communicate the news of Harriet Hapgood's death. She only hoped that Alice would find time, in all the busyness of being a new bride in a new home among new family, to write back.

Mr. Frederick Tierney pulled his watch from his waistcoat pocket and regarded it. He had been made to wait ten minutes already, and, apart from scurrying sounds and doors opening and closing abovestairs, he had no idea if the maid had even announced his arrival. There were no more gew-gaws in the room to be inspected, and he had already looked long out the windows.

At last there was a rattling of the door handle, and in paced the two younger Miss Hapgoods, dressed and neat. Edith carried her palette and a box of artist's supplies and Margaret a bonnet and her workbasket.

"I have taken you by surprise this morning, Miss Edith, Miss Margaret," said Frederick, making his bow.

"We are in some disarray," Margaret admitted. She took her usual chair and nodded at Edith to claim her easel.

Settling atop the ottoman used for Paris's perch, he continued, "Ten is an early hour indeed. My brother would be amazed to find I have become such a morning lark. It must be the country air that revives me. I hope Miss Hapgood is recovered from last night's activities?"

"I just woke her," said Margaret artlessly. "But it is not the hour that has us in confusion—our cousin's wife has died suddenly."

"I am sorry to hear that," he said, half rising again. "Forgive me—perhaps you resent my intrusion today."

"Elfie says it's all right," Margaret assured him. "We did not really know Mrs. Harriet Hapgood. In fact, we never met her above once or twice, and I was too young to remember her visits. We will wear mourning, of course,"—she held up her bonnet and the black ribbon she had found— "but we need not bother with crocodile tears."

"Margaret," came Edith's soft reproach. Placing a small corner table beside her, she began arranging her jars of pigments upon it. "I am sorry for my little cousins, in any case, now without a mother."

Mr. Tierney made a sympathetic sound as he resumed his seat. "Are there many little cousins?"

"Three," replied Edith. "We have never met them, however, and know of them only through letters. The oldest—Lionel Hapgood—is but a year older than I."

"That is sad indeed. I am very close to my mother—would be quite bereft without her." From his tone, Margaret could not determine if he was in earnest, but she saw from Edith's smile that her younger sister quite believed him.

"Mr. Hugh Hapgood—Papa's cousin—is the heir to Bramleigh, you know," went on Margaret, in what her sisters would call her know-all voice.

"Indeed?" said Mr. Tierney mildly. "And yet hasn't come to visit in some ten years?"

"I think Mama did not like Harriet. (Oh, hush, Edith—there is nothing to be gained by saying otherwise.) Until last night, when we first found she had died, Mama was wont to call her 'that woman who looks upon us as so many pounds and shillings.'"

Edith had an uneasy feeling that Margaret should not speak of such things to Mr. Tierney, but she only bit her lip and busied herself with compounding the paint for Paris's flesh. White, brown, red, and vermilion. She dipped the tip of her pallet knife in each and added it to the linseed oil.

"It would be unnerving, I suppose, to have the heir's wife about," he said, crossing one booted leg over the other. "But perhaps Mrs. Harriet Hapgood only looked so hard at things because she was shortsighted."

Margaret laughed. "Like Elfie? I will tell Mama that. Perhaps it will make her feel more kindly toward the departed."

Mr. Tierney had gone still. "I'm sorry—did you say Miss Hapgood is shortsighted?"

The sisters looked at each other, and even Margaret felt a stab of uncertainty. It was true that Elfie did not want to marry Mr. Tierney, but advertising her sister's defects did not, generally speaking, aid the Hapgood cause.

"She—that is—not very. Not—er—not particularly badly," fumbled Margaret. "It might only have been that our sister Alice is so keen-eyed in comparison. Ahem! Have you got that paint mixed, Edith? I'm sure Mr. Tierney hasn't got all day to sit."

"Nearly," Edith murmured.

Taking Margaret's hint, Frederick dropped the subject, and a silence fell, broken only by the scraping and mixing of Edith's compounding. Margaret was lecturing herself severely on the virtues of holding her tongue, while Edith was wishing Elfrida would rescue them—whatever could be taking her so long?

For his part, Frederick was subjecting the last several days to review. Miss Hapgood—myopic! Why, that explained all. Her vague, unfocused expressions. Her narrow concentration on whatever was at hand, whether it be her needlework or her supper or her playing cards. That way she had of tilting her head and narrowing her eyes, as if she were offended—she was probably only trying to see better from her stronger eye. And, chief of all, her inexplicable indifference to him. What he had imagined as lack of interest was likely no more than lack of opportunity to view him clearly. Frederick Tierney had been handsome too many years not to expect female admiration as his due.

But how near-sighted was she? If he were going to offer for her, there was no reason it should not be as pleasant as possible for both of them. That was, there was no reason she should not love him. He would present her with the opportunity.

When Elfrida quietly let herself into the drawing room, some twenty minutes later, she found the threesome innocently occupied.

Margaret stitched away; Edith applied the first strokes of flesh-colored paint to canvas. Mr. Tierney rose to his feet and bowed, despite her "please do not let me disturb you."

"Miss Hapgood." Not only did he not sit back down, he came across the room toward her. "I hope you are well this morning. You must allow me to express my condolences for your family's loss."

Peering around his shoulder to frown at Margaret, she replied, "Thank you, Mr. Tierney." He stopped directly in front of her. Directly. Without meaning to, Elfrida took a startled step backward and looked up at him, her middle section giving a curious contraction. She had not seen him this close before. Nor been swallowed up in the blue of his well-shaped eyes, darker at the center and radiating outward into paleness, his golden-brown lashes framing them like fine strokes from an artist's brush. She could see the lines of his mouth, hinting at private jests, and the shape of his jaw, stippled with traces of golden beard. Golden, like the crown of hair which brushed his forehead and ears. Elfrida found herself inclining back toward him, as if drawn by some invisible force. What remained of her field of vision he filled, with the breadth of his shoulders in his bottle-green coat and the sculpted drape and folds of his cravat, disappearing around his neck into the high, crisp points of his shirt. He was...immaculate.

Some inkling of warning rippled through her. She straightened in response. Whatever was he about, forcing himself upon her notice in this way? She only knew that if he were to overawe her now, she would ever after be at a disadvantage. Holding his gaze one bare moment longer, she turned lightly away.

"We thank you for your sympathy," she said again, patting the folded gowns she carried in her arms, "and I know you will pardon me if I work on these dresses. We have no mourning clothes ready."

Frederick retreated, satisfied. He had seen the alarm in her countenance and how she took him in as well, her breath quickening. However dim Miss Hapgood's eyesight, she had got a good look at him now. He would entrust the rest to time and reflection.

"No pardon is necessary," he replied, taking his seat and resuming his Paris pose. "It will be sad to see your family trimmed in black, however. You know my own tastes run to brighter colors and embroidery."

"Just so." Elfrida did not trust herself to say more. Shaking out the first gown, she examined the neckline to see how the lace might be removed, to be replaced with a band of black.

"Miss Margaret tells me you do not mind if Miss Edith continues her work as well, under the circumstances."

"No, I do not." The stitches securing the lace were too small for Elfrida to attack with her scissors unless she could hold the dress very close indeed, and she put the first frock aside for another. "I feel certain"—with an arch look at that sister—"that Margaret has told you plenty of things in my absence."

"Why should he not know?" countered the accused. Margaret tossed away her finished bonnet and took another gown from Elfrida, holding it up against herself. "I merely said that Mrs. Harriet Hapgood was our cousin Hugh's wife, and that we hardly knew her and were therefore not utterly prostrate with her passing."

"Well—we *are* very much acquainted with my father's cousin Hugh Hapgood," Elfrida pointed out, "and it is for his sake that we wear ribbons. Out of respect." To Mr. Tierney she added, "Cousin Hugh is the heir to Bramleigh."

He bowed in acknowledgement. "I certainly understand wearing mourning because of your deep esteem for your cousin."

Margaret snorted. "She did not say 'deep esteem.' I remember Mr. Hugh Hapgood little better than his wife, and I bet the same is true for Elfie. He was old, I think, and had Papa's bushy eyebrows."

With a repressed sigh, Elfrida said, "Say we wear mourning, then, out of respect for *Papa's* respect for Cousin Hugh."

"Nonsense. Papa has never mentioned him in my hearing without calling him 'that infernal man who—'"

Mr. Tierney here began whistling a lively tune and Margaret stopped in surprise. "Oh, do go on," he prompted. "You were saying, Miss Margaret...?"

"I—nothing."

"Sometimes I get a thought in my head, and I simply must act on it," he explained. "Impossible, really. I am certain that never happens to you young ladies."

Miss Margaret frowned at him, and Miss Edith looked uncertain, but he saw Miss Hapgood dimpling. An answering grin tugged at his mouth. "And the thought I have in my head this very moment is that I should give anything to see some jugglers and players. And I should like it still better in the company of my sisters-in-law."

"What jugglers and players?" asked Margaret, forgetting her embarrassment.

"You have but one sister-in-law," said Elfrida. "My sister Alice. We are merely the sisters of your sister-in-law."

"Then I long to see jugglers and players in the company of the sisters of my sister-in-law. Well put, Miss Hapgood. How the phrase rolls off the tongue."

"But what jugglers and players?" Edith asked, laying down her palette.

"The ones at the Taunton Fair. The younger Birdlows and De-Witts and Miss Porterworth make a party of going, and I hoped to lure the sisters of my sister-in-law into joining us."

Margaret and Edith whirled eagerly on Elfrida. "Oh, may we? Say we may, Elfie!"

She did not need to see their faces clearly to picture their expressions, and her shoulders drooped as she answered, "It would be peculiar, dears. We only just learned of Mrs. Harriet Hapgood's passing. I think our first appearance in public should not therefore be at the Taunton Fair."

"Could not we take one afternoon off our false mourning, and wear our ordinary bonnets and clothes?" Margaret wheedled.

"Certainly not."

"Then might we go before our black-trimmed clothes are ready to be worn?" she tried again.

"Margaret. No." Elfrida snipped her scissors decisively.

"'Let Fortune doe her worst, she will not rob me of this sable weed!'" pronounced Mr. Tierney in a dramatic mode.

"Oh, oh! It is too bad, Elfie," cried Margaret. "There is so much to see there. And how we all love the theater! I wonder what play they will put on this year."

"Remember when Uncle Alec took us?" said Edith. "How delightful we found it. It was *The Comedy of Errors*, I believe."

"With Uncle Alec it ever is," retorted Elfrida under her breath. And then, in a louder voice, "I'm sorry, girls. It won't do. Perhaps we will see them again next summer."

"Elfie—how can you be so stern?"

"Please, Elfie, please! Won't you at least let us ask Papa or Mama? Please, please, please?"

It was this scene of unpretended woe that Squire Hapgood interrupted, all unawares, having come from his morning ride and visit to the kennels. Indeed, he was not even in the house, but, when Frederick saw his stocky figure marching past outside, he sprung up to open the nearest window. "Good morning, sir!"

"What? Heh—oh, yes—good morning, Tierney." Tramping over, the squire stepped inside. "More art, eh?"

"Oh, Papa," wailed Margaret, jamming her needle into the gown she held and flinging it aside. Bounding up, she scurried over to throw her arms around her father's neck. "I hate this death and silly mourning!"

"Me, too, Papa," chorused Edith, her lip trembling.

"What's this? All this crying over some woman you wouldn't know, if you passed her on the street? I'm sure she's gone to her reward, and so on and so forth. Ahem."

"It's not that, Papa," spoke up Elfrida, slipping out the ivory ribbon from the French sleeve she held. "They are not a bit sad about Mrs. Harriet Hapgood—"

"I fear it is my fault," interjected Frederick. "Despite your family being at sixes and sevens over the loss of your cousin's wife, I was so imprudent as to mention an invitation to the Taunton Fair. Jugglers, animals, players, general merriment. All the young people of the other families going. Quite thoughtless of me. Miss Hapgood reminds me your daughters could not go, being in black ribbons."

Margaret wailed anew, and a tear slipped down Edith's cheek.

"There, there, dry your eyes." Clumsily the squire patted Margaret, though she was nearly as tall as he was. "Seen it all before at the fair, I suppose."

"Not this year's play, we haven't!" Margaret insisted. "You know it's different every summer. And we have been invited this time with the Birdlows and DeWitts. The young people of the county."

"At the time they devised the plan, however, they had no idea we had lost Mrs. Harriet Hapgood," Elfrida pointed out. "And certainly the Birdlows and DeWitts would be the first to understand why we could not accept."

"Oh, I don't know," wavered the squire, his brow troubled by Edith's unhappiness. Like his oldest daughter, Richard Hapgood was well able to resist Margaret's pleas because the girl waxed dramatic over every little thing. But Edith rarely wept and never whined, making it all the more difficult to refuse her on those few occasions when she did. "Fairs are busy places with much to see. I don't imagine anyone would notice. If you girls were calm and quiet and didn't draw attention to yourselves..."

His two younger daughters raised glowing faces to him, but Elfrida only shook her head. She regretted having this conversation in Mr. Tierney's presence, but if she did not state her objections now, her father looked in grave danger of giving in. If Mr. Tierney had any manners at all, he would excuse himself to go and look at the flower beds outside, or some such pretense, but instead he sat there cheerfully, examining his fingernails and brushing imaginary lint off his spotless sleeve.

"Papa," Elfrida began, resolving not to mind Mr. Tierney any more than he minded them, "the very appearance of black ribbons will give rise to questions about our loss, among the rest of the company, at the minimum, followed by astonishment that we are romping about at a fair."

"Then don't romp about," he returned. "You are ever too serious, Elfie. Why should not your sisters have some fun? For my own part, I resent wearing crape on my hatband for that woman. All she's done to me is produce an heir for my cousin, to ensure you girls and your mother will be exiled from Bramleigh for generations to come. Nay, let there be fairs and plays, I say."

"'Dost thou think, because thou art virtuous, there shall be no more cakes and ale?'" murmured Mr. Tierney to the window curtains.

"I beg your pardon? I did not hear that," snapped Elfrida, sweeping up her needlework and getting to her feet.

"What?" Mr. Tierney said with a feigned start. He stood up himself, politely, but Elfrida refused to notice his bow as she prepared to leave the room.

"Another fifteen minutes today, Edie," she said from the doorway. "We must not trespass more on Mr. Tierney's time."

"Farewell, Miss Hapgood! Until Tuesday," he called to her retreating back.

Elfrida halted and turned around slowly. She could make out nothing of his expression from where she stood, and she wished in vain that he could not read hers. "What is Tuesday, sir?"

"Why, the Fair," he replied. "We hope to make an early start of it. If you are not usually up and about by ten of the clock, perhaps I might convince the Birdlows and DeWitts to wait until eleven."

She took a measured breath, cursing Margaret inwardly for her heedless tongue. How else could Mr. Tierney have known she was still abed when he came?

"Ten o'clock will suit us admirably," she said, going again. "You will find me prepared."

CHAPTER EIGHT

The squire was right about one thing. In all the crowd and hubbub of the Taunton Fair, not a person took notice of a few black ribbons dangling from bonnets or bordering sleeves and necklines. Elfrida's greater fear was losing her younger sisters in the throngs, and she found herself grateful for Mr. Tierney's presence. His height and the rich blue of his frock coat made him easy to keep sight of, although she hated to think she was orbiting about him nearly as closely as Miss Birdlow and Miss Porterworth.

The former young lady graciously made room in her family carriage for the three Miss Hapgoods, while the gentlemen rode the four miles to Taunton. Miss Porterworth spent most of the journey remarking on Mr. Tierney's progress: "He has topped the hill there, behind us, and I do believe Mr. Roscoe DeWitt has caught him" and "Where can he be? Oh—there! No, no—that is Mr. Norman DeWitt, I am afraid, though what *he* should be doing, wearing such a similar shade of blue I cannot say. I had thought the younger Mr. DeWitt did not like to draw attention to himself."

"Please accept my family's sympathy, on the loss of your cousin's wife," murmured Miss Birdlow, gesturing at the ribbons and touches of bombazine marking the Miss Hapgoods. Margaret and Edith could only nod in reply, quite awestruck to be in the presence of the county's leading heiress. Miss Birdlow wore her favorite blue Indian muslin, with its braided trim of woven silver-and-blue fabric and smart sleeves *à la Mameluke*. (Margaret thought Miss Birdlow prone to gesticulation when she spoke, as if to draw attention to how the ruffle of the sleeve covered her hand.)

"Thank you," said Elfrida simply.

"So brave of you to venture out so soon," went on Miss Birdlow. "And on such an occasion. I do not know if I would have had the serenity or the courage."

Elfrida only bowed, biting her cheek in frustration. These were exactly the charges she thought would be laid upon them, but she had decided the least said about it, the better. Margaret was sworn up and down to let Elfrida do the talking—or not talking—and Elfrida did not suppose Miss Birdlow would trouble herself in any case to converse with younger girls who were not out. But she had not counted on Miss Birdlow's and Miss Porterworth's interest in Mr. Tierney as artist's model.

"It was a brilliant idea of yours, Miss Edith," began Miss Porterworth, "to undertake a painting of Mr. Frederick Tierney."

"It—it was kind of him to agree," Edith answered, shrinking back against Elfrida's side.

"What a noble Perseus he must make."

"Perseus?" echoed Edith.

Elfrida's breath caught. Her gloved hand reached for her sister's, even as she pressed her other elbow into Margaret's side. "Perseus," Elfrida repeated. "Darling—the subject of your painting. Mr. Tierney was pressed to tell these ladies about it the other evening, so we cannot keep it a secret. Perseus slaying the Gorgon."

"Oh," said Edith, returning Elfrida's squeeze. "Yes. He makes a noble...Perseus."

"His arm must grow weary," put in Miss Birdlow, "holding that lady palm." She raised her own arm, shaking the ruffle of her sleeve from her hand to pinch her fingers together.

Edith's eyes widened and Elfrida heard Margaret's indrawn breath.

"He only had to hold it thus for the preliminary sketch," interjected Elfrida quickly. "For the positioning of his arm. Edie will, of course, paint in the—Gorgon's head later."

Miss Porterworth raised her eyebrows. "I am not sorry you have not asked *me* to sit, Miss Edith. I should not like to be chosen as Medusa!"

"Indeed," agreed Miss Birdlow with a chilly smile. "Altogether such an odd scene to paint, for so young a girl as you."

"Extremely odd," muttered Margaret, earning another poke in her side.

"Does Mr. Tierney wear—is he draped in classical robes while he sits?" persisted Miss Porterworth. She stole a glance out the carriage window, as if hoping to spy him just so arrayed atop his bay mare Mignonne.

Going pink, Edith managed only to shake her head, and Elfrida had to interpose once more. "No—this is not such a serious venture. Edie simply has him sit—stand, rather—by the drawing room window, clad in his usual apparel, and she...captures him. Yes." Releasing Edith's hand to clasp her own together in her lap, Elfrida redirected the conversation: "Miss Birdlow, you and Miss Porterworth must be great students of art yourselves. Tell me, do you have a favorite work?"

Although Miss Porterworth looked like she would far rather return to the topic of Mr. Tierney, Miss Birdlow was too well-bred to ignore the hint, and the young ladies persevered in discussing the painters and paintings of the day until the carriage rumbled into Taunton.

"You had better each take an arm," Mr. Tierney said to little Edith and to Margaret, when their party was gathered before the Wayfarer public house. He had to raise his voice to be heard above the organ grinder. "It's quite a crush here, and we would not like to lose you." To the rest of them he added, "I own myself responsible for the younger Miss Hapgoods, having pressed our invitation to the fair against their elder sister's better judgment. If we become separated, shall we meet in this very spot? After the play, say?"

Miss Porterworth looked like she had no intention of being separated from Mr. Tierney, and she tugged Mr. Roscoe DeWitt to stand closer to that man. Miss Birdlow, on Mr. DeWitt's other arm, only pressed her lips together and wondered for the hundredth time why Mr. Tierney had to invite the younger Miss Hapgoods in the first place, when there were already too few gentlemen for the ladies. Fortunately the DeWitts' elder sister Miss DeWitt had pleaded headache at the last moment and begged off, or that would have made the imbalance that much worse.

Elfrida found herself on Mr. Norman DeWitt's arm as they plunged into the hurly-burly before the town's Market House. The fair had grown since their last visit with Uncle Alec and the noise was tremendous. Baaing of sheep and lowing of cattle. Hawkers of silks and woolens. The roars and taunts of the crowd when urged to pay their penny to see a five-legged pig. The raucous music from countless barrel organs and pipers.

Elfrida clutched her bonnet to her head, looking this way and that at the many sights and squinting all she pleased since no one was observing her, all the while endeavoring to keep an eye on her sisters. Bakers offered fair buns and beggars pleaded for halfpennies. Jugglers gathered circles of cheering onlookers. Painted signs advertised gambling tables, fortunetellers, puppet shows, and foot races.

"Elfie! Elfrida!" Edith whirled up before her, one small hand catching at her sleeve. "May we please go on the roundabout?" She pointed behind her to the large wooden ring suspended from a central pole. The circumference of the ring was fitted with wooden horses, on which sat laughing and hollering riders of various ages, while a walk mill of ten workers within the ring kept them in motion.

"Certainly not."

Mr. Tierney let the crowd push Elfrida toward him and then leaned to say in her ear, "I would be happy to accompany her."

Elfrida drew back from this intimacy, but the press of people did not allow much in the way of retreat, and the next moment she was thrust against his waistcoat, the buttons of which she could feel press into her bodice. She had lost hold of Mr. Norman DeWitt altogether.

"I thank you," she managed, finding herself short of breath. "But it would not be seemly."

There was his mouth again, at her ear, his warm breath raising the hairs on her neck. "Are you always such a slave to propriety, Miss Hapgood?" he asked. His low, leisurely voice filled her with something akin to panic. "Let the child have her fun."

Without a word, and actually squeezing her arm between them to push him away, Elfrida nodded. She felt as if she rode the whirligig herself, so muddled were her faculties.

Mr. Tierney and Edith had not long to wait. And when Miss Porterworth found they would be riding, she insisted that Mr. Roscoe DeWitt accompany her. As the roundabout only carried six people at a time, the sight of these four in their relative finery attracted some notice. The observers began as curious and admiring, but it was not long before Miss Porterworth, with her shrieks and lavish smiles, drew some unwelcome remarks.

"Halloa there, Doll! Your mount giving you trouble? I have another for you in my stable."

"Too rough a ride for ye, love? Thought you had enough padding to soften the blows!"

"Wish I were such a horse, with such a bottom atop me."

On his next go-round, Mr. Tierney stretched up on his wooden horse and produced a heavy twopence from his breeches pocket. With an easy flick of the wrist, he sent it flying into the onlookers, where it bounced off the forehead of the loudest wag, a beefy unshaven man clutching a mug of beer. The man spilled his drink on the brute next to him, and the two of them shouted at the injury.

"Oop! Lost my grip on it," called Mr. Tierney. "But a good reminder to keep one's wits, when ladies and children are about."

"I'll wit you!" cried the beefy man, with more anger than quickness. "And ring you, you flowered popinjay! You pretty fellow!"

"Ay!" yelled others. "Give it 'im, the perfumed Frenchie!"

"Now *there* you go too far," murmured Mr. Tierney, swinging easily from his wooden steed, without waiting for the roundabout to slow. Calmly he approached the roisterers, hands extended and palms up, while the crowd parted to either side, as if he were Moses at the Red Sea. "I do beg your pardon for throwing the coin at you," he said. "I quite lost my head. You see, I would not like any young ladies of my acquaintance to be publicly accosted."

Taken aback, the beefy man appeared uncertain how to respond, but soon his fellows were jabbing him and jeering him. "Ye gonna take that from Mr. Fine Words, Sam-o?" "Don't let 'im wheedle ye,

Sam!" "'Publicly accosted,' eh? Ye're the one who's been publicly accosted, an' ye have!"

Sam-o rallied with their urging. Thrusting his beer mug at the spilled-upon man, he pushed his way over to Frederick, balling up his hands in fists and hunkering down in a ready position. "I'll give ye 'publicly accosted,'" he bellowed. "Let's see if ye can put those prinked-up daddles of yers to any use."

Frederick frowned. "This won't do, my good man. You see, despite my well-groomed appearance, I do have some experience with this."

"Coward!" piped a hard-faced woman with gray-brown hair struggling from her mob cap. Flour dusted her face and the neck of her brown stuff gown. Frederick half expected her to step into the ring and take a swing at him with a rolling pin.

"Madam—"

He was drowned out by a swell of opprobrium. The roundabout had halted by this point, and Frederick found Roscoe DeWitt by his shoulder, a tearful Miss Porterworth clutched to his chest. As for Miss Edith, she flew to her older sisters, and Miss Hapgood wrapped a protective arm about her.

"You'd better get the ladies out of here, DeWitt," muttered Frederick. "Miss Porterworth looks about to faint. Norman's getting Miss Birdlow away. Don't let the Miss Hapgoods see this." No sooner had he issued his instructions than Sam-o's hand was on his waistcoat, whirling him around.

"Come on, ye scented coxcomb," growled his would-be assailant, his feet beginning to dance heavily beneath him as he bounced back and forth.

"Miss Hapgood," hissed Mr. Roscoe DeWitt, making his stumbling way to her side with Miss Porterworth hanging on him. "Let us go. This is no place for ladies."

Elfrida turned alarmed eyes upon him. "No."

"There is going to be a fight," he insisted. "Come now. Bring your sisters."

"Give 'em room!" ordered some among the crowd. Bodies shoved and staggered back. Mr. Tierney removed his blue frock coat and draped it over the saddle of a roundabout horse. He flipped a six-pence to one of the mill walkers, saying, "If you could keep an eye on that—one of my favorite coats, you see."

Upon hearing with what presence of mind Mr. Tierney went forth to his doom, Miss Porterworth gave a whimpering sigh and fainted dead away, leaving Mr. DeWitt to haul her up ungracefully below the bosom, mouthing curses.

"Go with Mr. DeWitt, girls," said Elfrida, wriggling from her sisters' grip. "Help him with Miss Porterworth. She may have salts in her reticule."

For her own part, heart in her throat, she shoved her way forward, determined to see the last of Mr. Tierney. She could not say what drove her; she only knew she could not bear to leave. What ailed the fool, to be so provocative in such surroundings?

Some heads turned, at the sight of the violet-eyed beauty among them, her brow furrowed with concern, but their attention returned to the combatants when a roar went up. Sam-o had landed the first punch, right in Mr. Tierney's silver-blue, waistcoated midsection. The latter gave a huff, as if the wind had been knocked from him (which it had), but he straightened up immediately, giving Sam-o a bow of acknowledgement before putting up his own fists.

The clamor swelled to deafening proportions. Elfrida glimpsed money being waved and changing hands as men laid their bets and cheered. She found herself smashed against an old man who did not even glance at her, but because he did not smell as others did of spirits and tobacco, she remained in his lee for the duration of the contest.

Sam-o held the clear advantage in size and strength, but he was somewhat fuddled by drink and had a tendency to throw all his weight behind lumbering blows which Mr. Tierney sidestepped handily. This happened any number of times, leaving Sam-o increasingly red, enraged and determined, and the crowd frustrated.

"Quit running away, ye princox!"

"Stand and fight, if ye be a man!"

Sighing, Mr. Tierney squared his shoulders and, on Sam-o's next charge, his fist shot out and caught his assailant in the throat. Sam-o doubled over, wheezing and running into the closest spectators.

"On yer feet, Sam-o! Have at 'im again."

Valiantly, Sam-o rose. He slapped his hands together and raised them high above his head, yelling, preparing to drive Mr. Tierney to earth in one powerful blow. The latter was forced to evade this attack as well, to the derision of the assembly, but he followed it up by spinning Sam-o about and driving him back, step by step, with repeated one-two blows to the gut, another box to the gorge, and a final straight punch to the jaw. Sam-o crashed through the ring of shouting onlookers like a mighty felled oak, the wheeling branches of his arms swiping and grasping as he went down. He managed to seize the tails of an old man's coat with one hand and, with the other, the skirts of the young woman who stood beside him. So caught, the two of them tumbled down upon him in one heaving mass of limbs and cries and petticoats.

"Good Lord!" exclaimed Frederick, forgetting all about the mill, even as the excitement of it continued to speed through his veins. He had one glorious glimpse of Miss Hapgood's linen drawers and slender white ankles before he rushed over to set her upright again. "What are you doing here? Are you hurt?"

Her bonnet hanging about her neck by its black ribbons, her hair in disarray, and her face utterly crimson, Elfrida could do no more than shake her head. The sooner she could flee this scene, the better, but Mr. Tierney had hold of her elbows, and he looked on the point of shaking her and giving her a good reprimand for her foolishness.

He *was* angry, all of a sudden. How could she chide him and frown at him for affronts to propriety, when she committed the greater breach by witnessing such a brawl? And then, if that were not enough, she had opened herself to further insult. It was one thing for him to admire, however briefly, her lace-trimmed undergarments and shapely legs, but another altogether, for every Tom, Dick or Harry at the fair to inspect them.

"You should have gone with DeWitt," he said curtly.

Elfrida's eyes widened. *He* involved himself in some ridiculous row with a perfect stranger, and then had the effrontery to scold her for waiting to see if he lived or died? "I—I cannot see how I am to—to blame here," she stammered, indignation tying her tongue.

"Can you not, Miss Prim? But this is neither the time nor place for explanations," he returned, tightening his hold. By George, she was lovely! And with his blood still high, he was hard put not to take hold of her by the waist and crush his lips to hers.

During their short exchange, the rest of the world might have faded to nothingness, so little did they heed it, but ignored or not, the crowd continued to exist. Winnings were paid out; the old man was helped to his feet and brushed off; the beauty of the couple was remarked upon and wondered at; Sam-o was taunted for his defeat. The flour-dusted woman harangued him especially, she being his fair lady, and, once he had struggled upright again, his resentful eye could not help but notice what good fortune was showered upon the victor. There stood that embroidered dandy, golden and unmussed, holding in his grasp an equally beautiful young woman, while he, Sam-o, was covered in shame and had only an evening of his wife's reproaches to look forward to. It was more than a man could bear, and Sam-o was not inclined to put up with it.

"Aaaawwwwrrr, have at ye!" Sam-o shouted, slinging off his wife's hand and barreling into Frederick. Caught completely off guard, that young man went down, Sam-o atop him, and the latter landed two heavy blows before his friends came to pull him off.

"Unsportsmanlike, Sam-o," one tut-tutted. "He beat you fair."

"Let's get another pint," suggested another, "though you'll be standing for it, as I lost my money betting on ye."

"Sure, and here comes the constable!" hissed a third. "Off we go."

Magically, the crowd dissolved, off to see the other sights, leaving Elfrida on her knees beside Mr. Tierney, dabbing at his bleeding nose and lip with her handkerchief. "Oh, look at you!" she whispered. "Miss Porterworth will surely faint again when she sees you."

As his vision slowly cleared, the blur of gold, ivory, violet, and rose resolved into the accustomed lovely lines of Miss Hapgood's hair and complexion and features. Without thought, he reached for her, placing his hand at the back of her head, his fingers burying themselves in hair as soft as he imagined it. He pulled her down and kissed her, the pain of his swelling lip giving way to pleasure at the touch of her mouth on his. Making a sound in the back of his throat, he tugged her closer.

"What's this here?" The constable's question broke the spell. Elfrida gasped, scrambling to her feet and wiping her mouth with the back of her hand. It came away bloody and she scrubbed it with her handkerchief.

"Nothing, sir," replied Frederick. "We had something of a quarrel here, another gentleman and I, but it has all been resolved and now needs only to be forgotten." Standing up, he retrieved his own handkerchief and fastidiously cleaned his face and hands. He nodded Elfrida's direction. "Naturally my betrothed was anxious, but all's well that ends well."

At the word "betrothed," Elfrida smothered a gasp. What the constable and Mr. Tierney said next she never knew, as her discomposure prevented her from something so mundane as listening to a conversation. Did he jest? Call her such, merely to cover for having exposed her to another public insult?

But he could not be jesting. By the rules of their class, kissing her in any setting, much less a public one, was tantamount to a proposal. He *must* offer for her now, whether that kiss were a fleeting impulse or something premeditated. And must she accept?

Elfrida had decided when she first met him that Mr. Frederick Tierney would not make a suitable husband for a respectable, practical, yet impoverished lady like herself. There was his bad reputation. His indifference to propriety. His provoking manner. There were the rumors of women and gambling and who knew what-all. There were those embroidered waistcoats. And then the final offense: taking advantage of her concern by grabbing her and kissing her senseless as she knelt over him. Her fingers flew to her lips, as if to wipe away the memory of warm pressure there, just as she had wiped away his blood.

The thought of marrying Mr. Tierney should fill her with horror.

And yet it did not.

What were those rumors of his exploits but rumors, after all? Elfrida knew what it was to be a victim of gossip. Her sister Alice's misadventures had educated them all in that. And had there not been more to Alice's story than what gossip would have? Could not also Mr. Tierney's reputation be stained by the same brush of envy and jealousy and pleasure at another's expense? He certainly showed no bent for heedless flirtation in Somerset. Indeed, she could only accuse him of flirtatiousness where she herself was concerned, and if there existed some women who could find fault with being the object of a handsome man's attentions, Elfrida was not one of them. Perhaps he could not be held liable for the reactions of women, if he was guilty of no more than being handsome and charming. Was it Mr. Tierney's fault that Miss Birdlow and Miss Porterworth admired him, if he had done nothing to encourage their admiration?

The whispers of gambling excesses troubled her, but she thought back to the Pattergees card party. There had been no gambler's zeal, no desperation in Mr. Tierney's play, as she would sometimes remark in her uncles' manner, if they had to surrender even a pile of steel pins to Edith. And Elfrida was not aware of any creditors pursuing Mr. Tierney to the country. Surely Lord Marlton would never shelter a hardened rake and gambler beneath his roof. Could not the viscount's hospitality be read as an endorsement, rather, of Mr. Tierney's character?

"Miss Hapgood."

She found him before her, as close as he had been in the drawing room when he offered condolences for Mrs. Harriet Hapgood's death. He wore his frock coat again, and the constable was vanished. Her eyes fell to his mouth, one side of which was swollen, and she saw it spread in a wicked smile that made her heart race.

Yes, she could get used to the idea of being his betrothed.

His fingers brushed either side of her neck, causing her to shiver and him to laugh softly. But he only took hold of her bonnet and set it on her head again, deftly tying the black ribbons under her chin.

"Although I have provided you with bountiful entertainment this afternoon, Miss Hapgood, I believe the official play begins shortly. Shall we find the others?"

Chapter Nine

**The Comedy is an imitation
of the common errors of our life.
—Sir Philip Sidney, *An apologie for poetrie* (1586)**

The first performance of *All's Well That Ends Well* was already under way by the time they reached the theater tent, but Elfrida was not sorry. She found herself drifting in a blissful fog, despite having exchanged Mr. Tierney's arm once again for Margaret's. One afternoon did not matter, when they would have a lifetime together.

She and Mr. Tierney found the rest of the party gathered in varying states of worry and disdain. Miss Porterworth flung herself at him, stopping short, with her hands fluttering against his chest and away again. "You have been injured!"

"My opponent had the final word," sighed Mr. Tierney. "After I had thought the discussion ended."

Looking from Mr. Tierney to Elfrida, while Roscoe DeWitt called for a description of what had passed, Miss Birdlow raised one arched eyebrow. "You stayed behind, Miss Hapgood," she said coolly. "Were you afraid your mourning might soon be for someone closer to your heart?"

"I confess I was solicitous," Elfrida replied tranquilly. "I felt responsible, as it was I who allowed Mr. Tierney to accompany my sister on the roundabout, against my better judgment."

"Hmm. And yet it was not Miss Edith's honor Mr. Tierney felt called upon to defend."

"I respect him for rising in Miss Porterworth's defense in any case," said Elfrida.

No more was said by Miss Birdlow. She affected an interest in a nearby display of apricots and cherries and paid not the slightest heed to Mr. Tierney, over whom everyone else was inclined to fuss. She had seen the glances Mr. Tierney threw at Miss Hapgood. The glances and the curl of his mouth when he did so. Something had passed between the two of them, and she, the Honorable Miss Agnes Birdlow, would not give him the satisfaction of knowing it vexed her.

She need not have feared. If Frederick had even noticed Miss Birdlow's agitation, it would have given him no satisfaction—his thoughts were too taken up with other matters. Or, to tell the truth, with just one other person. He ventured another look at Miss Hapgood, who stood silently beside her sister Miss Margaret, willing to let the rest of the group decide what they should do next.

He had kissed her and called her his betrothed, and she made no objection. The way was clear: he would call on her the next day and make his offer formal. The thought filled him with surpassing contentment. What had begun as a ruse of sorts, to stave off further threats from Lady Wimpole, now seemed an end in itself. After his letter to Honoria Braithwaite, informing her of his pending engagement, she had not replied. Perhaps the possibility of his marriage had been enough to put her off; perhaps he need not actually go through with it. Although he certainly would cross his sometime mistress' path again in the future, by then she might have resigned herself to his loss and would not care so much to learn he was still unattached. He could say, after all, that the betrothal fell through—that the lady cited insuperable objections. He could return to his former life as a single man, with all its freedoms and privileges.

And yet...why not marry? He must at some point, being both his father's and his uncle's heir. And why not marry Miss Hapgood? She was already connected to his family and would thus meet with his parents' approval, since they approved of anything related to Frederick's brother Joseph. She was not rich, but she had an ancient name and a lovely, lovely person. The unswollen side of his mouth curled again, remembering the press of her bosom against him, the feel of her hair and lips, the wonder in her forget-me-not eyes. Miss Hapgood was not demonstrative, but Frederick was fast becoming addicted to the pleasure of provoking her, and, after the likes of Lady Wimpole, a little reserve in a woman had its charms.

Impatience stirred him. If only he could be rid of the rest of the party and get Miss Hapgood to himself again. The morrow seemed too far away. Perhaps in the dark and cramped quarters of the players' tent he might place himself at her side, might grasp her hand in his own, tease off her glove and—

"I say—I'm famished," declared Miss Porterworth, waving off Roscoe's continued solicitude. "If we have so long before the play, why do we not have something to eat and see what else there is?"

They did exactly that. Elfrida and her sisters had Bath buns, laughing and wiping their fingers on Margaret's handkerchief. Elfrida's tongue darted out to lick lingering sugar from the corner of her mouth, only to hear Mr. Tierney murmur, "You have missed some—shall I help you?" and to feel his gloved hand brush the small of her back.

They wandered past the gambling tables and the feats of strength. Norman DeWitt paid sixpence to see the five-legged pig. Miss Birdlow purchased her sister-in-law a length of baize to sew into window curtains. The footraces proved amusing, until Elfrida recognized among the participants some of the scamps who called out remarks at the roundabout. All enmity seemed forgotten, however, washed away by ale and the festive music of the fair.

Weariness set in by the time they bought their play tickets and filed into the tent, and Elfrida was glad to see plain deal benches set out in rows so they would not have to stand. The light within was dim and dusty. When she discerned an elbow extended to her, clad in blue, she took it and let it guide her to the first row. Only when she was seated did she peer into her escort's face and find Norman DeWitt beside her, with Margaret and Edith to his right. Miss Birdlow glided down on Elfrida's left. Elfrida would not ask where the rest of their group had got to, but the blur of blue she caught on the neighboring bench, angled toward them, and the high titter of Miss Porterworth informed her they were not far.

When the benches had filled and subsequent spectators were filing in to stand in the back, two players strode from behind the curtain, a round little man and an elegant black-haired woman, both sumptuously appareled in velvet.

"Welcome, fairgoers," the man greeted them, bowing low and causing his gilt crown to tumble from his shiny bald head. The audience laughed and hooted, and the woman pretended to be mortified, chasing the crown as it rolled away. When she had clamped it back on his head, she dropped a curtsey and continued in a musical, thrilling voice that quickly hushed everyone, "By his majesty's pleasure, we, who during London's season have played these roles at Covent Garden, will here present William Shakespeare's comedy *All's Well that Ends Well*. We will begin after a brief musical interlude."

Applause and stomping broke out as the woman swept another curtsey and the man tried to give her a clumsy kiss that knocked his crown off again. When they had disappeared behind the curtain, the small orchestra squeezed against one side of the tent struck up some folk tunes, their tempo quickening as the rowdier sorts began to jig to them.

Fanning herself with the program Mr. DeWitt had purchased from the book woman, Elfrida found her view of the stage suddenly obscured by a silver-blue waistcoat from which a snowy shirt bloomed. Mr. Tierney stood before her. It was difficult to tell, with his back to the stage and the oil footlights behind him, but she thought his face rather drawn and his movements unquiet.

"Miss Birdlow," he addressed himself to the chief of their party. "I find myself concerned for you young ladies here. The audience is not much improved after a day spent drinking"—he nodded toward the jigging patrons—"and we will perhaps be better served if we forego the entertainment and return to Pattergees."

The viscount's daughter merely stared. "Forego the entertainment? I had thought that the sole reason for attending the fair. I am sure the rustics are no rowdier within the confines of this tent than they have been without. I refer, sir, to one incident by a whirligig some hours since."

Elfrida thought he colored, but that could not be the case with someone so worldly and at his ease as Mr. Frederick Tierney.

"I gave my word to Lady Marlton that she would have nothing to fear or disapprove of, if I brought you and Miss Porterworth here—"

"Nor does she," retorted the young lady. Having intercepted those mysterious looks between Mr. Tierney and Miss Hapgood, she was in no mood to humor any whims of his. If anything, she would like to flaunt her disregard for his opinions. "Mr. Tierney, I would like to see the play. If you find yourself too tired or too discomfited by your earlier injuries, I will excuse you, but I will remain. The Mr. DeWitts will provide ample chaperonage for all of us ladies. Unless, perhaps"—casting a sidewise glance at Elfrida—"Miss Hapgood also disapproves and would like to leave."

Puzzled by the undercurrents of the discussion, Elfrida tried to read her would-be fiancé's countenance. She found nothing there.

He did not meet her gaze, and his own eyes were shuttered, his bruised countenance still.

She fell back, therefore, on honesty. "I would very much like to see the play, and I know I would never know another moment's peace if I required my sisters to go now. Mr. Tierney—we appreciate your concern, but I think, for all their noise and riotry, no one here intends any further mischief."

Without another word, he tendered them a short bow and returned to his place beside Miss Porterworth.

The Hapgoods had never seen this particular play performed, and Margaret would later say she hoped never to see it again. The actors added what humor they could, but they could not, without violence to the script, rescue Bertram from his callow unworthiness or Helena from making him her object. It hardly comforted Edith that Helena won Bertram in the end, and she muttered to Margaret, "I understand now what is meant by the expression *a worse fate than death*. Such a husband!"

For her part, Elfrida was too distracted by Miss Birdlow's whispered commentary during the play to give it her full attention. It began when Helena took center stage to deliver her first monologue:

> *I am undone: there is no living, none,*
> *If Bertram be away. It were all one*
> *That I should love a bright particular star*
> *And think to wed it, he is so above me:*
> *In his bright radiance and collateral light*
> *Must I be comforted, not in his sphere.*

"Is it not strange," came Miss Birdlow's voice by Elfrida's ear, "how the actress fixes her eyes on Mr. Frederick Tierney as she delivers her lines? It seemed, when she came onstage, her gaze was more often on our friend than on this supposedly-beloved Bertram."

Elfrida made no reply, but after a minute, she leaned back slightly and tried to glimpse Mr. Tierney. His face was indistinct even when she squinted, but she saw that his arms were crossed over his chest and his head somewhat bowed. Was he annoyed? Bored? Asleep?

"There!" hissed Miss Birdlow. "See?"

"'Bless our poor virginity from underminers and blowers up!'" exclaimed Helena to Parolles, her hands on her hips. But even as she bantered him and made clever ripostes to his innuendoes, she glanced again and again toward Mr. Tierney's place, as if sharing private jokes.

Elfrida shook off a twinge of uneasiness. She cared nothing for Miss Birdlow's observations. But when that lady continued to poke her and murmur, Elfrida was obliged to say, "It might be no more than absent-mindedness, that she looks so often his direction. I suspect she cannot see much of the audience because of the footlights."

"Odd that she should always be absent-minded in the very same place. She looks his way no matter whom she is supposed to be speaking to."

"Then maybe she finds him handsome," suggested Elfrida stubbornly.

"Certainly she does. There! She did it again—did you note?—when she said 'my master, my dear lord he is.'"

Biting her lips, Elfrida set herself to studying the black-haired Helena of the thrilling voice, and after a half-hour of this, she was forced to admit the truth of it. Helena did look Mr. Tierney's way at every opportunity. And any line that might be interpreted as admiring she addressed to that same gentleman. How Elfrida wished she could also make out his reaction to these peculiar attentions!

As if she read her mind, Miss Birdlow pressed close once more. "He frowns. He shakes his head. He looks away—he looks *our* way."

"We had better not whisper anymore," urged Elfrida, drawing back. "We will disturb those around us."

Miss Birdlow met this suggestion with a lift of her eyebrow, and, indeed, Elfrida blushed to make it, as the rest of the playgoers in the tent kept up a constant stir of shuffling feet, laughs and hisses, and various remarks addressed to each other and the actors. The players only succeeded in making themselves heard by speaking so loudly and emphatically that Elfrida more than once saw spittle fly out. No—their conversation disturbed no one but herself.

"Check the program," commanded Miss Birdlow. "What is the name of Mr. Tierney's dogged admirer?" Elfrida made no answer but handed her the paper, and her companion lighted quickly on the information. "Mrs. Anne Gurdy," she muttered, tapping the name thoughtfully. "Mrs. Anne...Gurdy. I remember the name from my time in town, but I would not have remembered her face. Without the rouge and the velvets, she would be nothing. How impudent she is, to behave so outrageously! Could she possibly be acquainted with him? My brother was shocked by the behavior of some of the actresses he encountered at an inn in town..."

Elfrida heard no more, her twinge of uneasiness having metamorphosed into something far more troubling. Gone was her earlier bliss, the sensation of floating on a cloud of future hope. What could it all mean? Mr. Tierney and this Mrs. Anne Gurdy—they must have some manner of prior acquaintance, or even a stage actress would not behave so boldly, would she?

Desperately Elfrida clung to Mr. Frank Birdlow's comment—perhaps stage actresses were all this brazen. Perhaps Mr. Tierney had never seen this woman in his life, but she was so taken with his appearance that she dedicated the performance to him. No sooner had Elfrida deemed this idea passably plausible than she remembered Mr. Tierney's odd behavior before the play began—his inexplicable desire to be gone.

Miss Birdlow returned the program to her and observed with satisfaction that Miss Hapgood crushed it with unthinking fingers. Entirely forgetting her own assurances to Miss Porterworth that Pattergees would never shelter a known rake, Miss Birdlow enjoyed the smug certainty that, on the whole, it was hardly flattering to any young lady to attract a gentleman's notice, if that gentleman was so careless and indiscriminate with it.

Elfrida spent the remainder of the play sinking further into discouragement, before drowning in it altogether when her companion made one final remark. "There! He has finally acknowledged her! Did you see his little nod? And she has *winked* at him, the baggage." If Elfrida required any proof that this interchange was not simply a malicious invention of Miss Birdlow's, Mrs. Anne Gurdy provided it, subsiding thereafter into a straightforward playing of Helena, with no more significant looks or wanderings of attention.

"How late it grows. We had better get back to the public house," cried Mr. Tierney, beside them the instant the players left the stage, and while the audience continued to stomp and catcall. He had hauled up a surprised but willing Miss Porterworth and left Roscoe DeWitt stumbling after them. This time he darted a glance at Miss Hapgood, but her face was turned toward her sisters as she passed the word.

Without waiting for Norman DeWitt even to offer his elbow, Elfrida took hold of it, and he emerged from the tent into brighter light with the three sisters hanging off him as if he had crawled through a hedgerow of Hapgoods.

The crowds had not thinned noticeably, and it was not until they were gathered before the Wayfarer and the horses and carriage called for, that the group could converse.

"I cannot think why that play should be called a comedy," declared Margaret to her sisters. "Could there be a more tragic tragedy than Helena marrying Bertram?"

"Even more tragic was that performance," agreed Roscoe DeWitt, although Margaret had not addressed him. "Did you notice, Tierney, that the actress who played Helena kept looking our way whenever she was onstage, as if her lines were printed on banners above our heads."

"Did she?" said Frederick.

"She wasn't even that pretty," pouted Miss Porterworth, who had her own suspicions about whom Mrs. Anne Gurdy found so interesting. "If she didn't have those costumes and all that paste and gilt jewelry, she would have been quite ordinary."

Margaret frowned, the beauty or plainness of Mrs. Anne Gurdy being quite beside the point. Perhaps she communicated her feelings through the tension in her arm because Mr. Norman DeWitt glanced sidewise at her. "You did not find Bertram's redemption compelling, Miss Margaret?"

"Not a bit of it! I cannot imagine either Diana or Helena wanting anything to do with such a liar and...seducer of women. Such characters do not change overnight."

"I agree there with you," replied Norman, in his moderate, calm voice, and a silence fell on the party. Margaret stole a look at him, having never really noticed him before. He was as tall as she—perhaps a bit taller—with stolid features more strong than handsome. Elfrida had been wont to say he was a nice young man who rarely spoke, and Margaret realized with surprise that, when Norman DeWitt did speak, it gave a fleeting liveliness to his countenance. He lifted hazel eyes quickly to hers, catching her stare, and Margaret quickly dropped his arm in a fluster of embarrassment.

A creaking and clattering announced the arrival of the carriage, followed by ostlers with the gentlemen's horses in tow. Mr. Tierney brushed the groom aside to hand the ladies in, that he might murmur to Elfrida, "I will call tomorrow."

By neither word nor look did she acknowledge this, and he was left to wonder if the afternoon's excitement had been no more than a brief, anomalous departure from her increasingly tiresome calm.

But Elfrida was far from calm.

Once in the carriage, she removed her bonnet and lay her head back, wishing they could all be silent for the drive home. At Bramleigh she would excuse herself from a late supper—plead headache—and steal up to her room to try to order her thoughts.

Her companions nearly were silent, the four miles back toward Patterton, being most of them equally weary from such an active day. Only the indefatigable Miss Porterworth had energy left. She rapped on the glass and waved at the gentlemen as the carriage set out, her face so close to the window that her breath misted it.

"They'll be out of town before we are," she remarked, "for we must wait in the crush of traffic. Yes—Mr. Roscoe DeWitt is threading his way through. Mr. Norman DeWitt and Mr. Tierney hang back near us, so we will not be abandoned. Oh, look!"—the desultory note in her running commentary gave way so abruptly to eagerness that even Miss Birdlow sat up and craned her elegant neck to see out— "Someone has run up and grabbed Mr. Tierney's bridle! I think—I think it is—it is! It is! It is that dreadful actress! She calls up to him and now he leans down to her—"

"Shameless," interjected Miss Birdlow. "Constance, you have so fogged the window I can barely make anything out. No—don't wipe it! He will know we are spying."

"—How can it be spying," her friend countered, "if they will behave so in a public place?" She left the glass clouded, however, and merely half stood to peep through a clear spot. "Mr. Norman DeWitt pretends to see nothing. He goes on. Oh—how long will Mr. Tierney suffer her to address him? There. He says something to her and she releases his horse. Now he waves to her—a very small wave—and she—she blows a kiss! Gracious!" Triumphantly, Miss Porterworth plopped back into her seat and rolled her eyes at Miss Birdlow. "Did I not say the man had a reputation? *Now* tell me your Papa would never shelter a rake!"

"Constance, this is hardly appropriate," Miss Birdlow warned, inclining her head to where Edith and Margaret sat staring at their hands in their laps. Whispering audibly she added, "And you recall that Mr. Tierney is their near connection."

Miss Porterworth widened her eyes and pantomimed turning a key to lock her lips.

With difficulty Elfrida resisted telling her not to bother. The harm had been done. Margaret and Edith would now pelt her with questions when they were alone again at Bramleigh. And what would she say?

What would she say to them, and—more pressingly—what would she say to *him*, when he came on the morrow?

Chapter Ten

**No Man of common Sense will value a Woman the less,
for not giving up herself at the first Attack,
or for not accepting his Proposal without enquiring
into his Person or Character.
—Daniel Defoe, *Moll Flanders* (1722)**

Miss Elfrida Hapgood accused herself of cowardice.

What other reason could be given for rising earlier than was her wont and determining that her letter to Alice must be sent that very morning? It was a sad excuse for a letter in any case, filling only three-quarters of the sheet and failing to treat on anything near Elfrida's heart. But she folded it, sealed it, and set out from the house toward the Patterton post office, refusing the offer of her sisters' company, and cutting across the fields to avoid the main road.

Cowardly, yes. She was cowardly.

Mr. Tierney had not said when he would call, but Elfrida suspected it would be at the hour he came for sittings, and she was determined to avoid him. For all his shortcomings, he was not a booby. He would understand her absence to mean that his offer would be unwelcome. If she was not at home, he could not propose. He would thus be spared humiliation, and she would be spared being its agent.

It was a fine morning with a pearly sky and a breeze that played with the black ribbons of her bonnet. If Elfrida had not been preoccupied, she would have walked more slowly to drink it in, but she hurried now, throwing more than one glance over her shoulder for fear of seeing a blue-coated figure on a bay mare.

But she reached the post office unmolested and was delighted when the mistress handed her a double letter in Alice's writing. Waiting with difficulty until she was once more in the street, she slipped her finger under the wax to open it. Margaret would read the letter aloud to the family, of course—a hundred times—when Elfrida arrived home, but she wanted the luxury of reading it for the first time without interruption. Ducking under the awning of the grocer's, Elfrida unfolded the pages.

The second sheet was no letter at all, it so happened, but rather an illustration of sundry flowers and bugs. Alice had given the bugs whimsical faces and drawn little banners issuing from their mouths with jokes for Edith because Edith recoiled from the insect world.

Smiling over these, Elfrida tucked them away and proceeded to the letter. No one was about. She might hold it as close to her eyes as she pleased.

My dearest and still more dear Elfie,

If not for missing you and my family, my happiness would know no alloy. My Joseph is the kindest, cleverest, most talented, most thoughtful husband since the world began, and I would fill pages with his praise, if not for fear of growing tiresome or provoking barbed remarks from Margaret.

We are safely arrived at the parsonage in Stone Halt, and you must not imagine such a one as poor Father Thomas inhabits. Our home is in good repair, with a kitchen garden and orchard about one quarter the size of Bramleigh's. The chimneys do not smoke at all, nor does the roof leak, Joseph promises me. Best of all, my husband's study is a goodly size, and on our very first walks to meet our flock, we have begun to fill it with "s pecimens."Our corner of Buckinghamshire is charming indeed, with rolling fields and neat hedgerows. Joseph could see I wished for a trifle more wildness to my landscape and assures me I will find that, too. But in the meantime I am happy to see our parishioners modestly well off. Mr. Walter Tierney my father-in-law is a much-praised landlord here—several people said as much and were so kind to me that I cannot do otherwise than believe them.

I do wish you could meet Joseph's parents. His mother is graciousness itself. She has the curious Christian name of Evelyn because she is named for her grandfather Mr. Coningsby Evelyn, and I suppose they could not call her Coningsby! In any event, she is a model female, and Joseph's father a warm and just man. Now I understand how my husband came to be the person he is—thoughtful, modest, discreet. Oh, but I am praising him again! But, Elfie, you will too, when you come to know him better. I pray I will make him happy and thus give pleasure to his father and mother. It seems there has been much to grieve Mr. and Mrs. Tierney of late, in the conduct of their elder son Frederick—

"Miss Hapgood, good morning."

Elfrida fairly leaped, crumpling the letter to her bosom as she stared at the very same Frederick Tierney, conjured as he seemed to be from the page she had been reading. What he should be doing in Patterton, when he ought to be at Bramleigh, she couldn't say.

"Forgive me. I did not mean to startle you." He touched the brim of his beaver hat, the gleam in his eyes belying his apology. He looked astonishingly handsome in his well-cut coat (the bottle-green one) and buff breeches, and to her surprise he wore a plain black waistcoat with not a hint of embroidery. The swelling of his mouth was gone down, leaving only a reddish mark by his upper lip. Not that she was looking at his lips.

"Mr. Tierney." She curtsied.

"I have interrupted you."

"No. That is—I have a letter from my sister—from our sister Alice," she answered, vexed with herself for her fumbling speech. "I will finish it later."

"Indeed. I am surprised you took the time to stop and peruse it now. After all, you must have pressing business that draws you to town this time of morning."

"As must you," countered Elfrida, bristling at the mischief in his voice. "And I beg you not to let me keep you from it. Good morning."

"Wait—Miss Hapgood." He hurried the few steps after her. "Come. Imagine my shock when I rode to Bramleigh, only to have your good sisters say you had gone to town! I hoped to speak with you this morning—as I suggested yesterday, when I handed you into the carriage. I do not blame you for forgetting—a fatiguing day, was it not?"

She halted unwillingly. "Yes. It was."

"Though not without its...pleasant...memories."

Coloring, she concentrated on folding Alice's letter and stuffing it in her reticule. "What did you wish to speak to me about?"

"Nothing that could bear mentioning before a greengrocer's shop," he replied mildly. "I do not suppose you rode here this morning?"

"No. I will walk home."

"Then I will accompany you. Let me untie my horse, which is across the way."

"Mr. Tierney"—she took a deep breath and faced him— "it would not do for you to walk to Bramleigh with me." Any more than it would do for him to stand there talking with her, for longer than a polite greeting warranted.

Mr. Farnsworth the grocer emerged from his shop to sweep the walk. "Have you need of anything at Bramleigh, Miss Hapgood?"

"Oh—er—if you might add a packet of Kitchen Pepper in your next delivery, we would be obliged, Mr. Farnsworth. Thank you." The grocer nodded with alacrity, and Elfrida made haste to move on.

"There would be no crime involved in being seen together," Frederick began again when he had caught up and they were out of earshot, "as I am so bold to believe we might come to an understanding by the end of our stroll."

The line of her jaw, which few but her family ever saw appear in her soft cheek, appeared now. If Mr. Tierney had been to Bramleigh—if he knew she did not want to speak to him and had deliberately avoided him—and he pursued her still, he must be a booby after all. And with the dull-witted, one must be perfectly clear to avoid misunderstandings. Clear to the point of rudeness, if need be.

She stopped before the chandler's. Pretending to inspect the display of beeswax and spermaceti candles, she said, "Mr. Tierney, there is no understanding between us."

"I realize that," he agreed. "I realize that I rather put the cart before the horse at the fair. Forgive me for taking liberties, Miss Hapgood. You were so very beautiful, you see, bending over me like a compassionate angel."

His flattering words, spoken with every sign of sincerity, weakened something within her, and Elfrida hurried to prop it back up. *He might have made just such speeches to Mrs. Anne Gurdy*, she reminded herself.

Her long study of the chandler's window brought that merchant to the door as well, to greet her and ask if he might be of some assistance.

"Ah—thank you, Mr. Weeks. Perhaps if you could send to Bramleigh a dozen of the beeswax."

"Another dozen? Mrs. Button ordered six dozen not two weeks ago."

"The spermaceti, then," cried Elfrida. "We have been doing a fearful amount of reading in the evening. Thank you."

The chandler bowed and hurried away, and she scowled to find Mr. Tierney grinning. "This might be a very costly conversation for you, Miss Hapgood, if we do not continue it elsewhere."

Indeed.

Being in complete agreement there, she hurried on. "Mr. Tierney—I should not have allowed you the liberty of—I should not have allowed you the liberty. It goes without saying. We were both overcome by the drama of the situation, I daresay. But I do not consider you in any way obligated to—act upon it. To make something...permanent...of the impulse of a moment."

He did not answer immediately, but she felt his eyes fixed on her, trying to read her motivations.

A pair of ladies emerged from the stationer's across the street, chattering and laughing. Mercifully Elfrida was not acquainted with them, but she caught the second glances they gave her companion before their heads drew together to whisper. Feeling heat rise in her own face, she hissed, "I hope we understand each other now, Mr. Tierney, and I pray you would not refer to it again. Good day."

Without waiting for a response, she turned on her heel and strode away, avoiding the appearance of hurry, but chagrined to find she had set off in the wrong direction. Although she did not hear him following her, she had no desire to turn back across his path again and decided she would make a big circle once she was out of the main street.

Elfrida paused at the top of the rise, having emerged from the small woodland that bordered Bramleigh to the west. Her boots were damp from the stream, where she attempted to cross on the rocks before slipping and splashing in. The water was low, thankfully, now that August approached, but there was still mud to be scraped off against a tree trunk. How had Alice put it, in her letter? The Somerset landscape had "a trifle more wildness" than Stone Halt. Elfrida was not overly fond of wildness herself, but another pang for her sister struck her. Once home, she would finish reading Alice's letter and then write her a very long response, and she would tell all, this time. Except—in her mind she drew back again—except the part about Mr. Tierney kissing her and nearly proposing. That would never do.

When the last bit of mud was removed, she looked up in time to see a man on horseback approaching the house. A man in a bottle-green coat and buff breeches, who slid off and passed the reins to their boy Hal. For heaven's sake!

Hal tipped his cap, having received a coin for his troubles, and the two figures walked together, the man posing a question and Hal answering. Elfrida guessed the subject being canvassed, and she froze like a statue, her heart speeding.

She must have guessed correctly because the next moment, Hal nodded and pointed up the rise toward the woodland: *Miss Hapgood would come that way from town.*

Mr. Tierney waved.

"Good Lord," muttered Elfrida. "What more can the man have to say?" But she could hardly stand there and hope for him to go away, now that he and Hal had seen her. She raised her own hand and began to pick her way down the slope.

"Quite sensible of you, Miss Hapgood," called Mr. Tierney, when she was near enough to hear him. He had started up the rise as she descended and removed his hat altogether to gesture with it at their surroundings. "Much more privacy here than at the chandler's."

"Or there would be," she said, as she reached him, "if you were not shouting."

"Who is there to hear us now?" he asked in a quieter voice. "I have sent Hal on his way. But we have satisfied the proprieties because I imagine your sisters and the remaining servants are even now peeping out the windows at us. Chaperones galore. There—see the curtains twitch? Whose chamber is that on the west side?"

Elfrida did not need to see twitching curtains—even if she could at this distance—to know it was Margaret and Edith's. Mr. Tierney knew too much, and it was no use declaring that no one at Bramleigh would spy on them, when she could not say so with any pretense of honesty.

Ignoring his extended arm, Elfrida folded her gloved hands. "Very well. We will speak here, if you like. Although I am at a loss. What more can you possibly have to say to me?"

"After you were so discourteous, you mean?" he asked with an innocent smile.

"I *was* that," she admitted. "I always own it best to be straightforward, so there might be no misunderstanding."

"But Miss Hapgood, there is a misunderstanding."

"There is?" She looked up at him uncertainly, into his unreadable blue eyes, before dropping her own again as she tried to work out his meaning.

Had he not meant to propose to her, after all, then, despite what he said at the Taunton Fair? Had he meant, rather, only to offer some feeble apology for his behavior? But—no—he spoke of "coming to an understanding." What other sort of understanding could there be?

She felt the heat rising to her face again—heat which had nothing to do with the summer sun overhead.

No one in their circle had witnessed their kiss or Mr. Tierney calling her his betrothed—only some village constable. It was not like when Joseph had to offer for Alice—his hand forced by scandal and social pressure. But—if Mr. Tierney had no intention of proposing—then, did he look upon her as some Mrs. Anne Gurdy to trifle with? To embrace in broad daylight and then discard, as if she were no gentleman's daughter? Was the "understanding" to be that there would be no "understanding"?

To her confusion, her companion burst into a hearty laugh. "My dear Miss Hapgood—what can I have said, to anger you so?"

Her flush blossomed into full scarlet. "I am not angry," she lied. "It is warm out, however. I hope you will tell me what you have to say, for I have not all day to stand here."

"Of course not. How inconsiderate of me," he soothed, his tone such as one might use with a wayward child. "But I cannot fathom what you thought I was about to say to you. It must have been terrible indeed, to bring that fire to your eye." Grinning again as he saw her fists clench, he added, "But I digress. I only meant that I did not understand you. This was what I meant by 'misunderstanding.' Because I did not see how you could dismiss me so summarily before the chandler's, without knowing what I was to say in the first place."

Elfrida hardly knew how to reply. The man was impossible. She had gone from relief at being spared his proposal of marriage, to being insulted that he never meant to make one. Those who knew her would say Miss Hapgood was not an easy young woman to ruffle, gifted with a calm disposition that few things could unsettle, and yet Frederick Tierney was proving to be chief among those few things!

Struggling inwardly, she did not trust herself to speak until she mastered her voice. "Pardon me, then, for being hasty. I will hear you out."

"Thank you. Would you prefer to sit? I warn you I may go on at length."

"I will stand."

"Very well. Although the slope of this hill makes it precarious for me to lean far back," he sighed.

"Then pray avoid doing so," Elfrida said shortly, refusing to wonder at his meaning.

"But I must." He inspected the ground cursorily before—to her astonishment—going down on one knee. "My man will have a fit over this," he said ruefully. "Grass stains and so on."

Mr. Tierney reached as if to take her hand, and Elfrida withdrew a step in alarm. "What can you be doing?"

"Does not my posture speak for itself?" he asked with pretended amazement. "Small wonder we have been talking in circles this morning, if you do not know that when a man gets down on one knee before you, he intends to ask for your hand in marriage."

"I know what it means!" cried Elfrida. "But I cannot imagine why *you* should be doing it."

"Having little experience in the matter, I confess I thought it *de rigueur*," he said. "Would you prefer I stand?"

"Sir, you willfully misunderstand me. I do not refer to your posture. I mean to say that I cannot understand why you would propose to me."

"Strictly speaking," he rejoined, "I have not yet proposed."

Here Elfrida so forgot herself as to stamp her foot in frustration. She would not tolerate another instant of this farce. But as she made to sweep past him, he caught at her skirt.

"Release me at once, Mr. Tierney!"

He obeyed, but just as quickly stood to block her path. "Forgive me, Miss Hapgood. My conduct is abominable. I plead nerves. This is a novel experience for me, you see, and one for which I find that books and plays have little prepared me. When I am anxious, I tend to jest. I had best get right to the matter: will you do me the honor of becoming my wife?"

He tended to jest in *all* moods, Elfrida thought, and even now she would not lay odds he was entirely in earnest. She did not dare answer if he was not. And yet, he did seem anxious. There—the way he winced, as if his words had not come out how he planned—was that genuine? Was his offer, indeed, genuine?

"Customarily one should give reasons for asking, I suppose," he began again, more carefully this time. "To increase one's odds of being accepted. Ahem—Miss Hapgood, I am fortunate in being able to offer you a name as good as your own and the future hope of a title, as I am my baronet uncle's sole heir. The income my father provides me you would find—"

"Mr. Tierney—" holding up a hand, she interrupted. He was not mad—he was sincere. He was asking her to marry him. Now that she realized he had meant only to tease her earlier, Elfrida felt her anger give way to embarrassment. Embarrassment and wonder! But she did not have time now to sort out her feelings. She must not let him continue—it would only lead to regret and discomfort.

"For all your raillery," she hurried to say, "I see I did indeed understand you at the chandler's. I thought you…might feel obliged to offer for me after—after the fair. What happened there was—nothing. And seen by no one we need mind. I—thank you for your honorable intentions, but I excuse you from the consequences."

"No one we need mind?" he echoed faintly, striving for his former teasing note. "Is this how you refer to a constable, an officer of the peace?"

"I wish you good day, Mr. Tierney," she said. Biting her lip, she held out her gloved hand. "Will you shake hands with me, to show we are still on friendly terms?"

Instead he clutched at it, grasping her fingers, his brows drawing together. "Miss Hapgood, let me be clear: I do not feel compelled to offer for you simply because I kissed you."

"No," she murmured, trying unsuccessfully to pull away. "If you felt such a compulsion every time you kissed someone, I imagine you would have more wives than Solomon."

"I beg your pardon?"

"Nothing."

It was his turn to color. "Miss Hapgood—do you have a reason for speaking thus?"

"It was idle," Elfrida apologized. "And none of my concern." She tugged again at her hand, but he hung on.

"I suppose you refer to gossip you have heard of me."

"Mr. Tierney, forgive me. It was not the gossip—entirely—"

"What do you mean by 'entirely'? Have you another reason for your most—summary—refusal?" Slowly he released her. "Was it because of the actress in the play yesterday? No—I do not deny it—though I would rather not have had her go on so, as I am sure you deduced. I do not deny I had a...*liaison* with her. Such things are the way of the world, in town, but I am content to be done with that sort of life."

How easily he brushed it off, Elfrida marveled. She was no stranger to men behaving badly, having grown up hearing of her uncles' countless mishaps, but, just as with her uncles, she caught nothing in Mr. Tierney's tone or words to indicate he felt any remorse for his conduct. Keeping mistresses was simply what was done by men about town, it seemed, and she would prove herself the veriest provincial if she objected to it.

"There is no longer anything you need fear, between Mrs. Anne Gurdy and me," he went on. "You may rest easy there."

"I am not *un*easy," Elfrida said, drawing away. "You need not explain yourself to me. I have said it is none of my concern. Mr. Tierney—again, I thank you for your offer and the honor you do me—"

"—But you refuse," he finished her sentence, unable to disguise the amazement in his voice.

"I...I do."

For some moments he was unable to speak, and Elfrida found herself unexpectedly on the defensive. "Mr. Tierney—we are barely acquainted, the connection of our siblings notwithstanding."

"Then—I have rushed matters. You would like more time to consider, as we continue to know each other better."

"Oh, no," she said. "I do not mean to toy with your feelings thus. I—although our acquaintance has been brief, I suspect we should not suit."

"That is," he frowned, "we hardly know each other, but what little you do know makes you consider marriage with me repellent."

"For pity's sake," Elfrida floundered, "how dreadful you make it sound! Since we have not known each other above two weeks, this...idea of yours...surely it may be forgotten as rapidly as it arose."

If asked, she would not have been able to explain it, but she suspected she had wounded him. How could that be, however, when he spoke not a word of love? The playful gleam was vanished from his eyes, and two lines now flanked his set mouth. Her refusal might only be a blow to his pride, yet Elfrida could not help trying to make it better. "You are a very eligible young man, you know. You will easily find a much wealthier and fashionable wife than I am, and then you will be glad I did not take advantage of you."

"Yes," was his curt reply. He flicked at some speck on his sleeve and then stared off in the distance. "So considerate of you, to think of my interests before your own, Miss Hapgood. But will you give me no other reason, than that you think I might do better?"

"Mr. Tierney—"

"I suppose you also think *you* might do better?"

"Mr. Tierney, I must ask you not to cross-question me. I said I thought we should not suit." Clutching her hands together, she was grateful for the gloves which hid how white her knuckles must be. "I am a provincial girl, and you—you like town life. You like to...cut a dash, while I think I would prefer a—prefer a—"

"Prefer a very plain young man?" he interjected, one eyebrow raised, turning to regard her. His eyes had paled to icy blue. "Why, so I thought I was. A very plain young man. I do believe I heard you call me exactly that, the morning of our siblings' wedding."

If possible, her hands wrung each other even more tightly, but she only said in a low voice, "Forgive me an ill-advised instance of sarcasm with my sister Margaret. Mr. Tierney, you are anything but plain. You would more accurately be described as the *precise opposite*."

Abruptly he clapped his hat back on, the black beaver fur eclipsing his golden crown. "I see. Whatever our earlier misapprehensions this morning, Miss Hapgood, you make yourself perfectly comprehensible now. I am sorry to have taken so much of your time, and I wish you all good fortune in the future."

Would he go like this? she thought, half-panicked, reaching for him just as he started away. What on earth would she tell Alice? That she had, in the space of two weeks, succeeded in creating a rift between the two sides of the family?

"Mr. Tierney!" she cried, taking a step after him.

He stopped but did not turn to look at her.

"Hold—please. You are not angry, are you? You cannot be so, for Joseph and Alice's sake. Mr. Tierney, say we will still be friends."

There was a long pause. Elfrida feared she would have to repeat herself if he did not reply. He pulled at the cuffs of his shirt, which peeped from the ends of his coat sleeves, and then brushed his hands down his front, as if whisking the morning's trials, including herself, from his person.

"I do not know what we are," he said at last. "Neither friends nor enemies. There is no appropriate word. We are nothing to each other, Miss Hapgood."

Never seeing her outstretched hand, he touched his own to the brim of his hat.

"Please make my apologies to Miss Edith. I will not be able to finish the sittings. Goodbye."

CHAPTER ELEVEN

I knew not what I ayled, but I knew I ayled something more than ordinary: and my Heart was very heavy. —Thomas Ellwood, *The History of the Life of Thomas Ellwood* (1714)

The heat was unbearable.

Even in the dim quiet of White's, with the curtains drawn shut on the famous bay window that fronted St. James Street. The few gentlemen in the dining room grumbled about it over their potted shrimps and beef joints, but there were not many of them, as any who had the means or connections to escape town in mid-July had done so.

"Beastly unpleasant," rumbled Mr. Babcock to Mr. Hawkins, "I will see about this horse Ed Tattersall wrote me of, but then I'm off again. It may be hot as Hades in Kent, but there won't be all these beastly buildings and pavement to hold it in."

Mr. Hawkins, whose crushing debts prevented his own flight from London to the family home in Norfolk, only nodded. He would dearly love to accompany Babcock to Hyde Park Corner to see this vaunted steed, but it would not do for him to be seen about town—his creditors might think him in pocket again. As it was, their constant dunning forced him to hide for hours in the club, and his grandfather was threatening once more to disown him. "If I could just get up a game," he mumbled, half to himself, "my luck would turn. I know it."

"Well, I won't join you," said Babcock baldly. "You look too desperate, for one, and, for another, I can't bear another hour within doors."

Hawkins threw down his fork and surveyed the room. Two old gents, each at his own table—no gamers there. Lord Wantley in the corner—much too sharp, and Hawkins already owed him a hefty sum. But Wantley could make a third, if Hawkins was not his only victim.

"Say, Babcock—" Hawkins said, "who's behind the paper over there?"

Babcock made a great show of taking another shrimp, chewing it thoughtfully, setting down his utensils, and swallowing another sip of ale. Then he threw one glance over his shoulder in the direction indicated.

"Tierney," he said. "You'll want to let him alone."

"Why?" demanded Hawkins. "He's here, isn't he? Introduce me. He might like to play a hand or two."

"I won't introduce you," replied Babcock. "The man's in a fearful mood. Hasn't said a word to anyone for two days."

"Well, why not? What ails him? Money?"

"I didn't ask," Babcock said dryly.

"I will ask," declared Hawkins, pushing back his chair.

"Don't be a fool."

"I bet you five guineas I can get him to play me."

Babcock raised a skeptical brow. He had but little acquaintance with Mr. Frederick Tierney himself, but he thought that, judging from his recent observations of the man, he could hardly lose this gamble. Of course, Hawkins hadn't a farthing of ready money, and if Babcock won, the sum would merely be added to what was already owed.

So be it.

The waiter brought the betting book and the wager was duly entered.

Babcock mopped his front with his handkerchief and steeled himself to enter the fray. Gesturing for Hawkins to accompany him, he stood and approached the wall of *Morning Post* which hid their quarry.

"Ahem. Pardon me for interrupting your reading, Tierney," he began.

The paper was not lowered.

Babcock rolled expressive eyes at his dinner companion, but Hawkins only mouthed, "To it!"

"Ahem. Tierney. Allow me to present Mr. Leslie Hawkins. Mr. Hawkins, Mr. Frederick Tierney."

"A pleasure," said Hawkins, as if he had been bowed to and smiled over.

There was a sigh (Babcock would have characterized it as an angry one), and the *Morning Post* was lowered and folded. The Mr. Frederick Tierney who then faced the world was not the one the world was accustomed to see. Not only was his linen limp and his jaw bristling with stubble, he had shadows beneath his pale blue eyes, eyes which were lacking their usual gleam of humor.

"Babcock," he uttered, his voice somewhat rusty from disuse. He bowed to one and then the other. "Mr. Leslie Hawkins."

"Mr. Tierney," began Hawkins, "Babcock must away to Kent this afternoon, but there are so few of us in town that I wondered if you might like to join me for a game. In fact, we have a little bet riding on it: Babcock says you won't, and I say you will."

"What game?" said Frederick.

Giving Babcock a significant look, Hawkins rocked on his heels. "Oh—I don't know. Loo?"

"Most certainly *not* loo," declared Frederick, the corners of his mouth turning down.

"Oh!" said Hawkins, taken aback by the man's sudden vehemence. "Well—we haven't enough for whist or quadrille. Say...macao?"

"If you hope to lose a fortune, macao is your game," Frederick said, rising from his seat and signaling the waiter. "But you will have to do it without my assistance. I hear they would be glad to make a table for the susceptible at Watier's."

"Piquet, then!" suggested Hawkins as Tierney took his stick and donned his hat. "No? All right. Then faro, with Wantley. Do wait—You would prefer ombre? Dice—a nice game of hazard?"

There was no reply—not even a nod as he pushed past them.

Babcock shook his head after Tierney had gone. "I do not know the man well," he said, "but did I not warn you he was in a temper? Such a show of recklessness on your part." Reaching for the copy of the *Post* before the waiter could clear it, he thrust it at Hawkins. "If you dare not go out and no one will play, you had better spend your time reading. And, waiter, please add five guineas to Mr. Hawkins' tally."

Frederick climbed into the hackney coach hailed for him and gave orders to circle the park until instructed otherwise, ignoring the peculiar look the driver gave him. If Frederick did not care what impression he made on the other members of White's or on that sad man Hawkins, he could not be expected to interest himself in a hackney coach driver's opinion.

It truly was devilishly hot. Babcock was right to flee town as soon as possible. Frederick could hardly say why he himself was there, except that he had to get out of Somerset and had no desire to be with anyone he knew. That left London, where, for one of his class in a high, hot, dusty summer, one might have the place to oneself.

"A hot one," ventured the driver. "Can't remember such a one. Hotter even 'n yesterday."

"Mmmph," was the sole reply.

The coach bumped and rattled over the stones of Pall Mall, past St. James Square to the north and Carlton House to the south, before negotiating the traffic from Haymarket that approached Charing Cross. When they turned at last into the park, Frederick sank back against the split and stained cushions of the carriage and stared absently into the Mall, the shady double avenue of trees marking the northern border of St. James Park.

What was amiss with him? Why should he be so down in the mouth because some woman rejected him? Some woman whom he had not known even a month ago, and whom he had decided to marry for his own convenience?

Who was Miss Elfrida Hapgood, after all, but some penniless, myopic, provincial miss burdened with a similarly shortsighted understanding of the world? Her vision must be limited indeed, if she could not comprehend what an opportunity had been thrown in her lap. She would never again, buried as she was in Somersetshire, be presented with so eligible a suitor as he. Whereas he, with his name and his fortune and his connections and prospects, might marry whom he pleased next week, if he so chose.

I suspect we should not suit.

What country girl would rather sit at home amidst her mud and meadows, when she might have a house in town and lead the *ton* with her dashing husband? Why, any young lady with a modicum of spirit in her would leap at the chance! How eagerly Miss Porterworth would have accepted his proposal Frederick could well imagine. Nay, even the cool Miss Birdlow would have understood the stakes and thawed accordingly.

When Frederick had returned from his fruitless time with Miss Hapgood, he was in a reckless mood. Coming upon Miss Birdlow and her friend on their morning constitutional, the thought crossed his mind that he would teach Miss Hapgood a lesson. He would propose to Miss Porterworth or Miss Birdlow and find solace in the approbation of whichever young lady Fate decreed for him. Let Miss Hapgood learn what she had lost, in her desire for a plain husband and narrow morality!

And he might have acted on his impulse, had not the passage of half an hour and the too substantial presence of Miss Porterworth and Miss Birdlow checked him.

"La!" cried the latter young lady, when he joined her and Miss Porterworth and left his horse once more to trail after them. "You have become as early a riser as your brother, Mr. Tierney."

"It is the country air," he answered, almost succeeding in speaking with his usual lightness.

"Have you been sitting for Miss Edith Hapgood again?" asked Miss Porterworth. "Sly little minx—I am sure she draws the process out."

"I have not," he said shortly. "Nor will I again. She has her sketch and the beginnings of paint."

Miss Birdlow gave him a shrewd look (which he failed to see, as he was staring straight ahead) and smiled. "Then you have simply been riding or fishing or...hunting. And yet you have bagged no game. Tell me, Mr. Tierney—do you like the country?"

"I do not. Barring your presence"—he remembered himself in time to bow to both ladies and ameliorate the sting of his words—"it is frightfully dull."

"Yes, yes it is!" declared Miss Porterworth. "And how much worse it must be, if one is accustomed to constant excitement and dash, as you are."

"Indeed, Constance," said Miss Birdlow dryly, "it must be difficult to be buried in Somersetshire, when one is the beau-est of the *beau monde*."

For the viscount's daughter, this was as close to coquetry as she came, but Frederick could not bring himself to answer in kind. His feelings were still too muddled, too raw, after his encounter with Miss Hapgood. He merely turned to Miss Birdlow and said, "Do *you* prefer the town or country?"

"Town," she replied without hesitation. "What can compare? There is the court and the shopping and the theaters and the company of our greatest families—London is the pinnacle, our nation's *summum bonum* of culture and education, society and government."

"Yes," agreed Miss Porterworth. "Just so, Agnes. Town is precisely those things."

Well, this was exactly what Frederick had been wont to think, but this morning it irked him to hear it. He saw again Miss Hapgood's face, her blushing struggle as he spoke of his connection to Mrs. Anne Gurdy. *You like to...cut a dash, while I think I would prefer a—*

"What do you think, Miss Birdlow, then," he addressed her abruptly, "of town morals?"

"Town morals?" she echoed.

"They are somewhat looser," put in Miss Porterworth. "Are they not, Agnes? I could not be certain—I have never spent much time in town, and Agnes has had a season. But when I visited there, I was astonished at some of the things I saw. Some of the dress and...classes of people intermingling."

"Young men, in particular, might be accused of adopting—of adhering to less stringent mores there," Frederick went on, the frown which creased his brow deepening.

"Mr. Tierney!" shrieked Miss Porterworth. "I am sure we should not be speaking of such things."

"*Which* things?" he asked ominously.

"Young men's dissoluteness," Miss Birdlow replied. She had no certain idea what lay behind his mercurial temper, but she sensed he was testing them, and she was determined to pass. If he meant to know whether she, the Honorable Miss Birdlow, would begrudge him a past entanglement with a London actress, she must be clear. "Mr. Tierney refers to gambling and drunkenness and—debaucheries—I suppose, Constance. It is true such conduct is more often found in town than in the country, but it is not a young lady's place to notice such things. Though, if this *particular* young lady were to comment"—with a quirk of her lips and modest duck of her head— "she might argue that one could excuse such activities as, when in Rome, one must do as the Romans do."

"To be sure," Miss Porterworth agreed, not entirely following. When things were out of her depth, she always found it safest to agree with her friend.

There, thought Frederick. Miss Birdlow looked upon matters exactly as Miss Hapgood ought. Young men would have their adventures, particularly young men of fortune. Frederick was not, compared to some of his class, especially debauched. He had no mistress at the moment; he was not in debt above a quarter of his annual allowance; he was rarely in his cups. He could show Miss Hapgood "cutting a dash," if she wished! His conduct made her uneasy? Why, then let him demonstrate to her a true rake's progress!

For a minute Frederick waffled between one urge, to out-rake his own reputation, and another, to wound Miss Hapgood by marrying. Not to Miss Porterworth after all, mind. He did not think he could bear years of her titters and simpering. It had better be to Miss Birdlow.

A refined, understanding, lovely young woman was Miss Birdlow. So why should he not offer for her? She could serve the same purposes as a Miss Hapgood, in warding off Lady Wimpole, satisfying his parents, and providing an heir. She was wealthier and better connected— Besides, marrying would be better than pursuing a course in corruption. If he were to choose the latter, likely Miss Hapgood would only believe her judgment vindicated.

Marriage it would be. To the Honorable Miss Birdlow.

And yet—Miss Hapgood's forget-me-not eyes swam before him. Those eyes and the tender curve of her mouth, which he had pressed against his own—

He heard again her soft voice, never shrill or arch, never disdainful or petulant.

No.

He could not do it.

He could not marry Miss Birdlow, of the haughty eyebrows and self-satisfied smiles. Miss Birdlow, who always appeared to be calculating her words and actions for effect. He could not marry any woman, if he could not prefer that woman to Miss Hapgood. Never mind whom he ought to prefer. The matter simply was what it was.

Frederick took a measured breath and looked about for his horse. The sooner he could extricate himself from this situation to mull it all over, the better.

"I hope, Miss Birdlow, Miss Porterworth, that when either one of you is next in town, you will do me the honor of dancing with me," he said, taking hold of Mignonne's bridle. "That, and perhaps accompany me for a ride in the park."

Miss Porterworth unleashed a cascade of giggles. "How odd of you, Mr. Tierney! We may dance and ride with you here, you know."

"Ah, but I will not be here, after today," he announced. Hardly hearing their gasps and the succeeding flurry of questions, he swung himself up on his mount, touching his hat brim. "Business. Pressing business. Thank you for your company, my ladies. It has been...clarifying. If you will excuse me, I must go in search of his lordship. Good morning."

White sunlight glittered off the waters of the canal.

"Come, Fred," he muttered to himself, running a finger behind his neckcloth to loosen it. "Don't be stupid. And you are stupid, if you mope about, wanting her more, simply because she refused you."

The passage of several days and space of 150 miles had put an end to his initial anger and injured pride, leaving behind an enduring sensation of lowness. Of indifference to his usual interests. There was nothing he felt like doing and no place he felt he would like to be. For the first time in his life, his independence and leisure weighed heavy on him. He did not want to play cards, visit the tailor, bet on horses, find a new mistress.

He was adrift.

The coach emerged from beside the trees to circle the west end of the park, turning from the Queen's House, and Frederick grimaced as the summer sun beat full upon him again. This was madness. He would return to the Tierney home in Green Street and have Norton draw him a bath. A cool one. Norton had been beside himself recently to have an unshaven, rumpled Frederick Tierney abroad, bringing disgrace to the valet's reputation for immaculate workmanship.

Before Frederick could give the word to the driver, the sight of an approaching young woman on horseback, trailed by her groom, brought him up short. He straightened sharply, squinting through the ripples of heat, aware of the sudden race of his heart. The gleam of golden curls and the dance of black ribbons trimming the lady's bonnet and sleeves made him forget to breathe, but she was not five yards nearer before he realized his mistake. Not Miss Hapgood at all—who would have no reason to be in St. James Park, of course, he reminded himself angrily, and who, furthermore, walked, rather than rode, and had no groom to speak of! He must get out of this heat—it was beginning to affect his senses. Sitting back with a scowl, he looked away down the Bird Cage Walk until he heard his name called.

"Mr. Tierney! Ah! What a delight—it is you." The young lady drew abreast of the carriage, the black ribbons fluttering as she leaned in. "Whatever can you be doing in town now? Is not the temperature dreadful? I hope you are well—you do not look yourself, precisely. I have not seen you thus. That is—you left town with such unexpected suddenness! And I had hoped to see you at Lady Palmer's ball, don't you know, you cruel man. Things have been such a dead bore—everyone gone. I had gone myself, you know, but now my great-uncle Lord Bewick has died, and the service is tomorrow. Mama says it is just like the man to die at his own convenience and force us all to return to town at the very worst time of the year, but I am not sorry it has happened, if it has also brought you. Were you and Lord Bewick acquainted? The gout kept him confined to home nearly all the time. You would not imagine what a condition the house is in—my cousin Horace—the new Lord Bewick, that is, says it isn't fit to live in! But do say—Mama will want you to dine with us today, I am certain of it. She said you would likely never want to spend time in my company again, after I made such a cake of myself this winter, but I assure you I am all grown up now, Mr. Tierney. You need fear no more embarrassing notes or scenes from me. So, please, do let me tell Mama we may expect you at six—"

Frederick had long since signaled the driver to halt the coach, that Miss Tremont would not have to deliver the entirety of this speech at full volume as her horse sidled next to them. How he could have mistaken the girl for Miss Hapgood—mourning ribbons or no—was a positive sign of his madness, but Miss Tremont's chatter left little room for meditation. Her avowal of maturity must be taken on faith, as outwardly she appeared to be the identical, high-colored, headstrong, wayward debutante who pursued him the previous season. Miss Tremont had indeed made a cake of herself, writing him ill-advised love notes, devising little schemes to encounter him by "chance," once swooning as Frederick forced his way through the throngs at Carlton House, so that he would be obliged to catch her in his arms. Lady Wimpole had taken great pleasure in mocking Miss Tremont when the lovers were alone, always with an edge in her voice because she knew her beloved must marry some young woman at some point, and if it was not Miss Tremont, it would not be someone vastly different.

"—Pheasants," Miss Tremont had begun again. "I believe Mama spoke of pheasant for dinner, in honor of my great-uncle. He did love pheasant. Surely you will join us if you are free, Mr. Tierney, and you must be free, as here you are taking a drive in the park—?"

"But I am not free," Frederick broke in when he was able. He felt a wave of perspiration beneath his arms as he scrambled to excuse himself. "Forgive me—I was not in town for Lord Bewick's memorial. Indeed, we were not acquainted. But I am very sorry for your family's loss. Please express my sympathy to Mr. and Mrs. Tremont. I am—unfortunately—this very afternoon returning to my family's home in Buckinghamshire. I am expected. I only had the driver take this...detour through the park to avoid the crush of carriages and omnibuses in Picadilly—"

"But shan't you have to go back along Picadilly, to return to Mayfair?" asked Miss Tremont with trembling lip.

"Not a bit of it," interjected the driver, to Frederick's relief. "I was plannin' on turnin' down Stafford Row here. Go roundabout the Queens Garden and catch Park Lane up. Better be on our way, eh?" He gave Frederick a nod, which Frederick returned, inwardly promising the man a generous tip.

"Oh, no! Dear me—you mustn't be going just yet, must you? Mr. Tierney"—Miss Tremont stood in her stirrup—"how long will you be in Buckinghamshire?"

"No idea," he called back, doffing his hat to wave it at her and hissing to the driver, "All speed, man!"

"Might I—may I write to you there?" came one last question from the eager young lady, which was just faint enough above the rattle of the coach and crunch of the gravel for Frederick to pretend not to have heard.

Exhausted, he lay his head back and shut his eyes, muttering, "400 Green Street, if you please."

Green Street and on to Buckinghamshire, then. Cornered by fate, he was glad to have the next move in his wanderings decided for him. There would be no Miss Hapgood in Buckinghamshire, any more than there could be a Miss Hapgood riding through St. James Park in London, but at least, at home, neither would there be any Miss Tremonts.

CHAPTER TWELVE

...This day will pour down,
If I conjecture ought, no drizling shower,
But rattling storm of arrows barb'd with fire.
—Milton, *Paradise Lost* (1667)

"Read it out, Elfie," ordered her mother from the nest of pillows ensconcing her. "How silent and secretive you've become! Come—what has my brother Alec to say?"

Elfrida lifted a pale countenance, but her complexion escaped her mother's notice because Elfrida had been not feeling the thing the past week. In fact, this was her first day emerging from her chamber after the strange summer sickness that struck her down. The doctor Mr. Lewis had been confounded by it and fell back on ordering the squire and Elfrida's two younger sisters to be as silent as possible and to keep Miss Hapgood well supplied with cool compresses. It was this unnatural silence in the house, broken only by Margaret's furtive whisperings to Edith in the hall and Dorcas's complaints about Mrs. Hapgood's fussiness, that finally roused Elfrida from her bed. Margaret had done her best to run the household during her older sister's convalescence, but the girl was only fourteen, after all. Moreover, Elfrida was disgusted with herself. What was there to droop and languish about, in any case? That Mr. Tierney had gone? Well, he would have left Somerset sooner or later. That he had been rejected, then, and saw fit to give her up? So much the better—she had not refused him in order to be wheedled out of it. It was true that Elfrida was fearful of the consequences on the Hapgoods' relations with the Tierneys, yes, but it was also true that she was not fearful enough to lie abed with over-concern. Alice made no mention of the situation in her letters, and from this Elfrida concluded that Mr. Tierney had not made it known. Life must go on.

Although the sight of the daily post gave her a flutter of anxiety, there were but two letters this day, and the first came from her uncle Alec Arbuthnot. Across the reverse he had written "Private, for Mrs. Richard Hapgood," indicating that he did not want it read aloud in the drawing room, but Alec had forgotten his sister's troublesome tendency to headache. Even after Elfrida tried to persuade her mother to peruse the letter herself, Mrs. Hapgood merely put a hand to her suffering brow. "The heat, my dear. I could not possibly read under these circumstances. You must read it to me. I am sure Alec would not begrudge you knowing anything he might tell me. And do open the window wider, Elfie—I am sure there would be a breeze, if only it could be caught. The sky darkens. We will certainly have a storm."

"It is—it is not good news, Mama," said Elfrida at last, smoothing the sheet on her lap. "Would you not rather hear the letter from Papa's cousin Hugh to begin with? We will see how he fares after the loss of his wife."

"Nonsense. He probably only writes to ask if his inventory of our goods tallies with his memory," retorted her mother. "Give me Alec's letter."

Still Elfrida demurred. "Perhaps I had better fetch your hartshorn first."

"Nay, girl, I have it here at hand. Be quick—the suspense makes me all the more nervous."

"Very well." With a sigh, she read.

My dearest Augusta,

The fat is surely in the fire now. You must brace yourself, sister. There is one Miss Kitty Todd who accuses me of fathering her child, and I admit I had something to do with the girl, but who is to say ultimately that the child is mine? Unfortunately Miss Todd has a drunken father who does say—nay, swears—no one has been near his daughter save myself, and the man demands I provide both for Miss Todd and the bastard. He had the gall to suggest I marry her, as if I, an Arbuthnot, could contemplate such a connection as that! As it is,

*I see no way to avoid taking on Miss Todd's mainte-
nance. Alwyn says there is no help for it, else Mr. Todd
will make good on his threats to trumpet his daughter's
ruination and my supposed part in it.*

*I would not trouble you with this, Augusta, were I not
so terribly broke at present. You know it has been some
time since I asked Hapgood for funds, and I have been
on a cursed unlucky streak at the clubs. I must come
down to Bramleigh, only do you prepare the ground
with your husband. I think I could get Todd to accept
£35 per annum—possibly as low as £20 if Hapgood
could get Miss Todd a position somewhere thereabouts.
She says she will put the child out to nurse. I do not know
that she can cook or clean or teach, but perhaps she could
learn.*

Expect me on the afternoon of the 15th.

Your loving and much put-upon brother,
Alec

It should not be supposed Mrs. Hapgood received this epistle in
calm and silence. By no means. Elfrida had not finished the second
sentence before there were shrieks and sobs, the hartshorn bottle
knocked to the carpet in the struggle to retrieve it. Elfrida had much
to do, to soothe and quiet her mother enough to attend to the
balance of the letter, and even so Mrs. Hapgood appeared nearly

unconscious as she listened, only the rise and fall of her chest and her muted whimpers betraying that she lived on.

"Wretched woman," she moaned when some minutes had passed. "The wretched, designing woman, and her wretched sot of a father."

Elfrida bit her lip. Speaking her mind on whom she thought bore an equal, if not greater, share of the blame would be useless in the moment. She only knew that the 15th was upon them, and there might be only a few hours for her father to be informed, and not nearly enough hours for him to recover from what was certain to be a towering rage. As her mother lay weeping and muttering, "He will surely *murder* Alec! O Richard! What will become of us," Elfrida was inclined to agree. Her father might very well murder her uncle, and Elfrida would hardly blame him. Where were an extra £35 per annum to come from? This, after Uncle Alwyn had just wormed more money from the squire and Alice's wedding portion had to be paid out?

Foolish, *foolish* Uncle Alec! They should not give him a halfpenny, except who should suffer then but the wronged woman and her innocent baby?

"He does not even say if the child is a boy or girl," Elfrida frowned.

Her mother gave another wail. "Boy, girl—what does it matter, poor little bastard child? Oh, Alec!"

Patting her mother's shoulder, Elfrida turned the matter over in her mind. It would be better to supply Miss Todd with a place, that she might work for her keep and the allowance be reduced. But where could such a woman be employed? Bramleigh's own servants, Button and Dorcas, would resign in protest if forced to work alongside a fallen woman, even if the Hapgoods could afford to employ her. No—Miss Kitty Todd had better become Mrs. Todd the widow, and it was plain she could not be kept at Bramleigh, where she would have to encounter Alec Arbuthnot several times every year. She must be hidden away elsewhere. But where?

Time was a-wasting. Putting the hartshorn bottle in her mother's flailing hand and calling for Dorcas to attend her mistress, Elfrida went in search of her father.

The air was heavy under a dark sky, and she shivered despite the heat. There would indeed be a storm, but she did not imagine the sky could wreak greater havoc than her father in a temper.

Squire Hapgood was found where she expected him, down at the kennels, fondling a now-recovered Caractacus and feeding him choice scraps. "There's a good boy! At it, Crack, hearty-like."

"Papa."

"Elfie! Up and around, I see," he beamed up at her. "Two of my best beloveds, completely recovered. What joy. But what is it, girl? Still such a long face? You mustn't tax yourself so soon."

"Papa, Uncle Alec wrote that we are to expect him this afternoon."

The squire's smile evaporated like dew in the summer sun. "Ah...indeed? That can mean only one thing: he wants money, like his brother."

"Yes." She saw no reason to gild the pill that must be swallowed. Not when her uncle might arrive at any time. "He wants money, Papa. He writes to say so. But not for himself, especially, in this instance."

"For Alwyn, then? I'll be d—"

"No, Papa. For a Miss Kitty Todd." Elfrida wrapped her arms about her middle, wishing she could cover her ears with her hands instead. "It seems Uncle Alec got this Miss Todd with child and refuses to marry her, and Miss Todd's father insists that Uncle Alec provide a maintenance for her and the—"

"Wha-a-a-at?!" roared the squire, springing to his feet and causing both Elfrida and Caractacus to shrink back. "What's this? Fathered a bastard child with some hapless woman, and *I* am the one who must face the consequences? I'll be damned if they see one penny of my money!"

"Uncle Alec suggests a yearly allowance of £35," Elfrida pressed on. "But we might make it lower if we could get Miss Todd a position with some family—"

"I'll give him a yearly allowance!" bellowed her father, slamming about the kennel, kicking over Crack's bowl and setting the hounds to howling in chorus. "Why should I be putting up a brass farthing to support those who are none of my own? A curse on his £35 a year! My own blood daughter Alice, honorably married, got but £120 in a lump sum! Let him cast the woman on the parish and support her from the poor rates, a pestilence on him!"

"Papa—" holding out her arms, she attempted to arrest him in his storming about, but he threw her off, his tirade building. Some of his curses were unintelligible, but she understood enough. Something about *those confounded Arbuthnots—why a man should never marry—benighted debauchees—not a penny more!—time enough he*

*had let them push him to the brink of ruin—imposters—pretenders to
the name of gentleman—abominable—confounded—vicious—*

What other opprobrium the squire heaped on his brother-in-law's name was swallowed in a massive crack of thunder, as if the very heavens were rent open by his rage. Elfrida did squeal and cover her ears then, and her father took advantage of her distraction to shove past her, out of the kennel, waving his riding crop and raving and gesticulating in pantomime as further cracks of thunder drowned his words. She ran to the door and looked out as the sky suddenly broke open and sheets of black and silvery rain poured forth.

"Papa! Wait!" cried Elfrida. He either could not hear her or chose not to, for off he slipped in the midday darkness. She thought he might be headed for the road at the end of Bramleigh's drive, surely intending, as his wife feared, to intercept Alec Arbuthnot and wring his neck, at the very mildest. Flying back, Elfrida grabbed one of Crack's blankets to hold over her head, but no sooner had she emerged from the kennel under her odorous and fur-wreathed shelter than the downpour turned to hail. Stones of sufficient size and violence that Elfrida was driven back inside, calling to her father with all her might that he, too, might come in out of danger.

She had never seen the like. One hailstone bounced into the open kennel door, scaring the howling Caractacus, and when Elfrida picked it up, she thought it must be all of four inches in diameter! Larger than any apple or pear growing in Bramleigh's orchard. "The fruit," she whispered. The remaining cherries would be beaten from the branches by this onslaught, along with the unripe apples and plums. But regrets for the orchard were forgotten in her anxiety for her father. Suppose he should be caught in the open? His hat would not afford much protection. Ah—this was all Uncle Alec's fault, and Elfrida could not help thinking bitterly that, if anyone deserved to be struck down by a hailstone the size of a pumpkin, it was he.

After some time, the storm began to lighten, as it passed to the northwest. She would learn later that it reached Bristol by mid-evening, the hail breaking windows and frightening horses. When Elfrida thought she could risk venturing out with only the blanket for protection, she emerged, squinting and cursing her poor eyesight as her gaze swept the grounds. It was all very well to sit at home embroidering and not seeing anything, but here was her father's life at stake—

Soon the blanket was sodden with rain. She was on the point of throwing it aside, since her arms ached with upholding it and her gown was already soaked to the knees, when she stumbled against an obstacle in the grass. Peering down, she saw it was the body of her father, face-down and seemingly lifeless!

Elfrida tumbled over him, the smelly blanket slapping down to cover them both. She heaved it aside, tears and rain running down her nose, and managed to roll the squire onto his back.

His eyelids fluttered, and he gave a low groan, for which Elfrida exclaimed, "Thank God! Papa! How badly are you injured?" There was a cut on his forehead bleeding copiously, and under her hand she felt a lump the size of a goose egg. Frantically, she tried to tear a strip of linen from her petticoat to bandage her father's head, but the wet cloth would not give way. His neckcloth—she would use that—it must be choking him, at any rate. With care she unwound it, calling softly to him all the while, but even after she handled him and stanched the bleeding, he had not come to himself. Could this be simply the blow to his head? The loss of blood? Or had he also suffered a fit of apoplexy?

"I must leave you, Papa," Elfrida said, dashing a hand across her eyes. "Hal must get out the cart to carry you home, and Dorcas must go for Mr. Lewis. But I will return as swiftly as I am able." Wadding up the blanket, she lifted his head to push it beneath, but still he did not respond. Then giving him one last, anxious look, she hurried away.

"Brother! What grave misfortunes have overtaken us!" lamented Mrs. Hapgood, when Mr. Alec Arbuthnot found her by her husband's bedside, some hours later. Her tall, tailored sibling took hold of the hands extended to him, endeavoring to appear suitably woeful, but Elfrida guessed at her uncle's share of relief, to find his brother-in-law laid low and unable to get at him.

"I met Mr. Lewis in the hall," Alec replied. "He says Richard has suffered blows to the head and a fit of some kind."

"He has, he has! Oh, Brother, if he were to die...?" She threw herself against his well-padded chest and let him soothe and pat her. "We will be turned out by that cousin of his, that Hugh Hapgood. I do not know what should become of us. The girls and I would have to squeeze into your house in town."

With genuine alarm, and a full awareness that the London townhouse was supported by the squire's contributions, her brother said, "Heaven forbid, my love, it should come to that. Mr. Lewis said it was too soon to tell how serious the effects might be."

"We might live with Joseph and Alice," suggested Margaret from where she sat clutching Edith.

"I shouldn't like that," her mother sniffed. "To depend on the Tierneys' charity and to cram into a parsonage, when we have family of our own to provide for us."

Elfrida repressed a sigh. She knew her mother had no head for practical matters, but it was nevertheless painful to be reminded of it at such times. Stepping forward to greet her uncle, she asked, "Were you also caught in the hail, Uncle Alec?"

"I thought the barrage would penetrate the coach, my love, and I pitied those seated on the outside. We had to halt and wait in a grove of trees." After kissing each of his nieces in turn, he resumed his place beside his sister, and they watched the squire's even breathing. "Has my brother spoken yet, Augusta?"

"Not a word," she sighed.

"That's not so," corrected Margaret. "He said 'damn fool' once, and 'blast' another."

"Margaret!"

"I thought it was 'Darfur' and 'blast,'" piped up Edith, still hiccupping with tears.

This earned her a scathing look from Margaret's reddened eyes. "Don't be ridiculous. Why would Papa be speaking of the Fur peoples?"

"Well, why should he be speaking of a 'damn fool'?" Edith countered.

"Edith!" said her mother.

Hastily, Elfrida intervened. "Girls—you had better go downstairs and see that Mr. Lewis is offered something to eat before he goes, and ask when we may expect him again."

When they obeyed, Alec Arbuthnot settled himself gloomily in the armchair closest to the window and ran fingers through his thin hair, displacing it from where he had coaxed it across the barren expanses of crown and temple. "I assume, Elfie, you received my letter and shared its contents with your father?"

"Yes, Uncle."

"Was my situation the—er—a contributing factor in his fit?"

"I cannot say with certainty that it was not, sir," Elfrida admitted. "Papa was rather upset."

"You didn't cause the hail, at any rate," Mrs. Hapgood assured her brother. "And who knows but that being pelted with such enormous stones brought on the fit?"

Elfrida could hardly point out that her father would not have been found in the first place, ranting over the fields in a hailstorm like some Somersetian King Lear, had not his outrage driven him to it. But there was no use in saying as much. She took her father's hand, where it lay uncharacteristically still on the coverlet, and pressed it between her own. "He was upset," she repeated simply.

"Had he—ahem!—did he express any opinions on how he might address the situation," her uncle persevered, "before he was rendered unconscious?"

"Not as yet. I do know a yearly allowance would be a hardship at this point," Elfrida said. "He has just had to supply Alice's marriage portion, after all. But perhaps, as you suggest, a place might be found in service. In which case, I believe we had better refer to…your friend as Mrs. Todd, the widow."

"Sensible, sensible," agreed Alec. "What a girl my niece is! If anyone can find Kitty a place, I am sure it will be you, Elfrida."

"What would become of the child?" asked Mrs. Hapgood.

"A girl. Dolly, I think Kitty calls her. I daresay," her brother replied, "the nurse who has the child can be paid to maintain it, while Kitty works."

"And where does Miss—Mrs.—Todd live now?"

"She still resides in town. In her father's house—over a shop in Monmouth Street." He grimaced to name the ill-famed neighborhood.

And, indeed, his sister bristled for him. "Why—what has some Seven Dials shopkeeper to say to *you*, Alec? I'm sure the girl was no better than she should be."

Clearing his throat, he shuffled his feet along the thick carpet, tracing the outline of a rose with his toe. "It appears—that is to say—Mr. Todd undertook to pledge some of my bills for me." This revelation proving one too many for Mrs. Hapgood, she dropped with a cry into a chair and fumbled for her trusty hartshorn bottle.

"I will give the matter thought, Uncle," Elfrida said, waving the uncapped bottle underneath her mother's nose. "It would not do, of course, for her to work here or in the immediate neighborhood—not if she has a father accusing you of misconduct. That would be...uncomfortable for all."

"Clever girl, Elfrida. I trust you to manage this, during your father's incapacity. In the meantime, would you know of any pin money you had lying about? I have a pressing expense or two..."

It was when she reached in her pocket to withdraw her coin purse that she finally remembered the other letter the post had brought.

Brief though it was, this second epistle was a final blow in a day of blows.

My dear cousins—

Thank you for your kind remembrances. My dear wife Harriet, though she knew you little, would have been grateful for your words, and my poor motherless children are anxious now to know more of the family which remains to them. You wrote that you would be pleased to see us again in future, and I hope that such future may begin as early as possible.

Would it be convenient for you, my cousins, if the children and I were to pay a visit? I make no secret of the fact that I, now a sad widower, begin to think over what has passed in my life and what is still to come. When

I first married my Harriet, I know you bore me no grudge in choosing according to my heart. But now that I have been afforded a second chance to choose a wife, I believe my own desires and the needs of my greater family are both due consideration. In short, I propose selecting a second mother for my orphaned children among your lovely daughters. I believe they are all un-married but one. I would not wish my cousin Richard's life shorter by one hour, I assure you, but when that sad day should come to pass, I would feel the happier (and presume to believe my Hapgood cousins would as well) if it would bring no further disruptions to the family. When I do take up residence at Bramleigh, my wife's relations would naturally be welcome to continue there.

Forgive me for the baldness of my language. I am but a plain and plainspoken man, but you may trust that every word is true. Let me know when we may come to you.

Your humble servant,
Hugh Hapgood

Chapter Thirteen

Stern Daughter of the Voice of God! O Duty!
—William Wordsworth, "Ode to Duty" (1805)

"Cousin Hugh, I find I am not prepared to give you an answer."

The tall man with gray-streaked hair and forthright jaw beside her gave a solemn nod. His voice, when he spoke, was dry and rusty. "You are young, Elfrida, and I suspect my manner of offering has not pleased you. Young ladies nowadays have such romantic notions."

Drawing herself to her full height, she replied, "I beg your pardon for my bluntness, but you are mistaken. I do not indulge any 'romantic notions.' It is by no means your manner of proposing that causes my hesitation. I am simply...not decided yet. I realize the honor you do me," she faltered, "and the—the generosity behind it. I would understand if my response displeases you. That is, I understand if you would like to withdraw your offer."

"Now, now," he urged, lifting a hand and then letting it drop as he thought better of patting her arm. "Don't be getting in a pet. I have been precipitate, I see. I had not thought to wed, at any rate, until a year of mourning has passed. But I had hoped my letter, stating my intentions, would have prepared you."

The two of them faced each other across the squire's desk, but it was Elfrida's gaze which fell first. She fiddled with her papa's pen knife, nervously sticking its blade at random in the embossed leather blotter. The curtains were closed, veiling the room in a dim, greenish light which was quenched entirely where it encountered Hugh Hapgood's deep black mourning clothes.

When Elfrida said nothing, he made a graveled sound in the back of his throat and went on. "I would have preferred to speak to your father first, of course, but in his condition—"

"Yes," said Elfie. To his family's consternation, the squire had been feverish for some days, and Elfrida had not yet recovered from the heaviness of those sleepless nights. But the fever, thank God, had broken. Now her father lay still abed, weakened. Mr. Lewis admonished them all that they must keep him very, very calm, lest they provoke another fit. Ordinarily such a task would have been beyond the family's capabilities, but it was a sign of his continuing frailty that the squire manifested no restlessness, no impatience, no yearning to be up and about, shouting.

"It might settle my cousin Richard to know that his family would be provided for," Hugh persevered. "I am sure the uncertainty of what might become of you all, if he were to—were to—I am sure he would recover his strength more quickly without such a weight on his mind."

"Yes," she said again. She knew all this. Of course she did. He need not explain it to her.

His dark eyes ran over her.

There was some inexplicable catch in her throat, and Elfrida thought that if she said another word, something in her would snap, releasing—what?—releasing *everything*. Everything *everywhere*.

Because she did not want to marry her father's cousin.

That was the simple part. It was not that Hugh Hapgood was not a nice man—he was. He was...older, but still hale and upright, as her own father had been a week ago. He was serious and modest. He had been a faithful husband and a faithful steward of his own income and the money his wife brought to the match. To his children he was somewhat forbidding, but not through unkindness. He just wasn't the sort of man to romp about with them.

It should have been to the man's credit that Elfrida's beauty did not seem to be a deciding factor. He had come, willing to marry one of his cousin's daughters, and finding that she was the only available one of marriageable age, he settled on her. She almost thought he would have preferred her plainer, that his offer might be subject to no suspicions or whispers behind hands.

No—her cousin's character posed no problems. A steady, decent man. And his children required a mother. Marrying him, more-over, would ease her parents' minds immeasurably and provide a home—their own familiar home—for Elfrida and her sisters the rest of their days.

Yes. All the reasons were perfectly...reasonable. She could understand Hugh Hapgood's amazement that she did not leap at his offer, weeping with gratitude.

Is it that I am vain? she asked herself. *I am offended that he does not find me beautiful? That he doesn't say a word of love?*

The other one had not spoken of love, either.

The thought stopped Elfrida in her tracks and the pen knife slipped from her grasp.

She must not think of the Other One. Of *him*. But why did not thinking of him require such constant effort? She had heard nothing of Frederick Tierney since his abrupt departure, but that was hardly surprising, immured as the Hapgoods were by the squire's illness and their family visitors. With trembling fingers Elfrida had opened Alice's next letter, but her sister made no mention of the man either. And in her own reply, Elfrida could not bring herself to ask—it would have given the subject undue importance, full as her letter was with its account of their father's condition and Uncle Alec's dreadful contretemps, followed by reassurances that Alice must not worry.

What is wrong with me? Elfrida fretted. *Have I not always prided myself on my practicality? What could be more practical than accepting this good man's offer and saving my family?*

She did not doubt she could learn to love the children—she was halfway to loving them already. And she might—could—eventually love her cousin, if she set her mind to it. Why, then—

Breaking the silence with another rusty sigh, Cousin Hugh lowered himself into the armchair opposite the desk, placing his elbows on the rests and tenting his fingers. "It is a lot to ask of a young woman, I know," he began again, "to take on the role of mother to three young children. But as you have three younger sisters, I thought it might not be beyond your abilities. In time, God willing, there might be children of your own—"

"Cousin Hugh," she interrupted, hoping he wouldn't notice the color that rose to her face. "Your children are lovely. But they have only recently lost their mother. It would come as a terrible shock, I fear, to learn she would be so soon replaced."

"Their mother was not much concerned with them," he said shortly. "And I believe both Lionel and little Rosie are already attached to you." To say so was to put it mildly. Since their arrival at Bramleigh, both twelve-year-old Lionel and six-year-old Rosie were wont to keep very close to their eldest cousin. Lionel would talk at her continually, telling her of things and showing her things and demonstrating things for her praise, while Rosie would come quietly to slip her hand in Elfrida's, or to lean against her knee.

"The children are lovely," Elfrida said again, automaton-like. She pushed the blotter away from her and stalked to the window to sweep back the curtains, narrowing her eyes against the sudden light. "And they like me well enough as a cousin. But I suspect it would be a different matter to introduce me as—that is"—snapping the curtains shut and putting her back to them—"Cousin, I cannot give you an answer now. Forgive me." If her own eyesight had not hampered her, the abrupt shift from light to dark would have left her blind to his reaction in any case.

"Is it Hetty who gives you pause?" he asked, referring to the ten-year-old middle child. "She is a tetchy girl, but that is her way with everyone. We must not make decisions about the future based on Hetty's conduct."

"Please. It is not Hetty—alone."

He was quick to notice her qualification. "Then it is Hetty, in part."

Elfrida thought briefly of the fits the girl had thrown since her arrival and the mischief she created. Hetty was certainly not as winsome as her siblings, but Elfrida knew Hetty was not the rub. "I should not have said that," she amended. "Poor Hetty misses her mother, and I do not blame her for it."

"I see."

His mouth tightened in a way that boded ill for his second child, Elfrida thought. But before she could speak up again on the girl's behalf, he added quickly, "Then perhaps, cousin, you hesitate because your heart belongs already to another?"

"No!" cried Elfrida, taking refuge behind the desk again and straightening the mangled blotter. "How should I—whom, pray—no—it is not that. Certainly not. Only—do not press me, Cousin. I will give you an answer as soon as I am able, and I beg you will leave the matter until then. I promise you I will think very hard on all this and not keep you in suspense any longer than I can help."

"Very well. I will leave you then. Do you need anything? You are flushed. Shall I ring for the maid?"

She demurred, and no sooner was the study door shut behind him than she gave a groaning sigh and, crossing her arms upon the desk, lay her tormented head upon them.

Elfrida had not much time for reflection, however, before Margaret bounded into the room, pursued by Edith and two of their young cousins, one very spindly, tall boy and a smaller, rounder girl, both so fair as to be nearly translucent, with blue eyes and reddish-brown hair.

"Elfie!" Margaret cried over her clamoring companions, "You must come on the instant!"

"Is it Papa—?" breathed Elfrida, springing to her feet.

"No, no! But it will be, if he finds out!"

Taking her sister by the hand, Margaret dragged her back to the window and threw aside the curtains. Elfrida made out only streaks and blurs, though she squinted and peered for all she was worth. Lionel and Rosie got hold of her and tugged on her, speaking at once, Lionel jumping up and down and nearly banging his head into her chin and Rosie with tears running down her face, but Elfrida could only sputter against the noise and confusion until Edith took up the fireplace shovel and brought it down with a muted clang against the iron fire-dogs in the hearth. The surprise of the sound hushed the other children, and Edith blurted, "It's Papa's hounds, Elfie. Hetty went into the kennels and let them all out and set them after Button's two cats, and now we must catch them again!"

"Button's cats!" echoed Elfrida, horrified. Their ill-tempered cook had few soft spots in her surly heart, but two of them belonged to Ginger and Minx, the pair of spiteful orange fur balls who returned their mistress's exclusive love and scratched everyone else. Button had already been grumbling over the recent increase in mouths to feed, with all their guests—if her precious cats were injured, Bramleigh might find itself without a cook.

Forgetting her earlier woes, Elfrida joined in the chase. The dogs must be corralled and herded back into the kennels; the cats lured from hiding and returned safely to their mistress (this step resulted in many scratches to arms and hands, and Minx even slashed Lionel's cheek); Button herself had to be soothed and placated. Alec Arbuthnot charged about on his horse, shouting and hallooing as if autumn fox-hunting were under way, until Ginger clawed the length of one hound's nose, and Elfrida could send her uncle away to fetch Mr. Frick the veterinarian. Cousin Hugh stalked hither and yon, his face as dark as his clothing. All the while Elfrida urged everyone *Quiet, please!* and to be calm, calm, calm, for the sake of the squire's health. Then, when the animals were caged again, Lionel must be tended with sticking plaster and Mr. Frick spoken to, and her mother visited and settled. Altogether two hours passed before things were set to rights.

Shortly after the fracas, Margaret claimed a headache and disappeared, and Edith—bless her—took Lionel and Rosie up to the nursery where she promised to sketch them. Cousin Hugh was too much the gentleman to force his company on Elfrida after their earlier conversation, and he excused himself with an apology for the "trouble little Harriet had caused."

In all truth, Elfrida was not feeling too kindly toward naughty Hetty by the time peace was restored. When she finally collapsed on the chaise in the drawing room and reached for the comforting routine of her embroidery frame, yet one more shock awaited her. The scene she had been working on for months, of a shepherd pushing a shepherdess on a swing, lay blanketed under a thousand swipes of orange-brown earth color. Biting her lip, Elfrida touched the fabric with a tentative finger and sniffed at it. Paint. Edith's terra di Siena, if she was not mistaken, which she had been applying to Paris's sandals in her scene.

Well, there it was.

Months of work and many shillings of paint gone. Spoiled. All for nothing. At the whim of a child.

With a cry, Elfrida hurled the frame across the room. It struck the mantel with a crack and splintered apart.

A shriek, rapidly stifled, came from behind her, and Elfrida whirled to see the curtains of the window seat swing back into place.

"Who's there?" she demanded, though she already knew the answer by process of elimination.

When no reply came, Elfrida marched over and swept the draperies aside. Crouched upon the cushioned seat she discovered her cousin Harriet—Hetty—a taller, thinner version of Rosie, with the same pale skin and auburn coloring. But unlike Rosie, Hetty's face bore a cunning, pettish expression. Her features were narrow and pinched, and Elfrida suspected the girl often suffered by comparison with her winsome younger sister. Wariness flickered in the girl's blue eyes.

"Why did you throw that?" Hetty said abruptly. "You've broken it."

"It was mine to throw," retorted Elfrida. "One may do whatever one likes with one's own things."

"It was ugly," declared Hetty. "And stupid. That was why I ruined it. That was why I covered it over. So no one would have to look at such an ugly, stupid thing."

Though her words were provoking, the girl's voice gave a telltale quaver and, against her will, Elfrida felt her initial surge of anger ebbing. She remembered that Father Thomas, the curate of their parish, was wont to say that people grieved in as many different ways as there were people. Clearly little Hetty grieved by kicking up a row.

Elfrida sighed and sank onto the seat beside her cousin. "Perhaps you are right," she agreed. "I liked it—the scene—but my sister Alice would say she could never spend time stitching such farcical subjects."

"What does farcical mean?" came the unwilling question. Elfrida suspected that Hetty deemed it a sign of weakness to show curiosity.

"It means silly. Alice thought it silly. My sister prefers *real* things. Plants and animals and insects. Not that she embroidered those either. She hates needlework. And I suppose it is silly. After all, shepherds have no time to push shepherdesses on swings. They must look after the sheep. Hard, dirty, constant work."

"Well, why shouldn't they be thought pretty?" countered Hetty, switching allegiance. "Because they do unpretty things?"

"I hope that wouldn't be the reason," Elfrida answered. "After all, we all do unpretty things, from time to time."

Hetty said nothing. Elfrida kept her eyes lowered, watching the girl drag a fingernail over the velveteen cushion and dig it under one of the covered buttons. If she pried it off, it would be a nuisance to repair.

"My mother was pretty," Hetty began again, after another minute.

"I remember that about her," said Elfrida.

"—And she did unpretty things," Hetty went on, not appearing to hear her. "Like leaving us always with the nursemaid and then *dying*. I should not like another mother." Turning sharp eyes upon Elfrida, she added, "Everyone says Papa must marry again, but I wish he will not do so, for my sake."

"Have you told him so?" asked Elfrida.

"I have not. One does not simply tell Papa things like that. But I wanted you to know that you mustn't marry my father." Hetty remained alarmingly solemn. "That is why I let the hounds loose and why I painted over your work and why I have caused so much trouble since I arrived."

Not grief, then, motivating the girl. Not directly. Grief via spite and fear, perhaps.

"I see," said Elfrida. "You have indeed had us at our wits' end since you arrived. And what makes you think your father wants to marry me?"

"Mrs. Carstairs, our neighbor in Crawley told Papa he must not let duty rule him so," explained Hetty. "She said that heaven would provide a new wife for him and a new mother for the children, and that Papa needn't go trying to save the world by marrying one of 'those pitiful girls of Richard Hapgood.' I see Miss Margaret and Miss Edith are too young to marry, and Miss Alice is already married. So Papa must mean to marry you, Cousin Elfrida."

"The Carstairs must be very intimate with your family, to speak thus to my cousin," Elfrida surmised.

"Mrs. Carstairs always speaks her opinion on marriage. She has a grown daughter of her own—not married—you see, and has spent much time pondering the matter."

"Ah. I do see."

Hetty laid a small hand on Elfrida's sleeve. "I don't dislike you, cousin. In fact, rather the opposite. I think you are very pretty and even do pretty things. I should like to be good for you. Only, will you promise not to marry Papa, and, in return, I will stop misbehaving?"

Elfrida's breath caught. How she would love to assure Hetty she would never become Mrs. Hugh Hapgood! But could she make such a vow? The agitation caused by her cousin's offer returned to her in a blow, and she felt her breathing become shallow. Would it be right to refuse him, knowing their union might save two families from heartbreak and ruin?

Elfrida grimaced. She was being dramatic. It sounded like Cousin Hugh, at least, could recover from heartbreak in the arms of this Miss Carstairs, she of the opinionated mother. But what would become of the Richard Hapgoods? Did not ruin truly lie before them, with its gaping maw, if her father did not recover?

No. She could not make Hetty such a promise. Not yet. She needed to mull the matter of marriage over, as carefully and thoroughly as Mrs. Carstairs had. Besides, it would never do to let Hetty get her way by manipulation and threats. Elfrida might never be her mother, but such methods must be discouraged in any child, even a clever, grief-stricken one.

"I cannot promise you that, Hetty," she said at last, reaching for the girl's hand. "But I hope you will cease to make mischief for everyone's sake. We all of us wish the best for you and your family."

Snatching her hand away, Hetty leaped from the window seat. "You horrid thing!" she shrilled, the blood high under her translucent skin. "You wish nothing of the kind! You are not my friend. And I am not yours! We are at war now." This last she pronounced with frightening dignity.

Then, choking back a sob, she fled the room.

Chapter Fourteen

They began to cry out, A Rescue, A Rescue.
—Anonymous, *Cynthia* (1687)

I n such a small family party, the gentlemen did not leave the ladies long to themselves after dinner. The quiet and elegant Mrs. Tierney had not time to do more than stroke her daughter-in-law's shoulder and admire her sketches of different bird nest structures before her husband and two sons joined them in the drawing room. She would have liked another moment without everyone else about, to ask Alice what was troubling her, but she was not kept long in suspense. Her younger son Joseph took his seat beside his wife and clasped Alice's hand in his own.

"Now that the servants are gone," he began, "and before they bring in our tea, Alice and I would seek your advice, Mother and Father."

"Advice?" breathed Mrs. Tierney, looking at Joseph with a glow. Was he going to announce that Alice was expecting? Could that explain her pallor and depressed air—she was not feeling quite the thing? It was very soon, of course—Alice could hardly be certain yet, but—

"Have you run into some difficulties with Harrison?" asked Walter Tierney, a grayer version of his son Joseph, his mind running along altogether different lines than his wife's. "Paley heard the man grumbling about recalculating the modus when the vestry gathered next spring. One would think, in this year of bountiful harvest, he might wish to leave well enough alone."

"It is nothing of that nature," Joseph said. He ducked his head to catch his wife's eye, murmuring, "You still do not object to my telling them? We discussed this."

"I do not object," answered Alice quietly.

Then, to the rest of them: "It concerns my wife's family."

There was a muffled thud from the further reaches of the room, where Frederick Tierney had thrown himself upon a sofa and taken up a book. That volume had slipped to the floor, and he hastened to retrieve it, turning pages at random and affecting not to notice the attention he had drawn.

Mrs. Tierney turned back to regard Alice anxiously, her smooth brow furrowing. "My dear—I hope there is no turn for the worse in your father's condition!"

"No—no. I thank you," Alice assured her. "Elfrida says he remains steady, though weak. It is—other news—which she withheld from me because she feared my father's accident was enough to think on."

"Not bad news, I pray," Mrs. Tierney said.

Alice only shook her head, her eyes filling. Her husband's arm came around her shoulders, and he took up the tale. "It is bad news, rather. Or—one half bad and one half uncertain."

"We had better have the bad first, Joseph," said Walter Tierney. He began to pace up and down in preparation, while, for his part, Frederick abandoned the pretense of reading and sat up, very still.

Joseph took a deep breath. "I have told you, sir, before, of my wife's uncles?" This was met by Walter with a sigh, as indeed, who could hear of Alec or Alwyn Arbuthnot's misadventures without sighing? "It seems, sir, that my wife's younger uncle, Mr. Alec Arbuthnot, has run into some difficulties again."

"Financial difficulties?"

"Not primarily. He has...got a young woman with child, and the young woman's father threatens all manner of ruin, unless the family pays him off. This expense would stretch the squire's income—especially at such a time as he is not well. One possible solution"—he hurried on, to ease his wife's embarrassment and abridge his parents' exclamations of horror— "would be to provide this young woman with a position in service. The child has already been put out to nurse. Elfrida suggests rechristening her as one Mrs. Kitty Todd, a widow, and training her as a maid. But she cannot work at Bramleigh, you understand. We—Alice and I—have decided we might take this woman on at the parsonage."

"You take her on?" echoed his father. "This young woman of questionable background and morals? What sort of person would that be for a clergyman's family to have about?"

Involuntarily, Walter and Evelyn Tierney glanced toward their elder son, and Frederick had to feign unawareness once more. It seemed all questions of immorality reminded his parents of him, at present. He suspected they would like to say, *A young woman of questionable morals is the last person we should have about, with Frederick at home and unoccupied.* How little they understood—! His mind ran only to one young woman at present, and that young woman's morals were beyond reproach.

"Her background is indeed humble, but she has received some little education," Joseph replied. "As for her character—we would bring her here for a set period. A trial. If Mrs. Todd shows an eagerness for reform and a desire to begin anew, it would not be Christian to deny her the opportunity. And if such is not the case, we will have spared the squire her maintenance for that many months—until he might be fully recovered. You know that our Mrs. Brinkley has wished to retire and go into Hampshire with her daughter as soon as we might replace her."

"You have given this much thought," Mrs. Tierney said sadly.

"We have," her son admitted. But Alice reached a pleading hand to her mother-in-law. "Do not be angry, madam! I am ashamed that things have come to this pass. Joseph is so good to consider helping my poor family—"

"Angry?" cried Mrs. Tierney. "How could I be angry?" She pushed Joseph's arm off his wife and gave Alice a fierce squeeze. "I am only sorry it has upset you, my dear. Of course you may hire whom you please and we must do what we can, so your father is not worried right now. Let this Mrs. Todd come as soon as she may. If you cannot train her, I suppose I can send Mrs. Lloyd over to do it."

Walter Tierney did not appear as easily persuaded as his wife, but he let the matter lie for the moment. He had no more desire than his wife to see his daughter-in-law distressed and contented himself with saying, "Very well. A new servant and her extortioner father. That is the bad news, Joseph. What is the uncertain?"

Joseph gave Alice another look, and she knew he thought it fitting for her to explain this portion. Having the Uncle Alec-Kitty Todd debacle accepted with so little fuss encouraged her, however, and she ventured to shake off her lowness.

"We call it uncertain news because with Elfrida it can be hard to tell sometimes," Alice explained. "It happens my sister has received an offer of marriage."

A coughing fit took Frederick, and he lurched up from the sofa without quite knowing what he was about. His father strode over to thump him between his well-tailored shoulders, but Frederick waved this solicitude off. One glance at Alice told him that it was not his own proposal which was about to be discussed, but the fleeting relief this realization afforded was forgotten the next instant. Who in thunder had made Miss Hapgood an offer?

Mrs. Tierney brightened with the announcement, as she wished everyone as happily married as herself. "Was it an eligible offer?"

"Very eligible, I suppose," said Alice slowly. "Seen in a prudential light, Elfrida could hardly do better, for my family's sake." Briefly she explained Hugh Hapgood's situation as Bramleigh's heir and his recent bereavement. "I fear she will think it her duty to accept. You see, if she were to become Mrs. Hugh Hapgood, Elfie would ensure my family's future security, as well as be the very best mother those orphaned children could hope for."

"Money and mother both, at one fell swoop," Frederick snapped.

His tone surprised her, and Alice felt her cheeks grow warm. "I suppose prudence can sound mercenary," she conceded. "We Hapgoods are far from the wealthiest family in Somerset; therefore—money—has always weighed heavily with my father."

"How grossly large can this Hugh Hapgood's income be, that Miss Hapgood would be tempted to sell herself for it?" demanded Frederick.

"Don't be so abominably rude," said Joseph, over his parents' chorused reprimands. "You are hardly one to make pronouncements on the various motives for marriage. And you, who have never wanted for income, can hardly understand what it is to be without one." Joseph spoke from experience, having spent some months before his own marriage estranged from his family, with his allowance cut off and only a small naturalist's stipend to live on.

Frederick's mouth tightened, and he jerked away from his brother's gaze. He poured himself a brandy at the sideboard, the bottle clinking too loudly against his glass. His fingers were shaking as if he had already had several drinks too many.

As the spirits slipped blessedly down his throat, Frederick steadied himself. What a cake he was making of himself! Joseph was right—his comments were rude, and Frederick did not blame him for getting angry.

When he spoke again, he was pleased to hear how offhand he sounded. "I had thought, brother, you were a great proponent of the love match. Surely you would want no less for your new sister." He took another swallow. "Unless, of course, she fancies herself in love with the man."

"That is just it," said Alice. "Elfie is so practical that she could decide she will love Cousin Hugh because she ought, and that will be that. I fear she will draw up her list of reasons for and against, and if there are enough reasons *for*, she will marry him!"

"How easily and admirably Miss Hapgood manages her affections," drawled Frederick, forgetting himself again. "Like they are so many sheep to be herded into whichever pasture seems most green." He found his mother beside him, laying a firm hand on his arm. Yes—he already knew—he was behaving like an ass again, after just telling himself he would not, and Joseph's wife was too new to the Tierneys to be treated thus. Setting his empty glass a trifle too firmly back on the tray, he made an apologetic face at his mother and retreated to the sofa. What was it to him if Miss Hapgood made her calculations and found some other man a better bargain?

Frederick's comments might have annoyed his family, but Alice only grew thoughtful. "I, too, have found my sister's practicalness hard to fathom at times. She has a soft, warm heart. Among her immediate family she is playful and droll and affectionate. But she never lets her heart rule her head. Elfie would never have got into such a scrape as I did with Joseph." Her husband chuckled at this, sharing with his wife one of those little secret looks that made Frederick want to dash his head against the mantel. Nay, if he had hoped that retreating to Buckinghamshire would help him forget Miss Hapgood, he found himself utterly mistaken. Daily he was confronted with marital contentment. He noticed for the first time his father's consideration for his mother and her quiet reliance on him; and, as for Joseph and Alice, their newlywed bliss was too plain to be ignored. Why else would his mother fret herself, to see Alice, for once, unhappy?

"What sort of man is this Hugh Hapgood?" asked Mrs. Tierney. "Would it be so very bad if Miss Hapgood did—train herself—to love him? If she let duty rule her?"

"I hardly remember him," Alice said. "I have not seen him since I was a child. I could—would you mind if I read part of Elfie's letter aloud to you? You might help me judge."

Of course everyone assured her of his willingness to listen, and she drew the letter from her pocket. "I will not read it all. There is much about my father, which I have already told you, and about Kitty—about Mrs. Todd, I mean to say…"

…You ask what sort of man Mr. Hugh Hapgood is, and I will endeavor to describe him. He is older. Not so old as Papa, but older than other gentlemen of my acquaintance. I would imagine he must be in his middle thirties. But he is not fat or gouty, and he still has much of the hair on his head. He is not handsome, but he is distinguished. Cousin Hugh is a serious man, not

given to light talk or jesting. If you will pardon me for repeating gossip—even good gossip—his man told Dorcas that Mr. Hapgood bears a character "without stain" and that "any number of ladies where they come from would gladly take poor, departed Mrs. Hapgood's place and consider themselves blessed."

What do you suppose, Alice? If I were to accept Mr. Hapgood's offer, what ease I could give my father and mother! We need never leave Bramleigh. If something were to happen to Papa now, I am certain Cousin Hugh would not hurry us away, but I could not vouch for any future wife of his, and it would be right that the new mistress of Bramleigh should be mistress indeed. He is a kind man. I do not dislike him by any means. I am certain I could come to love him in time. Only, I cannot bring myself yet to say Yes. Perhaps I may only be asking myself for some reprieve, as Jephthah's daughter asked for two months to roam the hills and weep with her friends before she was sacrificed. Though I suppose she wept because she would never marry, and I weep because I will.

Or perhaps I hesitate because, however much Cousin Hugh's children need a new mother, the middle child Hetty is by no means convinced. She has told me plainly that I must not marry her father and continues to provoke and make mischief in order to drive me away. Father Thomas counsels me to bear her with patience, and I do try, but it seems hard to be blamed for something I would never suggest for myself, if Duty did not ask it of me.

"There is more," Alice said, folding the letter and replacing it, "but I have read enough to give you a sense of her dilemma. You see what I mean? Elfie perceives it as her duty, but I hate to see her marry for duty alone. If only I could help her!"

Frederick had not attended this reading in silence. He moved restlessly from the sofa to the fire to each of the windows, in turn, running fingers through his hair, his jaw locked to hold in heedless words. But there was a limit to what a man might bear.

"There can be no question of Miss Hapgood accepting him," he declared, startling the others with the abruptness of his speech. "How can there be? She compares herself to Jephthah's daughter—to a woman being sentenced to death! If—if I had proposed to Miss Hapgood, and she asked for two months to mourn and weep before she lay herself on the altar of marrying me, I would speedily interpret that as a No."

"I must say, I agree with Frederick here," Walter Tierney said. "Whatever benefits such a union might hold for both Hapgood families, surely those are outweighed by Miss Hapgood's reluctance? I cannot imagine your father would ever force her to marry against her inclination, no matter how shillingless he might think himself."

Alice bit her lip. She had grown up with enough of the squire's you-must-marry-and-marry-well speeches ringing in her ears to cause her some doubt in the moment, though she could not tell anyone but Joseph that much. "Perhaps not," she said. "But you see—my father cannot be consulted in his condition. Elfrida will not want to upset him. She will make this choice on her own, and I do not think mere disinclination will guarantee her refusal."

A soft knock was heard at the drawing room door, followed by the entrance of the footmen with the tea tray and a basket of fruit. Frederick was grateful for the interruption, as he had been on the point of saying something impulsive. Something like, *Miss Hapgood has proven herself more than capable of refusing a man for "mere disinclination"! And if she chooses to martyr herself now, she had better do it as soon as possible.*

Baskins and Tuttle withdrew. When Mrs. Tierney handed Alice her cup, with its two lumps of sugar, she said, "My dear, I have an idea. Why do I not invite your sister to visit us? Then you might judge for yourself how nearly her heart is involved. It will give her space to consider, without your father's cousin always at hand. Moreover, she might enjoy some relief from this Hetty child who plagues her."

"Oh, madam," breathed Alice, her mouth trembling, "that is too kind of you to offer. I did think I might persuade Elfrida to come—I want, if possible, to rescue her from a hasty decision. I was going to say she could help me settle this Mrs. Kitty Todd—but she need not trouble you. She could stay with Joseph and me at the parsonage."

"What—and have this Mrs. Todd preparing bad food for all of you?" Mrs. Tierney objected. "No—I won't hear of it. Let her come to Stone Halt. We have rooms enough. She will still see you every day, my dear. But you and Joseph will have enough to deal with, with this Mrs. Todd person."

Alice had no words to express her gratitude, so she simply put down her tea and embraced her mother-in-law. "How kind you all are to me! You will love my sister, if she comes. Everyone does. She is beautiful and sensible and quiet—not a harum-scarum like I am—"

"And don't forget, she plays loo like a hardened gamester," interjected Frederick.

Alice blushed. "We all do, I'm afraid."

"You've played cards with Miss Hapgood, have you, Frederick?" his father questioned.

Frederick was already berating himself for speaking out again. "I have, Father," he replied. "Once. The Birdlows had a card party at Pattergees before I left Somerset. Luck was with me, or I might have been quite fleeced by Miss Hapgood. You had better not mention that I am here, Alice, or she will devise alternate plans to save your family's finances."

"Oh, I will not mention you at all, Frederick," blurted Alice, "for I do so want her to come."

Nonplussed looks from her parents-in-law met this instance of gaucherie, and she blundered onward. "That is to say—er—I do not know why I said that."

Frederick's voice was unnaturally quiet. "Do you mean it would be better if I were not here when she comes—if she comes? Has

Miss Hapgood expressed more than a 'mere disinclination' for my company?"

"Nothing of the kind!" cried Alice, recalling guiltily Elfrida's written comment that *Mr. Frederick Tierney delights in teasing. He has none of his brother's gentleness, but he garners admiration all around. Of which I am certain he is aware.* "Elfie said you were—were—Elfie said you were delightful."

Joseph rolled his eyes, having always thought his wife hopeless at lying. "Well, if Elfrida is the only woman in England whom Frederick has not charmed from head to toe, I should like to witness it. By all means, love, do *not* tell her he is here."

The conversation moved onward, to spare Alice further embarrassment, leaving Frederick to reclaim the sofa and stare blindly at his open book. Well—what had the blasted woman said of him? And why should he care?

But he did care. He cared enough that he wanted to see her again, whether or not she disliked him. He cared enough, obviously, to make a fool of himself in front of his family. Of course it was all nonsense. He had built her up in his mind because she had refused him. Likely, when he saw her, he would wonder what his blustering and pother had been about.

Yes. It was best that he see her again. It was the surest route to recovery and total indifference, where the woman was concerned. Did not familiarity breed contempt?

He found his breath still coming to him quickly and the corner of the sofa upholstery quite torn out beneath his nervous fingers.

And what if she were to come?

Chapter Fifteen

Then be not coy, but use your time,
And while ye may, go marry:
For having lost but once your prime,
You may for ever tarry.
—Robert Herrick, "To the Virgins, to make much of
time" (1648)

It was a tired Miss Elfrida Hapgood who stepped down from the coach in the hamlet of Wendover, accompanied by a dark-haired, inquisitive-looking young woman who must have been her maid.

"Well, here we are, somewhat worse for the wearing," the maid said in a carrying voice. "Hope they won't be long in meeting us." She paid no attention to the coachman, who was trying to hand down their baggage, and the man finally hurled the four valises at her feet.

"What's that?" cried the maid, leaping like a deer. "Have a little respect, you! I've a mind to turn you inside out for that—you've surely been turning my insides wrong way about, with what you call driving. You couldn't have done better if you aimed for every bump and gully from town to here! Yaah! Sheer luck we weren't overturned and thrown in a ditch."

The coachman did not deign to acknowledge this critique, merely tipping his hat to Elfrida before he clucked to the horses to walk on.

"How do you like that?" the maid sniffed. "Rude. I hope you didn't tip him more than a ha'penny, Miss Hapgood."

"I do not know, Mrs. Todd," Elfrida replied wearily. "My uncle Alwyn arranged the fare."

"And an 'andsome uncle he was, too. Far prettier man than your other uncle, though the other one be the love of my life. Won't you call me Kitty?"

"We had better say Mrs. Todd. And please—remember—you must not refer to my uncle anymore. You are the sadly bereaved Mrs. Todd, whose husband—"

"All right, all right," interrupted Mrs. Todd. "Haven't I been practicing it enough, with you and with your 'andsome uncle? I am the sadly bereaved Mrs. Todd, whose husband got all spotted up and died in camp before his regiment left for Penobscot—"

"Portugal," corrected Elfrida through gritted teeth. "Penobscot was a naval battle in the American War of Independence. If your husband contracted measles and died before departing for Penobscot, we would need to explain why you were still with child thirty years later."

Mrs. Todd gave a high, whinnying laugh at an impressive volume. "What a merry one you are, Miss Hapgood! I was born but five-and-twenty years ago—an 'usband dead thirty years would require some explaining. Ha! Got me from beyond the grave, he did. Ha!"

Elfrida passed a hand before her brow, not sorry that no one had immediately come forward to meet them. Servants were such talkers. If she could not get Mrs. Todd to hush, and to stick to her story when she did speak, the jig would be up before it had begun.

"That would be curious indeed," she murmured, laying a cautionary hand on Mrs. Todd's arm. "Now try again, and more quietly. It would not do for anyone to hear you reciting."

Huffing out a sigh, Mrs. Todd put her hands on her hips and complied. "I am the sadly bereaved Mrs. Todd, whose husband died of disease before 'is regiment left for *Portagal*. Mr. Todd was the son of Mr. Alec Arbuthnot's groomsman, so Mr. Arbuthnot is taking my future in hand and putting me out to service." She muffled a snort. "To pasture, more like! What is this place? All grass and slopes. Can't imagine there's anyone out here to serve! Oh! 'Old up now"—she broke off with a sharply indrawn breath—"look there, Miss Hapgood! Here comes a one. And an 'andsome one, too. Look at the blue of that coat!"

Turning in the direction Mrs. Todd indicated, Elfrida made out an approaching curricle, drawn by a pair of bays. She could not, at this distance, make out the driver, but she assumed that, by "a handsome one" in a blue coat, Mrs. Todd did not refer to one of the horses.

Wendover was not a big village, but as the public house stood at the intersection of the high street and the Aylesbury road, the curricle driver was forced to slow and negotiate some traffic: a mail coach going the opposite direction, a flock of sheep and their shepherd, and one stray dog. Elfrida did not imagine Stone Halt would send a curricle for them, since it would be a squeeze for three people. Could her last letter have gone astray, and they were not expected?

After her one glance, Elfrida kept her gaze fixed straight ahead, but the irrepressible Mrs. Todd hopped up and down on the balls of her feet, hallooing. "Here we are! Are you come for us? Miss Hapgood and Mrs. Todd, for Stone Halt?"

The vehicle drew up, the horses stepping slightly to avoid the dog, and a warm, low voice replied, "I am indeed. Have I the good fortune to have found those two ladies?"

Elfrida's head snapped up, her eyes enormous. It could not be. But it was. Mr. Frederick Tierney, whip tucked under his arm, favoring her with a lazy grin.

"What—whatever are you doing here?" she asked faintly as he sprung down.

He tossed the valises into the trunk strapped between the rear wheels and extended a brown-gloved hand to assist her into the carriage. "My dear Miss Hapgood," he murmured, his mouth close to her ear, "I might ask the same of you. After all, I live here."

The curricle was as impractical as she feared, and she found herself nearly pressed against Mr. Tierney along the length of her left side. If she did not actively hold herself apart from him and cram against Mrs. Todd, things would be awkward indeed. As it was, at every jolt and turn she was tossed against him, whereupon she swore she heard him chuckling. Elfrida suspected he made no effort to avoid these hazards and seemed rather to seek them. She was glad he was no longer angry with her, but it was not long before she thought the return to his old manner was little improvement. It was altogether the most uncomfortable ride of her life, and she was too overcome with dismay to pay any heed to Mrs. Todd until they were well under way. Too overcome to press the woman's foot, or to elbow her, or to hiss any reminders. And so Mrs. Todd ran amuck.

"You know Miss Hapgood then, Mr. Tierney?" the woman ventured, leaning around Elfrida to smirk at him. "She said we would be visiting her sister's new family, but she didn't say a word about you! Oh—you're brother to her brother-in-law, then. Well, well, what a pleasant surprise. New experiences all around, wouldn't you say? I'm going into service for the first time—having just been delivered of my first child. Why, thank you. I'm not so slender as I was when Mr. Ar—when Mr. Todd knew me (my sainted husband burst with measles before he even set out for Penobscot, sir—died in camp 'e did), but I pride myself that he would still call me a fine-looking woman as he looked down from heaven, God rest him. And the child! A daughter, Mr. Tierney, as fat and pretty as ever may be. Oh, thank you for your sympathy, Mr. Tierney. Mr. Todd was a fine man. So sad, 'im going as spotted as a plucked goose before 'e pitched over the perch, and 'im so vain of 'is looks. Yes, yes, a shame. Thank you for the use of your handkerchief—what fine lawn it is. It is silly of me to cry when he is in a better place. But I do not know what would become of me, if not for the kindness of Miss Hapgood's uncle.

You've not met him? Mr. Alec Arbuthnot—bit shorter than you, half the hair, and not a quarter as fancy. Mr. Arbuthnot. My Mr. Todd was the son of his groomsman. It's in memory of my dear departed—and in charity for my fatherless child—that Mr. Arbuthnot found this position for me. Of course, my father was loath to part with me. I'm his precious jewel, he's wont to say. But Mr. Arbuthnot convinced him it was for the best. And this here Wendover isn't so far from London that my dear Pa can't come down sometimes, if the urge takes him. Are you often in town, Mr. Tierney? Fancy one like you. Oh—if you are just come down yourself you must have been there when there was that wretched heat. I was fair to melt like a tallow candle—all guttering pig fat, I felt that sweaty and faint! You couldn't know sir, but being with child and then having a newborn is like carrying around a piglet strapped to you. Warm all the time."

"And how was your journey, Miss Hapgood?" Frederick asked, when, after some fifteen minutes in this vein, Mrs. Todd had the misfortune to inhale a gnat and was forced to stop and cough. He turned to peer around the sides of Elfrida's straw bonnet, the contortion pressing his thigh against her own through her skirts.

"I—it was—fine." She tried to contract herself into a still smaller compass, only to find Mr. Frederick Tierney's limbs relaxing to fill the space. For a man who wore embroidered waistcoats and astonishingly high shirt points, he had a very firm, muscular leg. (Elfrida could have no idea how Mr. Tierney's man had nearly wept with joy to have his master's old fastidiousness return inexplicably at the eleventh hour.)

"You came by way of town, did you not?" continued Mr. Tierney, affecting not to notice her discomfiture.

"Yes. My uncle Alec took me up, that I might meet with Mrs. Todd and accompany her down to Buckinghamshire."

"I hope your family are all well."

"Yes."

Elfrida scowled. She must do better than this. She would not have him suspect how he disturbed her. "That is—no. My sister perhaps has told you that my father met with an accident and is quite weak. But we hope he will make a full recovery."

"I did learn of that," he said gently. "And I am glad he is recuperated enough to spare you for a little. You must be weary with nursing."

His concern took her aback, and Elfrida had to swallow a sudden constriction in her throat. Unless...by "weary," did he mean she looked as fagged and colorless as she felt? He, if anything, was more glorious than she remembered, from his shining beaver hat propped on golden hair, to his perfectly proportioned and tailored limbs, to the tips of his gleaming boots. In his blue-and-buff-and-rosebud-edged apparel, Mr. Tierney stood in contrast to her other suitor Cousin Hugh as a peacock to a crow.

"*Other*" suitor? she asked herself. She had but the one suitor now. Mr. Tierney had not then, or at any time thereafter, indicated that his suit would be renewed or left to her indefinite choice, as her cousin's was. Indeed, Mr. Hugh Hapgood had accepted Elfrida's proposed absence with equanimity, indicating with one solemn nod his willingness to wait for her response, protracted though it was.

Mr. Hugh Hapgood might wait and wait, but Mr. Tierney—perhaps his restored spirits resulted from his indifference to her.

Ignoring the sinking feeling this thought produced, Elfrida sat up the straighter and replied, "You are very kind. But things were not so bad as that—after the first week. And my mother and sister Margaret have been surprisingly helpful. I do believe my father's illness has made my mother forget her own more trifling ailments, and Margaret has done a great deal of growing up. Still, I would not have come, had my father not begun to grow irritable with inactivity—a very good sign, Mr. Lewis tells us." Elfrida neglected to mention that the squire's irritability stemmed from Hetty stealing Button's biggest pot and spoon and clanging them together in the dead of night as if she were beating to quarters, and Bramleigh the *HMS Victory*. (A great point in favor of Elfrida leaving home for a while was the hope that Hetty would observe a truce in her absence.)

"Oh, yes," put in Mrs. Todd, having got the bug in her throat down or out. "My pa is ever tetchy when he's been in his cups and has the splitting headache, but he don't yell until he's enough better that he can stand the row himself."

"Wise man," said Mr. Tierney. And to Elfrida's amazement, just as she was elbowing the voluble Mrs. Todd in her ribs, she felt a nudge to her own side. Startled into looking full at him, she found Mr. Tierney's eyes twinkling at her, and she felt her own mouth twitch in response. Mrs. Todd was simply too awful. This plan to place her in service—in a clergyman's house, no less!—could never prosper.

"I understand," he went on loudly, when Mrs. Todd again opened her mouth to speak, "that your father's condition has not been the only excitement at Bramleigh, Miss Hapgood. Alice tells me you have had other guests."

Coloring, she tried to read his expression, but his face had smoothed into a handsome blank. What had Alice told him? A sight more than she had told her own sister, in any case! Why had Alice not warned her that Frederick Tierney was at Stone Halt?

"We have," Elfrida said. "My father's cousin Mr. Hugh Hapgood—the one who lost his wife—has come with his three children."

"Such a time for a visit! I own myself surprised, Miss Hapgood, that this Cousin Hugh did not take himself off immediately, once he became aware of the inconvenience his family's presence might cause, under the circumstances."

To this Elfrida could make no possible reply. She brushed invisible lint from her wrinkled calico skirts while she cast about for a new topic.

Mrs. Todd took advantage of the pause. "There's nothing like family, I say. I don't know what would become of me, if not for me Pa looking out—"

"An apt observation, Mrs. Todd," interrupted Mr. Tierney with such friendly eagerness that she could not take offense. "How well you put it—nothing like family! Perhaps I am wrong to accuse this Cousin Hugh of being inconsiderate. Perhaps his stay at Bramleigh was prompted entirely by solicitude for the family. What would you say, Miss Hapgood? Has the man your best interests at heart?"

"My best interests..?" breathed Elfrida.

"*Your* best interests, Miss Hapgood?" wondered Mr. Tierney. "Oh—excuse me—I meant the best interests of your entire family. 'You' in the plural, not 'you' singular. Our language is so fearfully imprecise! It must be so much simpler to be his majesty King George. Then one might always respond with 'we' and never be corrected—if one dared to correct a king."

Elfrida barely heard out this nonsense before she said primly, her heart hammering, "Mr. Hugh Hapgood is a perfect gentleman. And, yes, I would say he has *our* best interests at heart."

"Your best interests, indeed, but perhaps not *your* best interests."

"I am completely confused," declared Mrs. Todd.

"I am little better," said Elfrida. Though she followed the maddening man exactly. Wherever he had spent his time since he left her, he had not lost his love of teasing.

He knew of Hugh Hapgood's proposal, then. Elfrida's hands itched to wring her sister's neck. What business had Alice to advertise the information?

"Well, God bless him, at any rate," continued Mr. Tierney blithely. "We would have no fairy tale endings if not for such knights in shining armor."

"Have you been long in Buckinghamshire?" Elfrida almost demanded, determined that he should no longer direct the conversation.

"Some two hundred years, I imagine. Not nearly as long as the Hapgoods have been in Somersetshire."

"I meant *you* in particular, Mr. Tierney, not the Tierneys in general."

"Oh! That imprecision of our mother tongue again. In that case, I would say twenty-five years, give or take a few months."

The line of Elfrida's jaw appeared through her soft cheek, but the brim of her bonnet hid it. "And on this particular visit?"

"Two weeks." There was a note in his voice that told her he was laughing at her. He cleared his throat. "What think you of our fair county, Miss Hapgood? The Chilterns are not so different from your Blackdown Hills, are they?"

Landscape appreciation had never been Elfrida's forte, given her poor eyesight, but the soft green outside Wendover did not look so different from the soft green outside Patterton, and she made agreement. "I do not share my sister Alice's specific and all-inclusive love for the natural world, sadly," she said, "but I daresay it looks pretty enough."

"I prefer more buildings myself," put in Mrs. Todd, yawning and patting her fingers against her mouth. "That's one more thing you and I have in common, Miss H."

Mr. Tierney began to point out features of their surroundings and to speak of escarpments and chalk soils and stands of beech; enclosures and vales; earth banks and thorn hedges that marked an ancient trail through the hills. He found an appreciative audience in Mrs. Todd, who "hmmed" and "oh!-ed" and "just so-ed" as if she had never set foot out of Shoreditch, which, in fact, she hadn't.

"What a fund of knowledge you are, sir!" exclaimed Mrs. Todd. "A regular cyclopede!"

Elfrida, too, was impressed, though she marveled only inwardly. It seemed Mr. Joseph Tierney was not the only member of the family who looked about him with interest when he went out of doors. It made sense, she supposed, as Mr. Frederick Tierney was the heir to Stone Halt. He must have long studied the swaths of countryside with a proprietary eye. But there was fondness in his tone as well. She wondered if such an attitude characterized landed heirs. Did Cousin Hugh regard Bramleigh in similar fashion?

"If you look over your shoulder that way"—Mr. Tierney lay his arm behind Elfrida's shoulders to point with his whip—"you will see Haddington Hill, the highest point in the Chilterns."

She straightened up once more, because the brush of his sleeve sent a small shock through her, as when Margaret would shuffle her stockinged feet on the carpet and then catch at her hand. Invisible sparks, Alice had called it. Electricity.

Mrs. Todd gave a screeching caw of derision. "Haddington Hill, you say? More like Haddington Bump. I would be surprised if Parliament Hill in town weren't higher."

"It isn't, as a matter of fact."

"Have we much farther to go?" Elfrida gulped.

"Not very. We will be to Stone Halt before dinner, which we eat at the shockingly early hour of four. Not very worldly people, my family. Joe and Alice will dine at the house with us today, of course."

"And I'll be shuffled off on this Mrs. Lloyd," declared Mrs. Todd without resentment. "Hope she's one for more talking than Miss Hapgood here. Not that you aren't lovely to look upon, miss, but I prefer the chatty type myself. My Pa always said I was like a bird for chatter. Ah, but he'll be lonely and quiet without me."

Elfrida thought Mr. Todd more likely to fall upon his knees in gratitude for this unforeseen deliverance, but she kept this opinion to herself. "We have missed Alice sorely," she said. "I am asked to be the eyes and ears for my family. They want to know all about her new home and family and husband, and Alice is never the most satisfactory correspondent. We, at this point, know more about the plants and bugs and beasties she has found near the parsonage and on the grounds of Stone Halt, than we do of any of its human occupants."

"Ah. Then I have not been telling you much that Alice has not already shared. Let me remedy that, Miss Hapgood. You will find your sister...vastly contented."

Elfrida looked at him to measure his sincerity and found he gave her a rueful smile. "Indeed, Miss Hapgood, I would not be surprised if the contentment of our brother and sister quite took away your appetite, it is so very...contented a contentment. Such as few others might ever hope to experience. Most, as I am sure you are aware, meet with disappointment in love. Tragic, really."

Her lips parted, but nothing emerged. Did he mean something by this speech? *Was* he disappointed by her refusal of his offer? It was impossible to ask, even if she were not sitting nearly in Mrs. Todd's lap. But not to know was painful. Elfrida could find no words, no offhand jest, to lighten the weightiness of the moment, and she feared her silence would give it added significance. Mr.

Tierney would think that she so labored under her disappointments in love that she could not string two words together.

Still, she could have screamed when Mrs. Todd threw herself once more into the breach. The fragile moment of unspoken question-and-answer fled away before that woman's trumpet call. "How right you are, Mr. Tierney," sighed Mrs. Todd. "'Tragic'—that is precisely the word for it. Look at me, for instance. How briefly did Mr. T and I enjoy the fruits of our love before this terrible war tore him from my bosom? If Mrs. Alice and Mr. Joseph Tierney have found true love together, so much the better, say I. I wish them joy of it. And so I would counsel all young people," she went on, as if she were a hundred years old. "Snatch at your chance at love, because it will be gone, soon enough. Gone, youth. Gone, beauty. Gone, young men. Just so. 'Gather ye rosebuds,' I always say—"

This was too much for Elfrida, who could not help interjecting, "Yes, Mrs. Todd. And how well you followed your own advice. I imagine you yourself gathered several bouquets' worth, before—"

"Before—"

"—before Mr. Todd got blown up with measles in camp," they finished together.

And with the fictitious Mr. Todd's sorry fate still ringing in their ears, they arrived at the gatehouse of Stone Halt.

Chapter Sixteen

**I have saide enoughe, especially to a learned governor,
to whome an inclinge weare sufficient.
—Edward Campion, *A Historie of Ireland* (1571)**

Mr. Walter Tierney repaired to his wife's dressing room, as was his habit, before turning in. The maid was just letting down Evelyn's waving hair, and Walter dismissed the woman with a nod, taking the brush from her hand, that he could draw it himself through his wife's tresses.

"Alice spoke the truth, did she not," he began. "Miss Hapgood is a quiet, amiable young woman."

"Beautiful, too," his wife agreed. "In a different way from dear Alice, of course, just as Frederick is so different from Joseph because of their coloring."

Any objective observer would give Miss Hapgood the decided advantage in beauty, but Walter and Evelyn Tierney were no longer objective. They had thrown themselves headlong into welcoming and loving their new daughter, and nothing so trivial as a sister's looks could topple Alice from her pedestal.

"Yes, beautiful," said Walter, as if his mind were elsewhere. As indeed it was. "I do not like this Mrs. Todd, however. We will let Lloyd do her best with her, but I do not think that woman has the material to be made into a decent servant. For one thing, she does not seem to realize her place. She spoke up as if she herself were the guest being welcomed to Stone Halt."

Evelyn sighed. "She spoke up a great deal too often. I do not think she will be able to maintain the fiction of her widowhood. Poor Alice! She and Miss Hapgood want so badly for this plan to work. We must not be the first to cast doubt, Walter."

"Certainly not. But neither have I any wish to see Joseph and Alice saddled with this creature. We will let the trial run its course and then wring an honest assessment from Joseph. If this Mrs. Todd proves as disastrous as we fear, and the squire still lingers in a weakened condition, you and I must come up with some means of getting rid of her." Laying the brush on the dressing table, he placed his hands on his wife's shoulders, their eyes meeting in the looking glass. "This Mrs. Todd is not the only thing you have on your mind, is she, Evelyn? There is something else. What is it?"

Turning, she took his hands in her own and pulled him down to sit beside her. Her lips formed a trembling smile. "It is—my dear—did you think Frederick was himself tonight?"

"Frederick? What of him? I admit I noticed nothing. He was talkative, perhaps."

"Yes! He was, as he used always to be," Evelyn beamed. "Walter, I think—nay, it is too soon to say—but I have an intuition about Frederick."

Her husband raised his eyebrows and waited patiently, thinking in the meanwhile that, when Evelyn looked so eager and abashed, the years fell away from her.

"He was not the same when he came home this time," she said. "Did you mark it? He was...subdued. Moody. There was none of his usual teasing and boisterousness, not even with Joseph. I confess I was pleased at first—I thought Frederick might be putting his wilder ways behind him at last. But as it went on, I grew concerned. He seemed...unhappy. But then tonight, Walter—tonight it was as if he...came back to life! He was his old self again. Still quieter, perhaps, but alive."

"I am not certain we want his old self resurrected," frowned her husband. "Do you remember that sheaf of bills presented to us some months ago? And the talk that reached us of his carryings-on in town? That letter you wept over? If anything, I have been pleased he chose to come down and keep to himself. I do not believe he's been to a single horse race since his return, nor has he seemed to miss any of his old companions in profligacy. *That* Frederick may disappear without a trace, as far as I am concerned—I would not shed a tear."

"Darling." Evelyn leaned her head against her husband's neck. "You know well enough how many tears I have shed over that young man in recent years. I would not rejoice to see him fall back into his sad habits any more than you. Yet to have him grow wiser, at the expense of his personality—at the cost of what makes him a distinct individual—I do believe I would mourn that loss equally."

Walter made no immediate reply, having always thought that Frederick had too much "personality" for his own good. It was a subject he and his wife had canvassed thoroughly over the years, with neither conceding any ground to the other. Rather than take up the tired thread once more, he said, "Well, then. What is your woman's intuition about Frederick? Is he reformed?"

"I do not know about 'reformed.' But I think—perhaps—yes—I think he may be...in love, Walter. And when has love never led to reforms of sorts? You yourself were as fond of the races as Frederick, before we met."

"That is neither here nor there," he objected, grimacing. "In love, you say? He?"

"Yes. I do not know—it is only a hunch—a theory, as Joseph would say."

"Our Frederick in love. Do you mean with Miss Hapgood? Mercy on me—you cannot mean with that Mrs. Todd creature."

"With Mrs. Todd?" cried Evelyn, springing to her feet and laughing. "Gracious! If I suspected Frederick had feelings for Mrs. Todd, I should be prostrate on my bed with grief. Though even Mrs. Todd might be an improvement on his previous attachments. You foolish man, Walter. Of course I mean Miss Hapgood."

"I don't think she said a word to him all evening, if she could prevent it."

His wife smiled at him. "My dear. I did not say Miss Hapgood loved Frederick—though I don't believe her wholly indifferent to him. I said only that I suspect *he* loves *her*."

"Well! Well." Walter rubbed a thoughtful finger alongside his nose. "Good heavens. I do not think her his sort at all."

"And why not, pray?" his wife pressed. "Did you not just say she was quiet and amiable and beautiful? She is not wealthy, which Frederick certainly would appreciate, as he often overspends himself, but apart from that I can think of no objection to her."

"Who speaks of objections? I said merely she was not the sort who ordinarily attracted him. She being neither married, nor older, nor shocking, nor worldly. Does not Frederick take singular delight in causing us anxiety? If he were to attach himself to Miss Hapgood, how could he bear with our approval? Our smugness? We must pretend horror, Evelyn, or it will never come about."

His wife laughed again, laying a fond hand on his shoulder. "Teasing man! We must say and do nothing, neither in approval nor disapproval. It is only an inkling of mine, you understand. A vapor. An idea which might dissipate and vanish if we look too hard."

"Thus speaks Mrs. Tierney," he rejoined, "as if her husband were the one looking too hard. But if preaching your sermons at me helps you better obey your own commands, my dear, then preach away."

Mrs. Walter Tierney was not the only woman with inklings that night.

"Joseph," said Alice, climbing into the bed beside him and curling up against his side.

"Yes, love?"

"Do you hear that queer sound? A sort of rumbling?"

He left off stroking her hair to listen.

"Could someone be dragging a dray of lumber outside?" she suggested.

Her husband muffled a laugh. "It does sound rather like that, but I suspect the noise originates from within the parsonage walls."

"Within?" Her childhood home of Bramleigh had known its share of hedgehogs and rats and mice over the years, but Alice had never known the unwanted denizens to produce such sounds as these.

"And as *I* am not making that racket, and as *you*"—he laid his head against her breast to listen—"are not, we must conclude the source to be Mrs. Kitty Todd."

Alice's eyes widened. "What can she be about?" she whispered. "Is she rearranging the furniture? Pulling the pianoforte across the kitchen flags?"

He paused in tracing the outline of her hip through her lawn nightdress, giving another chuckle. "My dear Alice, I will be brief: she snores."

Alice drew a surprised breath, which she expelled the next moment in a giggle, clapping her hand to her mouth. Joseph just as quickly drew her hand away, muttering, "Never fear—I doubt Mrs. Todd would hear the Last Trumpet in her current state. You mustn't cover your lips, love. I have business with them."

Some minutes passed before Alice was at liberty to say, "I have already decided, Joseph. Elfie cannot marry Papa's cousin."

"Your own marriage must already be grown something tedious for you," he murmured against her neck, "if you can think of your sister's prospects at such a time."

"No—never! Only—stop a moment, Joseph, or I won't be able to think clearly—"

"Such, I confess, was my aim."

"I am in earnest." She pressed him back against his pillows and scooted as far away as the bed allowed. "Did you see how pale and out of looks she is? For Elfie, I mean. And she embraced me far too long."

"She has not seen you for some time," Joseph countered, reaching for her again, "and I am certain I never get to embrace you half as long as I should like."

Alice captured his hand between her own. "You don't understand—Elfie is not expansive with her affections. To my mind, such a display spoke that she was more than happy to see me. She was relieved *not* to see someone else, to be away from the daily sight of something that caused her anxiety."

His wife's solemnity finally giving him pause, Joseph rolled onto his back and folded his arms behind his head. He looked thoughtfully up into the canopy. "Of course you have known your sister far longer and more intimately than I, Alice," he said, "but is it not a leap to say that Mr. Hugh Hapgood is the source of her anxiety? After all, your father has been unwell, and that little cousin has been wreaking havoc."

"Yes, yes," Alice agreed, sitting up and tucking her knees beneath her. "And certainly that has been wearing on Elfie. But I do not draw this conclusion out of airy nothings. It is not just the embrace—I observed her closely all evening and wait only to confirm my findings with her when I have an opportunity. But I do not believe Elfie wants to marry Cousin Hugh, even if she ought, because—"

"Because—" he prompted, when she broke off.

"You will not say anything, Joseph?" wheedled Alice.

"To whom? To Hugh Hapgood? He is three counties away and we have not even been introduced!"

"To your brother Frederick."

"Now I am truly lost, my love. What has my brother to do with this subject? I thought we spoke of Hugh Hapgood and Elfrida."

"But that is just it, Joseph—you mustn't say a word of any of this to Frederick because it would be calamitous."

"*What* would be calamitous?" Joseph demanded, laughing now. "Speak plainly, wife, or I will be forced to extreme measures. Under cover of Mrs. Todd's snoring, who should hear your cries for mercy?"

"I will be plain, then. I think my sister cares for your brother. And for this reason, she cannot marry someone else."

Her husband, who had risen to one elbow to grasp her by the ankle, forgot all thought of tickling the little foot he held. "Cares for *Frederick*?" he echoed, when he found his voice.

Alice nodded, her brow knitting, to see how horrified he looked. "Would that be so very dreadful? It would, would it not?"

"I would not...recommend...such a course to any young gentlewoman," said Joseph finally. "Though I grieve to say it of my own brother, whom I love. But you know as well as I now, of Frederick's habits and reputation. I do not say he would trifle with her affections—not deliberately—but the effect may be the same in the end. No—the sooner Miss Hapgood—Elfrida—the sooner she can overcome this fondness, the better. Be assured, I will say nothing to him. But are you certain of this, Alice?"

Her shoulders sagging, Alice gave a slow nod. "Elfie is never loud in company, but she is always at ease and gracious. Tonight she was not at ease, and she seemed to...avoid...your brother."

"She might only have had the headache," Joseph suggested hopefully. "No wonder, if she rode down from London to Wendover in Mrs. Todd's company. And Fred was something of a rattle tonight."

Alice only pressed her lips together, and Joseph made a sound in his throat, unhappy to see her worried. "I will not say a word to Frederick," he assured her again. "And perhaps more time spent in his company will serve to cure her of her complaint. A surfeit of sweets, as it were. But I am completely persuaded by you, my love, that no matter how misplaced her affections, Elfrida should not be forced to marry Cousin Hugh if he is not the object of them. I daresay—if your father were to be taken before his time—we could squeeze your mother and sisters in with us here at the parsonage. Heaven knows they could not make more noise than this Mrs. Todd."

Throwing herself upon him, Alice wound her arms about his neck and bombarded his cheek with kisses. "Oh, Joseph, you are the kindest, most loving, most generous husband in all England! How you comfort me. I love you with abandon—no woman is more blessed than I."

She felt him chuckle again, even as he tried to turn and catch her wild kisses with his own mouth. "I had better beware," he murmured against her lips. "If such will be my reward, I may not stop with inviting only your mother and sisters."

Although the objects of these controversies had not the slightest awareness that anything was in the wind, they, too, were making resolutions.

Frederick slouched in the armchair closest the fire, stretching long legs toward its dwindling blaze and giving it occasional listless pokes with the iron. He had dismissed Norton after the man helped him out of his coat and boots, but there was little use getting further undressed when his mind was troubled.

He knew he had talked too much that evening. He knew his mother had remarked the change in him, but he could hardly restrain himself. Being around Miss Hapgood again was like uncurling himself after having long been cramped in too confined a space. His every nerve prickled; his wits danced; he was restless with impatience to hear her speak, to draw the gaze of her dark blue eyes. And when she hardly spoke and seemed intent on *not* looking at him, it only increased his unrest. And so he had rattled on, rambled on topics which might interest her, baited her once or twice.

This would never do.

Acting like a fool who had drunk too much wine was no way to attain his goal.

And what goal was that?

Why—to make her violently in love with him. To make her regret bitterly her matter-of-fact dismissal of him, and to put forever out of her head any thought of marrying this dried-up cousin of hers. Because Miss Elfrida Hapgood must marry him and him alone, Frederick Tierney!

Stabbing at the fire once more, he threw down the poker, that he might rise and pace the rug, his hands loosening and unwinding the intricacies of his cravat.

He must be methodical about this. Miss Hapgood was a dutiful young lady. Practical. Too clear-headed for her own good. He must take care to present himself as everything she would desire.

This Hugh Hapgood could provide a home for her family? What of it? Why, Frederick was heir to both Stone Halt and his uncle's Halton End. Each of them far grander and more tidily kept than Bramleigh. He would make sure she both knew and saw the homes he could provide the Hapgood women. Neither would replace Bramleigh, of course, and the Hapgoods' history there, but either would be close to Alice, and all the family could remain together. Miss Hapgood could not lose there.

And this cousin of hers was "kind"? Well, Frederick did not consider himself *un*kind, particularly. He was no Joseph, of course, but most likely this Hugh Hapgood was not either. Frederick must try to impress Miss Hapgood with acts of kindness during her visit.

As for that other part Miss Hapgood had written in her letter: that her cousin "bore a character without stain"—

Frederick scowled at the ormolu clock on the mantel as if it were that same stainless Cousin Hugh. Really—of whom were such things entirely true? Consider Honoria Braithwaite's husband, Lord Wimpole, the "Silent Saint." Even such a publicly peerless man as he neglected his wife and child, or at least was cold to them. Was he, Frederick Tierney, truly so much worse in character than most other men (excepting his brother Joseph, again), or had he only been less careful about maintaining a reputation for virtue?

The memory of Miss Hapgood's reference to Mrs. Anne Gurdy rose to trouble him. He suspected Miss Hapgood would indeed consider Frederick's past amours as stains on his character. Well—possibly—but they were behind him now. And, if he meant to behave honorably by her evermore in the future, she must learn to give over her complaints. No woman could ask for more. Besides, what did men who never sinned know of virtue? Was not virtue the more virtuous for having been chosen deliberately, after having known vice? Yes, indubitably. At least, it must be true because he needed it to be true.

He threw his neckcloth aside.

There remained only the underlying question of *why* he must make these prodigious efforts to win her. He, who had never before been obliged to exert himself. To answer such a question required self-reflection—never Frederick's forte—and he struggled with it now. Did he...care for her?

His inamoratas had ever insisted on the word Love. They Loved him, they said. Did he Love them? It had always seemed simplest all around for him to say yes. He Loved them. He had cast the word about, as lightly and widely as they, and found that it satisfied them. To apply such a word to Miss Hapgood at this juncture meant little to him, if anything. If she were to insist on it, surely he could and would use that word with her as well. And yet—he balked at the idea. To him, Love implied that fencing of coquetry and possessiveness that led to possession. Love was desire—easily sated and diminishing with time, in inverse proportion to familiarity. The latter definition, he supposed, was exactly the state to be found in marriage. And the fortunate few—his own parents, for instance—found their way to companionship and trust.

He ran his fingers over the carving of the mantel, following its swoops and points. He suspected, if he were to marry Miss Hapgood, they could find their way there. That is, to that serene equilibrium which characterized his parents' marriage. Although Miss Hapgood was beautiful as poetry, and desire played no small part in Frederick's pursuit of her, he was almost equally drawn to her peacefulness. She was by nature a quiet woman. Calm. Utterly sensible. She would be the grounded counterweight to his own flights of recklessness. These qualities of hers might drive him mad when they worked against him, as they did now, but he could not help admiring them, and wanting them the more, the rarer he found them to be.

There: let the word for his feelings be Admiration. He Admired her.

His waistcoat, breeches, shirt, and stockings lay in an untidy heap on the floor by this point, and, after donning his nightshirt, Frederick kicked them aside, yawning elaborately.

He had his plan. He would begin tomorrow.

And for now, he could sleep.

For her part, Elfrida had long ago retreated to the charming rose bedchamber Mrs. Tierney assigned her, undressed with a housemaid's assistance, extinguished her candle, and climbed into bed. But sleep came no more easily to her at first than it did to Frederick.

She was, however, more in the habit of introspection than he, and she gave herself over to it now, unpleasant though it might be.

Admit it, Elfrida Hapgood, she admonished herself. *You have conceived a most ill-founded and regrettable* tendre *for Mr. Frederick Tierney, one which you must work very hard and very speedily to conquer.* What good could come of rekindling his interest and forcing him to renew his offer, even if she had the power? What good had come to Kitty Todd, for yielding to Alec Arbuthnot? Not that Elfrida imagined Mr. Tierney would dare to seduce and abandon her, gentlewoman as she was, but that did not mean he did not have Kitty Todds of his own, stashed in other corners of England. *Stashed!* Elfrida grimaced in the darkness. Mrs. Anne Gurdy could hardly be described as "stashed," when she stared and winked and mouthed from every provincial stage in the country.

Did it matter, however, if Mr. Tierney had numberless Kitty Todds, and had, perhaps, peopled all the kingdom with illegitimate offspring, if he now chose to pursue a proper union? (Elfrida thought she was safe in assuming that she was the first person he had ever proposed marriage with, because someone so eligible as he could not possibly have been rejected before.) That is, did the number of former mistresses matter, if there was only ever *one* wife?

Ah. Therein lay the rub.

Elfrida had no way of knowing if a man who kept mistresses ceased for all time to keep them once he was married. Apart from her two uncles, she had never been acquainted with any man who kept mistresses, and as her uncles had not yet married (and possibly never would), she could not even consult them on such a point. She knew very well that, however much she might care for Mr. Tierney, she should be exceedingly miserable if his bachelor ways persisted after marriage.

Rolling to her stomach, she let out a lengthy sigh. How could her thoughts even tend this direction? She would not, could not, be so foolish as to marry a man so like her uncles! A spendthrift. A rake. Charming and thoughtless. Had her experience taught her nothing? And even to consider it, at such a pass as the Hapgoods now found themselves —!

Nay—it was clearer than ever that she must put away this schoolgirl weakness. It mortified her to discover she was not above such things.

She would pay her visit. She would sit with Alice and endeavor to train this Mrs. Todd to her new station, and then she would return home.

And engage herself to Mr. Hugh Hapgood.

A slant of moonlight slipped through a gap in the damask curtains, bathing Elfrida's arm as it hung down in silvery blue. She moved her fingers through the light, thinking they looked like mysterious reeds waving in the current, far below the water's surface. Feeling a first wave of drowsiness, she wondered if mermaids had such problems as she.

If she were a mermaid, then Mr. Tierney was a shark: sleek, graceful, dangerous. No, no—he was not so sinister as that. If he were ever to injure her, Elfrida did not think it would be premeditated. For he was playful as well, and sharks were not playful. Perhaps he was an otter: quick and lively and winning. Otters meant no harm. And yet—Alice once told her she saw an otter catch a bird. "I would not have believed it, Elfie, if I had not seen it! I thought, at first, the otter meant only to play with it. Because he certainly did play with it, until the very moment he popped it in his mouth. And that was the end of the bird."

Elfrida's thoughts were drifting now. But one final one meandered ahead of approaching sleep, so fleeting it was gone as soon as it came.

If one must be eaten in any case, I should prefer the otter to have me.

Chapter Seventeen

Cleannesse..is the thing that bringeth her into most estimation: as contrariwise slutterie and filthinesse breeds her most hatred.

—G. de la Perrière, *The Mirrour of Policie* (1598)

"Were you born in these parts, Lloyd?" Elfrida asked her guide and companion.

The sturdy woman with her long face and thinning hair nodded. "Yes, Miss. I am the third generation of my family to serve at Stone Halt. A good family. Much respected hereabouts."

"Yes," agreed Elfrida, a little out of breath. The housekeeper set a fearsome pace, despite her advancing years. And though the path connecting Stone Halt with its parsonage wound over level ground, Elfrida still found herself trying not to break into a trot. She suspected Lloyd thought it more proper to lead the way and not engage her master's young guest in conversation, but the Hapgood girls had lived too many years with too few servants on too great terms of intimacy to be comfortable thus. "Mr. and Mrs. Tierney are wondrously kind and genteel," Elfrida gasped, "and one cannot speak too highly of Mr. Joseph, I imagine."

At this, Lloyd halted so abruptly Elfrida nearly collided with her. Turning, the housekeeper fixed the young woman beadily. "Indeed, Miss. I hear naught but praise of them. But *all* of the family deserves their neighbors' approbation, in my opinion."

"Oh! I am sure," faltered Elfrida. "I have not yet made the acquaintance of the baronet, however—Mr. Joseph's uncle."

"Him?" Lloyd snapped her fingers. "Sir Crispin will do, naturally. But I spoke of the young master. Not so very young anymore, I suppose—Mr. Frederick."

"Of course. Mr. Frederick," repeated Elfrida, unable to prevent a flicker of surprise crossing her features. What Mr. Frederick Tierney had done to deserve praise from the housekeeper, when he seemed to cause his immediate family only anxiety, was cause for wonder. But she had not long to be curious, for Lloyd soon resumed both her swift pace and her train of thought.

"So charming and agreeable and high-spirited as a boy," sighed Lloyd, a nostalgic near-smile pulling at the corners of her mouth. "And he's become a charming and agreeable and high-spirited young man."

"Quite," said Elfrida. Mr. Tierney was all those things, to be sure—to the peril of her own peace of mind.

"And certainly he has sown his share of wild oats, Miss," Lloyd marched on, "but what young man of his handsomeness and station has not?"

"Mmhh," was Elfrida's more noncommittal reply this time. (She could have said something to the effect that Mr. Tierney seemed still mid-harvest of his oats, but she forebore.) She was sadly aware, however, that she delighted to hear him spoken of, and spoken of so approvingly.

"You would never know it, Miss, but some called his father Mr. Walter Tierney something of a scamp in his day, and hasn't he proven a wise and just one since he became master? I have not a doubt the same will prove true of Mr. Frederick in due time. Nothing good comes of a young man being idle for overlong—why, look at his majesty the Prince!"

Lloyd struck home with that one, Elfrida admitted. Compared to England's expensive, idle, disastrously-married Prince George, Mr. Frederick Tierney appeared a paragon of thrift and virtue. But would the Prince of Wales be magically cured of his excesses whenever he ascended the throne, anymore than Mr. Frederick Tierney would rise above his? The comparison with the royal heir had its disadvantages as well: certainly marriage had had no effect in reforming the prince.

"I say, Lloyd!" called out the very subject of their discussion, emerging some distance behind them from the stand of ancient oaks. "Is the parsonage afire? Why such haste this morning?"

Mr. Frederick Tierney strode toward them, hat in hand, but apart from the sunshine falling upon his golden head, Elfrida might not have recognized him, so soberly was he dressed. The vivid blue frock coat was nowhere in evidence, replaced by plain buffs and whites and black broadcloth. She wondered idly if he had plundered his father's wardrobe. But as he drew nearer and resolved into distinctness, she made a second observation: muted attire could not disguise the fineness of his form. On the contrary, his expert tailoring only emphasized it, without the distraction of color and embroidery and sheen. Charm and handsomeness indeed.

Casting her eyes down, Elfrida was nonetheless aware of Lloyd's sharp glance at her before the housekeeper bobbed a curtsey, calling, "No haste, sir. I was making certain Miss Hapgood found her way, but if you are going the same direction, I will leave her to your care, for I'm dreaded to hurry over and see what mischief that Todd creature has got to."

"If I know your capabilities, Lloyd, you will have the mischief well in hand before we catch up. Do not let us delay you. I will guide Miss Hapgood."

Another bob and the housekeeper scurried off, leaving a bemused Elfrida to note that her presence had indeed been checking the good lady's pace. But Lloyd was quickly forgotten when she found Mr. Tierney abreast of her, and she was only too aware of the rush of blood to her face and the faltering of her midnight resolution.

He fell into step beside her and silence descended upon them, broken only by the calls of birds and their own footfalls. Elfrida carried herself stiffly in anticipation of another round of his irrepressible teasing, but to her surprise, he said nothing.

She could have no idea, of course, that Frederick was ill at ease as she was, as he cast about for a way to open the conversation. Sober dress was easy enough—but how did one begin a sober conversation? Although he wanted most of all to ask about her cousin's offer, he saw no smooth approach to the matter. Venturing one sidelong glance at her availed him nothing, as he could see nothing of her face around the brim of her bonnet. How to begin...?

"You say your family have been here some two hundred years?" Elfrida blurted, at the very instant he uttered, "How goes Miss Edith's masterwork?"

Their eyes met, each of them laughing ruefully, and Frederick said, "You must answer my question first because you only asked something you already knew."

"Very well," she submitted. "I cannot say how Edie's painting fares now, but two days ago it was a disaster."

"Disaster?" he cried. "How could that be possible, in the hands of so talented an artist? And with such models as she had—I heard they were peerless in beauty."

His wry tone made Elfrida wonder if he was mocking the compliment he paid himself or the ones he paid her and her sister. "It was not the fault of the peerless models," she replied, "but rather that my young cousins have come and Edie let them 'assist' her. I am afraid Paris has a mustache and bicorne hat now."

"Never say! And Aphrodite?"

Elfrida laughed. "Wings."

"Wings?" echoed Frederick in pretended outrage. "Have you—pardon me—has Aphrodite also a halo?"

"...Something like," confessed his companion.

"I see." He swung his walking stick with a flourish. "Do you mean these cousins of yours deemed Paris some sort of whiskered Bonaparte, but Aphrodite they thought an angel?"

"I suppose that is exactly what they imagined, Mr. Tierney. Although you—that is to say—*Paris*— more resembles General Blücher now. The mustache, you understand. It is quite a swooping one. General Blücher, therefore, but wearing Napoleon's hat. Quite odd."

"I see," he said again. "I suppose the hat symbolizes Blücher's defeat by Boney at Auerstadt. Quite the prodigies, these cousins of yours, to be so schooled in contemporary military matters. And perhaps the presence of the angel Aphrodite indicates that they hope Blücher might be saved from his predicament by the holiness of his love."

"I know nothing of that," Elfrida choked.

"I daresay you wouldn't." He could not see her face, but he heard her stifled huff of exasperation. They were treading on dangerous ground again, and Frederick gave himself a mental shake. *No more of that!* Serious and sober must win the day.

They continued beside a meadow where sheep grazed, and Elfrida was startled to see a coarsely-dressed young ruffian spring up from nowhere to bow at Mr. Tierney. "Sir—g'day, Mr. Frederick, sir."

"Good day, Jack. How fares the flock?"

"Most satisfac'ry, sir. Be taking this hunnerd of 'em out of the park to pasture tomorrow, like."

"Very well. Keep up the good work."

Mouth popping open, young Jack eyed Elfrida as she passed, and Frederick sympathized with his curiosity enough to add, "We are on our way to my brother's, at the parsonage. I'm bringing Mrs. Joseph Tierney's sister to her."

"Miss," croaked Jack, scraping another clumsy bow.

Elfrida gave him a shy smile and nod, causing Jack's mouth to fall further open. Frederick gave a silent laugh and retraced a few steps to flip the boy a coin and whisper, "On your guard, Jack—let your mouth hang like that, and you'll catch flies."

"Sir," gulped Jack, almost forgetting the vision of the lovely lady when he caught the twopence. Examining his windfall, he looked up to see Mr. Frederick had already resumed his place beside the alluring maiden.

Frederick cleared his throat and began anew. "These cousins of yours—are you as fond of them as Miss Edith is? (At least I hope Miss Edith allows them to paint over her work because she is fond of them, and not because they cannot be made to mind.)"

"They are good children. Lively."

"And missing their mother, I daresay."

Elfrida stumbled over a root in the path and his hand flashed out to steady her. Without thinking, she twitched away from his touch and then scolded herself for making a show of her discomfort.

"That is, they grieve in their own particular ways," she managed after a pause. "The oldest Lionel and the youngest Rosie follow us about and yearn for affection—which we are only too happy to provide—they are very dear, winning children. It was they who transformed Edith's *Judgment of Paris* into *General Blücher Meeting the Angel.*"

"And the other child—I believe you once said there were three—?" he prompted, trying to quash an unhandsome resentment that Lionel and Rosie should so pull at his companion's heartstrings.

"The other," sighed Elfrida, biting her lip. "Hetty—Harriet—distracts herself by making mischief." Pulling her shawl closer, though the morning grew warmer, she hurried on. "She is but ten, after all, and not of so easy a nature as her siblings."

"Mischief of what sort?" prodded Frederick.

"Oh—childish pranks," she fumbled evasively. "Annoying, but not of lasting harm. Waking the family with a great midnight ruckus, for example."

"Did you not hesitate to leave Somerset, then, Miss Hapgood? To abandon your family to this little sprite? With your father ailing, I suspect that she would be far likelier to obey you than Miss Margaret or Miss Edith. But perhaps her...father...keeps a steady hand on her."

How long was this walk to the parsonage? Elfrida fretted. Mrs. Tierney had said it was not above three-quarters of a mile, but she would gladly be on its doorstep now, to avoid the direction of Mr. Tierney's questions. Of what concern was her family to him?

No humble cottage sprung up to deliver her from the necessity of answering, however, and Elfrida was compelled to reply. "Papa's cousin has not been used to bringing up the children, I suppose. And I—I thought it...acceptable to leave Bramleigh at Hetty's mercy because Hetty obeyed me least of all."

"It cannot be so. Little Lionel and Rosie Hapgood worship you as an angel, while Hetty—" he paused, studying the side of her bonnet as if he believed it might provide a clue to her feelings. "Tell me, why would she not prove as willing as they?"

Elfrida's unwilling, murmured response was delivered to the tips of her boots.

"Forgive me, Miss Hapgood. I could not catch that."

"I *said*," she nearly growled, "that Hetty likes me least."

"Least!" Mr. Tierney's amazement seemed to know no bounds, and Elfrida wished she might rap him across the shins with that walking stick he swung so jauntily. "You will understand, Miss Hapgood, if I confess myself astounded. To hear your sister Alice speak of you, you are all that is perfect."

"Alice is too generous," said Elfrida shortly. "No one is perfect, of course."

"I would hate to gainsay any young lady, you understand," he replied, "but I must say the balance of evidence lies with you in this case."

"Indeed?" She nearly stumbled again in her surprise. Elfrida might believe, in theory, that all people fell short of perfection, but she had not much practical experience, it must be admitted, with others finding fault in *her*.

Ignoring her quelling tone, Frederick sighed. "But Alice is nearly right, Miss Hapgood. You are as perfect as it is possible for a young lady to be, except perhaps for those occasional lapses of temper I have witnessed in you—"

"I beg your pardon!" she cried, whirling on him, her dark blue eyes sparking under her furrowing brow. "I do not see what right you have—"

"—Added to a tendency to vagueness in speech at times that is most confusing—"

"This is hardly courteous of you, Mr. Tierney—"

"—And lastly a sad tendency to censuriousness in your view of the world. One might even call you strait-laced."

Bosom heaving, she halted in the path to fix him with a narrow gaze. Giving a half-bow of courtesy, he also stopped and regarded her mildly. His resolve not to bait her lay forgotten once more, and he could hardly be expected to recall it now, when she glowed at him with such becoming anger.

"And I suppose you have no flaws, Mr. Tierney?" Elfrida demanded. "Though I do not think even our family connection justifies you taking me to task thus."

"Perhaps not," he agreed. "Yet if I have overstepped, I give you permission to do so as well. What are my flaws? Do enumerate them, Miss Hapgood. I should dearly like to know your opinion."

"Then you will have it," she declared, struggling against her tight lacings to master her breath. "Why, you—you—nothing is ever serious to you. Life, death, love, marriage—it's all the same. Subjects for teasing and merriment."

"And if I said you had broken my heart," he rejoined swiftly, "making life meaningless, if it could not be crowned by marriage with you..?"

"Precisely," she snapped. "That levity is precisely what I speak of." Tossing her chin, she resumed walking, and even Lloyd might have marveled at the pace she set. Yet—some treacherous part of her wondered if he spoke with any sincerity. Had he been disappointed, then, by her refusal? He did not behave like a broken-hearted man, or one who found life meaningless, did he?

With his long legs he kept up with her easily. "A grave failing on my part, to be sure, for one so serious as you." Elfrida began to sputter again, but he continued as if he had not heard her: "We are nearly to the parsonage now, Miss Hapgood, and although we have made a good beginning, we cannot hope to reform each other in so short a space. It will have to be the work of another day. Therefore, let us return to our conversation about your cousin Hetty. What can be her possible objection to you?"

Not for the first time did she tell herself the man was impossible, and that she had better give up understanding him and the circumlocutions of his mind. Abandoning her attempts to penetrate his thoughts, she suppressed her confusion with an effort and took hold of his question.

"Hetty dislikes me," she explained, "because she does not want me to marry her father."

He was silent for some yards, and when he spoke again, his voice was altered, flat. "I see. Yes. And—what of you, Miss Hapgood? Do you want to marry her father? This fear of hers must have its origin in something."

"Her father has asked me to marry him," she answered, avoiding the question, "and I have not yet given him a reply."

"And yet you were so prompt in sending me about my business," he sighed, twirling the walking stick and catching it in his fist. "How I envy your cousin the indecision he causes you. Because indecision leads more often to acceptance than outright refusals, you know. I would be wont to make a jest at this point, Miss Hapgood—something along the lines of, 'Haste me to know't, that I, with wings as swift as meditation or the thoughts of love, may sweep to my revenge'—but I know how distasteful you would find it."

She was spared forming a response to this latest irreverence by their arrival at the parsonage.

The path rounded a small copse of beech, and the house hove into view, a trim little cottage beside a trim little kitchen garden which was enclosed by an ivy-covered wall. Neither the wall nor the ivy, however, was sufficient to prevent Frederick and Elfrida overhearing voices raised in argument: one firm and stern, the other high and put-upon.

"What right had you to interfere with Mr. Joseph's specimens, when he had not asked you?"

"Don't know what you might mean by 'specimens'! Where I come from, we call that dirtiness. Never saw the like! Bottles and boxes and oozes and dead creatures. Dead flowers, dead bugs, dried up nastiness. Thought I was doing the master a favor, I was! I could have had that room in right order, in another hour—"

"Mr. Joseph is a naturalist, Todd. He collects such things. *On purpose*. And you are never to touch or order or rearrange any of his things unless he expressly instructs you—much less throw them out! I imagine he and the missus will have it all to do over again—"

"I might tell 'em they can spare themselves," Mrs. Todd retorted. "Hasn't the world enough filth and sluttery without bringing it all within doors? All over the desk and tables and shelves it was! And I don't see what right you have scolding me when I'm sure Mr. Joseph and Mrs. Joseph will thank me when they get back."

"Thank you, indeed! You'll see, when the two of them come back with more such 'filth and sluttery,' as you call it. When they see what you've destroyed and tossed out, you had better prepare yourself to be dismissed!"

"Dismissed!" scoffed Mrs. Todd, giving her braying laugh. "That's all you know. I *can't* be dismissed, by you or anybody else!"

Elfrida, one hand covering her mouth in horror, forgot her wrangling with Mr. Tierney and laid the other upon his arm. He covered it with his own, briefly, his eyes meeting hers, and then he was opening the door in the garden wall and stepping through.

"Mr. Frederick!" cried Lloyd, "Only see what the woman has done—"

"I'll 'woman' you, I will! (Good morning to you, Mr. Frederick, Miss H.)"

"—Mr. Joseph's collection in disarray! Half of it gone to the rubbish pile—"

"I've straightened things up right nicely," said Mrs. Todd stoutly, "and this creature here seems to think I've bungled the job. But you'll see, Mr. Frederick, Miss H. The study is all better for Mr. Joseph to write his sermons. Got rid of the clutter—at least the bits that were nasty or wet. So please to tell this person *I'm* the housekeeper here, and she had better not be threatening me with dismissal when we both know, don't we, Miss Hapgood, if you don't mind my saying, there'll be no dismissing of *me*."

"Mrs. Todd," interjected Mr. Tierney, "or 'Todd,' rather, as I suppose we must call you now, if I might have a word with you?"

Giving Lloyd a superior look, Mrs. Todd gladly went aside with the handsome gentleman, and Elfrida hurried Lloyd indoors again, out of earshot. Mr. Tierney knew the dreadful circumstances of Mrs. Todd's situation, she supposed, and she was only too grateful to have him take the matter in hand, as Elfrida had had little luck bending Mrs. Todd to her own will.

She and the housekeeper had but stepped into a small vestibule at the end of the hall when they heard Joseph and Alice coming in at another door, talking quickly and laughing. There were noises of buckets and satchels and various items being set down—the slosh of water and an "Oh, dear, Joseph—catch it!" Then they were in the hall and Alice exclaiming and dropping her appurtenances and rushing to embrace her sister.

"You have found us, Elfie! Isn't the parsonage darling? And look what Joseph and I found this morning in the fish basket—an eel! We will have Todd cook it after we have had a good look at it. Such rich country! Come and see what we've collected in only a few weeks."

Not daring to glance at Lloyd, Elfrida trailed her sister and brother-in-law with their many pieces of gear into Joseph's now-purged study. What followed, when they saw Mrs. Todd's handiwork, was as unpleasant as she feared. Not that Joseph raged or Alice fainted or cried—quite the opposite—but their pale, stunned faces and inability to form sentences (for what seemed an hour but was probably no more than one minute) grieved her more than hysterics and histrionics possibly could have.

Lloyd broke the silence first. Although she knew it was not her place, she could no longer suppress her indignation. "Mr. Joseph, I beg you will forgive me. I should have come much earlier, and this could have been prevented."

Joseph only blinked at his bookcase. It had been nearly empty the day before, all the volumes removed and used to press flower specimens, but now the books were back, evacuated of their botanical contents and replaced in no particular order.

Alice was biting her lip, her hand placed proprietarily on a case of insects under glass which Mrs. Todd had not disturbed. Those which had merely been pinned to a board were vanished, as was the board. The range and quantity of all that had gone missing was bewildering, and Alice could only stare, dumbfounded.

"But where—where has it all gone?" she asked. Her voice held still a note of unreasonable hope, as if Mrs. Todd might merely have moved everything to the kitchen or spare bedroom.

"The rubbish pile, madam," answered Lloyd inexorably. "And I've already seen what could be salvaged, but it's all a topsy-turvy, mixed up jumble that the chickens and pigs lost no time getting in to."

Unable to absorb this, Alice's mind could only catch at the loss of their most recent findings. "Jo—Joseph," she croaked, after another minute, "the Brimstone butterfly—and the orchids we found at Halton End—"

"We will have to replace them. It is as simple as that."

"You said the orchids would not bloom much longer."

"Nor will they."

"Then we must pay our uncle another visit, and speedily," came Frederick Tierney's voice from the door. Elfrida could see no Mrs. Todd lurking behind him, and she took a step nearer to read his expression. He gave her a tiny nod and half-smile, and she felt the knot of tension within her relax a touch.

"Yes," he went on, "It has been too long since I have visited my uncle. If I do not pay my respects soon, the man may cut me from his will and leave everything to you, Joe. I will write to him. We might stay several days, so you and Alice can collect more butterflies and blossoms than one housekeeper could ever throw away."

Joseph gave a wordless grunt. Frederick suspected he only half attended him, so he crossed the room to give his brother a bracing clap to the shoulder. "I have dressed Todd severely, Joe. She will never cross the threshold of your study again, I suspect, even if you should beg her to mop up a cup of spilled tea herein."

"Surely you won't keep her on, Mr. Joseph?" blurted Lloyd. "You speak of 'dressing' her, Mr. Frederick, but I'm certain you were too kind and jocular to do the thing proper. The woman has no training. This will only be the start of it, mark my words."

"Always such a doomsayer, Lloyd," Mr. Tierney teased her. "Did you never make mistakes when you entered service?"

"Yes, and got my wages docked and my hand slapped when I did, as well I should have! I learned right quickly and kept a civil tongue in my head while I was at it."

"Well, well, not every home can be run as smoothly as you manage Stone Halt," he soothed. "But since I have dressed her as I saw fit this morning, won't you follow Todd to the kitchen now and begin teaching her? I hope you'll find her biddable enough for that."

Her lips compressed in disapproval, Lloyd slipped past Elfrida from the room.

"You don't really mean it, Frederick, do you, about paying my uncle a visit?" Joseph asked, finding his voice at last. "Alice and I should be glad to come—we were so very delighted with those orchids. Everything else"—he gestured with a sweep of his hand—"came from nearer to hand and can be found again at our leisure."

"Of course I mean it," said Frederick roundly, remembering well his plan to overawe Miss Hapgood with all that he was heir to.

"He might not welcome us before the orchids are past blooming," mused Joseph. "When last we saw him, he was grumbling about the annual day he holds for tenants and neighbors."

"Indeed, nothing troubles Sir Crispin so much as conviviality and the outlay of money, but if our visit coincides with one of his dreaded House Days, he will already be so put out that we will add to his burden but infinitesimally. Think no more of it, Joseph. And, Alice, you shall have your Brimstone butterfly and ephemeral orchids. I will write to him today."

CHAPTER EIGHTEEN

Of all Gods workes, which doe this world adorne,
There is no one more faire and excellent,
Then is mans body, both for power and forme
Whiles it is kept in sober government.
—Edmund Spenser, *Faerie Queene* (1590)

Ever after, Elfrida would remember the days that followed as halcyon. She and Alice would go for walks, usually accompanied by Joseph and Frederick, or they would sit in Alice's snug morning room, Elfrida sewing or writing letters and Alice poring over some natural history book as she scrutinized the latest insects or plant bits collected. In the evenings they dined at the house and passed the time pleasantly in music or card-playing, reading, or even, once, in dancing. On the Sundays they heard Joseph's early attempts at sermons and saw with pleasure the small congregation's willingness to hear him. The sisters spoke of their family, of Joseph's plans and new curate, of Alice's experiments in housekeeping, of the kindness of Walter and Evelyn Tierney. More than once Alice wondered how to broach topics nearer her sister's heart, but she allowed Elfrida's outward serenity to lull her.

"I believe the danger is past," Alice told her husband, when Elfrida had been over a week in Buckinghamshire. "Away from Cousin Hugh, Elfrida does not seem to think on him at all, and if what Margaret writes be true, that Papa was well enough to call Uncle Alec a 'sponging fop'—! I prophesy it: Papa will recover, Cousin Hugh will depart Bramleigh, and Elfrida may go on with life as she pleases."

"And what of her supposed passion for Frederick?" Joseph asked, setting down the magnifying glass through which he had been inspecting a beetle.

"I never said it was a passion—only that she was uncomfortable with him, and that worried me. But I say—Frederick has been an entirely different man of late. Well-mannered and thoughtful when we are with him...talking business with your father and his steward...arranging the coming visit to your uncle. He teases as much as ever, but I begin to think he is only tempted by what always tempted me: that Elfie is so unruffled, one simply must ruffle her! If he were not so handsome, no one would accuse him of flirting, but I suppose that has ever been his fate."

Her husband grinned at her. "Fred has certainly won you over."

"And we must not forget," Alice went on, as she came to rest on the arm of his chair, "his being so helpful with dreadful Mrs.

Todd—how well he handles her! She listens to him when she will not listen to anyone else."

"I do not think even Frederick's charm can transform Todd into an acceptable servant, however," Joseph sighed, thinking of the woman's constant chatter by day and snoring by night, and the tremendous banging and stomping and crashing that accompanied her work about the parsonage. As for her decimation of the study, the weeks of lost work, he could not bear to dwell on it. Putting the thought from him, he took Alice's hand between his own. "You are right about Frederick, I hope. I agree he is much improved of late. He has always interested himself in the management of Stone Halt, and if he would only settle here and give up seasons in town, he would be the better for it."

"Do you suppose he might think of taking a wife, Joseph?"

"He spoke of doing just that not two months ago, but I assumed him to be in jest. I considered it unthinkable. Now, I cannot say. But if a rural life improves Fred, I would vouchsafe that a good wife would be the making of him."

Which good wife that might be, neither one said, but couples as fondly attached as the Joseph Tierneys do not always require words to understand each other.

Joseph and Alice were not the only ones who thought Frederick Tierney changing for the better. Elfrida, too, made careful note, at first with doubt and uneasiness, and then with a tremulous flickering of something she did not yet call hope. Could these changes be enduring? Could they be for her sake? *Anyone may behave himself for a week or two,* whispered the skeptic in her, to which the sentimentalist retorted, *But what reason would he have to do so? He seems never to have troubled himself to please his parents heretofore, so it cannot be* their *presence which influences him.* Indeed, it could hardly be their presence, as the Tierneys left the young people often to themselves, only sharing the lingering summer evenings with them.

"You had a letter from your sister today, did you not, Miss Hapgood?" Evelyn Tierney asked her guest one supper, after the footman had served up the meat pie. "I hope it bore good news. How does your father?"

"Better—I thank you. Margaret says he even shooed them all away and ventured out for the first time, but of course, being Papa, he overdid his exertions and has been bedridden once more. Mr. Lewis—the doctor—says he must not attempt it again for another week."

"And Papa threw a slipper at him for his pains," put in Alice, who had read the letter for herself.

"We rejoice to hear it," said Walter, after a pause, as if hurling footwear were the best news possible. He caught his wife's nod and added, "Because we wish that you might extend your visit, Miss Hapgood."

"Three weeks is not long enough," cried Mrs. Tierney, not at all satisfied with her husband's mildness of tone. "Especially if we are to lose two days when you young people go to visit Sir Crispin. If your father truly does so well, we hope—nay, we *insist*—you stay longer. You see how happy Alice is to have you."

"Oh," breathed Elfrida, wishing she could squint at them and read their expressions properly. "How kind of you. I did not—that is to say—it's very kind of you."

"Then you'll stay another fortnight after your return from Halton End?" persisted Mrs. Tierney, laying down her fork to lean forward and smile at Elfrida.

"I—" Elfrida glanced at Alice beside her, who only looked eager. "I do not like to be gone so long," she ended weakly. She could hardly explain that she must give her cousin an answer. It would be unkind to hold him longer in suspense, even if she did not yet know what her answer would be. Laying her own fork down, she nervously arranged her wineglass nearer her plate, causing a footman to leap forward and fill it up.

"It's not a decision to be made lightly," came Frederick Tierney's low voice, directly opposite her, his eyes meeting hers above the arrangement of fruit and flowers.

Elfrida felt that tremulousness in her midsection and wondered for one scattered moment if he had read her mind, a fear not laid to rest by his next words.

"How does it go in Congreve's play? 'Married in haste, we may repent at leisure'?" His gaze still held hers as one corner of his mouth curved up. "The same, I suppose, might be said for tarrying. Tarry in haste, repent at leisure. You need not make your answer now, Miss Hapgood."

"My answer?" echoed Elfrida faintly.

"To my mother."

"Oh. Yes. That answer." Breaking away from his steady look, she gulped down too large a sip of the currant wine and was forced to cough into her napkin.

"Surely they could spare you longer," coaxed Alice. "It sounds like Margaret is managing superbly, and you know how Margaret loves to feel in charge of all. She has never had the opportunity before, Elfie, because you are always so capable."

"All—all those children," coughed Elfrida.

"Margaret writes that my cousin Hugh seeks a school in Somerset or West Sussex for them," announced Alice to the table. "She says that Lionel and Rosie and even Hetty are dear ones, but that they do make a terrible rumpus, and Bramleigh will be like a tomb if they are sent away."

"Furthermore, I suspect it would be easier for your cousin to find a second *Mrs.* Hapgood to be their mother," Frederick suggested, "if he did his courting without three rumbustious urchins nipping about his ankles."

"Oh, it's too soon for him to think of remarrying," Alice said with elaborate indifference.

Joseph only shook his head, amused, but Elfrida shot her sister a warning glare. She saw whither this talk tended. While Alice had not yet broached it in any of their *tête-à-têtes*, Elfrida could read her well enough to know that her sister did not want her to marry Hugh Hapgood. But that was pure Alice, a girl into whose mind duty had never entered, and who had only been convinced to do her duty to family and society when it chanced to coincide with her heart!

What would become of the world, if everyone behaved as heedlessly as Alice? Or as Mr. Frederick Tierney?

"Well, let Miss Hapgood postpone her response to your invitation in any case, Madam," Frederick said to his mother. "She may well wish to be shut of us Tierneys after she has met my uncle Sir Crispin."

"Then let her be rid of Sir Crispin and not hold him against the rest of us," Evelyn retorted, smiling at Elfrida. "You will see, Miss Hapgood. Sir Crispin is my husband's much older brother, and a very retiring, odd little man he is, too. I am astonished he has agreed to a visit from all you young people, when he has seen Joseph and Alice so recently."

"It was no small feat, persuading him. He would not hear of it until I assured him we would come the day after his dreaded House Day."

"As he *has* agreed," interjected Walter Tierney, "and as Miss Hapgood has not *yet* agreed to prolong her stay, let us make the most of this evening. Frederick, Joseph—shall we dispense with the port and sherry and retire with the ladies? I should like to hear the girls play again, and sing, if they will."

Of the four Hapgood daughters, only Margaret showed any talent for music, and "talent" might be an exaggeration there. Edith cared only for painting; Alice's attention wandered; and Elfrida grew weary of peering at the tiny notes, trying to distinguish between the squiggles and blots. But they had all endured years with a long-suffering music master and could stumble through a small repertoire with adequacy. Elfrida committed her pieces to memory, that she need not bother with reading music, and that evening she was prevailed upon to play two of Mozart's Viennese sonatinas, which, truth be told, she had already performed shortly after her arrival.

Alice, having heard them countless times before, was guilty of humming along and occasionally playing an imaginary pianoforte on the armrest of the chaise, but the rest of the party listened in attentive silence. When Elfrida had finished the first, there was applause and praise, and, while Evelyn Tierney fussed with the tea things, Frederick drifted to stand beside the instrument.

"You have a light touch, Miss Hapgood."

"If I do, it is no credit to me. I fear it comes from a long-held fear of striking the wrong keys. Although even my blunders sound beautiful on this pianoforte. We have only an ancient spinet, you know, at Bramleigh."

"Do you miss Bramleigh?"

"Certainly," she murmured. "I have never been from home before, without my family beside me. We would spend part of the year in town when I was much younger, but for many years we have only stayed down in Somerset. Papa does not like to visit my uncles, you see, and the former Mrs. Hugh Hapgood was not overfond of visitors to Crawley, even if Mama could be convinced to go. You, I suppose"—she played a little trill upon the keys— "have traveled much."

Leaning upon the instrument, he regarded her with those unsettling eyes. "I have been away to school and university, of course. But with all the trouble on the Continent, I had no Grand Tour. I made plans when the peace came, but before they could be carried out, we were at war again. Therefore I am afraid London has been my Paris and my Rome, and England my entire Continent. What then, I wonder, would that make Bath?"

"Your Vienna, perhaps," suggested Elfrida. "I hear there are many concerts in Bath."

"So there are. Yes—Bath was my Vienna, then. My musical education. What should we call Somerset? What part of my Grand Tour was Pattergees and Patterton?"

"Hmm..." she ran through the opening bars as she considered. "...Somewhere more remote. And sublime. And rustic. The Alps?"

"Precisely!" He gave the pianoforte an approving thump with his fist. "Somerset was the Alps. Miss Birdlow put me in mind of an ice maiden, to be sure."

They smiled at each other.

"One day I should like to see the real things," he said, "but I hope it may not be alone. My domestic travels have taught me that the company one keeps is the greater part of the enjoyment."

"Yes," she breathed, in order to say something. Just as swiftly, she realized he might suspect her of appropriating his comment as flattery, and she looked away in confusion. How long would he lean over her? She found herself wishing he would take himself off and, simultaneously, that she might sit and speak with him forever. He had been so very pleasant the last few days. So very pleasant always, it seemed to her now.

"I had better play this second piece," Elfrida said reluctantly, after another pause. "If I am to be relieved of my duty."

"Very well," agreed Mr. Tierney. "I know how important duty is to you. Would you mind very much if I listened to you from this vantage point?"

"I'm afraid I would. It would remind me of my music master, who used to stand precisely *there* and drum his fingers inexorably to the tempo, while my trembling hands tried in vain to keep up."

Giving her a bow and another smile, he withdrew and left her to plow through the Sixth Viennese Sonatina. As her fingers danced and pounded and trilled, moving purely by the power of habit, she still felt his gaze upon her, and herself warming under it.

When she had finished her piece and given way to Alice at the instrument, she accepted her cup of tea from Mrs. Tierney and took a seat beside her. But it was not long before Alice abandoned playing anything serious, and Joseph and his parents soon gathered around to join her in singing "The Yellow Hair'd Laddie" and "Betsy Belle and Mary Gray" and other popular songs.

"I've often thought," began Frederick, close behind her, "that if the yellow-hair'd laddie were worth his salt, he would have helped the lassie milk her ewes and get her work done."

Elfrida started to find him so near, leaning over the back of the sofa, his breath stirring her hair. Feeling the color sweep up her neck and face, she blurted, "I—I think thoughts of work were far from them that day."

"Thoughts of work and...duty," he murmured.

"Yes, precisely," managed Elfrida.

"I wonder if the yellow hair'd laddie's beloved was a yellow hair'd lassie," Frederick went on. With one finger, he reached for one of the curls trailing from her high chignon, tugging it gently and releasing it, his hand brushing her bare nape as he did so.

Elfrida shut her eyes, her breathing shallow. She should pull away, of course. Object. Freeze him with a quelling look. But though these thoughts flitted through her mind, she could no more act on them than if she had been paralyzed.

"And it's no wonder the laddie could 'crack and kiss' with the lassie by the hour, if her 'claithing' was as fetching as that gown, Miss Hapgood. Have I told you how utterly lovely you look in blue? As if your eyes weren't blue enough—a man might drown in them."

"Mr.—Mr. Tierney—"

"My words run away with me." His voice was so low she found herself turning to catch them. "Forgive me—but it has not been a simple matter to hold myself in check these last few days."

She felt it again—the feathered touch of his hand, tracing the line from her neck to the hollow between the tops of her shoulder blades. Elfrida shivered and bit her lip to keep back any sound.

"I am trying, you know. To please you. To be the very plain young man you prefer."

"Mr. Tierney," Elfrida said, her voice scarcely audible, "you are under no obligation—"

"But I am, Miss Hapgood. You see, I found that your rejection of me only increased my admiration for you. Admiration." He repeated the word slowly, to watch its effect on her. "Of your firmness of character. Your loyalty to those you love. Of the calm that surrounds you."

She felt anything but calm at the moment. And as for firmness of character—how firm could it be, if she thought she might forget caution, forget family loyalty, forget all, to love him?

Love.

The word woke her from her trance. She loved him?

She loved him.

But he—he still spoke not a word of love. What cold feeling was admiration? Was that not what one felt for a work of art? A statue? A painting? Were these the colorless words he used to lure the Mrs. Gurdys of his life?

"Miss Hapgood, I may not have been as good or as plain a man as you might have wished in the past, but I ask only that you might allow me to change that opinion."

Then he did mean to renew his offer. The candlelit scene of the singers gathered at the pianoforte blurred, but this time it had nothing to do with her shortsightedness. As Alice shut the instrument, Elfrida felt one last brush of Mr. Tierney's hand on her bare shoulder as he straightened to lead the applause.

He admired her and he would ask again. She did not need to search herself to know what her answer would be. Whether it was wise, whether it was dutiful, whether it was a decision she could explain to herself without blushing—she knew what her answer would be.

Chapter Nineteen

Left to himself, Sir Crispin Tierney, Baronet, would never have suggested opening his house annually to the ruckus and depredations of rejoicing tenants and neighbors. But the yearly occasion at Halton End had been traditional since the time of his great-grandfather, and he would not be the first baronet to forgo it. The buffets were prepared, certain rooms dusted and aired, the general invitations issued, and the doors and gates thrown open. He had only to greet all comers and nod benevolently before he was allowed to retreat to a quiet arbor along the rise to the south of the house, from which he could watch in grumbling consternation as his rooms were overrun, his grounds trampled, and his boisterous guests given more drink and rich food than was good for them. Over the years, the House Day had been supplemented with an assembly the following night at Stoke (Sir Crispin having resolutely ignored all hints that he should add a ball to his own efforts at hospitality), for which the Right Honorable Lord Risborough traditionally catered and put in an appearance. Unlike Lord Risborough, Sir Crispin had neither votes nor a seat in Parliament to secure through the goodwill of neighbors, and therefore he never attended this additional occasion for merriment. He merely retreated into his house, shutting the doors and gates and letting his staff tidy up, until the turning of the globe brought the next year's crisis upon him.

When his nephews intruded themselves following the House Day, accompanied by his new niece and her sister, Sir Crispin squirmed at the thought of the ladies but made few objections. He often found Frederick too obstreperous for his tastes, but the boy—the young man, rather—seemed to have settled down somewhat. On this occasion he wore sensible clothing instead of his usual peacock feathers, and while he rattled away as he always had, Sir Crispin saw him make efforts to contain himself. The young ladies were as unexceptionable as it was possible for young ladies to be. His new niece had the dismaying habit of kissing his cheek in greeting or pressing his hand, and from time to time she would give little glows and thrills and enthuse in a bewildering manner over such unladylike topics as bugs and animals' private habits, but she confined these quirks mainly to her discussions with Joseph. As for his niece's sister, though Miss Hapgood was quiet and unobtrusive, her beauty terrified Sir Crispin, and he hoped to have as little to do with her as possible.

"What say you, Uncle," Frederick accosted him after the introductions and greetings and family messages had been got through, "did it do your soul good to have all the county trampling the grounds yesterday? I hope they didn't empty your larder entirely, for we will make a dinner before this assembly of Risborough's."

"First things first," put in Joseph, when his uncle made no signs of replying. "Alice and I only agreed to this assembly if we have our orchids in hand."

"And so you shall," said Frederick. "Uncle, if you have no objections, we will spend the afternoon gathering your weeds and then off to shake our heels and jink in Stoke."

"Won't you join us?" asked Alice kindly.

Sir Crispin dissolved into wordless stammering at the earnest gaze his niece fixed upon him, and Frederick, amused, came to his rescue. "We mean the weed-gathering, sir. Not the assembly. We would never ask you to endure standing up for a set with Lady Risborough or her exalted guests."

"Oh. Oh. No, thank you—to either," Sir Crispin responded to the figured ceiling of the drawing room. "Saw enough of my own grounds yesterday. And assemblies—" he shuddered.

"Who has Risborough brought down this year?" Joseph asked. "Did they come to the House Day?"

"People. Just people," muttered Sir Crispin. "Important sorts, I suppose. They came briefly, yes, but I—I didn't have much speech with them. Lady Risborough..." He waved away the rest of his speech, but his nephews took his meaning. Lady Risborough was a daunting woman, even to men not mortally afraid of the female sex, and if she had "important sorts" with her, they were probably equally formidable.

Leaving the retiring baronet to retire, the four young people spent the afternoon exploring Halton End, Joseph and Alice replenishing their decimated orchid stock and Frederick leading Elfrida to the best vantage points of the house and landscape to measure her response.

"Has your uncle never been inclined to marry?" questioned Elfrida, looking out over the ha-ha to the forested slopes rising green-gray in the distance. Behind them spread the vast, grassy lawn, dotted with sheep and stands of trees. The house at Halton End was grander than Stone Halt, as befitted a baronet's dignity, but it made Elfrida smile ruefully to think of the shy Sir Crispin alone, both master of and mastered by his domain.

"Father says there were women inclined to marry Sir Crispin," Frederick answered dryly, "only he could not be prevailed upon to agree. The only lady I have ever heard him speak more than ten words to—besides his housekeeper, and even there he is reticent—is my own mother."

"It would be impossible to be afraid of Mrs. Tierney," said Elfrida. "She is so gentle and kind." Even as the words left her lips, she blushed, to think he might construe them as making up to him.

"She is that," agreed her companion, his tone thoughtful. He paced a few steps away from her, regarding the fluffy bundles of sheep, and then turned and paced back. "I never meditated upon the charms of a gentle and kind woman when she was raising me, of course, but I begin to understand them now."

A flutter in her stomach greeted this comment. Crossing her arms over this treacherous part of her body, she cleared her throat. "His gardens and grounds must be your uncle's true love, then. Is that pond a natural feature?"

They spoke determinedly of the landscape, although neither one's heart was in it. Frederick was debating whether he ought to offer for her again that moment, or wait, as he had planned, until the day after the assembly, when she had observed with what respect and honor he was treated because of his future prospects. He had planned his campaign carefully and could almost taste the success which would crown it. He could wait one more day, could he not?

If only she were not so appealing in her spotless white muslin, clocked with silver at the sleeves and hem. Climbing the slope brought color to her cheeks and parted her lips. He thought she had never seemed so lovely, so tempting in her figure. Surely he might venture another kiss, without jeopardizing anything?

For her part, Elfrida was all uncertainty. So close to hand, she could not miss the heavy-lidded look in his eyes or the curve of his mouth as he spoke to her. He had looked exactly thus at the Taunton Fair when she leaned over him as he lay on the ground. If Mr. Tierney wanted to kiss her again, she had to admit she would dearly like him to—but surely he would not take advantage of her without first renewing his addresses?

He drew nearer.

Elfrida held her breath, not daring to raise her gaze above the covered buttons of his plain buff waistcoat. She rather missed the embroidery, now that she thought about it, and that bright blue frock coat that made his eyes dance with liveliness. If he asked her to marry him, she would tell him he might dress as he pleased, and she would love him all the better for it.

She saw his hand reach for her own and then hesitate. She waited, her own hand almost vibrating with anticipation. But his did not move.

Disappointed, she glanced up and saw he was looking over her shoulder. At what? At whom? Turning, she squinted with all her might and saw two figures approaching. She could only tell they were a man and a woman, so they must be Joseph and Alice. *Blast.*

The moment slipped away.

Mr. Tierney took a step back from her, before raising an arm to wave in response to their distant halloos. But she heard him murmur, "All in good time."

Some might grumble that Lord Risborough would do better to hold a ball in his own house, if he wanted to secure the goodwill of his constituency, but those less covetous had no fault to find with the vast Market Hall at Stoke, decorated, catered, and supplied with musicians, all at the baron's expense.

The company was as various as Sir Crispin welcomed to his House Day: town shopkeepers and schoolmasters and -mistresses rubbed shoulders with yeoman farmers, the gentry mixed graciously, and whispers and wagers passed in all directions as to when Risborough's party would arrive and who they might expect to be among it.

The Tierneys and Elfrida caused no small stir when they entered the hall, and for a time the imminent arrival of the greater Risboroughs was forgotten. Through their uncle, Frederick and Joseph were acquainted with two or three gentlemen in the room, who—upon noting their wives' significant looks—hurried over to greet them and to perform introductions. While Joseph and Alice met with open warmth and congratulations on their recent marriage, the covert attention of most soon turned to Mr. Frederick Tierney and Miss Hapgood. What a tall, handsome gentleman—and the heir of their own Sir Crispin! To dance with him would be a signal honor, if he were to ask—*sit up straight, girls*! He seemed, alas, attentive to his sister-in-law Miss Hapgood, but he must, they supposed, she being family. Any gentleman in earshot who made the mistake of saying, "Tierney can hardly be blamed—a fine looking girl, that one," was hushed with a frown and a "Certainly—well enough in her way, but they say the Hapgoods haven't a penny to their name. Mr. Joseph could have done much better."

"Will you do me the honor?" Frederick asked, bowing over Elfrida's hand as the master of ceremonies called for the first dance.

While not fond of other forms of exercise, Elfrida loved to dance. Here her eyesight could not hamper her. There were only the long-familiar figures and pleasantries to be exchanged with one's partner. She was always light on her feet, but this evening she felt she barely touched the uneven boards of the hall as she took hands with Mr. Tierney or wove around him or stood as he circled her. Everything fell away. Worries about her family, guilt over her cousin's offer, misgivings about the man who stood opposite her.

Mr. Tierney had made one concession to the evening's assembly—he abandoned his buff waistcoat for a gray one striped with silver, and Elfrida made bold enough to compliment him on it.

"Softly, Miss Hapgood," he cautioned her. "If you profess to admire it, I might never take it off again. For my part, I am glad you have left off the black ribbons tonight."

"Alice and I agreed it would make an unseemly parade of our family's loss, to wear ribbons into this corner of Buckinghamshire, where we are unknown."

"What sacrifice! Fortunately your erstwhile Cousin Harriet will live on, unseen in your hearts." Seeing the contraction of her brows at this flippancy, he hastened to add, "I would remark upon your own appearance in that gown, and how you should wear that ivory sarsenet all the days of your life—but I must not weary you with compliments."

She wondered how he came by his peculiar knowledge of women's evening gown material—had he ordered gowns for his mistresses? For Mrs. Anne Gurdy, say?—before putting the thought firmly from her. Waiting until the figures brought them together again, Elfrida said, "My ear would be jaded indeed, Mr. Tierney, to be tired of flattery, since you are more wont to find fault with me." It was the closest she had come to flirting with him, and she saw the answering challenge in his eyes.

"Fault?" he echoed, passing her in the hey.

"Fault." She gave him her hand for the turn.

"Remind me again of these supposed *faults*. The perfection of your features when you smile at me—thus—quite drives other thoughts from my mind."

She obliged, naming one of her purported flaws with each turn and pass, even as her pulse raced and skipped.

"Ill-tempered, I have been called."

"You, Miss Hapgood? Surely not."

"Then there was ill-*mannered*."

"I'll strike the varlet who dares say so!"

"Provincial." She ticked it off on her fingers.

"If it were permissible to correct a lady, I would point out that *you* called yourself that."

"Priggish."

"I believe the phrase was 'strait-laced.'"

"And...too serious."

"I never said *too* serious. Come now—with a man such as myself, one can never be *too* serious."

They had reached the bottom of the room and waited for the other dancers to go through the series. Aware of the many curious and admiring onlookers turned their way, Elfrida kept her gaze trained on the lines of weaving figures, only the color in her cheeks and the ducking of her chin giving any hint that Mr. Tierney still spoke low to her and that she still listened.

"If I ever said any or all of those things about you, Miss Hapgood," he murmured, "you must make allowances for a foolish young man. One who has never encountered your equal. You have the temperament of an angel, to my misfortune. Had you any vanity or frivolousness or calculation about you, you would have thrown yourself at me when I offered for you. And were you not so...good...and...estimable yourself, you would not have the power you do."

"I do not know what you mean by power," Elfrida ventured, smoothing her gloves and glad they hid her flying pulse.

"Power," he said. "To make me...regret... portions of my past and wish to be a better man."

Here her eyes flashed up to his, but the intensity of his gaze and the utter unguardedness of his countenance threw her into confusion again, and she looked away. The room was warm. Very warm. Or the dancing had made her so.

"Miss Hapgood—I have never...admired another woman—another person—as I do you."

There it was: that word again. And yet it did not strike her as so chilling as it had previously. How could it, when spoken in that low, throbbing voice that awoke an answering throb within her? How could it, when it must be a prelude to much more? Had it been in her power to respond, which it was not, the dance would not have permitted her. Just as he spoke this last, the couple above them circled to the bottom of the room, compelling Elfrida and Mr. Tierney to rejoin the figures. But it must show on her face, surely, she thought, that she could hardly draw breath for joy.

It did.

Fortunately for Elfrida, the arrival of Lord Risborough's party had stolen the attention of the assembly. While the baron himself was neither handsome nor particularly winning, he took care to surround himself with those who were, and his company this night was no exception. There was Lady Risborough, of course, grand and handsome as a ship of the line in her purple silk, bestowing condescending glances and nods as she surveyed the room. And behind her—a ripple of whispers and muttering swept the crowd—was that not Lord Wimpole, the Silent Saint, and his famously beautiful wife? Following them, some other MP, probably a rising star, rounded off the group, but the latter's star was not risen nearly enough to distract from the glittering figures who preceded him.

Those not dancing made way for the party, bowing and curtseying, and the musicians quickly skipped to the closing bars, despite all couples not having progressed down the length of the room. Preoccupied as they were, Frederick and Elfrida were the last to register the change in their environment, and when all heads in the room turned and bobbed courteously, theirs were conspicuous for their nonconformity. Lady Risborough raised an eyebrow, but the sharp intake of breath was not hers. Rather, it came from beside her.

"Lady Wimpole," the baroness drawled, "has something startled you? You appear pale."

"Not in the least," was that woman's quick rejoinder. "The room strikes me as overwarm. They should throw open the balcony doors. How eagerly your husband's constituents regard us! We must keep them contented, Emma. Risborough must make introductions, and we must dance."

Elfrida could not say how it came about, but even as she danced every dance with a succession of men whose names she would not later recall, even as she conversed and curtsied through introductions and smiled her thanks when dances ended, she thought of little else than Mr. Tierney. Without watching him, she was always aware of his precise location in the vast hall. He did not often dance—once with Alice, once with a friendly matron, and once with Lady Risborough—rather, he stalked about the edges of the room, frowning. The frowning puzzled her. She could not imagine he objected to her dancing, and he had already secured her for the supper dance. Why did he not share her own feelings, after what had passed? Did he not feel, as she did, that he nursed a secret warmth which threatened to overflow and spill out at any moment?

As she took hands with her partner for a turn, she caught sight of Mr. Tierney speaking intently with his brother. Joseph seemed to be persuading him of something, and then the two of them disappeared, possibly to the card room.

Whirling to her right, to circle down the hall, Elfrida was brought up short and stumbled.

"Do forgive me! How clumsy of me!" cried the woman below her. "I fear I trod upon your gown. I have torn your hem."

To Elfrida's dismay, a good four-inch length of lace was now trailing along the floor, but before she could decide what to do, the woman had clutched her by the elbow and was leading her away. "Do excuse us," she called back to their respective partners, adding in a delighted whisper to Elfrida, "We have cast them all in confusion by abandoning them, but I daresay they will sort it out."

Elfrida did not see what their forsaken partners could do but decamp themselves, along with the two neighboring couples who could no longer make up a square. But the status of her abductor was such that no one gave voice to any objections.

"Please do not trouble yourself," Elfrida gasped, as her companion darted glances in either direction and then tugged her through a narrow doorway. They appeared to be in a servant hallway and their sudden entrance forced the footmen carrying trays to squeeze against the wall to pass.

By the light of the candles in their brackets, Elfrida saw that she had been spirited away by an elegant woman clad in thinnest russet silk, taller than she, with auburn hair and eyes the color of sherry. Eyes which scrutinized her appraisingly. "So clumsy of me," the woman said again. "I am sure we can compel some maid here to repair your lace presently. In the meanwhile, I have not made your acquaintance. I am Lady Wimpole. Please tell me, whom have I had the honor of injuring?"

"Miss Hapgood," answered Elfrida, dropping as graceful a curtsey as the narrowness of the corridor and the tray of cold meats floating by permitted.

"Miss Hapgood." Lady Wimpole gave a small nod in return. "Just so. You must be a resident of these parts, Miss Hapgood?"

"No, I'm afraid. I mean to say, my sister is. She is lately married to Mr. Joseph Tierney, nephew to Sir Crispin Tierney, a neighbor of Lord Risborough's."

"Charming," Lady Wimpole purred. "But have you yourself no closer connection to the Tierney family?"

"I don't understand," replied Elfrida, drawing herself up nevertheless at her ladyship's insinuating tone. "Are you acquainted with the Tierneys, my lady?"

A maid carrying a pitcher made to edge past them, and Lady Wimpole arrested her with a raised hand. "You see Miss Hapgood's dress wants repair. Fetch a needle and thread, girl."

Nodding, the servant backed away, nearly spilling her pitcher's contents in her haste.

Lady Wimpole touched delicate gloved fingers to the beads twined in her curls. "I am not acquainted with the Tierney family as a whole, but Mr. Frederick Tierney I have long counted as a very good *friend*."

A very good *friend*? Lady Wimpole's words might be innocent enough, but the way in which they were spoken, paired with the unblinking regard of her handsome eyes, made Elfrida draw back. A painful little knot began to form in her chest, and she shook her head slowly, as if doing so might prevent it from gaining purchase.

"Indeed," murmured Lady Wimpole, "in one of Frederick's recent letters to me, he mentioned that he thought of marrying soon. Every good son and heir's duty, you know. So naturally, when I saw you standing up with him and casting him such tender looks, I thought, *Surely this must be the fortunate young lady*."

The knot tightened and would not be shaken off. Elfrida felt it take hold and expand.

Letters? This woman corresponded with Mr. Tierney? Not only corresponded with him—called him Frederick! But Lady Wimpole—this woman—was married! What married woman corresponded with a man who was not her husband or relation?

Part of Elfrida knew the answer even before the rest of her could acknowledge it. Lady Wimpole couldn't be—she wasn't—she *must* be—what was it that Roscoe DeWitt had said of Mr. Tierney, weeks and weeks ago at Lord Marlton's Midsummer Ball? All that gossip racing through the Pattergees ballroom—

Elfrida racked her brain. It was something about Mr. Tierney leading "the devil's own life" in London. Well, this she knew already. But what more? Ah, yes. Mr. DeWitt mentioned "opera dancers and actresses and even a liaison with one—"

"Lady W," mouthed Elfrida, turning her appalled gaze upon the woman beside her. Lady Wimpole had been studying her like a cat at a mouse hole, and when she saw recognition dawn on Elfrida's face, she could not suppress a curving of her lips.

Another waiter bearing a tray of cakes pressed against the walls to avoid brushing them, and Elfrida did not even note his furtive glances at them, so anxious was she. When he was gone, she said only, "You are mistaken. I am not engaged to Mr. Tierney."

"Oh! What a surprise! What a shame!" glowed Lady Wimpole. "It can only be a matter of time, my dear, for I know he means to go through with it. 'What cannot be cured must be endured,' after all. Such a charming man, and so handsome. No woman I ever knew could resist his words of love."

The creature inhabiting her chest unfurled its claws, and Elfrida heard herself gasp, "Indeed. So charming. I must return to the hall. My sister will be wondering where I have got to."

"Do wait, Miss Hapgood—your gown. Here comes the maid again."

And Elfrida was forced to resist her urge to fly. She made muddled, curt responses to the maid's questions, not trusting herself to speak at length and unable, in her distress, even to look her thanks. Lady Wimpole, however, suffered no such difficulties, and talked on as if the maid were not even present.

"A *friend of mine*—I will spare you her name—said she was so *beleaguered* by that gentleman's heartfelt professions that she almost grew weary of the word Love. Imagine. She told me it was always *he loved her this* and *he would be lost without her* that. He loved her, he loved her, he loved her! Heavens! Would not any woman begin to wish the word tabooed?"

"If he was so taken with her," Elfrida retorted through gritted teeth, "I wonder that he did not offer for the lady."

"Oh, he would have, you enchanting girl," Lady Wimpole gave a light laugh, "only she was not free herself, at the time. Very complicated, these Society affairs. You understand. Or perhaps you do not. Where did you say your family lived?"

The maid scratched Elfrida's ankle with the needle, but she did not even notice. She kept wringing her skirts between her fingers, however, until the seamstress uttered, "Please, ma'am." Releasing the sarsenet folds, Elfrida made an apologetic sound in her throat.

"Somersetshire. What—became of the friend?" she managed, after another pause.

Lady Wimpole was playing with the clasp to her garnet bracelet, her brow smooth and untroubled. "A little absence on his part made her heart grow fonder. It is all part of the game, you see, and Mr. Tierney is a great dab at the game. I suppose my friend will wait until he has chosen his intended bride—for men like him must marry, naturally—and then she will send word that he may return and recommence the siege of love. Is that not the way of the world, Miss Hapgood? Look at my good husband, the 'Silent Saint.' We marry whom we admire, but we cannot govern where we love. We cannot rule our hearts."

At the word "admire," Elfrida jerked away, causing the hapless maid to cry, "Miss—you've torn it again! It's ruined now."

"Yes," whispered Elfrida. "Better leave it, then. It's ruined."

Heedless of her gown, the maid's surprise, or even the require-ments of etiquette, Elfrida fled. She could not put enough distance between herself and the woman she was ashamed to call a rival.

Alas.

If only she could flee as easily the woman's words.

Chapter Twenty

Once more unto the breach, dear friends, once more.
—Shakespeare, *Henry V*, III.i (1599)

Frederick Tierney had disappeared with his brother into the adjoining card room not for a hand of whist, but rather to beg his advice. As this room was peopled mainly by those too old or too infirm or too married or too dignified to dance, the appearance of the brothers attracted no more than a glance or two, and Frederick hardly needed to retreat into an alcove of potted palms as he did for privacy.

Joseph let out a low whistle when he had heard all. "I cannot believe this is the same woman who wrote you those mad, mad letters. She appears entirely in her right mind and perhaps hopes you will forget her past effusions as thoroughly as she wishes to."

"I think," Frederick answered, recalling with a shiver the fiery glance his former mistress bestowed on him when she caught his eye (he had dropped Miss Hapgood's hand in inexplicable guilt), "she has neither forgotten nor wished to, what passed between us. I will have the devil to pay tonight, and you will not let us escape while we may."

"Running away will only make you more guilty and Lady Wimpole more furious," Joseph returned. "No, I do not counsel it at all. You must speak to her, Fred, I'm afraid."

"Lady Wimpole?"

"Yes, Lady Wimpole! Whom else could I be referring to?"

"Joe—how can I, when I am neither married, as I hoped to be, or even betrothed? I wrote her that I was soon to be one or the other, and I had every intention of making that lie into a truth, only—"

Joseph had plucked a dried sprig from the palm and been turning it over in his hand, but at this speech he paused in his unconscious study. "—Only what, Fred?"

"Only Miss Hapgood would not have me," admitted his brother. "At the time. I have not abandoned all hope—"

"You *offered* for Elfrida?" demanded Joseph. "When? How? And she refused?"

"At Bramleigh, before I came. It was hasty. Both the offer and her refusal."

"You offered, after I urged you to leave her in peace?" The palm sprig fluttered to the floor.

"Yes. Sorry. I do apologize," Frederick said. "But as my intentions were honorable toward her, my disobedience to your wishes scarce gave me pause."

Joseph shook his head. "Why does that not surprise me? So—you say she refused, but you still have hope?"

"I do." The words came less easily now. "I had no intention of renewing my addresses, not after her summary refusal, but I find I—I—well—I had much rather be yoked with Miss Hapgood than any other young woman of my acquaintance."

Here his brother gave so loud a laugh that heads turned at the nearest card table. "Worry no more, Frederick. Miss Hapgood will not be able to resist a second time so passionate an avowal of love."

To Joseph's astonishment, Frederick colored. He smoothed his sleeves and plucked at the potted palm himself. "As it happens, I have not yet made Miss Hapgood an avowal of love. She seems a practical girl, with no need for scenes from a play between us. And she is, I hope, increasingly attached to me. Therefore, I have hinted at my *admiration* and thought I would try my chances again tomorrow."

"Frederick, did Miss Hapgood give a reason for her refusal, the first time?"

Another leaf of the palm fell prey to Frederick's nervous fingers. "She did. Several, in fact. But chief among them, I suppose, was her objection to what she deemed my wild manner of living in town. You see I have tried to alter that opinion of hers." He gestured at his clothing. "I've been sober as a pilgrim these past few weeks. Not only in my dress, but in my conduct. I am ready to renounce all: foppery, seasons in town, gambling—"

"Other women?" prompted Joseph.

Frederick's sigh was half a shudder. "Other women. Have not I realized that one woman is handful enough? Miss Hapgood, with her serenity and reasonableness, would not be one fraction the trouble I have found elsewhere."

"Then one last question, and I have done," Joseph said. "If we are to be brothers, twice over, the cautions and concerns of my wife weigh equally with my own. Tell me honestly, Frederick: do you love Elfrida? If you say yes, Alice and I will give our unalloyed blessing. And, for heaven's sake, quit torturing that plant."

Frederick released the mangled palm and began next with picking at a corner of the striped wallpaper. "I hardly know what the word means anymore, Joe. I have used it so lightly and so often—even with that Wimpole woman out there!—that it ceases to signify."

"It might hold no significance for you, brother," Joseph said wryly, "but I assure you Miss Hapgood would be well-pleased to have you use such a word with her. Let me put it this way—you prefer her to any other young lady you know. You enjoy her company?"

"Yes. If 'enjoy' means I would rather be in her company than anyone else's."

"You care what becomes of her? You wish to help her family for her sake?"

"Yes, yes. Though I wish her cousin Hugh Hapgood at the devil."

"You find her attractive? Alluring?"

"God, yes."

"Not only in her person, but in her character?" Joseph persevered.

"Haven't I said as much?"

"And you should hate to see her marry someone else?"

Frederick's only response was to tug the shred of wallpaper in his grasp so hard it tore, and Joseph laughed again. "Very well, very well. There is no need for vandalism. Here is my counsel then, and it is in two parts: firstly, you must ask Elfrida again *tonight* to marry you, thus winning the bride of your choice and staving off the revenge of the ferocious Lady W; and, secondly, you must certainly tell Miss Hapgood that you offer for her because you love her. In cases such as these, mere 'admiration' will never do. Elfie might be serene and practical, but she is, in the end, a woman."

"Tell her I love her," repeated Frederick blankly.

"You love her," Joseph agreed. "I assure you."

A wild, leaping look came into Frederick's eyes and his breath quickened. He loved Miss Hapgood? These dizzy heights and bottomless lows, the sensations of terror and restlessness that alternated with surges of hope and sleepier periods of contentment—this was love!

"I will—I will find her straightaway," he blurted. "But where—I can hardly renew my addresses in a card room, and still less in an assembly hall, under my former mistress' baleful watch."

"Alice and I discovered a little balcony leading off the bottom of the room, with stairs down to a pretty sort of walk. You had better do it there, Frederick. Ah! There is my wife now, looking for me. I will have her deliver Elfrida to you."

Without any memory of how he came to be there, Frederick found himself pacing a torch-lit graveled path between hedges. If it was indeed a pretty walk, he didn't notice, but it must have been so, for a few other couples wandered its length. He drew a handkerchief from his pocket and mopped his brow. When she came, he would say—he did not know what he would say. He would say, *Miss Hapgood, you must have guessed that my feelings for you have continued to deepen, and I have dared to hope that—*

"Frederick, dearest!"

For an instant he thought his fumbling words would not even be necessary. She had come to him and intimated, even from the summons, what he intended. All that remained was to press her to him—

But it was not Miss Hapgood before him, her face in shadows as the light spilled from the balcony at her back. This woman had auburn hair and garnets about her neck and wrist. She rushed at him, even as he imagined Miss Hapgood might, and he stiffened, thinking he would have to fend her off.

Lady Wimpole stopped short, however, her silken skirts rustling about her. "I cannot greet you as I would wish, Frederick, even after so long a separation," she mourned. "Who can say what tale-bearers surround us, and Rodney—Rodney is inside with that blockhead Risborough. Suffice to say, it has been an *eternity*, my love. And we might have been even longer apart, had I not convinced Rodney that his ridiculous summer progress must encompass Buckinghamshire. Where were you yesterday, say? We went—I with my heart in my throat—to your uncle Sir Crispin's House Day. Tedious Day, I should call it, rather, without my—"

"Lady Wimpole," choked Frederick, peering over her shoulder with rising panic. He must send her away quickly, or take her where they would not be seen when Miss Hapgood emerged. Seizing her hand, he pulled her onto the grass directly below the balcony.

"Darling!" she cried, now losing no opportunity to throw her arms around his neck. "How can you be so formal? Say Honoria, my love."

"Honoria," he grated. As gently as his urgency allowed, he detached himself from her.

"How cold your letter was," she reproached him, still keeping one gloved hand upon his sleeve. The garnets glittered upon her wrist. "But I told myself that your sense of duty made it so. You spoke of marrying. Very well. All our kind must, naturally. But not a word did you spare to temper your cruelty—to say what it would cost you to be apart from me, even for a time."

"Honoria," he began again, more firmly this time. "To 'spare' such a word, as you put it, would have been more cruel. It would have been deceitful. Because we must, in truth, put our time together behind us. You are married. I hope soon to be married—"

"To that blonde doll you were standing up with, the one with the vacant eyes?" she cut in.

Much as he disliked hearing Miss Hapgood thus described, he knew better than to be lured in. "Our moment has passed, Honoria," Frederick said with finality. "You are a beautiful, witty, ardent woman. I am grateful for our time together"—he permitted himself this small lie—"and wish nothing but your future happiness. "

"Do you, Frederick?"

"Sincerely."

"And you can spout such nonsense to me, in such a voice, after what has passed between us?"

"Honoria, I have said nothing now that I did not already say when we parted in June, or in the letter that I sent you since. You must forgive me if the repetition of it begins to make it sound rote."

"Then you no longer love me."

Wincing, he felt a new wave of heat break out on his forehead. Why, in the name of all that was holy, must he be pressed to apply this word to this woman once again—now, when he had finally learnt its true meaning? Even if he had been able, he would not. Not when Miss Hapgood might chance upon them at any instant. No. That word would never cross his lips again, Frederick vowed silently, until he spoke it to *her*.

She must have sensed his resistance.

For an instant there was a flash in her eyes that made him think she prepared again for an attack. But as he observed it warily, he saw it waver. Dilute in a gleam that might have been tears. He watched Lady Wimpole retreat into herself and gather her dignity about her like a shawl. She smoothed her gloves, touched the beads in her elaborately dressed hair.

Frederick felt the familiar self-reproach for causing pain to a woman, but he was obligated to suppress a sigh of relief as he added, "We are friends, I hope. Not enemies."

She took a moment to master her voice. She had pleaded and threatened to no avail, sacrificing what remained of her pride. There was nothing left but retreat—and the hope that he would suffer heartbreak one day, at another's hands, if not her own. That she had broken the *girl's* heart she was certain; whether the damage would reach him remained to be seen.

When she could speak she whispered, "Never enemies, Frederick." Pulling his unresisting form close, she pressed her lips to his. "This is good-bye then."

"Good-bye."

Her mouth curved in a bitter smile, and she gave a soft "ah" before turning to go. He suspected the woman might vacillate again the next day and shoot off another flaming bolt of accusation, but for the moment she was resigned. And, *Deo volente*, by the next day the question would be moot.

In another moment he was alone, his last memory of his former lover being the sound of her slippered feet padding swiftly up the steps and across the terrace.

Frederick took a rapid survey of the scene and exhaled in relief. Miss Hapgood was nowhere about, and the other couples crunching along the gravel were not even turned his direction. Hastening back to the path, he scraped the grass from his boots and looked up at the balcony expectantly. How long could it take Alice to fetch her sister? Even if Miss Hapgood had been standing up with some rustic, surely the dance must be ending soon. Of course, Frederick had laid claim to her for the supper dance, but he would prefer to have things settled before then.

He drummed his fingers along his thigh. The music spilling from the open doors gave way to soft applause. *Now,* he told himself. *Let her come now.*

As if he had conjured them, people began to emerge from the hall, laughing and chattering. Frederick scanned their faces, but saw no sign of the only person who interested him. Which must explain why he failed even to pick out his brother Joseph until the latter called down the steps to him.

"Fred."

Frederick raised his palms questioningly.

"She isn't coming, Frederick." Joseph hurried down to stand beside him. His brow was furrowed. "Alice is having my uncle's carriage called. Elfie has the headache, apparently."

"Miss Hapgood is unwell?"

"I suppose. Alice thinks—"

"What does Alice think?"

Joseph ran a hand through his brown curls and shrugged. "Alice thinks something has happened to upset her sister because she says Elfrida is too flustered for a mere headache. She says when Elfie has a headache, she is usually more inclined to turn white and suffer in silence."

"That, I can imagine," said Frederick. A dread suspicion roused in his breast. "Has Miss Hapgood been within doors this entire time? I did not see her come out here."

Joseph dismissed this. "Oh, yes. Alice found her beside the refreshments, drinking glass after glass of orgeat. Perhaps she really has the headache."

If Miss Hapgood had not ventured out, she could not have seen or overheard him with Lady Wimpole. He was safe there. And, given Lady Wimpole's presence at the assembly, Frederick would like nothing better than to depart early—Miss Hapgood's headache was convenient indeed. He would not like her to be truly unwell, of course, but a well-timed headache was in this case a blessing.

"I am afraid you will have to put off your addresses until tomorrow after all, Frederick," his brother said.

"Very well," he agreed, trying not to sound too cheerful. "I should like Miss Hapgood to be feeling as well as she possibly can when I ask her, in any event. Who knows if even words of love can overcome the crossness caused by a pounding head?"

Miss Hapgood neither looked at him nor thanked him when he handed her into Sir Crispin's coach. The squeeze he gave her hand before releasing it was not acknowledged. Frederick thought she did appear paler and drawn, but that might have been the moonlight bathing her. When all of them were seated and the coach creaked into motion, he ventured to say, "I am sorry to hear you are unwell, Miss Hapgood, and hope the headache may pass off quickly, with rest."

"Yes."

In consideration for her, the ride home proceeded in silence. It was only when the carriage struck a rut in the road and bounced Alice almost into Elfrida's lap that anyone spoke.

"Did you hit your head, love?"

"I think the coachman might have had one cup too many of sack."

"I'm all right, Joseph. Oh, but Elfie—what has happened to your gown? I did not do that, did I? The lace is all torn from the hem."

"It must have been some clodhopping ploughman, treading upon you as he cast round," teased Frederick.

"It was a lady," Elfrida murmured, her gaze fixed out the window. "And I rather think she did it on set purpose."

"A lady trod upon your hem?" asked Alice. "A clumsy one, I should say. She might at least have called someone to help you stitch it back up."

"She did. I could not wait for it, however."

Something in her sister's tone silenced the questions rising to Alice's lips. Here was the mystery, then, behind Elfrida's sudden desire to leave. Glancing at her husband, Alice saw he was looking in turn at Frederick, his eyebrows raised. And Frederick—Frederick was staring at Elfrida, with something like apprehension on his face.

"What—what did this lady look like?" Frederick stammered. "Were you—we—acquainted with her?"

"*I* was not acquainted with her," was Elfrida's only reply. "Though she seemed well known to others." She shook out her skirts where Alice had crumpled them and folded her hands in her lap.

"Well—whoever she was—fortunately you are so very good with your needle," Alice put in, her voice higher than usual. She had no idea why her brother-in-law was suddenly so nervous, or Elfie so ruthlessly composed, but she had her fears. "If anyone had trodden upon my hem, the damage would have been irreparable."

"I can repair the dress," Elfrida agreed. "A simple matter, with needle and thread. You are right, Alice. There has been no lasting damage done."

Silence fell again, and Alice could not help feeling that, Elfie's declaration notwithstanding, something had indeed suffered lasting damage that night. A fragile something, a something not yet put into words, which now lay broken beyond repair.

Chapter Twenty-One

**The great Gulph between You and Me
cools all News that come hither.**
—Lady Mary Wortley Montagu, *Letters* (1717)

Sir Crispin Tierney was unpleasantly surprised to find the breakfast room occupied when he entered the following morning. Even more alarming, the occupant was the person he knew least and feared most of his guests, the beautiful sister of his niece.

The baronet shuffled at the doorway and gave a tentative clearing of his throat, but as the young lady was occupied in reading a letter, he was forced to rattle the lid of the chafing dish.

"Ah, Sir Crispin, good morning," cried the young lady. "You find me here alone. I believe Joseph and Alice are already out of doors, gathering some last-minute specimens before we depart. You have been so hospitable."

In the furtive glance he threw her, he was alarmed to see her eyes were rather heavy and her complexion pale, and he sat as far from her as the table allowed, careful that the arrangement of flower and fruit should block their vision of each other. "The—uh—assembly. Was all right?" he muttered.

"Delightful," she answered. Her saucer rattled as she replaced her tea cup. "But better than that, Mrs. Tierney has forwarded me a letter from my sister. The news is all good, Sir Crispin. You see, my father has been ill, but now Margaret said he is almost himself again. He went riding and spent time among his hounds, which will cure him more completely than any other remedy, I am sure."

"Er," said Sir Crispin. He did not bother to butter his toast but hastened to take a bite.

"Margaret—my younger sister, you know—goes on to say that my uncle Alec Arbuthnot has caught a miserable summer cold, moreover, which can only add to my father's well-being."

"You don't say." Loading a forkful of kippers, he jammed it in his mouth.

"My uncle—uncles, I should say, for his brother Alwyn is little better—have often caused my father anxiety," Elfrida explained. She did not know why she should burden the baronet with this information when he clearly wished her to be silent, but she could not help herself. Her tired mind was energized by Margaret's letter, and in her restlessness she latched on to the news it contained as a way out of her own troubles. She must go home. Not in three weeks, as Mrs. Tierney requested, but immediately. *Today*. Or, if that were impossible, the next day.

"My uncles' spendthrift and ne'er-do-well ways have worried my father," she repeated. "I wish they might stand on their own two feet. I wish they might bear the consequences of their actions. They ought to. Everyone ought to. Bear the consequences of his own actions, I mean."

"Mm. Yes." The poor man stooped a little lower, that the pineapple would line up with Miss Hapgood's head and thwart further conversation. "Is—is my nephew Frederick up and about yet?" Perhaps Frederick might come into the breakfast room and endure these confidences instead.

The mention of Mr. Tierney's name sent an unpleasant jolt through Elfrida, and she hurried on, hardly knowing what she was saying. "My father has been rescuing my uncles from their scrapes as long as I can remember, but it must stop now. Papa is not as young or as healthy as he used to be. It must stop. Uncle Alec must be told to solve his own problems. I will tell him so. I will *make certain* it is so. Yes. And Mrs. Todd will not remain in Buckinghamshire to cause distress any longer."

Sir Crispin had no idea who Mrs. Todd should be, but she was not the only one he hoped would remain no longer in Buckinghamshire to cause distress. Blowing his nose in his napkin, he emerged to find Miss Hapgood rising from her seat, and Sir Crispin was forced to jump up as well.

Elfrida pushed her dishes away and folded up her letter. "That is not all Margaret writes, Sir Crispin. It seems my cousin Hugh has found schools for the children. I would rather they not be sent away. Not even Hetty."

"Not Hetty," echoed the baronet woodenly.

She clasped the letter against her bosom as if someone might snatch it from her. "You understand. I pray you will excuse me, Sir Crispin."

"Please, please!" he urged. "You have much on your mind."

"Yes. I must write back right away. I find I cannot bear to be from home any longer. Even if the news be good, the distance between us..." She found her throat closing.

"Yes, by all means, Miss Ha—Miss Harwell. Only have your letter be given to Tuck and he will post it straight away." And then, to his horror, tears welled up in the girl's eyes and she flew at him just as her sister was wont, pressing a hasty kiss to his dry cheek and fleeing the room.

An hour afterward, Tuck was off to the post with not one but two letters, and three hours afterward the Tierneys and Elfrida had taken leave of Sir Crispin and departed on their return to Stone Halt. It was a fine day. The beginnings of autumn's crispness had chilled the morning, but that was all forgotten in the afternoon's warmth. As the landau was considerably more crowded on this journey, Joseph and Alice's replacement specimens now packed in boxes at their feet, Frederick elected to ride alongside and let Joseph drive the ladies. One glance at Miss Hapgood's drawn, still face assured him that, whatever passed in her encounter with Honoria, it had not been forgotten overnight.

He wondered if his own face was as pallid as hers, because he had lain staring at the canopy of his bed as the hours chimed, cursing circumstances and the timing of it all. If he had not been so bent on showing Miss Hapgood all that he was heir to—if they had remained safely at Stone Halt—he did not think he overreached in imagining she would have accepted him. Or if they had stayed safely at Halton End and not ventured out to the public assembly. Or if the Wimpoles' summer progress had not brought them to this corner of Buckinghamshire at this precise time. Or if he had only not decamped from the hall to the card room—Honoria would never have dared accost Miss Hapgood with him standing watch.

There was no use proposing to her again in this mood of hers. Scowling, Frederick flapped the reins irritably across Mignonne, and she flicked back questioning ears. No. He must wait. Let time pass. Regain Miss Hapgood's trust and good opinion. Let Honoria's scratches heal—but he would have Joseph ply his wife for information, that Frederick might know exactly what was said between the women, and how he might best go about remedying it.

He had only himself to blame, he supposed. Chaucer might say, *Murder will out*, but Frederick would add that Illicit Passions showed much the same tendency.

The sound of Miss Hapgood speaking roused him from these unhappy meditations.

"...I have already written to say I will return, after Mrs. Todd and I visit my uncle in town."

"But what can you be thinking, Elfie?" Alice demanded. "Mrs. Todd has only just got here, and I thought the whole plan was to hide her away in the country."

"You cannot make me believe you find her satisfactory as a servant, Alice."

"Of course not! She's dreadful. Only look at what she did to Joseph's study! But that doesn't mean you can take her back to my uncle!"

"And why should I not?" Elfrida countered, the first color touching her cheeks. "We have spent too long taking care of Alec and Alwyn. Why must it always be Papa who pays the price for their indiscretions? You see at what hazard he has done so. Mama ought not to allow it, but Mama will never resist her brothers, so I will do it."

"But—but—" Alice let tumble from her numb hands the jar containing a streaked moth, and it struck a box and rolled around at their feet before she could scramble after it. Peering through the glass to ensure she hadn't killed it, she tucked the jar away beside her and turned back to her sister. "But supposing you drop Mrs. Todd back with my uncle, Elfie. What is to prevent her from spreading scandal far and wide? Will that not cause Papa grief as well?"

"Have you not noticed, Alice? It is only by the grace of God that everyone in Buckinghamshire does not already know Kitty Todd's true story. I say, let her broadcast her tale in London. It cannot harm you here, where you are already married, and by the time Margaret and Alice are of age, the story will be shrouded in cobwebs."

"But what of *you*, Elfie?" Alice persisted. "Would not my uncle's conduct harm your prospects?" Here she could not help stealing a glance at her brother-in-law Frederick, whose head had turned several degrees toward them.

Elfrida tightened the bow of her bonnet beneath her chin. "It will not matter to me, either."

"Of course not," Alice came about suddenly. "Because, if a man loves you, he will care nothing for the misconduct of your relations. You would still have married me," she called to her husband's back, "wouldn't you have, Joseph, no matter how many bastard children my uncles fathered?"

He looked back with a grin. "My dear girl, your own misconduct quite overshadowed what any of your family might be guilty of." He, too, glanced Frederickward at this point, but not so swiftly that Elfrida did not catch the motion. "But you are right," Joseph went on. "No man who truly loved a woman would be put off by a little taint of scandal."

"I know nothing of love," Elfrida said, a thread of steel entering her voice, "but the whole case is moot because I am already betrothed. To one who knows all."

Alice gasped and clapped her hands together, lurching up in the landau to pound her husband joyfully on the back and to wave at Frederick. The moth in its jar rolled off the seat to pitch around again. "How wonderful!" she hollered. "How too wonderful! But why did you two say nothing? Joseph and I rejoice at this, do we not?"

"You've been a sly one, Fred," Joseph said to his brother. "Allie and I worried that—"

"There is no cause to congratulate Mr. Tierney," Elfrida broke in coolly. "I speak of my own betrothal—not his."

"But—but—" sputtered Alice for the second time, dropping back into her seat beside Elfrida with a bump. "But are they not one and the same?"

To this question Elfrida made no reply, although her throat worked and she bit the inside of her cheek. No reply was necessary. Joseph and Alice had only to witness Frederick's ashen countenance and death grip on Mignonne's reins to have their answer.

For several minutes there was nothing but the steady clopping of the horses, the creak and rattle of the carriage, and the unnatural silence of its occupants. But when they had passed the crossing of the Aylesbury road, Frederick uttered abruptly, "I congratulate you, Miss Hapgood." Touching the brim of his beaver hat, he saluted her, a frightening hardness in his eyes that she fortunately would not have been able to discern at that distance, even if she had the courage to look up, which she did not.

"You will forgive me, Joseph, Alice. Miss Hapgood," he went on in the same muted manner. "I will see you again at Stone Halt. I find I cannot hold my horse to this pace." And, digging his heels most discourteously into Mignonne, he was off in a clatter of hooves.

Joseph let out a heavy sigh. He would gladly have followed Frederick—not to comfort him—Frederick was not a person one comforted—but to show his sympathy in wordless companionship. As it was, he let his brother put distance between them and tried his best to be invisible, that the sisters might converse.

"You have decided to accept our cousin Hugh Hapgood," accused Alice, when she had mastered her voice.

"I have already accepted him. I wrote so today."

"Oh, Elfie!" whispered her sister, throwing her arms about her. "It cannot be. You do not love him."

"I do not *not* love him," Elfrida retorted in an equally low tone, submitting stiffly to the embrace. "Cousin Hugh is a well-meaning, respectable, kindly gentleman. His income makes him independent, and his future fortunes are tied to our own. I already begin to love the children. Perhaps I can persuade him not to send them away. I could hardly do better than this match."

Alice only shook her head and buried her face in Elfrida's shoulder, heedless of her own bonnet, which fell off and hung by its ribbons. "You mean you could hardly do worse. I hate to see it, Elfie. There! I admit it. I hate to see it. And I hate Cousin Hugh and wish he had never come to Bramleigh with his good intentions. Why can you not love the children without becoming their mother?"

"Shhh...it's all right, Alice."

"It's not! It is not the least bit all right. Because not only do you not love Cousin Hugh, but you love somebody else! You love Frederick. I know it. I have not been your sister for eighteen years without gaining some insight into your heart—"

"You *hush*!" hissed Elfrida, pushing her sister away and raising a significant eyebrow to remind Alice of Joseph's presence.

But Alice refused to hush. "Joseph can hear this, Elfie. We have already discussed it. We neither of us wanted you to care for Frederick at first because he has been such a sad rapscallion, but only see how his feelings for you have amended his character and conduct! His love for you has made him a new man. No—don't turn away—I say his love for you. Why should you take such sudden, heedless action?"

"It is not heedless," Elfrida insisted. "On the contrary. I have deferred my duty too long."

"But Papa is himself again, or nearly! You need not marry Cousin Hugh now. You might wait and see if you prefer someone else," pleaded her sister. "It need not be Frederick, if you are so obstinate. But someone like Frederick—someone you can love without being compelled to."

Not trusting herself to speak further, Elfrida only shook her head and leaned down to rescue the moth in its jar. It was too late, it appeared. All the tumbling and jostling and rolling about at their feet had been too much for it, and it lay upside down at the bottom, perfectly still, the pretty streaks of its wings hidden from view.

An hour later, the landau reached the house at Stone Halt. The first to greet the party was none other than Mrs. Todd, who bounded down the steps, her arms a-flutter.

"Miss Hapgood, we are to return to London, then?" she hallooed, despite the nearby footmen and the coachman hurrying forward.

"What—are you doing here?" Elfrida asked, nodding her thanks at the footman when he handed her out. "Why are you not at the parsonage?"

"Oh, I was," said Mrs. Todd as she bobbed a heavy curtsey. "But Mr. T rode up and wanted a word with me, and next thing I know, I'm to pack my bags again and come back to the big house."

"Can you mean Mr. *Walter* Tierney?" Elfrida was all confusion. She knew Walter and Evelyn Tierney disapproved of Mrs. Todd as a servant for their clergyman son, but she thought it unlikely they would make such a high-handed decision without first consulting Joseph. But the alternative—that Mr. Frederick Tierney should, in his eagerness to be quit of her, take matters thus in his own hands...

"Not he," said Mrs. Todd stoutly. "To be sure I meant the handsome *young* Mr. T. We've come to an understanding, we have. But not a word more on it"—she tapped her nose—"be assured, though, Miss, I'll be happy to accompany you *back to town* tomorrow morning. See my beloved pappy again. But whisht! Not a word more. There he is."

Elfrida glared up to the house, where a tall figure loomed in the open door. Not bothering to take leave of Alice and Joseph, she marched up the stone steps, blood pumping, letting the hot words spill from her lips. "How dare you! I do not recall asking your assistance in engineering a plan."

"Miss?" croaked the man at the door.

Eyes widening, Elfrida faltered as she reached the porch, the man before her, in his solemn black coat and buff breeches being not Mr. Frederick Tierney at all, but rather Mr. Walter Tierney's steward. He had no hair at all on his head, and she could not imagine how she mistook him. She would have herself fitted for spectacles the instant she was at Bramleigh again, if she had to steal from the church box to make it happen. She would! "Excuse me. Forgive me. I thought you were—that is, I was looking for Mr. Frederick Tierney."

The steward only gave her a wondering look and gestured to the golden head poking from the study window.

"Were those dulcet tones summoning me?" drawled Mr. Tierney.

Dropping a mortified and apologetic curtsey to the steward, Elfrida hurried past him into the house, stepping into the study to confront her actual nemesis while her anger was high.

Mr. Tierney shut the casement and turned to face her, taking a seat upon the sill. "Whatever can be the matter, Miss Hapgood? You appear all of a fluster, and you quite terrified Mr. Langley."

"I want to know what you mean by withdrawing Mrs. Todd from the parsonage before I have spoken with her, and then having the nerve to determine when she and I will set out!"

He gave an elaborate shrug. "I only thought to save you difficulty. You know I have a way with the impossible woman—who better than I, to convince her of the absolute rightness of abandoning this foolish plan to enter service? As for setting out tomorrow, why, forgive me if I supposed you would want to settle matters as soon as possible. You have ever been a practical young lady, and I guessed you might be eager to relieve yourself of Mrs. Todd and regain the bosom of your family."

While she could not in honesty contradict any of this, his presumption in managing her affairs rankled. "That's as may be," Elfrida conceded, "but I'll thank you to let me make my own plans and communicate them."

"Certainly, certainly, in future," he agreed amiably. He gave the globe beside him a spin, trailing a finger along the Tropic of Cancer. "You are of age, of course?"

"What? What has that to do with anything? I am not...yet...but I have been the female head of household at Bramleigh since I was twelve—my mother being frequently invalided. I am perfectly capable of—"

"Just as I thought," he interrupted, studying her closely. "Not yet one-and-twenty."

"I fail to see what my age has to do with this discussion, Mr. Tierney."

"Everything, I'm afraid. Would you care to sit down? My father's chairs are quite comfortable. No? Very well. I too will remain standing, then, to maintain my advantage of height. You see, Miss Hapgood, twenty is quite young. Young enough to make impulsive decisions one might later regret. Decisions like *marrying for spite*."

He delivered the last part of his speech without raising his voice, but the words struck her with the force of a lash. Before she could recover, he closed the space between them, and, though he did not touch her, it seemed to Elfrida the very sliver of air between them hummed with heat and electricity.

"I am not marrying for spite," she said weakly. She wished she could back away from him, but he must not think her faint.

"What did Lady Wimpole say to you last night?" he uttered, so low it felt more like his thoughts pressing upon her own.

"Nothing of consequence." She shut her eyes, as if that might close him out. He smelled of summer sunshine and horse and sweat.

"Whatever it was," he persisted, "it was enough of a nothing that you and I have lost the understanding I thought we shared these past many days."

"There was no understanding," Elfrida lied. She turned from him and walked away, on the pretense of examining Mr. Walter Tierney's bookcases. Taking a volume down, she caressed the leather binding absently. "How often we have bandied that word about, Mr. Tierney. We have never had an understanding of what the other meant by 'understanding.'"

"Did she say she and I were lovers?" Frederick demanded to her back, ignoring her attempts at raillery. "We were. I do not deny it. You have known of my...irregular past already. If I might remind you, it was the reason you refused me some weeks ago. But the past is precisely that—the past. And it seemed to me"—he hesitated—swallowed—"it seemed to me you had begun to forgive me and find me acceptable."

She had. She could not deny it, but nor could she give voice to Lady Wimpole's further painful confidences: that Mr. Tierney yet besieged her with constant professions of love; that the two of them continued to correspond; that he meant to continue their liaison once he married and did his duties as a son and heir.

"Elfrida."

"I did not give you permission to call me that," she whispered, thrusting the book back on its shelf, grateful her skirts hid her trembling limbs.

"Before Lady Wimpole's inopportune appearance, I was on the point of renewing my addresses to you," he went on, low, urgent. "You must have realized this. I made no secret of how I admire you—"

There it was again! His infuriating "admiration"!

"—but I hesitated to call my feelings for you by another name. In short, Elf—Miss Hapgood, rather—I ask you not to marry your esteemed cousin. I ask you to marry me—because I—er—I—love—you." Frederick found that, the word, when required to be spoken with genuineness, was not altogether easy to produce. It seemed to stick in the gorge, then lurch forth without warning, dropping into the quiet air of his father's study with all the subtlety of a boulder smashing a china basin. No sooner was it said than he turned all-over crimson. The next instant, the blood drained from his upper half, leaving him white as paper.

But his rapid color variations in pronouncing the word were as nothing, compared to Elfrida's reaction on hearing it.

This? He said this now?

A mere day ago she would have wept tears of joy to hear him. A mere day ago she would have marveled at the contrast between this offer and his previous one. A mere day ago she would have flung herself at him and declared he might call her anything he pleased, so long as he did love her, and not just "admire" her. Feeble, pallid, ineffectual "admiration"!

But now, this day, she could not hear him speak that long-awaited word without remembering Lady Wimpole's poisonous complaint: *She told me it was always* he loved her this *and* he would be lost without her that. *He loved her, he loved her, he loved her! Heavens! Would not any woman begin to wish the word tabooed?*

Revolving to face him, Elfrida's usually mild blue eyes flashed arctic fire. Frederick started and even retreated a step.

"I will *not* marry you, Mr. Tierney," she declared, the words bursting from her. "I am already betrothed to my cousin, and I intend to keep my word because my words still have meaning. I do not toss them about or use them for my convenience. It is wrong of you to make me declarations of love—altogether wrong. I beg you will never do so again."

Why, the woman was glorious! If her sister Edith were to see her now, she would paint Miss Hapgood as an avenging angel on Judgment Day. (That Frederick himself felt like a soul cringing before the angel's wrath did not detract from his appreciation.) Moreover, some remarkable transformation was taking place within him. Having produced the all-powerful word once, he could not—would not—suppress the urge to speak it again, even if it should provoke Miss Hapgood to spontaneously combust.

"I must disoblige you straight away, my dearest love," he breathed, approaching her again, though he half felt he should cover his eyes from the brightness of her. "Because I find I do love you. Love you entirely. Love you—"

Scurrying to put the desk between them, Elfrida shrilled, "How dare you! Stop saying that—"

"—with every ounce of my heart's blood, my darling—"

"I will not stay to hear this!"

He made a lunge to capture her and she darted away. "—Love you and wish past hope that you love me in return." Another rush at her, and Elfrida escaped to the door.

Grasping the filigree door knob, she made to turn it.

"Tell me you don't love me," he called. "Your words still have meaning, you declare. Then say you don't love me, and you may go."

Certain that her feelings must be written on her countenance, and not in command of herself enough to lie, she could only gasp out, "You, sir, have not the power to prevent me."

With her defenses in ruins about her, she escaped. And if some willful, rebellious fraction of her wished he might pursue her, call her back, it received the punishment it deserved. Because Frederick did neither.

He let her go.

Chapter Twenty-Two

It is difficult to determine whether (in the fashionable

Vices) the fine Gentlemen imitate

the Gentlemen of the Road,

or the Gentlemen of the Road the fine Gentlemen.

—John Gay, *The Beggar's Opera*, iii. xvi. 75 (1728)

"Nice to travel in style, innit, Miss?" sighed Kitty Todd happily. "So kind and thoughtful of the family to lend us their coach. Beats traveling post. Especially nice, considering how Mrs. Tierney looked fit to cry with us leaving so suddenly. Spanking pace Terrence and Orkins are setting, but you wouldn't hardly know it, with how well-sprung this coach is. Hope you don't mind if I lower the shades—might keep it a little cooler in here."

Elfrida hardly cared what the woman did. She only wanted to be alone with her own thoughts until she could be rid of the voluble

Mrs. Todd, and the best way she could think of accomplishing this was to rest her head against the seat cushions and pretend to doze off. Not that her own thoughts provided much solace. The last twenty-four hours were a painful blur, from her encounter with Mr. Tierney, to the explanations and excuses and apologies to be made to his parents, to the tearful leave-taking with Alice, to the flurry of packing. But it would all be over soon. She would restore Mrs. Todd to her uncle's care where she belonged and return to Somerset, accompanied by a servant Uncle Alec would have to provide. Once there, she would treasure up every last minute at home before marriage to Mr. Hugh Hapgood took her off to her new life in Crawley, Sussex.

Two hours had passed before the coach made its first stop to change horses and Orkins assisted Elfrida down. Blinking, she took in the unfamiliar inn yard and crossroads. It was not the same one the mail coach had frequented on its route out of town, but that was hardly surprising, as this was a private coach. Nor could she see make out much past the immediately neighboring buildings, but Elfrida had no reason to suppose they were not in Uxbridge as she picked at her cold nuncheon. Orkins trundled her back into the coach, Mrs. Todd resumed her place and her monologues, and they set off once more.

"I forgot to ask Terrence," Elfrida said, after another hour, interrupting Mrs. Todd's complaints against the Tierneys' housekeeper Lloyd, "when he thought we might reach Ealing?"

"Ealing?" Mrs. Todd's eyes widened. "Oh, not to worry, Miss. He said it might be some time. Traffic will get heavier, the closer we are to London, you know."

Raising the blind nearest her, Elfrida peered out. "I daresay traffic could hardly get lighter, in any case." They appeared to be one of the very few vehicles on the road. She studied the soft rural landscape for a minute, squinting, in a vain attempt to bring its features into sharpness, before sitting back with a frown. "Isn't that peculiar."

"What, Miss?" Mrs. Todd shifted in her seat and snapped the blind down again.

"The sun," Elfrida replied. "We are going east, and the sun should be above and slightly behind and to the south of us at this time of day, and yet I glimpsed it from my window, which would put it to the north of us."

"What?" said Mrs. Todd again, waving off this information. "Compasses and the like. Never could make much sense of them. But I'm sure you're mistaken, Miss, begging your pardon. As if Terrence and Orkins couldn't find London, when every signpost in the kingdom points you there!"

Before Elfie could protest this cavalier dismissal of her concerns, the coach swayed suddenly, tossing her against its padded walls. Terrence and Orkins gave great cries and shouts and, with a groaning and rattling of parts and whuffling protests from the horses, the carriage jerked to a halt.

"What can it mean?" breathed Elfrida. Reaching for the latch of the door, she was thrust peremptorily back into her seat by Mrs. Todd.

"It's highwaymen, Miss! I know it! You mustn't stir from here. Leave us to handle the matter. I've seen all kinds in Shoreditch. Hide your jewels!" She made to spring out, only to have Elfrida thrust a leg before the door.

"You fool," she hissed. "I haven't any jewels to hide, and I am not going to let you go out there by yourself. You have your child to think of."

"That's it, Miss. I'll plead my poor babe and see if they'll let us go." Seizing Elfrida's parasol and shoving the young lady's foot aside with the coach door, Mrs. Todd valiantly sallied forth. A series of clunks outside told Elfie that her parasol was being jammed through the door handle to fix it shut.

"Mrs. Todd! Mrs. Todd!" called Elfrida, hammering on the door. Finding herself ignored, she twitched aside the blind and peeped out, certain she would see caped and hooded gentlemen of the road surrounding the coach, pistols pressed to the heads of the servants.

No one was in view.

Setting the coach rocking, Elfrida flung herself across it to peer out the other window.

No one!

Breathlessly, she sat back, trying to gather her wits despite her hammering heart. Had the brigands already dispatched the servants without a sound? Gagged and bound them and thrown them in the ditch? How they might have done so without a peep from the loquacious Mrs. Todd was nothing short of miraculous!

The silence unnerved her. Would they approach the coach door the next instant? She dug in her reticule for a weapon, any sort of weapon, but the small beaded bag contained only discarded black ribbons, a spare pair of gloves, and a scanty store of half-crowns, shillings, and various pence. Well, the highwaymen were welcome to whatever they liked of her possessions, but she feared her relative poverty would provoke them. The Tierneys' coach was a fine one, and the robbers must be expecting a rich haul. When they turned her out and discovered but a few coins—!

She shut her eyes and muffled a groan. They would take vengeance for their disappointment on her person, and she could not—a woman alone—do anything to stop them. *Imagine refusing Mr. Tierney because he did not meet your high-and-mighty moral standards,* jeered a voice in her head, *only to be victimized and put beyond the pale yourself!*

Mr. Tierney.

The thought of him brought her up short, and she felt another emotion pierce the fog of her fear. If she were never to see him again..?

If she had not been such a jealous—yes, jealous—fool, she would never be in this situation! She might have been sitting even now beside him, her hand in his, as their family rejoiced with them. But her pride and stubbornness had led her to this pass—she had thrown away her chance with the man she loved, and what would become of her now was anyone's guess. If these highwaymen attacked her—ruined her—would even Cousin Hugh marry her when it was all over, if she still lived?

Clasping her hands together, Elfrida sent up a hasty, bargaining prayer: "Dear Lord, only deliver me from this situation—let me not be ruined—and I will give my dowry to you. Entirely. To Joseph's church—if my husband will allow me. And, if possible, could that husband be Mr. Frederick Tierney after all?" She did not see how it could, since she had already twice refused him and had now given her word to marry Hugh Hapgood, but she thought if God were in the mood to grant miracles, it could make little difference to Him whether He were to grant two, rather than one.

A rattle at the door handle startled her from her reflections. Shrinking back in the farthest corner of the coach, Elfrida had wild visions of kicking and scratching and screaming, but before she had decided on any of these, the door flung open, and there stood Mrs. Todd, flushed and eager.

"What has happened?" cried Elfrida. "Are you hurt? Have they gone? Where are Terrence and Orkins?"

"That was right terrifying, Miss!" Clambering in, Mrs. Todd clutched her chest with one hand and laid the other to her brow. "Terrence and Orkins have been sent on their way *at gunpoint*, that is, and you and I are now hostages!" Just as she delivered this pronouncement, there was another series of clunks outside the carriage to the door handle.

Elfrida's hands flew to cover her mouth, but no leering bandit face appeared.

"That'll be him, locking us in," explained Mrs. Todd. "If I could borrow your smelling salts, Miss, I feel that faint."

Before Elfrida could tell her that she never carried hartshorn, her ears caught the sound of footsteps alongside the coach and the creaking of wood and leather as someone swung himself up into the seat. A snap of the harness, and the coach rumbled into motion again, soon setting a pace even more "spanking" than Terrence's.

"Who is out there, Mrs. Todd?" Elfrida whispered. "And how many of them are there? Where are they taking us? How was all this effected in silence?"

But the unsatisfactory Mrs. Todd was now lying across the rear-facing seat, fanning herself with a handkerchief and moaning inarticulately.

"Stop that at once!" ordered Elfrida, slapping at the woman's hands and cheek to rouse her, even as the motion of the vehicle threatened to land her atop Mrs. Todd. "You may not give way to this weakness until you explain to me what has happened."

"Here," said Mrs. Todd. Without opening her eyes, she thrust a crumpled note at her. "He gave that to me, the—er—ringleader. I don't know what it says—I can't read a word. Not even my own name. Terrence and Orkins couldn't neither. The fellow had to pantymime what he wanted us to do."

Bewildered, Elfrida raised one of the blinds, smoothed out the sheet and held it right up to her chin. She trusted Mrs. Todd was too overcome by nerves to notice anyone's shortsightedness, though it hardly mattered now, in any event.

Begging your pardon, you are hereby given notice that you have been taken hostage, to be held until a certain ransom is paid. My men accompany your attendants back to your kinfolk, to inform them of this situation.

If you keep quiet and do not try to escape, you will not be harmed.

McElroy the Mute

The first two times she read it, the note made so little sense to her troubled mind that Elfrida might as well have been as unlettered as the servants. "Begging her pardon"? "Hostage"? "Ransom"? "Kinfolk"? "You will not be harmed"? *"McElroy the Mute"*? By the third time through, however, pieces began to fall into place.

"We are hostages, and this villain requires a ransom for our release," Elfrida breathed.

"Didn't I just say as much?" retorted Mrs. Todd crossly.

"This—this 'McElroy the Mute' says he's sent Terrence and Orkins back to Stone Halt with his demands. On *foot*? If he hopes to receive any ransom for us before the world's end, he should have planned that part more carefully."

"Terrence took his horse," blurted Mrs. Todd, sitting up. "I mean to say, McElroy's followers took Terrence and Orkins. That was what I meant about gunpoint. And they went on horseback. All of them."

Elfrida stared at her. "Are you saying McElroy brought all this about without saying a word?"

"Well, he says he's mute, doesn't he? And I said he used pantymime."

"But why should his men also say nothing?" Elfrida insisted. "And why did I not hear horses riding away?"

"Maybe it's their style—total silence," suggested Mrs. Todd. "Remember Dick Turpin and the Essex gang? All these outlaws have their peculiar ways. Supposing one of McElroy's men had a distinctive voice, and you was later to identify him by it? I assure you, Miss, I saw the pantymime and I saw them ride away with Terrence and Orkins. Let's just hope the Tierneys will pay the ransom."

"But of course they shouldn't pay any ransom!" declared Elfie, her fear diminishing as her irritation increased. "This is none of their doing, and they aren't even my 'kinfolk,' as McElroy puts it."

Frowning, Mrs. Todd shook her head slowly. "Begging your pardon, Miss Hapgood, but they're as near as you have to it, because of Miss Alice marrying Mr. Joseph. If the Tierneys have to send on to Bramleigh, that'll take another several days, and we'll be dead in a ditch by then, make no mistake. Not to mention, the news of it will kill your father—drop him like a blow to the head. Heart, more like."

Elfrida inhaled sharply. No—her father must on no account be told! Even if ten McElroys the Mute set upon her. But suppose she were to die? Her father would surely follow hard after, and then what would become of the Hapgood ladies? Margaret was too young to marry Cousin Hugh—

"The Tierneys would not dare tell my father," she said. "They know what is at stake."

Mrs. Todd threw up her hands. "All right, then. If you say the Tierneys shouldn't pay the ransom and they won't ask your father to pay it, what is to become of us?"

"Mr. Frederick Tierney will think of something." The words were out of her mouth before she realized it, but no sooner were they said than a peace stole over her. And why not? He said he loved her—even if he only intended to marry her as an interlude between his carryings-on with Lady Wimpole and her ilk. If he loved her enough to want to marry her, let him come and rescue her. And if he no longer loved her or wanted to marry her, let him rescue her nevertheless! It was his duty as a gentleman.

Her mind made rapid calculations. How long would it take Terrence and Orkins to reach Stone Halt again? Surely McElroy's men would ride the horses as hard as they could. And just as surely, Mr. Tierney would set out as soon as he heard, even if he should have to ride more slowly at night. Why did this stupid McElroy drive on so fast? He had not changed direction, as far as Elfrida could tell, which only put more distance between the ransom and his reception of it.

It took her a minute to remark that Mrs. Todd was struggling to repress a smile. When Elfrida raised questioning eyebrows at her, the woman occupied herself with plucking a loose thread from her cuff. "You're perfectly right, Miss H. Mr. Frederick will set everything in order. We have only to wait."

They drove on. And on.

With both blinds raised, Elfrida looked out first one side and then the other. She never glimpsed McElroy the Mute, but what she did see was enough to set her fretting again. They were most certainly heading northeast. The countryside flanking the road was wholly unfamiliar to her, but the sun's path through the sky could not otherwise be explained. How would Frederick ever catch them? This outlaw was peculiar indeed, if he kept to the public road and preferred absconding with her in this unwieldy coach to collecting his reward.

On they drove.

They passed crossroads and villages and larger towns, slowing only when necessary. Even had Elfrida set herself on disobeying McElroy the Mute's injunction to keep quiet and not try to escape, she did not know how she would have managed. Most signposts were a blur to her, but she caught a name here and there: Hockliffe, Woburn, Ampthill.

Outside Ampthill she could endure it no longer. The sun was low in the sky; she was hungry; she needed badly to relieve herself. Moreover, another voice in her head whispered, if she could only get the outlaw to halt for just a few minutes, that was a few minutes more Frederick Tierney would have to overtake them.

"What did McElroy the Mute pantomime that we were to do, if we needed him to stop?" she demanded of Mrs. Todd, after shaking the woman awake.

Giving a great yawn, Mrs. Todd patted fingertips against her mouth. "I'm sure I didn't ask a lot of questions, Miss H. But I suppose we must wait until he pleases. He'll have to change the horses soon."

"I can't wait any longer," Elfrida said simply. "He must allow me two minutes, or I will begin to scream, and he may shoot me if he pleases. We're so far from Stone Halt now I don't think lightning could catch us anytime soon."

Ignoring Mrs. Todd's protests, Elfrida squeezed onto the rear-facing seat on her knees and began to beat on the ceiling of the coach with the palm of her hand. "McElroy! Mr. McElroy! Stop this coach, please."

To their mutual surprise, the carriage slowed almost immediately. After it ground to a halt, they heard someone climb down.

"You had better let me handle this, Miss H," said Mrs. Todd, sliding around her on the seat to be nearest the door.

A face appeared in the window, pale and freckled with eyebrows nearly invisible, they were so light in ginger color.

"Why, that's Orkins, isn't it?" expostulated Elfrida. "I thought you said McElroy's men rode off with him and Terrence."

"So they did," insisted Mrs. Todd as the footman fumbled with the door handle and whatever had been used to secure it. "He must have escaped."

"Don't be ridiculous."

When Orkins got the door open, the two women accosted him, but Mrs. Todd succeeded in drowning out Elfrida.

"So you got free of McElroy's men, did you?" she bellowed. "Not bad, for a slip of a boy such as yourself. And we're the happier for it, to see a familiar face. Miss H here has to make water, don't you know? You men wouldn't, since you may do it whenever you please."

Orkins stared, unable, it seemed, to explain himself or reply in kind. The questions Elfrida peppered him with, once she could edge out Mrs. Todd, only threw him into greater confusion. He shook his head violently and threw apprehensive looks back toward where McElroy the Mute sat on the front of the coach.

"Have you been stricken with McElroy's muteness?" snapped Elfrida, seeing that she would get no answers from the lad.

"Hush, Miss," hissed Mrs. Todd. "He's clearly affrighted. What did McElroy say about keeping quiet? You'll get us all killed with your chattering."

"M—M—he says you can take her over there," Orkins blurted, indicating a small woodland atop a rise, some distance from the road. "And—er—don't be thinking of running off, or"—he drew an illustrative finger across his throat.

"How could McElroy say anything of the kind to you," was Elfrida's next demand, "when he claims to be mute?"

But Orkins was spared answering because Mrs. Todd vaulted from the coach, hauling Elfrida after her. "I wouldn't have thought it in you, Miss," the woman huffed, hurrying her along, "but now is not the time for this show of willful spirits. Just be glad the villain stopped for you and allows you some privacy. Stop trying to look back! What if it makes him angry?"

"If he murders me for trying to see what he looks like, there was never much chance I would survive in the first place," retorted Elfrida. She could not make out more details than that he was a tall man in a caped greatcoat (on such a warm day!) with a hat pulled low. When she perceived his face turning her direction, however, her courage faltered, and she left off squinting at him.

"Everyone has lost his mind," she grumbled. "Or I've lost mine. Highwaymen! Servants who escape being driven at gunpoint, only to return and put themselves in danger again! A robber who demands ransom and yet runs away from any possibility of it, at top speed!"

"I'm nearly wild too, Miss H," said Mrs. Todd in a placating voice that only irked Elfrida more. "Who knows what will become of us."

They plunged through the thorn hedges into the trees, and with less embarrassment than she would have thought possible, Elfrida attended to her most pressing need. No sooner had she done so, than her stomach gave a fearful rumble. "Look here, Mrs. Todd! I do believe this tree—yes! Wild plums. I am going to pick us some."

"You'd better not, Miss H," chided her companion fretfully. "We should be getting back in the carriage. He'll be sure to check on us."

"Nonsense. Who knows when we will be given anything to eat. Let me see...I've never done this without a ladder before, but my sister Alice does it all the time, and I'm in a reckless mood." Ignoring Mrs. Todd's hand-wringing, Elfrida threw her bonnet aside and began to scramble for footholds into the branches. Slipping several times and snagging her frock, Elfrida could see why Alice preferred wearing breeches for such escapades, but hunger was hunger.

"That's enough of them now. Come down!" commanded Mrs. Todd a few minutes later, as plums bounced around her. "I'm sure McElroy the Mute wants to get a move on."

"Mr. McElroy's wants are no concern of mine," replied Elfrida, climbing still higher. "He has greatly inconvenienced *us*, if you haven't forgotten. We should have been in London hours ago. Now do make yourself useful, Mrs. Todd, and collect all those. We will want them later, if our kidnapper proves as little inclined in the future to make stops. I have no idea where he is taking us—who snatches his kidnapping victims so very far from his criminal lair?"

Perching on a limb, Elfrida bit into a plum and shut her eyes with the relief and delight of it, sweet and tart and juicy. She could eat ten of them. No—a hundred. Edith had been right: Paris would have given Aphrodite a plum. And why had she ever reprimanded Margaret for eating as many fruit as she picked? Life was too uncertain; a plum in the hand was worth two in the preserves.

She lost count of how many she had gobbled when she finally noticed the silence which had fallen. Mrs. Todd's whines and wails had faded away—even the sound of the woman's steps, as she scrabbled in the undergrowth to collect the fruit.

"Mrs. Todd?" called Elfrida, peering down.

There was no answer. Where could that woman have gone?

A ribbon of fear unwound in her now plum-filled midsection. Could anything but death silence Kitty Todd? But that was ridiculous—surely McElroy the Mute would not bother to do away with her. He wasn't even the one who had to listen to her, around the clock! It was eerie, though, how the man conducted his business in utter silence. Was he even now below her, creeping about and "pantymiming" his sinister intents?

She was trembling.

Well, if the wicked highwayman was in the mood for violence, hiding in this plum tree would not avail her long. She had better—*what*? What had she better do? She was unarmed, alone, on foot, and shortsighted. What was more, there were perhaps but four hours of daylight left.

What to do what to do what to do. The question raced around pointlessly in her head.

If Elfrida's sisters had seen her then, they would have recognized the expressions which gradually stole over her features, as she willed herself to stop shaking.

Resignation.

Fortitude.

Practicality.

Elfrida Squaring Her Shoulders and Accepting Fate.

If she was deserted and at the mercy of her kidnapper, she would just have to do her best. She certainly had no intention of going as quietly as Terrence or Orkins or Mrs. Todd. She would scream to set the birds cawing in alarm; she would scratch out the man's eyes and bite his hands and do what she could to ensure he could not continue in his criminal career. She would fly at him and see if her best efforts could not coax one roar of pain from McElroy the Mute.

Yes, and she would not wait here in this tree, for her courage to leak away.

Wiping the sticky plum juice from her hands and chin, Elfrida took a deep, slow breath and began to climb down.

As anyone who has climbed trees knows, it is far trickier to come down than to pick one's way up. Trickier still, is to descend into uncertainty and danger. Elfrida probed for each foothold with her booted toe, as her suddenly clammy hands slid on the tree's dark, glossy bark. Her heart accelerated with each slip, but she went on. Tapping her toe here and there, she would find a spot that would bear her weight and release her stranglehold on the forking trunk to reach lower. Halfway down, however, where she expected her fingers to encounter the empty crotch of a branching limb, she felt instead something fuzz-covered that flexed. Something *moving*.

Rather sooner than she imagined, Elfrida let fly the shriek that might have been heard in four counties. Snatching her hand away from the caterpillar with no thought of her own safety, she lost her balance. The tenuous position of her boot on the ridge of bark below gave way, and she found herself falling, tumbling, twigs and leaves catching at her sleeves and hair as her arms wheeled.

With a *whoomf!* and a thud, she struck ground—or not quite ground because, in fact, she had landed upon someone. A tall figure in a greatcoat whose hat, a moment ago, had been pulled low, but which now popped off and rolled away.

Even as stars spun in her vision, Elfrida gathered her breath to scream again, but McElroy the Mute was too quick for her. He laid long gloved fingers over her mouth at the same time that his other arm snaked about her waist.

For the first time that day, he spoke.

"None of that now. Hello, my lovely. Once again I have something to tender you, if you have had your share of plums."

Before her head was set to rights she was struggling against him, and, with a muffled laugh, he relinquished her.

Panting, Elfrida sprang to her feet. "You!"

"Come now, Miss Hapgood." He rose to a sitting position, bending one knee and picking a twig from his golden hair. "You don't mean you would actually have preferred to find McElroy the Mute?"

Chapter Twenty-Three

Though butter, and cheese, and a' should gang sour,
I'll crack and I'll kiss wi' my love ae hauf hour;
It's nae lang hauf hour, and we'll e'en make it three,
For the yellow-hair'd laddie my gudeman shall be.
—Folk Song, "The Yellow-Hair'd Laddie" (18th c.)

"You great, lying, tormenting, vicious, kidnapping *ogre!*" cried Elfrida, punctuating each epithet with handfuls of whatever lay within reach: leaves, twigs, rotten plums, clods of dirt.

Still laughing, Frederick ducked under his greatcoat, and the sound of his mirth only added fuel to her anger.

"What can be the meaning of this?" she demanded, out of breath. There was nothing more to pelt him with, and she was obliged to loom over him, glowering, fists on hips. "You pose as some highway-man—you abduct me—you subject me to terror and uncertainty and discomfort for hours—to what end? How dare you do this!"

"Come now," he said again, his tone cajoling. He got to his feet and brushed off his coat and breeches. "Surely you weren't terrified. I tried my best to avoid that. There was no violence, no shouting. I did advise Mrs. Todd not to lay it on too thick—"

"Mrs. Todd? You mean she *knew* you were no McElroy the Mute?"

"She did," he said simply. "We have an arrangement, you see. She assists me in my scheme, and I get her a role with a traveling acting troupe. Mrs. Anne Gurdy's troupe, to be precise. I know you looked forward to forcing Mrs. Todd upon your uncle again, but I thought this solution more convenient for all. Let us hope she makes a better stage-player than housekeeper."

"The woman says she cannot even read!" cried Elfrida, stamping her foot.

"Of course she can read. Did she claim she could not? Well, I suppose she felt it necessary for the authenticity of the role," he mused. "Won't she make a wonderful Mistress Quickly? Playing a barmaid should come rather naturally. As for my other accomplices, Terrence was glad enough to help, and I should have had him stay, rather than Orkins. Orkins cannot act his way out of a corner, I'm afraid." Observing the rapid procession of emotions across her countenance, he waited patiently to see if her sputtering would develop into speech. When it did not, he added, "And I do apologize for the discomfort, but the sooner we cover the miles, the sooner I will have achieved my goal."

The sudden swing from terror to rage to bewilderment seemed to have robbed her limbs of strength, and Elfrida sagged against the plum tree trunk. "What—what goal could that possibly be, Mr. Tierney?"

Taking her nerveless hands in his, he replied, "The goal to ruin you, of course. And then to rescue you from ruination by marrying you. As you are not yet one-and-twenty, and as time presses and precludes me from obtaining your father's consent, I find I must elope with you. Therefore, we are headed for Scotland, as quickly as the turnpikes allow."

They *what*?

The whole notion was so preposterous that Elfrida wondered if she suffered a blow to the head when she fell out of the tree. The man was mad. Completely demented. Her mind was so awhirl with confusion that she could hardly grasp at any one thought to object to first. Yet there he stood, looking perfectly sane, if a little apprehensive, as if all this were quite an unexceptional way to court a woman.

At last she said, "We have covered this ground before, Mr. Tierney."

"So we have," he admitted. "Extensively—figuratively speaking. (I assume you do not refer to our literal jaunt through Bedfordshire.) But you will note that I am not asking you to marry me this time—that strategy having failed so resoundingly on my other attempts. This time, Miss Hapgood, I am *compelling* you to marry me.”

“I am betrothed to my cousin. I wrote him my acceptance,” she pointed out feebly.

Here Mr. Tierney fidgeted and made a production of recovering his hat from the patch of grass into which it had rolled. Plopping it back on his head at a rakish angle, he said, “Well—here is my other confession. You’ll like this one still less, I fear.”

“Can that be possible?”

He cleared his throat. “Er—you might have written your cousin such an assurance, but I—ahem!—I suspected you might...act impulsively after the assembly at Stoke. I—you see, I intercepted the letters you entrusted to Sir Crispin’s servant. I have them, even this very moment, in my waistcoat pocket. I promise you I did not open them.”

Her eyes grew entirely round. “You stole my letters from Tuck? By what right did you do such a thing?” It did not make her less angry that she was conscious of a wave of relief sweeping her. Then she was not engaged to Cousin Hugh..? *I am not engaged to marry Hugh Hapgood!*

“No right at all—” he grimaced, “except—”

She thrust out her hand, palm up, and, with a sigh, he retrieved her letters and returned them to her.

“No right at all, except for the one you cannot bear to hear me say,” he muttered. “You did not like the word ‘admiration’ when I applied it to you. Still less did you like it when I said I loved you. Yet I do not know what else to call it. Whatever it is, I have never felt it before, for any woman. It is...an appreciation of everything that makes you Miss Elfrida Hapgood. Your dignity. Your beauty. Your love for your family. Your peace with yourself. It is...a vast contentment that fills me, when I think of spending my life beside you, and an—abyss—that yawns at my feet when I think I might never win you."

Her lips parted, but no sound emerged. Encouraged by her silence, he drew closer. "I know I have been insupportable, Elfrida. Interfering and managing and downright criminal toward you, but you see how desperate I am. And despite all, I will not force you, if nothing I say can persuade you to forget your objections to me." He took her hands again and, seeing she did not resist, he went on. "If you cannot love me or give me hope that one day you might—well, then Mrs. Todd is here. And Orkins. I can unhitch one of the horses and ride away, leaving you in their care to go where you wish, with no harm to your reputation. Rather, the only lasting damage would be to my heart."

Then she found herself gathered to him, her head resting on his shoulder and that heart of his beating against hers, as rapidly as her own.

"You would not answer me when I asked before," he murmured against her hair. He might have been kissing it. "Can you say in all truth that you do not care for me?"

It was the remnants of plum juice on the side of her mouth that decided her. She felt her skin adhere to the fabric of his waist coat, and she had to give it a tug to tear it away, ruefully licking at the wild, sweet flavor.

"I cannot," she admitted. "And I am sorry to have to confess it. You are altogether not the sort of young man I ought to marry, but it seems it cannot be helped."

She felt him chuckle, and then he was indeed kissing her hair, and her forehead, and her ear and cheek and mouth. When he tasted the plum juice on her lips, he gave a laughing groan and pressed her more tightly to him.

"You delicious hoyden," he whispered. "I am not entirely certain you are the sort of young woman *I* ought to marry."

"Frederick—" she interrupted this flood of sensation after some minutes, her eyes troubled and lost—"Lady Wimpole says that you only seek a wife because it is your duty, but that you will take up with her again as soon as ever you may."

"Does she?" He was beginning again at the base of her neck.

Elfrida's head fell back, but she managed to say, "I won't stand for it, you know."

"You won't have to," he growled, his lips brushing the length of her neck to her jaw. She felt one of his hands splay across her back and press her still closer, while the other buried itself in her hair, causing it to tumble from its pins. Elfrida grabbed hold of his lapels for fear her knees would altogether fail her.

"I should—Mr. Tierney, hold a moment—if that is the case—you have finished with her—I should very much like to be your wife, then." It was difficult to make such a declaration with any shred of the dignity and peace he attributed to her, not when her face was flushed and her hair disheveled and her pulse fluttering, but Elfrida did her best.

Frederick left off kissing her then. He grasped her by the shoulders and held her away from him, his eyes searching hers. "Yes? You mean it? You understand I was only half-teasing about the kidnapping plot—I really would let you go, if you truly wished it. I might trail after you some miles, beating my breast and bewailing my fate, but I think I would let you choose in the end."

Her lips curved into a tentative smile. No sooner did she give a tiny but definite nod, than he whooped and swept her up, spinning her around once. Elfrida's squeal then was not the least bit dignified or peaceful, but her smile blossomed into a glow.

"What was Joe's text for the sermon last Sunday?" he asked, releasing her to swing her hands in his.

"How your mind does wander, Frederick. Were you not attending, then?" she teased.

"No—I have it: 'I am made all things to all men, that I might by all means save some.' Apt, do you not agree? For your sake, my unutterably dear Miss Hapgood, I am made a very plain young man, and it has served me well."

"Even if that were a permissible reading of the verse," Elfrida laughed, struggling to pin her hair back up, "apart from your new wardrobe of dull blacks and buffs, I do not see that you are made a very plain young man at all."

"Then you are more shortsighted than I thought," he rejoined. "Ah—don't look so surprised, my love. Your secret is safe with me. Although, if you should like to be fitted for spectacles, I would make no objection. It might even be advisable, for the sake and safety of our children."

Enjoying her blushes, he led her from under the cover of the trees, and they started down the slope, where she could just make out Orkins on the box and Mrs. Todd idling about, dangling her bonnet by its strings.

"I am made a very plain young man," Frederick went on, "firstly by my modest attire (which I will be glad to abandon, if you find it dull). Secondly, by my renunciation of all other women ('Sufficient unto the day is the evil thereof'—I believe the Lord said that about taking even *one* woman to one's bosom). Thirdly, by my renunciation of town life (unless my wife should like to go up once a year). In short, by my renunciation of all wild living and extravagance. I will instead rusticate in the country with my beloved helpmate, growing blissfully plainer, fatter, balder, and happier as the years pass."

"Upon further consideration," Elfrida interposed, hanging back to remain out of the servants' hearing, "I would like to revise my preferences. Firstly"—she ticked them off on her fingers—"I would like you to wear whatever you please, and I am particularly fond of your blue frock coat and the waistcoat embroidered with leaves. Secondly, in return for your renunciation of all other women, I will renounce all other men, beginning with my cousin Hugh. To justify this, I cite the same verse, for our Lord might have meant it to apply to both sexes of spouse, if He had meant anything of the kind. Thirdly, I should very much like to accompany you up to town, if it pleases you to go, having only ever visited my scapegrace uncles in Hill Street. In short, I wish you might not be such a *very* plain plain young man, and that you will not grow any fatter or balder than I do, though I give you permission to be every bit as happy."

Under the curious gaze of Orkins and Mrs. Todd, the two of them closed their bargain with a solemn handshake, over which their eyes danced.

"Now I ask you to make one last decision," Frederick said. "We may continue on from here and properly ruin you, making Gretna in perhaps two days, or we may return to Stone Halt in all propriety and proceed separately into Somerset, to face your cousin's ire and beg your father's blessing on a proper marriage, banns and all."

Elfrida thought about the to-do there would be at Bramleigh—her father's astonishment and the possibility of over-exciting him, her cousin's wordless disapprobation, little Hetty's triumph. With all that unpleasantness in the balance, what was a little scandal? To be Frederick Tierney's wife in two short days! To be kissed and more than kissed, and rightfully so. There was clearly no choice in the matter.

Hoping he wouldn't notice her crimson cheeks or feel the tremble in her hand, she answered in a low voice, "It had better be Gretna Green, Frederick. At all possible speed."

He grinned. "That's the girl. Next stop, Conquest."

"Frederick!"

"Whatever can you be thinking, my dear young lady? I meant only that the next town is called Conquest—Houghton Conquest. Where we will get you a proper meal and a room for the night. I might ask for one good-night kiss, but surely no more. Your insinuations put me to the blush."

Elfrida had not heard this speech out before she marched away from him to hide her smiling embarrassment. Orkins leapt down to open the carriage door, but Frederick pushed him aside and handed her in himself. "And you, Mrs. Todd—keep Orkins company up on the box, if you please. Orkins—Miss Hapgood bids us make all speed to Houghton Conquest and beyond. You can handle this, I suppose?"

"Sir."

Frederick climbed into the coach after her, and no sooner did it lurch into motion than he swung across to join her on the forward-facing seat, twitching the blinds down. "Where were we?" he frowned. "Ah, yes, you were saying that we were embarking on a new career. I, as a not-so-very plain young man, and you"—his lips found her the tender lobe of her ear—"as a perfect renegade."

The adventures of the Hapgood family continue with Rosemary's story in *School for Love*.

THE HAPGOODS OF BRAMLEIGH

The Naturalist
A Very Plain Young Man
School for Love
Matchless Margaret
The Purloined Portrait
A Fickle Fortune

THE ELLSWORTH ASSORTMENT

Tempted by Folly
The Belle of Winchester
Minta in Spite of Herself
A Scholarly Pursuit
Miranda at Heart
A Capital Arrangement

PRIDE AND PRESTON LIN

www.christinadudley.com